LIGHTNING IN THE FOREST

The Offset Series
Book 2

By
Douglas M. Morrow

Cover Design by Doug Morrow

Cover Photography by Brett Sayles

First Edition 2024

This book is dedicated to my wife Janice without who's constant love and support this book might never have happened.

BBNK Publ.

Chapter 1

The fairies were having one of their Fairy Days, which really, for them, was just about any day. Fairies like to play. Deep in the Offset forest, far from the roads and the traffic, the river slowed to a crawl and the fairies had gathered to play their most favorite game, Skimming. There were several hundred of the winged creatures filling the trees, the bushes and lounging along the river banks all ready to see who would be the best.

Bali-elle stood on the log that traversed the river. She was far upstream from the main group of fairies waiting for her. Her golden hair matching her golden wings, she stood with both fists on her tiny hips. Her skin was only slightly darker than the shade of gold in her hair. She was the record holder and everyone loved her. She punched both fists high above her tiny head and shouted "Kloo kalooo!!" and the crowd of fairies echoed her call, "Kloo Kalooo!!"

With all four wings working overtime, Bali-elle jumped and flew straight up from the log. She looked down only once or twice as she flew to see if she was positioned right. This was a dangerous game if not done properly. Soon she reached the tree canopy; this was the point of no return. She waited a few more seconds, flying even higher above the treetops, before folding her wings to her back and allowing her body to turn in a graceful backward somersault.

With her upward momentum lost, she did the only thing possible. She fell, head first. She watched as the tree line came at her and slipped by and opened her hands to use them like sails against the rushing air to position herself for the final move. The river rushed toward her impossibly fast, even for such a small creature.

When the log bridge was about to slip by and Bali-elle was about to hit the water face first, she opened her wings for just a moment, using them to change her trajectory by ninety degrees and, just as quick, closed them as she flew under the branch that stretched across the river. The branch was partially submerged, but a small area near the center allowed just enough room between wood and water for a fairy to slip through, so long as their wings were folded. With no wings to lift her up, she landed gently on the surface of the river and began to slide along it, barely leaving ripples as she skimmed along the surface.

Fairies don't sink in water, so it was easy for them to slide upon the surface which was also why the fairies enjoyed this game so much. The real danger was missing the fall and hitting the log face first, though that has never happened.

Bali-elle pulled her arms in close. This was her technique for skimming the furthest along the river. She strained her neck a bit to look up and see how far she had come, watching for the first bunch of cottontails that grew along the river. Last time she had made it to the first of them, and today she was determined to make it further.

Sure enough, there was the first one, almost overhead. She slid along a lot slower now, and she lifted her feet and both arms to reduce her contact with the water in an effort to skim along far enough to take a new record.

She knew it was time to give in when the river

edge stopped moving past her. She rolled over on the water and looked up. She shouted and leaped off the river and onto the cattail above her head.

"Kloo Kalooo!" She shouted. Above her head, flying low was Rodri-gelle, one of her best friends. He flew along helping her to mark her distance. He now shouted along with her as he flew in excited figure eights above the river.

"Kloo Kalooo!"

And the rest of the fairies shouted along too. It was a cacophony of fairy voices cheering both the game and the new record holder.

"I'll beat you yet!" shouted Rodri-gelle and he flew, quick as an arrow, back to the branch in the river. As he turned to stand on the arched log, he looked down along the water and saw something that brought him up short. A large black hand reached out of the rushes and snatched Bali-elle from her perch on the cattail. Rodri-gelle immediately took to the air, sounding the alarm as he raced back to where he had last seen Bali-elle.

"SHADOWMANNNN!" he shouted as he flew. "SHADOOOWMAAAAAANNNNN!"

His alarm caused the fairies all to take to the air at once, forming a cloud of colored bodies and golden fluttering wings. Like a murmuration of sparrows, the colorful collection moved as one, high above the river, out of reach of the one they called 'Shadowman' but determined to save one of their own.

Rodri-gelle watched the ethereal figure of Shadowman as it moved through the underbrush and trees. The Shadowman was just that, a creature of darkness, which no light could penetrate. He was stooped, with broad shoulders and long arms almost giving him the look of an ape. But ape he was not. He wore a wide black fedora and a long black coat making him appear more like a human from one of their old moving pictures than the creature of darkness that he truly was. His face was also missing any features as there was no play of light and dark with which to create even the illusion of facial attributes. Even his teeth and the whites of his eyes were indistinguishable from the darkness surrounding them. He could usually hide in the shadow of a tree, or beneath a rock, but today was his most unlucky day. The fairies were keen in the eyes, and one had seen him.

Rogri-gelle wouldn't let him get away with this again. Several other fairies had disappeared over the recent weeks, and he was now sure that Shadowman was behind it! The proof was right there, moving through the forest!

He paused, mid flight, pointing back to the crowd of fairies. "YOU!" he pointed to one of the fastest fairies, a blue hued fairy known as Beri-elle. "Get help! Get the Old Man!" Pointing to another couple of fairies, he continued "You two, find the Knight! We need to save her!" And with that, he turned and continued to follow The Shadowman across the forest staying high and out of reach.

The three fairies took off like miniature guided missiles toward the center of the Offset. The rest of the fairies spread out and watched Rodri-gelle as he pursued the kidnapper. Even as far up in the sky as they were, their keen eyesight kept them apprised of his location at all times.

Rodri-gelle watched Shadowman as he slipped through and under the brush, over and around the trees, trying as he might to keep Rodri-gelle from tracking him. Finally, Shadowman crested a small rise, and down the other side. The protective fairy knew this area, and flew higher to protect himself from its aura.

The Shadowman was angry. He all but ran through the forest, headed for the one area he might be safe from those stinkin' flying things! Fairies were the worst! He ducked down and slipped over the top of a rise and there before him lay the Dead Lands.

It was here that the trees had stopped growing and stood like frozen shadows of their former selves, branches akimbo. The ground was just dry, sandy dirt, where nothing ever grew anymore. It was her doing. That old woman. Ever since she had come here everything nearby had died, leaving these damn trees. Nothing that he could hide in. Part of him wished to be back in his own cavern, deep within the mountain, safe in the darkness that bore him.

Even the fairies knew this area and kept their distance. They chanted and sang songs about it.

> *Down past the river*
> *where the trees no longer grow,*
> *Lives an ugly old woman*
> *With a heart as cold as snow!*

They would sing and laugh, and dance on the breeze and irritate the Shadowman until he could just about scream! When the old woman coerced him into catching them and bringing them to her, he was more than happy to oblige. Five times he had already come to the river's edge and spirited them away. This was the first time he had been caught, and chased, but now he was almost there. If he could just make it across the Dead Lands.

The Shadowman finally smiled to himself as he ran down the small hill and in among the dead trees. He ran left and right zigzagging across the dry dirt, beneath the blackened trees almost giggling at what he must look like from above. Finally he came to the big rocks at the edge of the field of dead trees, near the center of the Dead Lands, and crouched down with his back to the rocks. He wasn't tired or even breathing heavily, but kept his head down so the flying things wouldn't see his grin. He tilted his gaze up just enough to see the one had been able to follow him, and smiled a satisfied smile.

Rodri-gelle smiled too, realizing that the Shadow Man was at last caught. Sitting down at the rock formation, he didn't know where to go where Rodri-gelle wouldn't find him. Rodri-gelle glanced back to the cloud of fairies to see if the Knight or the Old Man had finally arrived. He looked back to the – Rodri-gelle nearly fell from the sky in shock!

Shadowman was gone!

#

While the crowd of fairies watched with excited trepidation as Rodri-gelle tracked Shadowman, another of the fairies took off across the river and into the vast Offset Forest. Mari-elle, one of the bright red fairies, knew Mother Nature was just over the hill and may offer some help, as the fairies were her favorite creatures.

Mother Nature was doing what she loved, communing with the flora and fauna. She lay face down, floating in a small lake, listening to the fish tell fish stories. On the shore, the Green Man lounged against a stand of trees and watched the water lap at the shore. He knew that she had been listening to the fish for a few hours, and didn't seem to be ending any time soon. The Green Man accepted this and turned his thoughts to what to have for lunch. He stared at a patch of dirt to one side and in a moment he had lettuce, celery, tomatoes and even some broccoli growing quickly.

Mother Nature felt something brush against her head and rolled over in the water. There buzzing about just above her face was one of the Fairies of the Woodland. She recognized the little creature at once.

"Mari-elle, how nice to see you!" She smiled and put out a hand for the fairy to land on. The Fairy instantly landed on her palm and launched into a long speech about Shadowman and the Dead Lands.

"Please," she entreated, "You must come and save them!"

The Green Man knew lunch would be delayed when he saw the clouds rush over the mountainside. He smiled at the way in which her moods could be reflected in the weather. He put their salad lunch together while he waited for her to join him.

Mother Nature rose up in the water, her anger on full display. The cascading water turned instantly to clothes as she gained the shore. She gave a look to the Green Man, who merely smiled and went about eating his salad. When two are part of one such as they, there is no need for words.

"Mari-elle," the great woman calmed a bit. "You must go into the Earth realm and get the knight. Tell him to bring his sword and meet me at the edge of the Dead Lands."

"But two others have already been dispatched to

_”

"They won't make it in time." Mother Nature poked a finger at the air before her and a small circular light appeared. "Now, child!"

Mari-elle knew this circular opening to be a door to Earth and hesitated only a moment before flying through.

The opening vanished as soon as she was through.

Chapter 2

Dave Nicklaus sat up in bed. As always, he turned to check out the other side of the bed, what he always thought of as his wife's side. Now, he considered it Sheldon's side of the bed. Sheldon was a big tuxedo cat who helped Dave overcome the loss of his wife after her death more than a year previous.

Sheldon, however, was nowhere to be seen.

"Uh oh," thought Dave, "I'm late getting his breakfast. He's going to have a lot to say about that." Dave chuckled at the thought. He threw on some lounging slacks and a tee-shirt as he thought of the actual conversation he had with his talking cat just the day before.

A talking cat. Dave hadn't had time to discuss this with the entity who had given Sheldon the ability to talk, Mother Nature. It was just another mental note he pinned to his 'to-do' list.

Dave stood in front of the mirror in the bedroom and ran a brush through his thick, long, white beard. It was the beard that made him consider being a part time Santa Claus in the first place. He had only wanted to find a way to make some extra money to pay some bills. Thanks to Todd, his best friend, he found and joined the S3 Company to become a Shopping Center Santa. There he met Edgar, one of Santa Clause's real honest-to-goodness Elves (with the requisite capital E) and in so doing, he also met the 7 major beings including Old Man Time, Reggie the Easter Bunny and Mother Nature. It was a gift from Mother Nature to Sheldon that had given him the gift of speech.

Dave stopped brushing and thought again on

their first actual conversation.

Sheldon had knocked Dave's silver sword onto the kitchen floor by the time Dave had joined him. Dave made a few comments about Sheldon's ability to talk and Sheldon, for his part, merely laughed. They talked a bit about Dave's adventures in the Offset and set about having breakfast. There was a moment of silence after breakfast while Dave waited on his coffee.

"This is strange." He said.

Sheldon jumped up to the kitchen island to be more in Dave's line of sight. "Yes, I suppose it is." Sheldon said.

"You don't feel strange talking to a human? To me?"

"At first, I felt strange when I woke up, but then it sort of became…natural."

Dave made a second mental note to speak to Mother Nature, the practical joker. "This may sound weird, but it's nice to have someone to talk to on a regular basis again." Dave took a moment to remember his life with Naquinta, talking all hours of the night. He brushed it away, careful to keep those memories, but not dwell on them. "Talking to Todd and the neighbors is nice, but having a friend at home is much better." Dave laughed. "I can't imagine what Lori would say if she heard you speaking to her one day. Can you imagine her face?" There was a pause while Dave studied Sheldon's response. "You do remember Lori, right? Little girl next door?"

"You know," said Sheldon, "I can't remember much before the change. Mother Nature's spell, if that is what it is, changed me so that I can't remember much at all before. Or maybe it's just I'm unable to put my new knowledge in line with what I felt… then."

"You remember living here, here at our house? You remember -" Dave stopped short, having trouble saying her name. "Naquinta?" Naquinta was Dave's late wife. Sheldon had been more her cat than Dave's.

Sheldon didn't need to think about it. The mere mention of her name caused his eyes to soften. "She always referred to herself as Mommy." Sheldon lost himself for a moment in the reflections of what had been. "I remember the sounds, sights and feelings; but couldn't really put meaning to them until the change." Sheldon stopped and looked Dave in the eye. "I remember the day we lost her. I remember your grief, your tears and I remember her suddenly not being around. Also not being able to do anything to change any of that. For a house cat, that was pretty... traumatic."

Dave looked at his newest confidant as he put his hand on the side of Sheldon's head and scratched him between his ears. Sheldon purred. "I'm sorry. I never knew how it affected you." The two shared a moment of silence.

"I still had the house," Sheldon remembered. "Which, for a cat, a house cat, is everything. A place to be, to own. And, of course, there was you."

"It always seemed that she was your favorite." Dave smiled.

"She was always willing to have me on her lap." A pause. "But at night, I slept between the two of you many times. We were..." Sheldon thought for the right word, "a... family."

The word family caught Dave right in the solar plexus. He had only just reconnected with Naquinta's family at Christmas. He had been lax in keeping up with them and had vowed to do better. Another mental note to contact his own kids was added to the list. That mental note list was getting long.

Dave shook his head as if to clear the previous day's conversation from his memory. Time to get on with the current day.

Just as Dave put down the brush, he heard some noise coming from the living room. He chuckled once again at the thought of Sheldon getting angry at not having breakfast. For just a moment he thought, "Why doesn't he come and get me?" But it was just a passing thought. He headed out to greet the day and his talking cat.

Dave found Sheldon in the living room running from couch to floor to cat-stand to kitchen counter and back to the living area and up onto the couch just to start it all over again. There was something flying around that Sheldon was determined to catch. Dave had just noticed the frantic activity when Sheldon made a leap off the kitchen island higher than Dave's head! Sheldon is a large cat, larger than most, with powerful long legs. Dave was almost taken aback at seeing his cat flying so high in the air, and worried for just a moment at his ability to land without hurting himself.

Sheldon caught whatever it was in mid jump. He landed easily on the big ottoman that sat between the island and the couch, holding whatever it was in his teeth. The little creature screamed, startling Dave. Even Sheldon dropped the creature when he heard the scream, but quickly held it down on the ottoman with both paws while Dave came to investigate.

"What is it, Sheldon?" Dave looked at the creature waiting for Sheldon to respond.

Sheldon said nothing. Dave looked at Sheldon, taking in his demeanor and, most importantly, his eyes.

With growing understanding, Dave realized that the intelligence and ability to speak were gone. They had only had one day to discuss things. Perhaps that was the real prank that Mother Nature had intended, though Dave wasn't sure at this point if, indeed, it was a prank. Rather than dwell on it, he turned his attention to the bright thing beneath Sheldon's paws. Probably a cardinal, a lot of them in this area, he thought. He also wouldn't dwell on how the bird got into the house during the night; he needed to save it from the big furry lug that was holding it down.

Sheldon had returned to his 'cat ways' and wouldn't let the creature go. To get the bird out safely, Dave had to pick the cat up and carry him to the laundry room and shut him in. Sheldon yowled the whole way. When Dave came back he thought that the flying thing would be up and trying to get away out the windows. He was surprised to find it on the kitchen island, waiting. He was even more surprised when it turned out not to be a bird.

"You are Dave Nicklaus, First Knight of the Offset?" The small creature asked. Dave stared at it with his mouth open. Somehow he knew that this creature, only slightly larger than his hand, was a fairy and he had no idea what to do about it. Wings flickered and it floated up to eye level, like a hummingbird. One arm was held with the other. Dave was, at once, concerned that Sheldon had hurt the poor thing.

"Um."

"Oh," said the fairy sadly, "I've come to the wrong place."

"Wait!" Dave came to his senses. "Yes, I'm Dave. Uh, Sir Dave. First Knight of the Offset."

"Really?" The fairy wasn't convinced. "You

don't seem too sure." The fairy threw its arms out to the side. Dave was amazed to see that neither arm was hurt.

"Yes. I really am." Dave tried to reassure her, "Oh, wait!" Dave rushed to the hall closet and reached in the back and pulled out the sword from where he had stashed it the day before. It gleamed in the light as he held it out and showed it to the fairy.

"OH MY!" The fairy wings fluttered quicker and she floated toward the sword. Her eyes were big and she was taken in by the gleaming silver as well as all the stones. "You are the Knight!" After only a moment more, she flew up in front of Dave's face. "You must come at once! Mother Nature has sent me to get you to come and save our friends, who have disappeared – taken captive by Shadowman. She asked you to meet her at the edge of the Dead Lands at once!"

Dave had questions, but he knew how things worked in the offset. Dave only found out after the fact most times and only then because he insisted. He also knew he was able to help them only because he was human, and they were not. They were held by the rules set in place so long ago, where he was able to work around those rules. Just when the fairy was about to give up, Dave nodded.

"First, are you hurt? I saw you holding one arm."

"Fairies heal very quickly, Sir Dave. But we must hurry!"

"Give me 5 minutes." He laid the sword on the kitchen island and went about getting ready.

"What of the beast?"

Dave turned back to the little fairy. "He's a cat, and he won't harm you. I have a plan." First, he had to get changed. Jeans replaced the lounging pants. An old pair of thick soled hiking shoes replaced his slippers. He almost left the tee shirt on, but decided at the last minute to put on one of his good polo shirts from when he was working. It gave him a boost to think he was actually working again, even if he wasn't paid. A knight should always look his best, he thought.

Next, he had to get Sheldon out of the Laundry room and feed him without him chasing the fairy again. He gave in to one of Sheldon's loves, tuna. A full can of tuna could distract Sheldon from the end of the world.

While the big cat gobbled down the tuna, Dave picked up the sword again, slipping the long strap up over his shoulder and his head. He gripped the sword where it met the sheath and joined the fairy in the living room.

"Ok, let's go."

The little fairy rose up in the air and waited. Dave nodded for the fairy to go ahead, but the fairy gestured to Dave to go first. Dave was dumbfounded as there was no door other than the door to go outside his house. Edgar, his friend and boss at S3 always opened one of these magical doors by simply touching the wall. Dave tried it, touching the wall and waited. When nothing happened, he turned and just shrugged to the fairy.

"Use the sword, Sir Dave?"

Dave gave it only a moment's thought and pulled the sword from its scabbard. He held it before him and touched it to the wall. It felt right that the door would need to know where he was going, so he added aloud, "The Dead Lands."

Immediately a door formed before them. The lines grew up and out from where he touched the wall.

Soon a solid wooden door was set into the wall. It was made of dark wood, with strap style hinges much like Edgar's door, but larger. Also different was the carving in the door of a knight holding a sword, the Knight's Sword.

Dave looked at the fairy, who merely smiled and gestured for him to try the door. Dave reached out and pulled on the door. It opened quite easily for the way it looked. When it was fully open, the two of them could see that the doorway was filled with a bright light.

Dave didn't hesitate; he had been through these doors before. He stepped into the bright light quickly followed by the bright red fairy. The energy crackled around them.

When they were gone, the door closed behind them and disappeared.

Sheldon never looked up from his bowl of tuna.

Chapter 3

The dark tunnel accepted him as one of its own. Both devoid of light, the two became one when the Shadowman entered. The ceiling was low, but Shadowman was unbothered by this as he moved down the tunnel quickly. He was supremely pleased with himself at how easily he had evaded the fairies. He hadn't planned on the little bug glancing away at that very moment, but the look on his face when he turned back and found the Shadowman gone must have been priceless!

The darkness didn't hide anything from the Shadowman. He moved down the tunnel as if it were fully lighted. He turned the corners and moved with confidence. This was his element: The Dark. It was his home, his companion, his mother, and his womb. He followed the corridors left and right, seemingly at random; but he knew the path that would take him to her.

Finally, he turned through a door into a large room, but far from being dark, this room was well lit with candles sporadically placed along shelves made of old wood. She stood, hunched over the workbench with nothing in front of her, as if waiting on the delivery the Shadowman was bringing.

He approached her carefully. Even one as dark as his soul might be, hers was darker. She had no patience for anything that wasn't done her way and done quickly.

The old woman turned as the Shadowman entered the room, her muddy, brown hair held tight to her neck and blended in with the dirty clothes she wore.

Her face was dark as if carved from an old piece of wood, the grooves deep and dirty. The grooves ran down her face, her neck and into her old dirty collar. She stood hunched over as if holding a great weight upon her shoulders.

"You have them?" she rasped. Her voice was rough, as if she had been coughing non-stop most of her life.

Without a word, Shadowman reached into his long coat and pulled the four fairies out. They tried their best to escape, thrashing to and fro, but he merely reached over and rapped them sharply against the edge of the table, rendering them unconscious.

"Careful!" the old woman screeched. "They're useless if they're dead!" She pulled one of the stunned fairies out of his grasp and turned to the workbench. Laying the fairy down on its stomach, she held it down with one hand while she slipped the gnarled thumb of her other hand under the wings. She got a good grip on all four of the dainty translucent wings down near where they connected to the creature's back and without preamble, ripped them off.

The fairy screamed and thrashed about, no longer stunned, but the old woman held it to the workbench until it had passed out from the pain. She handed the limp body back to the Shadowman and took another from his grip. Each one, in turn, held to the workbench and wings extracted in exactly the same violent manner.

When she was done, the Shadowman took the four fairies to the side of the room and extracted a large glass jar from a shelf under the workbench. He placed it carefully on the bench and checked the contents. Inside were sixteen more wingless fairies. He opened the lid and simply dropped the others in. Those inside the jar were quick to take care of their brethren, seeing to their well being and tending their wounds.

Back at the table, the old woman was still at work. She pulled out a weathered old box and carefully opened the lid. Turning the box up, she allowed the contents to fall gently to the workspace. Fairy wings, removed from all the fairies in the jar floated to the surface, golden in the faint light of the workroom. The flickering candle light against the falling fairy wings brought an evil smile to the old woman's face. It looked at once foreign and repulsive on her.

Next she pulled a long wide knife from a drawer. With care and expertise, she cut the bloody pulp from the edges of the wings. She didn't want any blood left on the wings and didn't want any part of the wings left mixed into the pulpy mess. She was exacting in her efforts, but quick in her movements. When she was done, she used the knife edge and pushed the pile of bloody pieces onto the floor.

The Shadowman glanced down at the mess on the floor and watched as all the pieces were pulled under the workbench by a set of dark claws. He could hear them being consumed by whatever was under the bench. He stepped away from the workbench a bit, unsure of what might be down there.

"Your job with me is done." The old woman growled to him as she went about her business, taking down a large mortar and pestle from its place on a shelf. The Shadowman didn't need to be told twice. He nodded to no one in particular and made his exit, slipping into the darkness of the tunnel and disappearing.

At the workbench, the old woman added all the

80 wings to the mortar, laying them in a pattern as she worked. She spoke softly to the wings and held one up to the light every so often to examine it for flaws.

When at last the wings were laid properly, she picked up the pestle and went to work, grinding the wings to dust. She hummed as she worked and her gnarled fingers moved the pestle about the mortar to the rhythm of the melody. She twisted and pushed and ground and mashed the wings until all that was left was a fine, golden powder in the bottom of the bowl.

She turned her hunched form to the shelves across the room, filled with all manner of glass jars, bottles and bowls. She pored over the bottles one by one, searching for just the right shape, just the right size. She also wanted one with a stopper, thus many were pushed aside. Finally, she found the one she wanted, and carried it to the workbench. Upending the heavy bowl, she allowed the fine golden powder to slide into the bottle, tapping the pestle against the side of the mortar to get every last grain. There was a purpose to her work, something that was older than she, older than perhaps even the caves themselves.

The mortar made a loud thump when she set the big crockery down. She reached into it and wiped her hand around the insides slowly. Holding her hand up to the candle light, she could see her palm and fingers dusted in a light glitter of gold. Keeping her hand aloft, she moved to the large glass jar that the Shadowman had left at the end of the workbench.

Opening the jar with one hand, she leaned over and looked at the frightened little fairies. The fear the fairies had for the old woman was palpable. She grunted in satisfaction as she laid the lid on the work area and, holding her hands over the jar, brushed the gold powder into the tiny prison and then waved her hands over the opening, murmuring soft sounds of languages long dead.

The effect was immediate. The gold powder turned into a golden glow and the fairies were energized by it. The blood from their wounds congealed and their backs scabbed over. In moments, small new wings could be seen sprouting from the scars. Those still comatose from the old woman's recent rough treatment opened their eyes and stood with their friends. The pain of their treatment only visible in their eyes as they stared at their captor.

The power of the golden powder was all the proof the old woman needed. She replaced the lid on the jar and pushed it firmly into a corner, adding a couple of old books on top to keep the fairies trapped. She pushed on the jar and pulled at the lid a couple of times to be sure it was secure. She turned and hobbled back to where she had left the small bottle.

Tipping the bottle, she gently poured a small bit of the powder into the center of her palm. Carefully, she put the stopper into the top of the glass vial one handed. Turning to the room behind her, she held up her hands before her face and blew into them, sending the golden bits into the air in a wide cloud. The golden bits twinkled in the dim light like stars in the night. Again, the murmured words joined the floating dust as they swirled beneath the dirt and rock ceiling.

She waited only a moment before stepping into the glittering cloud as it began to settle. Holding her hands out, she turned so that all of her was covered in the gold powder. Again, the effect was immediate. The old woman threw herself against the workbench as the powder took hold of her. She held herself erect, both arms straight out before her, braced on the edge to keep her balance.

The power of the fairy dust started at the top, and worked its way down. The mud and dirt matted in the old woman's hair disappeared allowing its long length to fall past her shoulders. The deep grooves in her face began to fill in, the darkness in her complexion lightened.

The fairies in the glass jar crowded to the sides watching the changes come over the old woman, restoring her youth and vigor. They stayed quiet, afraid of what might happen if they were to cry out. A small bit of hope also played across their faces as they wondered if, when the powder had done its job, the old woman would release them.

The old woman's bones grew straight and true. Her fingers, legs and even her spine straightened as the fairy dust did its work. Finally the old woman stood up and away from the workbench, no longer old. The true power of the fairy wing dust came to the fore as not only did it renew the old woman, but her clothing, as well. The dusty and dirty rags were replaced with fine leather and hand woven linen.

She raised her hands to view the work. She looked closely at her wrists and picked a bit at the clothes that now adorned her tall and vibrant form. She ran her hands through her long hair, renewing its color. As her hair renewed its purple hue, so did the color of her eyes as she turned and locked her glowing gaze on the jar full of frightened fairies.

Druscilla, the Hallowitch, laughed at their frightened little faces.

Chapter 4

The river flowed gently past the very spot where Dave entered the Offset. Overhead the fairy cloud moved and followed the action of those nearest Rodri-gelle's position, waiting for the arrival of The Knight. Waiting for Dave was also Mother Nature.

"Dave!" she called out from the opposite side of the river, "How is that wonderful feline of yours?"

"We had a wonderful conversation yesterday, Mother." Dave replied, "You and me, we gotta talk about that, too."

Mother Nature laughed, and added, "Dave, you're one of us now. Call me by my name. Gaia."

Dave would have said more, but Rodri-gelle called out from his high vantage point.

"He's gone! He's Gone!"

The excited voice of Rodri-Gelle guided Dave to the edge of the Dead Lands. Dave had never felt an area of land give off such energy as this. It was a feeling of death and despair. He stopped for just a moment, taking it in and trying not to think of the nightmares he had during the months after his return from the war so very long ago. But, that was dream energy. The feeling here, this…this was real… too real.

He knew he needed to get past the feeling and address things, so he turned instead to the little fairy and listened to him explain what had happened.

"Show me where he disappeared." Dave didn't know Shadowman, and didn't know what powers he may have, if he had any at all, so his only thought was to start with what was known: his last known position. He watched the little fairy fly up over the black trees and thought to himself that having wings right now would be much better than crossing the Dead Lands on foot. "I really didn't want to have to go down there." He muttered to himself as he started down the dry dirt hill.

Once among the skeletal woods, the feelings given off by the trees became a background, counterpoint to the mystery of what had happened to Shadowman and where he took the kidnapped fairies, and, of course, why. After only a few minutes, Dave came to the rocks below where Rodri-gelle now floated, wings working overtime as he flitted to and fro trying to understand how his prey had escaped.

Dave knelt down and examined the spot where Shadowman had stopped. A pair of big footprints were quite well defined pressed into the dirt where he had apparently stopped and leaned against the rocks. Dave took note that Shadowman didn't sit, as much as squat there beside the rocks. The dust and dirt that formed the footprints was deeper at the front of the print, thus more weight on the toes. The center of the print was without definition, flat and smooth.

Looking up across the Dead Lands, Dave also couldn't understand how Shadowman could have gotten out of sight of the little fairy flying right overhead. Even running as fast as he could, he would not have gained enough ground to be out of sight let alone out of the Dead Lands. It was quite an area, encompassing many hundreds of acres, larger than Dave could even guess at. Could Shadowman run faster than a fairy could fly?

He examined the rocks, poking his sword into the rock crevices; pushing and pulling on the rocks themselves in an attempt to find some sort of secret door or hidden opening, but it was to no avail.

As puzzles go, this was a good one, and Dave did the only thing he could think of at that point. He put his feet in the same spots that Shadowman had to see if he could figure out what happened by gaining the same viewpoint. He looked left and right, turning this way and that. Nothing could be seen that would explain the quick vanish of the Shadowman. Even the closest of the dead trees were too far away to even grasp or lean against, let alone hide behind.

"He was sitting when I turned to look away!" shouted Rodri-gelle from up above.

The information was enough to get Dave to crouch down. He looked down at the dry lifeless dirt, and again left and right. He still had no idea how someone could just disappear like that. He looked up at the angled branches that gave this area some sort of shade. Could he have some sort of power, akin to Reggie's ability to slip away unseen? Dave thought to himself. Rodri-gelle had looked away for only a second. Perhaps a second is all he needed. Dae shook his head, sure that the fairies would have known of such a power and told Dave as much.

Above and across the dead trees, the fairies looked to Dave as their savior, or at least the savior of their friends. Dave wasn't so sure. At that moment he felt more like just an old man with a long beard and no clue as to how to proceed. He was afraid to have to tell them that he had struck out. Here he was, the newly anointed Knight of the Offset and he had nothing. Feeling even more upset with himself, he leaned back against the rocks to think a bit more before returning to the fairies and Mother Nature.

And found himself in the dark.

Dave landed on his back, laying in the dark, more than a little surprised at this turn of events. Unsure of exactly how he had accomplished this maneuver, he rolled over and tried to figure out where he was. Sounds of his efforts came back to him easily. This told him it was a room, and not outdoors. The smell told him it was a cave of some sort, dirt and stale air. His hands and his knees told him this was rough stone. The room or cavern was completely dark. He couldn't even see his hand in front of his face.

"Hey!" he called out. There was no response. He reached out with one hand and found the wall and tried to stand. This, he found, was a mistake. The ceiling was so low he hit his head rather soundly and found himself again on his hands and knees. Stars danced before his eyes.

When his vision cleared, he was still in total darkness. By pure happenstance, he took hold of the handle to his Knight Sword, if only to assure it was still attached and wasn't lost in the dark.

Taking hold of the handle of the sword changed everything. Immediately, a bold white light shone from the gem embedded in the pommel of the sword. It shone like a beacon, or more correctly to Dave's point of view, like a flashlight. The dark was gone and suddenly Dave was able to see. It blinded him for a moment, and it took a few seconds for Dave to know what had happened.

The light showed him the walls of a short ceilinged passageway which had been carved out of the solid rock. The ceiling, just overhead, was so close Dave could touch it with one hand. The floor, if it could be called that, was also hewn from rock, but was at least passable. The tunnel was dusty, musty and dank.

The light offered a direction. To his left, Dave could see the tunnel ended, but to his right, the tunnel extended on, entreating him to follow. Unable to stand, Dave moved along on his hands and knees, one hand on the sword to keep the light shining, even from floor level.

After a few hundred feet, Dave's knees were screaming for a rest and thankfully, the ceiling had gradually gotten higher and higher. Dave was finally able to stand, holding one hand up over his head to be sure he didn't see stars once again. It was still short, and he was bent over but at least not on all fours. This would allow him to move a bit quicker down the rough tunnel. His knees thanked him for small favors.

Time after time the tunnel would divide, and Dave would need to figure out which direction. It was the light from the sword that gave him the answer from when the ceiling was too low to stand. Holding the sword in one hand as he moved on his hands and knees, he could see the dust disturbed by the most recent passerby – most likely Shadowman.

Dave knelt at each juncture, his knees groaning every inch, and held the light low, the dust showing footprints which pointed him in the right direction. Finally, after far too long, the ceiling rose enough for him to stand upright. He rubbed his neck and bruised head as he trudged on. He would have turned back, but he had no idea how to get out once he got back to where he started.

He cursed himself for not at least trying the walls where he had entered. Somehow he had gotten through them into the tunnel so there had to be a way out at the same spot. He should have at least checked around a bit before blindly moving on. The only option, keep going.

Noises came to him in the dark up ahead. Dave stopped and listened. He wasn't sure what the noises were, but felt he had to find out. As 'The Knight' he felt it was his duty, if duty there was. The light from the sword was bright, but as the tunnel turned and twisted, it was difficult to see far enough to know what was up ahead. He moved cautiously. If the Shadowman were not alone, there could be a problem.

Another turn, another choice. It was obvious that the noises, though soft, were coming from right around the bend. Dave stepped forward this time and shined the light around the corner as he looked. He was surprised to find a room with shelves made of wood. Lit candles were scattered about, giving a faint light. The shelves were filled with a myriad of bottles and boxes and books and as Dave scanned across a big glass bottle on a wide shelf there was sudden movement.

The bottle had something in it, something moving and making small noises. Unable to see what was in the jar, and curiosity being what it was, he moved into the big room, using his sword-light to check all the corners for Shadowman. Dave chuckled at the thought, because he really had no idea what Shadowman looked like.

Dave froze standing at the center of the room. He breathed slowly. There was a scent, a scent he had smelled just recently, and one which he should not be smelling. Lavender and Sulphur! The only time he had smelled this scent combination was when Druscilla, the decreated HalloWitch, had been close by. He turned, shining his swordlight across the room and into the passageway. He sniffed again. Yes, it was there, faint, but there, nestled within the musty smell of the rock walls and dirt floor.

Dave had a moment of disconnect. He had watched as Druscilla was turned to dust at the hands of the Headless Horseman, the true owner of Halloween. Nothing left, no reason to smell this smell unless… Could it be a leftover, something she had left long ago, which was captured in this room?

Again, noises from across the room reacquired his attention. He turned and moved even closer to that corner of the room. The jar was clear glass, though dirty on the outside. When he was close enough, Dave showed the light directly on the jar. There was enough transparency to see that there were fairies trapped within.

Quickly removing the books and other objects which prevented the jar from being opened, Dave released the fairies. There was a great rushing of wings, golden fluttering, shouted thanks and in moments they were gone. All but one. A deep maroon colored fairy stopped to say thanks and took time to talk to Dave. She landed lightly on the workbench, folding her golden wings behind her slowly. She ran a hand carefully down the wing as if checking it.

"Thank you, Sir Dave!" she said with a bow, "I am Marie-elle and I am... we all are in your debt!" The name 'Sir Dave' still was new to the Knight of the Offset, and he passed it off with a quick gesture.

"Where is this Shadowman?" He asked. "I think I need to arrest him or something."

"It's not the Shadowman!" said Mari-elle, "It's the old woman! She's the one who wanted our wings!" Marie-elle explained. "She tore them from our persons! Such an attack has never happened to any fairy! She ground them to a fine dust. She knew that the powder made from our wings carries every bit of power that the fairies themselves carry!" Her eyes grew wide, "She used it with a knowledge that none of us fairies thought anyone else had."

Dave cocked his head, pointing, "You mean… those wings?'

The fairy laughed, a gentle melody in a dark and dismal place. "Fairies heal quickly. We grew new wings."

"Where is she?" Dave's anger bubbled out as he looked around the room again.

"Gone. She sent Shadowman away before she used the powder on herself and revealed her true form!"

Dave looked at the small fairy. Mari-elle seemed to be leading up to this reveal. "True form?"

"Yes." Mari-elle flew up in front of Dave's face, giving more emphasis to her message. "She used the powder to reveal that all this time, the old woman was really, Druscilla, the Hallowitch!"

Dave somehow knew this was coming. It seemed to sync with what he had smelled earlier. But then, he thought of what Mari-elle had said. "What do you mean: all this time?"

"The old woman has lived here in these caverns in the center of the Dead Lands for as long as any of us has known."

"I saw Druscilla just a couple of weeks ago." Dave said quickly, "I watched her die, too." He added, but he wasn't so sure anymore.

"No." Mari-elle said quickly. "What you saw was not her. It was a… a spell, a shade, a trick of the light, but not really her. Druscilla has been in these caverns all these years disguised as that old woman. She created the Dead Lands to keep others away perhaps to protect her secret."

"But why?" Dave was confused, trying to put this new information together with what he had seen and witnessed. Mare-elle shrugged her tiny shoulders and, opening her golden wings, flew to the door.

"I must catch up with my friends." She said, "Thank you again for rescuing us!" and with that, she was gone.

Stepping to the door, he watched the golden light of her fluttering wings slip down the dark tunnel. He noted they had gone back the way he had come. Perhaps they knew something about how to get out that he did not.

Happy to have released the fairies and still unsure of how to get out of this cave system, Dave decided that he had a bit more time to investigate where this tunnel might lead, or who it might lead to. "Shadowman and Druscilla," he thought, "One or both might still be in here somewhere." He shined his light in both directions. "How much more of this tunnel can there be?" He said out loud, and listened to an echo chase itself off through the darkness.

Dave took a deep breath to begin his investigation and renewed his grip on the handle of the sword. The bright sword-light filled the tunnel. He shined the light down the passageway and began walking. The tunnel narrowed slightly but Dave kept walking. After a few minutes, when Dave was about to turn back, he heard soft noises, like something soft hitting something else soft. A puff of sound, but followed quickly by another and another. It continued unabated. The sound was not regular, but was assuredly there.

Dave stopped to listen. Taking his hand off the sword plunged him into darkness again but it allowed him to concentrate on the sound rather than the visual of the cave walls. He listened as his eyes once again grew accustomed to the dark. Down the tunnel, far off in the darkness, was a glow. The glow pulsed a bit and was gone, repeating itself in an odd pattern. He decided to keep to the dark and follow the pulsing light.

The light was further away than he thought. The walk was long and the floor of the cave uneven. His feet moved slowly to keep from stumbling in the darkness. But as he walked on, the glow grew brighter and brighter.

Finally, he turned a long arc and found himself in a large room with a very high ceiling. Here the walls were not hewn from rock, but were decorated in a fantastic mosaic of tiny stones. Swirls and circles, crosses and stars, mandalas and shapes of nature all adorned the walls and the ceiling; all made with the same small stones. The spaces in between the patterns and shapes were filled with more of the stones. Not a space anywhere was left open.

In the center of the room was the source of the light. It was an arch about the width of a door. A soft yellow light came from the arch on both sides, but what was more fascinating to Dave were the soft yellow specs going through the arch. They appeared to be very small winged creatures, smaller than the fairies, no larger than his palm, but they moved too quickly for Dave to study them.

The lights entered the room from a large circular opening in the wall on one side and flew through the arch and out a large circular opening on the other side. The flow was incredible. There were hundreds moving through the arch at any one time.

Dave was about to take a step to view it from

another angle, when a loud voice shouted at him.

"WHAT! ARE! YOU! DOING! IN! MY! ROOOOOOMMMM!" The voice was eerie in that it was more sing-song than shouting and went up and down the scale without reason. By its volume, he could tell it was also filled with a lot of anger. Dave found the sound grated on his nerves. There was also no doubt in the threat it implied. He worked at trying his best to control his impulse to yell back at... who was this anyway?

By moving to one side, only a half step, Dave could see beyond the arch. Across the room was a large flat surface molded out of the elements of the cavern. It was as big as a bed but table height, like a wide altar. It was adorned with the same pebbles that were pressed into the walls all around. The light from the arch also revealed someone crouched behind the table.

"I had no idea this was-"

"MYYYYYY ROOOOOMMMM!" shouted the voice. "MINE!" A head rose above the table followed by a long thin body which crawled up onto the wide altar. It stayed crouching down, its knees almost behind its shoulders. The thing's long thin arms wrapped under its legs and around the calves protectively; arms which ended in long thin fingers. The fingernails were dull, lifeless and dirty. It leaned forward and looked pointedly at Dave.

Dave almost stepped back, but held his ground.

The creature was overall ghastly. The head was larger than a normal head, with stringy long black hair framing and partially covering a pale face with black lips and wide, angry eyes that bulged out of their sockets, totally white with a black crust around them.

In absolute incongruity, the creature wore a

white dress, now dirty and torn, with matching torn and dirty white leotards. The style was something a small girl might wear to Sunday school with a full skirt and puffy sleeves. On its feet were old scuffed mary-jane style shoes. Dave could also see broken and dirty wings folded on its back.

"Forgive me," Dave bowed his head a bit, playing for time, "I'm lost here in these caverns."

"LAWWWWWWWWWST?" it intoned again moving up and down a scale of its own choosing. Its head moved jerkily back and forth, looking to Dave and then away.

"Yes." Still unsure of whom or what he was talking to, Dave waited for an opening and then went on. "I was tracking the Shadowman."

"SHADOOOOOOWMAAAAAN!" the thing screamed and thrashed about up on the altar, pounding its palms on the walls and the altar itself. It was quite evident that they didn't like Shadowman anymore than Dave did. With a quick movement, it stepped off the altar with only one foot, and Dave was suddenly aware of exactly how tall it really was, dwarfing Dave with its height.. It leaned in toward Dave and bared its teeth in a wide, angry grimace.

Dave was immediately repulsed. The teeth were a dark ashen yellow, misshapen and set in gums that were bleeding and swollen; but more than that, the teeth in front were long and sharp and there were more teeth than he had ever seen in one mouth. The grimacing lips stretched back and nearly touched its earlobes, it was so wide.

"Annnd   Juuust   WHOOOOO   ARRREEE YOUUUUUUU!" It screamed. Its eyebrows slammed down against the bridge of its nose expressing anger.

Dave stepped back involuntarily and inadvertently grabbed the handle of his Knight's Sword.

The room filled with light. This was not the flashlight light, this was Silent Lightning light. It filled the room for only a moment and then plunged all into darkness. It took a moment for both of their eyes to regain their vision in the wan light of the arch. The little flying things flew on, unfazed by interaction of the other two.

The creature was back behind the altar, lifting it's big head up just enough to see Dave.

"What waaaaas that?" it asked in a voice almost nonexistent.

Dave noted a difference in the way it spoke. More calm, less angry and without the strange sliding up and down the scale. He didn't know how to respond really, so he tried just the basics.

"Light." He said.

"Where did it coooooome frooooom?"

"From my sword." Dave didn't want to stand here all day. "Can you tell me how to get out of here?"

"No out. Only the little clones can leave."

"What clones?"

The thing behind the altar rose up, crawled to where it was before and spoke softly, "There." He was looking at the tiny winged lights. Slowly he slipped off the big altar and approached them, holding out one long fingered hand. He allowed one to alight on his open palm. Holding the little thing as if it was the most important and beautiful creature in the world, he just walked through the flow of lights as if they weren't there. The light flow slowed while he crossed and returned as if nothing had happened.

Dave wasn't exactly sure what he should do, but

allowed the tall thing to show him what was in his hand. It turned out to be a miniature version of the tall being itself. But instead of this nightmare creature, he saw a little perfect creation. Bright pink skin, curly black hair down to its shoulders, it even wore an identical outfit although clean and without tears or scuffs. Complete down to the mary-janes. Its wings were golden, like the fairies' wings and gave off a soft yellow glow.

The little creature had been gleaned from the lights that were moving out of the room, and Dave noted it was carrying something. A closer look showed him it was a tooth. Dave looked up at the bigger of the two and realization hit him.

"You're the…" he began.

"Tooooooth Fairy." He looked at Dave for a moment, closing his mouth to hide his black teeth. He gestured to the winged clones. "They briiiing the tooth baaaaack, carry it toooo the faaarrrrrthest corner of the caverrrrrrn and set it in the waaaaall. Thennnnn they returrrrrrn to the flowwww and gooooo back ooooout again." He was calming with every moment, and looked down at the floor, gesturing with his other hand. "The Miiiiice tooooo."

Dave looked down at the floor and noticed a moving carpet of little furry bodies. Mice. Moving in the same path that the flying creatures above them. "Mice?'

"Ah, yes." The Tooth Fairy replied calmly. "Many areas, they expect the mouse." He calmed even more. Dave wondered if he was calmed by the aura of the Knight's Sword or the Silent Lightning. "Just as the little fairy collects the tooth from under the pillows and leaves money in return." The tooth Fairy released his little clone back into the flow. "Ratoncito Pérez retira el diente de debajo de la almohada y deja el dinero a cambio!" The Tooth Fairy spoke the words in Spanish perfectly. "La Petite Souris récupère la dent sous les oreillers et laisse de l'argent en retour!" And again in French. He did not offer to translate.

"They take the money from those that have it there. Mother's purse. Father's pockets. Grandma's cookie jar. It's a transaction, but the money is theirs!" He winked and chuckled as if it were just the greatest inside joke.

Dave didn't know what to say. "I always wondered." He smiled. There was a long pause while the Tooth Fairy watched the flow of mice across the floor and into the arch.

"You also wonder why," he looked at Dave with his wide white eyes, "why they don't look... like me." He turned back to the flow. "Or maybe why I... don't look... like them..."

Dave didn't respond, but not because he wasn't curious. He was, but he was just unsure of what to say.

"They are clones." The Tooth Fairy said finally. He turned to look again at Dave. "Clones." He took his time, looking over the flow of fairies and mice, like a doting father. Finally, he turned back to Dave and stepped closer.

"I collect the teeth offered in the Human Realm. I have always had that power; but I have one other power. I asked for it when the human population got too large. I create these creatures to collect the teeth for me." He stopped again to look at the flow, the lights flying by adding a bit of golden hue to his pale complexion. He took a big breath, let it out. "In order to create them, I must put a little of myself in each one, yes, even the mice. They need to be me to be me to be me in order to do their job and in order for me to be there with them with them with them."

He looked to Dave again and moved very close, as if to impart some great secret. "The Teeth? They are part of the power of The Offset."

Dave knew of the power of the Offset. He knew the Old Man set each year in motion, and each of the Major 7 used their powers to keep the flow of energy between the Offset and human realms using special amulets they called Quedrets. He didn't know what to make of this new information.

"They powerrrrrr the OFFSET!" he moved again through the flow of fairies and mice, crossing to the altar. "NOW GET OOOOOOOUUUUUT!" he leaped up on the altar and turned to again show his full mouth of long deadly teeth to Dave. "MY ROOOOOOM!   MINE!   MINE! MINNNNNNNNNNE!"

Dave knew at once that the power of the Knight Sword and the Silent Lightning had worn off and it was time to go. He backed away without another word and into the dark passageway. He could hear the Tooth Fairy wailing and shouting mindlessly back in 'his room.' Dave glanced back a couple of times as he moved deeper into the maze of underground corridors. He was unsure if the Tooth Fairy would suddenly come after him into the dark maze.

Unsure of where the tunnel would eventually lead, Dave tried to remember anything from his long trek through the mountain that would help him find the exit. He was far from the Tooth Fairy's 'room,' when it suddenly occurred to him he could simply use the sword to create a door to get out, if only to his house.

He raised the Knight Sword before him, and touched the wall. The door appeared and in moments, Dave was through.

Back in the darkness, the shadows moved and watched him go.

Chapter 5

A few days later, Dave found the weather to be just about right for early morning coffee and texted Todd to join him. Todd rounded the corner on time as usual, and plopped into a chair, but quickly got up again.

"Wait," Todd said, "Am I supposed to bow or genuflect or something?"

"Don't start." Dave had already told Todd everything that had happened in The Offset, including being knighted. The two settled into their chairs, with a few small asides, laughs and sips of coffee. The conversation waned and died altogether as they both took in the day.

Dave knew he needed to tell Todd the news he had, or thought he had. He hesitated before speaking, hoping his friend would take this the right way. He had come to rely on the tall man, and didn't want to lose his friendship or his insight.

"Look, I know I told you about some of what happened in The Offset," started Dave, "at Christmas." He paused, unsure of how to approach the issue. "But some things have changed."

"How so?"

"Druscilla."

"I thought you killed the bitch?" Todd stopped with his coffee half way to his mouth. "Turned her to dust or something, right?"

"Yeah, that's about it." Dave took a deep breath and let it out. "I got some new information that she may have… somehow… eluded death." His eyebrows rose in emphasis.

Todd stared at Dave. "I'm waiting for the punchline."

Dave said nothing.

"It's a joke, right?" Todd smiled an uneasy smile. "How does someone elude death when they are basically turned to something the maid wipes up on Mondays?"

"That," Dave pointed a finger at Todd, "is exactly what I need to find out."

Todd still sat with his coffee held up, staring at his friend. "So, does this mean what I think it means?"

"That I will have to try and stop her again? Maybe kill her? ...again?" Dave sighed heavily and leaned back in his chair. "I can't really answer that just yet." Dave went on and recanted the story of what the fairy had said about Druscilla showing up in the dark caves below the Dead Lands.

The two men sat in silence and finished their coffee, staring at the little forest behind Dave's house. It was Todd that broke the silence. "You really sure it was her?"

Again Dave shrugged.

"Maybe an ...evil twin?" Todd smiled.

Dave made a moue and went back to staring at the forest.

"Now, wait!" Todd pressed, "Weren't the Wicked Witch of the East and the Wicked Witch of the West both sisters?"

"From what I know of Druscilla's lineage," Dave replied, "she had no siblings."

"Ok, then." Todd looked out at the forest, studying it carefully. He got up and paced out onto the grass and back. He stopped at the table as if to say something but merely turned and paced back out onto the grass, partway down the hill, where he stopped and stood, both hands in his pockets, his eyes on the forest.

Finally he turned and walked slowly to the patio where Dave sat. He stopped at the edge of the patio.

"You expecting trouble here like last time?" Todd knew of the attacks that had happened on Dave. Druscilla had sent a giant nightmare creature to kill Dave, who instead, killed the evil thing just a short distance from where they now relaxed.

Dave looked to Todd without answering, which as far as Todd was concerned, was all the answer he needed.

"I need to know, Dave." Todd lost his joking, easy going manner and was more serious than Dave had ever seen him. "For Carrie, for the grandkids and for me." He paused for a moment. "I'm gonna be honest, I think you lucked out last time, and if she sends another of those …those things,or something else? You're gonna need more than an old used bow and some hunting arrows. You know what I'm saying?"

Dave stood and walked over to his friend. He stood there next to him, face to face, trying to put into words how he felt. Both of them turned toward the forest.

"I know I was lucky." Dave said. "She didn't know a lot about me, but now she does. She's going to come after me, and come for whatever this is I have, with everything she's got.

"Then I would expect it's time to get your tools out again." Todd looked at Dave meaningfully. Dave nodded. They both returned to the table. "Maybe we need to add to that 'tool box,' if you know what I'm saying." This time it was Todd who raised his eyebrows indicating more.

After a few moments more Dave broached a new subject. "You know any good knife sharpeners in the area? Someone that won't ask a lot of questions about what and why?"

Without a word, Todd fished into his pocket for his wallet, took out a card and wrote on the back. "Knives, shears, he even sharpens surgical equipment, so I'm told." He started to slide the card to Dave, but stopped and pulled it back.

"There's not a lot I can do to help you." He fingered the card, still not handing it to Dave. "We can train, and I can help you prepare, but in the end, we both know it's up to you to carry it through… protect the world, so to speak." He smiled at this, as if it were some kind of joke.

Dave, for his part, still had his hand out, waiting for the card. In the back of his mind, the two facts fought. Todd had helped Dave prepare for the Christmas battle and had trained him and had trained with him; but Todd was not able to move about in the Offset as Dave was, even if the dangers that lurked and hunted him there were to come to this world.

Todd finally put the card in Dave's hand. "Drop those mugs in the dishwasher and get your tools. The least I can do is introduce you to the man and make sure you're treated like the VIP you are."

"Don't you have some kitchen remodel to work on?"

"HA!" Todd rose and started around the house. "That's the neat thing about being self-employed. I can take the day to 'research materials" for the job. Meet you out front!" Todd headed off around the north end of the house, which was closest to the driveway.

When Dave came out the front door, Todd was

waiting in his truck. The truck was one of those large oversized contractor's trucks with a lockable everything and lots of room for both tools and materials. The body of the truck was dented and the paint job was, in a word, horrid. The rocker panels, doors, and sides were each a different color. The tailgate was a dull primer gray.

"I thought your job was doing good last year." Dave said as he climbed into the cab and tossed his leather 'tool' bag between them.

"It is."

"Ok, then, explain the truck!" Dave laughed.

Todd put the truck in gear and they were moving. The truck ran better than it looked. "A month or so ago, I was giving a homeowner a quote on a bathroom. He took the quote, looked out the window and then at the quote, and then at me. He asked me how much of the quote went to my truck!" Todd laughed.

"Well, what did you tell him?

"I told him the truth and he understood. BUT, I got to wondering, so I called a few of those people who had declined my quote and, with very little prodding, found out that many of them thought I was overpriced, not because of the amount, but because of the truck I drove!"

Dave laughed along with Todd. They both knew that the jobs Todd took only supplemented his income. His basic income came from cement work in the spring and summer.

"I went right out and got me a handful of spray paint. Nothing neon, just different dark colors. I taped off the windows and the lights and I gave it a few dents with my 15 pound sledge. Worked it over with some sandpaper, primed it and then told my grand kids 'have at it' – my only stipulation was that each section had to be a different color." Todd glanced at Dave who was following every word. "I wanted it to look old and used."

Dave couldn't take the suspense. "And the result?"

Todd smiled and waited a moment before answering. "I haven't lost a quote since!"

The two men laughed and joked some more as Todd drove them further out in the country. A turn here and a few miles there and in no time, Dave was lost, but trusted his good friend. Dave glanced at him to make another joke, but his tongue dried up and his heart jumped into his throat.

Todd's eyes were glowing purple and they were locked on Dave's! Remembering the altercation he had with Miss Merry at S3 just a few short months ago, Dave immediately knew two things: That Todd was no longer in control of Todd and that Druscilla, the Hallowitch was, indeed, not dead!

Todd's right hand came up with an obsidian dagger! He swung his arm backhanded at Dave but Dave was quick to block the attempt. Without even thinking of it, he had pulled the Knight's sword out of the bag and used it to block Todd's swing. The obsidian blade cut a deep groove in the edge of the silver blade, shooting purple sparks out at the same time. Todd was much stronger, but Dave had been quick on defense.

Dave grabbed Todd's wrist to try to immobilize him but Todd pulled his wrist back with surprising speed and strength, pulling Dave with it! With a quick move, Dave released his seat belt and now the two men were now almost face to face in the center of the truck, the blade of the dagger held tightly between them!

"I told you I'd kill you!" Todd screeched, but it was not Todd speaking. Dave recognized the voice of the witch that had tried to kill him at Christmas. To answer her, Dave pulled the hand holding the knife a different direction and slammed the blade against the steering wheel, breaking it off. Druscilla/Todd screamed.

"Is that all you got, Witch Bitch?" Dave shouted. Leaning against Todd to immobilize the arm, he pulled himself further into Todd's seat, pushing the tall man against the driver's door. He reached his own foot over and stomped on the gas pedal. "Come on! Let's do this!" The truck dropped a gear and took off like a horse out of the starting gate.

Dave glanced out the front of the truck and saw a hard 90 degree right turn dead ahead. Bright yellow and black arrows pointed to the right, fastened to a large and imposing cement barrier. Either make the turn or hit the barrier at full speed. Dave made his peace with the result he saw in his mind.

The truck was still speeding up when the strength returned to Todd's arm. Druscilla, still in control, threw Dave into the passenger side of the truck. The door pounded him in the back, knocking the wind out of him. He shook himself and regained his breathing just as Todd spoke again.

"Whoa!" Todd's voice. "Wasn't paying attention there!" He braked the truck hard as the turn approached. "I didn't even know this truck could go that fast!" Todd laughed and Dave almost laughed with him. Dave's stomach dropped when Todd didn't take the right turn, but instead veered left.

What Dave had not seen in that quick glimpse out the front, was that there was a side road to the left of the big barrier. Over a short bridge spanning the creek and a long aggregate drive curved back behind the road barrier to a modern brick home hidden by the trees. Todd drove it easily, having been here before.

The scenery slid by in the short drive, and Dave watched Todd carefully. In the back of his mind was the realization that he had made the quick decision in the middle of the fight to allow himself to be killed rather than give up the power he had been gifted. He didn't know if this was a good thing or a bad thing. He knew Naquinta would not be happy to hear it. A mental note was added to bring it up to the good Doctor Pat next time he saw her. At the same time, he thought that might not be such a good idea, as she'd probably have him committed on a 72 hour hold at the mere mention of this 'death run' decision.

The truck slipped by the home around to another building, a Quonset hut building twice as long as it was wide. It looked like a barrel lying on its side and half buried. Two windows framed the door below a sign which said simply "Metal Shop."

For just a moment or two Dave was transported back to the 70s when his army squad lived in an identical Quonset hut during training. Dave tried not to let the thoughts of that time intrude on what they were about to do, or what had happened in the truck only moments before. He remembered that Miss Merry had no memory of the attack and had been her old jovial self as soon as she was no longer under Druscilla's control. He hoped Todd was the same. He was finally breathing a bit easier by the time they parked in front of the gray building; but he kept his eye on Todd until they entered the business's front door.

Inside Dave was taken by surprise. The outside

of the gray building gave the impression of a slap-dash put together affair, the old Quonset design coupled with a dull paint job and weeds sprouting in every crevice. Inside, the story was different. The inside was smooth walls of drywall, with soft tan paint, white trim, and a professional air. The walls created a retail space with the work area being in the back. They could smell the ghosts of smoke created by the machines used in the building, though currently there was no noise from the back. A counter ran through the front space cutting it in half. The counter itself wasn't as kept up as the walls and showed its wear proudly.

Todd rang the small bell on the counter. The bell hadn't even stopped ringing when a man stepped through the open doorway behind the counter. He was average sized, though easily the same age as Todd or Dave. He wore a tee-shirt with a lumberjack's shirt over it and ubiquitous blue jeans. He introduced himself as Mike, no last name, just Mike.

"Hey, Mike!" Todd shook hands with the man. "My buddy, Dave, here needs some knives sharpened." Dave began opening his bag when Todd's phone went off. He looked at it, and nodded for Dave and Mike to continue. He answered the phone as he stepped outside. "Mrs. Wright! I had hoped to call you before now. I got a bit sidetracked with this tile order. I think they may have miscounted." And with that, he was out the door.

Dave took each of his 'tools' out of the bag and laid them side by side on the counter. Mike watched the knives come out, picking each one up and examining it closely. After laying each knife back on the counter, he'd look at Dave closely from under dark brows.

"This blade is all wrong. Too long." He picked up the Gerber Combat Knife with the extra long blade.

"Where'd you get these – and don't say the Army. I know my knives."

Dave smiled. "Got them at knife shows, garage sales, you know how it goes..." It was easier to lie than to tell the story. "Bought that one because of its length. I like it that way."

Mike nodded understandingly. Dave glanced over his shoulder to see that Todd was still talking to his customer. Hoping they wouldn't be interrupted; he pulled the Knight Sword out of the bottom of the bag. Mike's eyebrows went up.

"It's purely ceremonial," Dave said quickly, "but it does need some attention." Again a glance over the shoulder. The blade had been damaged in the fight with Todd in the truck and Dave didn't want to have to tell his friend all about it - at least not yet.

"This is some of the best silverwork I've seen in a while." Mike said, examining the blade closely. Eager to get this settled before Todd returned, Dave quickly explained what he needed done with each blade, including the repair of the sword. He left a deposit and turned to the door, just a bit concerned about the ride back with Todd.

"If you ever think of wanting to add to your blade collection, you let me know." Mike didn't look up from his examination of the Knight's Sword.

"Well," Dave turned back to the counter, but again, glanced back out at Todd. "I'm always interested. What ya got?"

Mike moved his notes and the sword aside, showing Dave the display cabinet beneath. "I just started making these." He opened the back and pulled out a large vicious looking thing that had a long light brown handle and a big hooked blade. It had ZK engraved on the side of the blade. "I'm calling these Zombie Killers for the moment. Here, feel." He handed the ax to Dave.

The weapon was only slightly longer than a hand ax, with a wrapped handle of leather that felt like it was made to fit his hand. The ax blade was long and curved and the back was a flat surface, square, with sharpened corners. Dave hefted the ax and flipped it back and forth feeling the balance and weight.

"This is really something." Dave smiled. "I could kill a lot of zombies with this." The two men chuckled at the joke. Dave almost mentioned how he had battled a zombie horde just a short time ago, but he didn't want Mike thinking he was any crazier than he already did.

"I made the blade separate, strongest steel I got so it should hold its edge through just about anything." Mike was the salesman now. "The handle is a composite - same stuff they use on the equipment Firemen carry. Added a couple of finger holes to give it versatility. The head has a long hook to it and is balanced by that flat, square Poll."

"Poll?"

"The back part of an ax is called the butt or poll." Mike wasn't one to spout technical terms. Most of his clients were local farmers and homeowners needing things sharpened, but he knew Dave was a collector of odd blades. "It should take a lot of abuse and dish it out." Mike ducked down again. "Oh wait, I forgot the sheath."

The sheath turned out to be just a wide pocket with no real shape. It was thick, dark leather with a couple of reinforced holes near the top. Mike took back the Zombie Killer and showed Dave how it slipped into the sheath. "See? I made the sheath wide like this for a quick draw and quick return. No need to turn the blade back and forth, looking for a fit. The whole thing is as wide as the head."

Dave was impressed. He glanced out the window again as he pulled his wallet. Unsure of what the future may hold, he wanted to be prepared on all fronts. He didn't care what the ax cost, it was the perfect weapon for a Knight as well as protection for the drive back.

Dave carried his purchase out the door. Todd had just hung up with his client. "You ready to rock?" he asked as he headed back to the truck. Noticing the sheath, he added, "Ooooo new toy?"

Dave told him about the addition to his 'collection' as they drove. He just hoped he didn't have to show him why he bought it today. He was nervous and on guard the entire trip home, holding the new ax in his lap with the sharp blade pointed toward Todd.

Chapter 6

Druscilla sat in the dark. She was angry. She stared out the window at the dark clouds and dark forest. She had taken a chance that Dave would not be ready for another attack and had used the opportunity in the truck to catch him unaware and defeat him. But it had not worked...again. The power he carried so casually also was not hers… again.

She knew that Dave's friend Todd was physically taller and stronger than Dave and could easily overpower the shorter man. Even as strong as Todd might be, she was still unable to take Dave's power, even with the use of the obsidian dagger. Dave had merely turned the attack back on Todd, forcing the big metal vehicle into a death run! If she wanted his power, she had to let him live. He may have won this time, but his luck was running out. This, she vowed.

She remembered back to the night in the mall when Dave had sent one of the blasts of Silent Lightning chasing her into the Offset; catching her on the arm. The power she had felt jarred her to her core; thrilled her like the day she had been created and first felt her own magical energy. It was a power she had never even known existed, let alone in the hands of a human! She was saved only through use of her own abilities, both in healing and absorbing the brunt of the attack.

A small portion of that power now resided inside her, mixed with her own powers. She had to have it all! She ran a hand over the arm that had caught the bolt of light, closing her eyes hoping to feel the power again. All she felt was the dark satin covering her arm.

Dropping her arm to her side, she rose and stepped to the window.

The window looked south into the black sky. She watched as the clouds moved quickly, pushed by a firm, but unseen wind. Druscilla pushed against the pane and it swung open easily. She leaned forward on the window sill and took in the dark hills and dark sky. Reaching into a pocket, she produced the bottle of gold powder. She pulled the cork with her teeth and poured a small amount into her palm. She jammed the cork home and returned the bottle to her pocket.

Holding her hand to the sky, she began chanting in a language no one had ever heard - a language written for evil, all consonants and guttural grunts. It was only for a witch's spoken spells, and she was more than fluent.

Sar ra sen chu
Dah na ru chugh
Sar ra sen chu DU!
Gar MAH dan sen jah!

She chanted loud, unintelligible words, and soft whispers of breath; silently repeating the words again and again until at last the powder began to glow in her palm. She repeated it once more, bringing the light – and the power - to full. Smiling at her prowess, she leaned out the window and, cupping her hands together, she blew the golden glowing dust into the night sky.

The wind swirled the golden dust into the dark firmament in a glittering helix. Druscilla followed their progress as they danced on the heavy wind. Though she couldn't see it, the powder coalesced in small bits, turning the gold powder to golden orbs. The orbs defied the wind and slipped against its flow to return to the field outside Druscilla's window. Slowly, they began sucking the energy from the world around them. Druscilla watched with a mother's care. She wanted them to be correct, complete, death dealing creatures of darkness.

The darkness gathered into each of the globes turning from a glowing gold to a dark and menacing black. They were both part of the darkness and apart from it. Finally, they became creatures of shade themselves, borne on a now dark and evil wind. They gathered in the air close by where Druscilla watched. Bereft of definition, they were merely black holes in the dark air. They settled on the weed-filled ground outside Druscilla's window.

They sat and waited for Druscilla's approval as well as her commands. While waiting, the creatures grew wings and long spindly legs. Dark purple eyes marred their perfect black symmetry; some had two eyes, others three and others, innumerable. They sat perfectly still beneath the Hallowitch's gaze, awaiting the signal that would send them on their way.

Druscilla checked each and every one making sure there were no mistakes. When she was sure, she folded her arms and gave a quick nod of approval. Without a sound, the creatures disappeared. Druscilla smiled an evil smile and closed the window.

Chapter 7

The microwave beeped and Edgar pulled his lunch out and onto a plastic tray. He closed the microwave door and headed off to his office. Lunchtime. Edgar had a habit of bringing in a 'store bought' microwave meal at this time of year, now that their main season was over. The days of report writing, meetings and decisions were months away. Today, he was relaxing in solitude. The third floor cubicles of S3 were pretty much empty save for a few 'skeleton' staff seeing to the leftover paperwork from the season. He smiled and nodded to them as he walked by and turned into his office, the steam from his meal clearly visible to any who glanced his way.

He set the tray on his desk and closed the door, adding a "No calls for the next hour, please," to his secretary. The little black tray sat on his desk, steaming from its visit to the microwave, with unidentifiable lumps of…what was it this time, turkey? Edgar shook his head and tossed the dish and its contents into the trash. Cooking and carrying the thing through the office was a bit of theater for the city hired workers that needed to see him with a dish of normal looking human style food. Though in reality an elf who works for Santa Claus, city hired workers saw him as their more average sized and rather bland boss. No one even knew he was a vegetarian.

Edgar climbed up into his desk chair and pulled a large plastic container over to him. He pulled open the lid at the corner and, putting his nose right at the small opening, took a deep breath, letting out a long "aahhhhh" at the end. He pulled the lid completely off and leaned back, setting the bin in his lap. He took out the first cookie and bit in, eyes rolling in appreciation of the repast. He chased it down with hot chocolate.

Edgar tried to be the perfect human. He enjoyed dressing in suits and ties and polished shoes rather than those awful outfits of red and green. He had even tried to eat human food like the lunch which now sat in the trash. More often than not, however, he returned to his roots, bringing in a big bin of fresh cookies which he ate with hot chocolate – even in summer.

Just as he had raised the next cookie to his mouth, a door appeared across his office. The door bore the visage of a knight. It opened and in stepped Dave, First Knight of the Offset. His cookies momentarily forgotten, Edgar simply stared at the man and the quickly disappearing door.

"Dave."

"Edgar." Dave came across the office and sat in one of the chairs that Edgar kept in front of his desk, laying his newly repaired sword on the floor. The two stared at each other a moment before Dave made a motion like brushing crumbs off his shirt. Edgar looked down at his shirt and realized he was covered in cookie crumbs.

He looked back to Dave and the two just began to laugh. Cookies were shared and eyebrows were raised. Edgar, Dave had learned long ago, lived for cookies and hot chocolate. Having lived in the real human world for some time, he had learned to eat other things, but always found himself returning to his love of sweets especially right after the holidays.

The conversation was congenial and eventually waned, giving Dave the opening he was looking for. "Edgar," Dave started, "There's been a development."

Edgar brushed crumbs off his shirt once more and took a final gulp of his lukewarm hot chocolate. "Development? Pray Tell, Good Sir Knight of the Offset, what new development?"

Dave rolled his eyes at Edgar's attempt at humor. Edgar had been there when Dave had been chosen the Knight of the Offset. The only human ever to set foot in the Offset Realm, Dave had saved both the Offset and the Human realm from the evil plot Druscilla had to take control of both.

Before Dave could continue, another door appeared behind him. Edgar leaned to one side to look at it, which told Dave something was going on. He turned just as the door opened and Reggie walked in. Dave had once described Reggie as a "5 Foot rabbit in a 3 piece suit" which was more accurate than just about anything. Reggie, or rather Reginald Weatherby Van Oester, was, in fact, better known as the Easter Bunny.

Dave rose from his chair. Handshakes all round, conversation, jokes and finally, silence.

"Dave here was about to tell me something…" Edgar looked from Reggie to Dave, "important?"

Dave hesitated. The three had been through a lot. As one of the Major 7 in the Offset Universe, Reggie had been the target of Druscilla's evil schemes on more than one occasion. Her supposed demise brought them all a sense of peace. He wasn't so sure he wanted to destroy that peace, but needed the input of these very special friends.

He looked from Edgar to an expectant Reggie.

"Yes." He cleared his throat and again looked from one to the other. "An update…so to speak… It's just that…"

"My goodness, Man!" Reggie exploded,

"Would you just come out with it! I'm growing new whiskers just waiting for you!"

Edgar smiled. Reggie's outbursts of passion were things of legend. He was almost comical in his three piece suit, coupled with his angry expression, real or not.

"Ok, Ok, Ok. " Dave took a deep breath, and grabbed the arms of his chair. "Druscilla may still be… alive." Reggie looked to Edgar who looked to Dave who looked back. The silence in the room hung like a bad smell.

Unable to take the silence much longer, Dave launched into the story of how he had been called to the Dead Lands and what he had learned from the captured Fairies.

"Personally," Dave concluded, "I'm as confused as the two of you."

"Can we believe the fairies?" Reggie asked Edgar.

Edgar shrugged, "I guess. They've been around longer than either of us." He smiled at Reggie. "Well, at least longer than me."

"Don't start!" Reggie fell back into his seat, both furry hands held up before him as if warding off an attack.

"I thought you two came around about the same time." Dave said.

"No." Edgar fought to keep a smile off his face. He lost. "Reggie was here before me."

"Edgar, please." Reggie spoke fervently, raising his eyebrows meaningfully. "This is not the time." He turned back to Dave and attempted to change the subject. "Was there more the fairies had to say?"

Dave looked from Reggie to Edgar and back.

"Look," he started, "we may not have known each other very long, and the fact that I'm human and you two are … are… not, may come into play here, but if we've learned anything it's that information is key to me understanding everything I can about the Offset and well, protecting it." He held his palms up, waiting for a reply.

Reggie turned his head slowly to Edgar, who was almost bursting with laughter. He scoffed a bit, but nodded.

Edgar took a moment to reclaim himself. "You see," he finally said, "long before I came along, Reggie here was not what we see today."

"Out with it, Ed." Reggie said, closing his eyes.

"As one of the Major 7, before he was a rabbit," Edgar said, "you know, the Easter Bunny?" Edgar looked to Reggie and back to Dave. "He was a goddess!" Edgar laughed out loud and Reggie again scoffed to show his annoyance at the admission.

"Eostre! Goddess of Spring!" Edgar laughed a bit more.

Dave chuckled a bit. "So, what does that mean?"

Edgar was brought up quick, and stopped his laughter. "Mean?"

It was a generally accepted bit that Reggie and Edgar were old friends and picked on one another, this Dave knew. They also shared this camaraderie with Dave, but Dave needed information, even if he had to be a bit blunt to get it. Quick anger was part of his PTSD, and he was careful to try and keep it in check. Today, it was merely an irritation.

"Yes," Dave persisted, "What does that tell me that would help in this situation?" Dave stopped and realized he was being, perhaps too pragmatic. He relented. "Look, we can make all kinds of jokes later about Reggie in a dress –"

"Naked." Edgar added. Reggie made a face.

"- But what I need is to have information that will help me find and get rid of this … this… danger to us all. She's going to try to destroy both worlds, just as she tried before, I know it." Dave added the story of Todd and the attack Druscilla had tried, just as she had with Miss Merry.

They all sat in silence for a few moments, the gravity of the situation finally making its mark. Dave could hear muffled murmurings in the room outside the door, noises of office workers working, and the air conditioning kicked on making a hum. It was a long time before any of them spoke.

"Well," Edgar offered. "In a way, there is something to be gleaned from this." He pulled the container of cookies over and took one out. As he continued, he pushed the container to the center of his desk motioning for the two to partake. Edgar waved his hand over his mug and fresh hot chocolate appeared. He picked it up and looked at Dave. "One of my few… powers." He toasted the two and sipped the concoction.

"Now, where was I?" he set the mug down and leaned back. "Druscilla, herself, is a creation that used to hold one of the more powerful Quedrets, sixth in line." Dave and Reggie nodded; they both knew that the energy from the human world was gathered by the 7 Quedrets held by the Major 7 beings and how the energy was returned by each during their time of the year. Druscilla, representing the harvest or Halloween energy, held one of those Quedrets for many years. It had only been recently that she had been deposed and –

they thought – destroyed.

"But, and here is our salient point," he bit into his cookie and chewed a bit. "She no longer holds the Harvest Quedret. This means that she no longer gets power from the Harvest Quedret. Therefore," he leaned forward to make a point, "the only power she has is from the fairy dust she harvested."

"Ok," Dave agreed, reaching for one of the cookies. "This means she has limited power unless she kidnaps more fairies, right?" Edgar and Reggie nodded agreement.

"The fairies should be more wary," Reggie also reached for a cookie, "now that they know who's after them. I'll stop by and speak to them and I'll suggest that Mother Nature send Boo, her… uh… watch-bear to protect them."

"Watch… bear?" Dave's eyebrows went up.

"Big thing." Reggie said.

"Big as a house!" added Edgar. "But as long as you are no threat to Gaia or her fairies, you're safe."

The three chewed cookies in silence, ruminating on the situation.

Dave finally stood. "I have to do some more research as well as searching more in the caves under the Dead Lands. It would probably be better if I found her before she finds me." He picked up the Knight's Sword and turned to the wall.

"Dave?" Edgar started. Dave turned back with the Knight's Sword held up ready to create a doorway. "Is that the Knight's Sword?"

Dave knew that Edgar saw it was different, but he didn't want to admit he had to have it repaired. "Yes, it is." He offered with a smile. "Why do you ask?"

"Oh, I thought it looked a bit different."

"Well, I did have it polished and cleaned..." Dave looked at the sword as if trying to see what Edgar saw, turning it quickly back and forth, up and down, to keep them from seeing it too long.

"Yes, well," Edgar went back to his cookies. "Looks good."

Dave nodded and turned back to the wall. He created the door and left as quickly as he could. Behind him Edgar and Reggie's eyes met in silent conversation.

Chapter 8

In the back of the basement in Dave's house, away from the tools and steel, shadows collected and moved about in the already darkened space.. In the cement wall, a large dark square appeared. A hand pushed open a door and Shadowman floated fully into the room.

He sneered at mundane things Dave had in the basement, his own dislike of humans bubbling to the fore. The Knight had not taken care of that Hallowitch and needed to be brought to task and he was the one to do it. He sneered at the very idea that The Knight was above his head this very moment sleeping like a babe in arms.

He floated about the cement basement, taking in the myriad human things, tools, boxes of… who cares? Humans gave off a stink, he hated them. They spoke in sounds that were abhorrent, he hated that. They hated one another over the very things that should give them individuality. Skin color, thoughts and philosophies. They hate to see someone who looks different, acts different, thinks different. Hate it. Actually, that he enjoyed. When humans hate, he grows in power.

In a corner, on a shelf, the Shadowman encountered a large box. Metal edges made of brass kept him at bay. Nothing in this world could touch him, he was as ethereal as smoke, but he had to be careful, the Knight was not to be trifled with. Smart, and powerful. He might have crafted this mysterious brass protected box that drew him in and could be the cause of Shadowman's demise. He would draw near to examine the energy.

The box sat on a shelf, energy surrounding it, slipping out the cracks. Powerful energy of love and cherishment. He turned away in disgust. If he had a human stomach it would turn at the very thought. Humans and their emotions of love were not part of Shadowman's makeup.

Rounding the corner, he could feel the power, the true power of the Knight. Above, just above his head, here. He floated up in the center of the room, turning to crawl along the rafters, touching the wood here and there.

Yes, This is it. A dark smile crossed his lips. Just here, above the wood, the Knight sleeps.

WAIT!

A new energy. Large, powerful. What was this? He slipped a bit of shadow through the cracks in the wood, just enough to check the power.

Darkness. Darkness. And then…

Shadowman pulled back in surprise. A giant beast lay beside the Knight's bed! A pet? Too large. A guardian? Yes! The beast was full of Offset energy! Who was capable of creating such a beast to protect the Knight? Surely, not the Knight, himself. He had to have help!

He must move carefully lest the beast know he was here!

#

Dave was dreaming restlessly. He kept having this odd dream where he couldn't breathe because of a pillow stuck over his face. He opened his eyes to find the dream was true – only the pillow was furry. He pushed the big pillow off his face only to find Sheldon staring at him. The pillow had been one of Sheldon's paws, now big enough to cover his entire face.

"Shh!" Sheldon whispered, which came out more of a hiss. "There is something downstairs." Sheldon looked to the doorway and pulled back, his head rubbing against the ceiling.

His eyes darting from the darkened hall to his now giant cat, Dave crawled out of the bed, and moved to the door, slipping on a pair of jeans and a tee-shirt. He turned back, unable to fathom the change in Sheldon. Looking him up and down, he whispered back, "What caused this?"

"Converse later, danger first!" Sheldon instructed, urging Dave on with a push of his chin and Dave stepped out into the hallway. Sheldon pushed his head through the door, but was pretty sure he'd destroy the doorway if he went much further. "It's pretty obvious this is tied to the Offset and the 'gifts' I was given last New Years!"

Dave nodded in agreement. Moving down the hall, he slipped past the stairway and moved quickly to the front closet. His tool bag produced the buck knife and his gun. He was pretty sure the danger was the magical kind, but the gun was always a good bet in the middle of the night. Steel jacketed ammunition was an additional protection from Offset entities. Feeling more protected, he moved back to the stairs, standing to one side.

"Ok," he said, loud enough to be heard by the neighbors, "I'm armed and I'm coming down. I plan to shoot the first thing I see and then gut you for dinner!" Dave looked back down the hall where Sheldon nodded his agreement and showed his teeth.

The stairway in Dave's house isn't open to the basement, so he had to go most of the way down the stairs to peer around the corner. He was almost at the bottom before he snapped on the light.

Nothing.

Moving carefully around the boxes, the old vacuum and the tools leftover from his last uncompleted project, Dave moved around to the back of the basement.

Still nothing. But…

He felt the vestiges of leftover energy. Something had been here. Something that got out through the wall. Dave put his hand on the wall where he felt the most energy. It felt warm and thoughts rose in him he didn't like. Thoughts of the jungle, the bodies, the killing appeared before him with wild abandon. Whatever had been here had enjoyed these kinds of thoughts. He pulled his hand away quickly and the thoughts abated… somewhat.

Now he was tired and angry. Angry that something could bring those thoughts up in him as he tried so hard to keep them at bay. Anger as part of his PTSD he could deal with, but unknown entities who can pass on this kind of energy were something else.

Dave made one more tour of the basement to make sure that there was nothing that didn't belong. As he passed by, he ran his hand lovingly across the trunk where Naquinta's blankets were stored. The energy he had stored in it calmed him and chased most of the anger away.

Though there was nothing concerning in the middle of the night, the entire ordeal left him bone tired. Not just sleepy tired, but emotionally tired. He trudged up the stairs to check on Sheldon. He found his big cat laying on the bed, about half the size he left him.

"When the energy leaves, so does my size."

Sheldon noted.

"And speech?"

"That, too, I expect." Sheldon turned a couple of times, pulled his claws at the pillow and blanket and finally lay down.

Dave climbed into bed, and slipped under the covers. He lay a hand on his quickly shrinking cat. "Maybe you'll be a more normal sized cat in the morning.

"Fat chance." Sheldon said. "I am never normal sized."

Dave chuckled and slipped off to sleep. Sheldon stayed awake a bit longer, watching the doorway for intruders.

Chapter 9

"So," Dr. Pat began, "You had a good Christmas with your wife's daughter? Oh, and how did the new job work out?" Dr Pat ushered Dave into her office and closed the door.

"All good, all good." Dave sat down on the couch, putting his Styrofoam cup of coffee on the side table and leaned back. "The Santa gig surprised me. The teenagers I expected were a bit older and really knew what they were doing. I'll be going back and doing this as long as I can."

Dr. Pat made some notes on her pad. She looked up at Dave after. "And the nightmares you had been experiencing?"

Dave thought a moment before answering. "Fewer and Fewer, and frankly, they're becoming a bit boring."

The silence in the room was overwhelming. Dave looked at Dr. Pat. She was staring at him immobile. For a moment, Dave wondered if Druscilla had found a way to get to her, too. He checked her eyes for a color change, but found them to be their normal blue.

"Ok." She lowered her book and pen. "What's that from? Some TV show or movie I haven't seen? Is it found on the internet on a page entitled 'How To Get Your Doctor To Relent on the Treatment of Your PTSD Nightmares?' What?" The color rose in Dr. Pat's cheeks.

Dave just stared at the Doctor. She was never this emotional.

"Look Dave," Dr. Pat leaned back in her chair,

calming a bit. "I've been at this for almost 50 years. I'll probably retire soon, but so many of you seem to need my help, that I'm reluctant to do so. But my point is that I've heard it all. And I have a great memory." She looked at Dave and raised an eyebrow. "For the last few years I've heard that exact phrase dozens of times. 'The nightmares are becoming fewer and fewer and frankly they're becoming a bit boring.' It's the 'frankly, they're becoming a bit boring' part that is so memorable. So the only thing it has to be is some place they all got it from, Internet? TV? Book? What? Tell me, I need to know."

Dave chuckled. He had forgotten about the origin of the phrase, but when he had heard it parroted back to him, it all came back. "TV Show. Naquinta found it on one of the streaming services. Can't remember which one. Some Australian show about a pathologist. He's shot and a friend tells him to say that to his shrink to get them to let him go back to work." Dave chuckled again, but cut it short when he saw Dr. Pat's face. "Sorry, Doc, I really meant no disrespect."

Dr. Pat nodded, picking up her pad again. "Well, at least now I know." She made a few notes on the pad. Taking a deep breath, she let it out and continued.

"So, Dave," she hesitated, "the last time you were here, you told me of this power, what you call 'silent lightning' that you saw in the jungle. I want to explore this subject a bit more."

"You don't believe me." Dave leaned forward and cocked his head to one side.

"No, it's not that."

"Then what is it?"

"Was it only the one time?" Dr. Pat wouldn't

relent on the subject, something that both irritated Dave and endeared him to her. He decided to let her in, and examine it all with her bit more.

"Actually, no." he leaned back, looking up, remembering. "I mean, not counting the times I've had it happen just recently, I've been able to explore my own history a bit and more things keep popping up. Ever since I … released… that story, in the jungle, it seems to have opened the doors to more memories."

"Care to share one of them with me today?"

Dave really hadn't planned on going that route today. He had hoped to just stop in and talk a bit with the good Doctor. Dr. Pat and Dave had a Doctor/Patient relationship going back to the 1970s. He shook his head to clear it a bit, looking for something to start.

"A few months after I got back from Vietnam, I had to get out of the house. I spent way too long hiding from people. My hair had grown out a bit and I had really left military life -" Dave laughed, "what little there was of it, behind. I was like a lot of the guys who came back from that war. We all wanted to just leave it behind, hide and try to get a handle on life again. Most… couldn't. 'Nam had crawled inside them and continued to live on. Most of them were proud to have gone, and to have that inside while the people on the outside were tormenting them… that would do a number on anyone. To me, 'Nam was just a two month summer outing compared to what some of those guys went through, though at times I get a bit up set that so little time created such a big problem."

His eyes met the Doctor's in silent understanding. He knew what she was saying inside. The amount of time in the war is not the problem. He knew this, too.

Dave paused to get his thoughts together. A car drove by on the street outside. Dave listened to the motor fade in and out. Concentrating on the sound gave him a way to focus. He'd been having fewer problems focusing, and used another moment to relax before beginning. Finally he had his thoughts in a sort of arrangement.

"What finally took me out of the house was the fact that I figured I needed a job. I had applied to a school to go to college and was waiting on paperwork to go through for the GI Bill to pay for it, but I knew I'd need some money to pay for things such as gas or pizza." Dave smiled and looked at Dr. Pat, who looked as blank as ever.

"There was some rumor about a restaurant opening up near my house. Supposed to be some big thing, very fancy. I headed on down to see what it was, and see if any jobs were available. Turned out it was just a mile or so from my house.

"The place was designed to be like a big French farmhouse that had been taken over by the RAF during World War I. Huge building, even an old biplane sitting in a field off to the side. I didn't like the army and war references, but as long as it wasn't jungle oriented, I figured I could get by. So, I put my head down and headed on in. Once inside, the military aspect wasn't as pronounced, so I was able to relax a bit more.

"They weren't open yet, but I could see people doing things in preparation. Tables being arranged, glasses being unpacked, you know, stuff like that. I asked a couple of people where I might find the manager and they directed me to a little office off the kitchen.

"I asked him if there were any positions he

hadn't filled and he said matter-of-factly, 'Can you cook?' to which I answered a firm, 'Yes, sir, I can.' He gave me a few papers and said 'Grand Opening is Saturday night, be here by 4 to give us time to get this paperwork filed.' So, just like that I got the job.

Dave glanced at Dr. Pat, whose expression was one of skepticism. "Now, to answer the obvious question, No, I don't know how to cook, or at least I didn't then. I showed up Saturday at four on the dot. They gave me a chef's hat and one of those white jackets with the double rows of buttons and, after filling out a few forms, sent me out to cook. The cooking was done out in front of everyone, in what is called an 'exhibition kitchen.' All the diners watch you cook. There I met the other two chefs.

"These guys were right out of culinary school. But, me being me, I know I can't hide from the truth. So, I told them straight up. 'Guys, I can't cook, and you have two choices. You can tell the manager, who will fire me and you'll be shorthanded until he can find a real cook, OR you can teach me how to do what I need to do. I'm a quick learner.

"They look at each other for a minute and then they take me over and show me everything. I picked up one of those big chef's knives and I felt right at home. I cooked there every summer between years at college. I got really good at omelets and worked the brunch crowd most Sundays."

Dave took a moment remembering the fun he had. "It was quite a place. The building was located right next to the big runway out by Denver's Stapleton Airport. It was less than a hundred yards to the runway itself. The restaurant's entire north side faced the runway and the walls were big glass panels, 12-14 feet tall. The tables were all on tiers, so that everyone could watch the planes as they landed. The planes went by so close it felt like the wings were right outside the windows. At night, with the plane's lights flashing, it was quite a sight.

"The one thing this place had that impressed me, hell it impressed everyone, was a way to take care of little kids. This was long before cell phones that had games or movies on them, so kids could be a handful, especially in a fancy sit-down restaurant. They had about a dozen headphones that plugged into the wall and the kids could listen to the live air-play between the airport tower and the planes. They were all told that the runway number right outside the big windows was Two Niner, using the vernacular of the controllers, so that the kids knew when a plane was about to land.

"Kids ate it up. Literally. They would sit there eating quietly, listening to the tower. They'd stand up or crane their necks just before some airliner went by right outside. It was incredible."

Dave lapsed in talking. He was remembering that night. He looked at the floor and took a breath. "Those headphones may have saved a lot of people. At least I know they saved me.

"It was a cloudy Tuesday, just before dusk. I remember because the place wasn't really busy. They had a good steady clientele, but Tuesdays were always the lightest nights. Sitting just a few feet from us just outside the exhibition kitchen, on the center tier – the center tier had the kitchen so it was wider, but it also had the best views other than the tables next to the windows. There's this family of a Dad, Mom and a kid, about 12-14. He's got on the headphones and he's intent with the conversations he hears.

"The kid stops eating. After a minute or two, the Dad asks him to please eat. He won't. Kid keeps looking out the windows. Dad finally asks what's up. The kid explains that the tower is having problems contacting some plane. A plane called a Windecker YE-5. Now this was odd because they kept using its name, no call letters. In fact, the kid goes on to say they called it 'Air Force YE-5' at one point and even 'Air Force Windecker YE-5' another. Return contact was intermittent; the pilot was unable to control the craft properly. They had directed him to the big runway, Two-Niner in hopes he would have a better chance of getting control and setting it down with more room and distance.

"The kid says loudly, 'The tower keeps saying he's too far south, he'll miss the runway. Dad, aren't we south of the runway?' Dad looks at mom. Mom nods and the three get up and leave. Just like that. By this time the manager is out there and he stops them. After a couple of quiet words, he lets them go, and then he gets everyone out. Cooks, waitresses, everyone gets out, either by the front door or the side emergency exits.

"Me? I'm stupid. I go down to the lower tier, off to the east wall, where there is a 4 foot section of the main window facing east. I look up into those dark clouds wondering if I can really see this plane. I'm studying the clouds as a voice in my head keeps saying 'get moving, get out.' Then, I see it. It drops like a rock out of the clouds and yeah, it's south of the runway, but not by much. It's lined up in a straight line to the window where I'm standing. I'm whispering to myself 'turn north, turn north turn north' but the thing keeps coming.

"A moment later, a piece flies off the plane.

Looking back, I figure it was the canopy, and following that, something else. The pilot. His parachute opens and I can see the shape of the small plane for just a second in the white of the chute behind it. The plane now has no chance of anything but a crash. And it's going to hit the building, right where I'm standing.

"By this time I have both hands up on the window, I'm watching this thing get closer and closer wondering why it doesn't crash into the dirt fields to the east and then I realize it must be on some kind of autopilot. I know I should run, I should get out, but there is something in me that says I need to stop it, I need to fix it, I need to do something.

"I'm pressing on the glass with both hands and my emotions are welling up and there is really no time, I can almost see the rivets on the front of the aircraft when it all comes out and suddenly I shout 'NO!' and press my palms forward, willing the thing to turn or land or – something."

Dave looks at Dr. Pat to see if she's following along. Sometimes her stony demeanor is hard to read, but he knows she is listening.

"Two bolts of that Silent Lightning shot out of my hands and hit the plane dead on less than 50 yards from the restaurant. They tear through its hull, which just melts. I later learned that the hull was composite, very light. The lightning then hits the engine a millisecond later, tearing it apart. The fuel left in the tank explodes, ripping the thing right down the middle.

"One of the wings ends up stuck in the ground near the restaurant, upright in someone's backyard. The other slides by like so many of the aircraft we watched going down the runway. I stepped aside and up a tier to watch it go by through the north windows and that's when I noticed two holes in the window where I'd been standing. These weren't broken, they were melted. Two holes right where I had my hands on the glass. I could see where rivulets had run down and solidified partway to the floor, still red hot.

"For just a moment I wondered how I would explain that, when some large piece of metal slams through the window, sending glass shards across three tables. If I hadn't moved to the side to watch that wing go by, I'd be dead. That's the point where I realize I had better get out of there.

"When I turned around, standing there up one more tier was the one waitress I worked with so much, usually on Sundays. I was sure she had seen the two bolts of lightning and her giant eyes were on me, so I was trying to think of what to say. She grabs my hand and shouts, 'You idiot! We need to get out before more pieces of that thing come flying in here.' We ran out the side exit."

Dave took a deep breath. "It's amazing to me that no one saw a thing. Not her, not the pilot, No one. Even the people in the parking lot had moved too far south to see the plane when it exploded. Fire engines from the airport came and then the FAA investigators as well as Air Force investigators. The Air Force investigators took over and it was all labeled as an "accident during a classified project.' I thanked my lucky stars for that. I figure they found some melted glass and decided to hide everything because they just have no idea what happened.

"I looked up the Windecker YE-5 not too long ago, after the memory surfaced. Nothing much I didn't already know. 'Experimental craft. Crashed during a classified project.' Not much else." Dave stopped and rubbed a hand over his face to clear his thoughts.

"You don't wonder why an experimental plane was flying at that particular airport?'

"What do you mean?"

"From your own research, the Windecker YE-5 was experimental. Why was an experimental plane flying at a public airport?" Dr. Pat was trying to say something or was trying to get Dave to see something.

"Lowry Air Force base was nearby. As for the testing, well, I read it was used for testing surface materials against radar. Best radar to test with would be the civilian radar, I expect." Dave relaxed. "I read that they had problems in that the coating would hide the plane, but not the engine." He chuckled at that.

Dr. Pat just looked at him.

"What?" Dave said.

"Dave." Dr. Pat laid her pad aside and leaned forward. "There is most likely a better reason that the plane was labeled 'crashed in a classified project' than finding a couple of melted pieces of glass."

"Yeah, I guess. So?"

"So. As much as we both want to understand this power you say you have," She leaned back in her chair, "perhaps this one time no one is conveniently covering for you. It's very possible that no one did see the bolts of 'silent lightning' and that the craft really was in a classified project."

Dave hesitated, he really did want to give the Doctor proof of this power, but he could never use it when he wanted. He'd tried many times. He could not just call it up unless he was connected to the offset or found himself in danger. No one saw him send a bolt after Druscilla last year, and no humans were present when he used it to cut Jungar in half on Christmas Day.

It occurred to him now that Dr. Pat may not really believe in the silent lightning so much.

"Ok." He said, leaning forward. "But that doesn't mean this silent lightning I keep talking about doesn't exist. And somehow," he rose to leave. "Somehow, I'm going to prove it to you." And with that Dave walked out.

Dr. Pat didn't like it when a patient walked out like that, but she'd become used to it with Dave over the years. She made a few notes on her pad as the shadows under her desk quickly slipped out and followed Dave down the hall.

Chapter 10

It had been several weeks since Dave had rescued the little fairies. During those weeks, he had spent every day in the Offset, trying to find Druscilla. He had walked through the small city center, past each house, looking inside and even checked each of the large houses where the Major 7 lived. It took the better part of a day for Dave to check all the nooks and corners of Doc's huge mansion/library.

Doc and Dave sat in the center area, light streaming through the large windows, sipping on iced drinks and playing chess. Dave had yet to win against Doc, who was one of the Major 7 and was the recipient of all energy pertaining to beliefs and knowledge. Every book ever published in the human realm also had a copy here in the vast library of the Offset, which was also Doc's home.

Doc sat in a large comfortable chair, switching from one game to another while Dave studied the board. Chess boards were spread out across the area, some even hung on the walls.

"Checkmate." Doc pointed to the board, "you should have moved your knight here 5 moves ago. At that point, your bishop would have been in a better position to attack." He paused looking over the game, and began resetting the pieces. "I would still have won, but you wouldn't have lost so badly, yes?"

"No doubt." Dave toasted Doc with a tall glass of lemonade and sipped lightly. He put the glass on the table beside him and stared out the big windows to the gardens beyond. "I'm telling you Doc, I have no idea where to find her."

"Hmm?" Doc had not been paying attention.

"Druscilla."

"Oh, that."

"I have looked in every place imaginable." Dave threw up his hands in exasperation. "I even got Gaia involved. She's positive Druscilla is nowhere inside the forest. She would know." Dave shook his head.

"Well," Doc adjusted his glasses, "Where haven't you looked? As I always tell Reggie, when he's lost something and can't find it no matter how much he searches, there is one place you haven't looked."

"Oh?" Dave looked skeptical. "Where?"

"Where it is!" Doc rubbed his hands together. "Another game?"

Dave was still stuck on the line Doc had used. "Where it is." Dave said again. "So, you're saying that even though I've searched the entirety of the Offset, that Druscilla is hiding some place I have yet to look?"

Doc looked up from the chess board. "Did you find her?"

"No."

"Then you haven't looked where she is!"

Dave made an exasperated face and rolled his eyes.

"Well, let's take this one fact at a time." Doc set the chess set aside, working hard not to look at it. "What do we know about Druscilla?" He ticked things off using his fingers. "One, she's not yet able to permanently cross over to the Human World."

"How do you -"

"If she had, dear boy, your world itself would have collapsed already into chaos. Has there been a change?' Even a minor but noticeable one?"

"No..."

"Then we know she has yet to make that journey. She's still here." Doc nodded firmly. "Q.E.D. Quod erat demonstrandum." He looked at Dave to see if he was following and believing he was, he continued, "Two, she no longer lives within All Hallows Gates as the Horseman would surely have told you."

"Yes, I guess so."

"And, Three," Doc ticked off another finger, "we know she likes to have a place of her own, evinced by the rooms you found in rescue of the kidnapped fairies. She needs a center of operations, a place to scheme and even to rest and recuperate."

"Yeah," Dave acknowledged, "What does that leave?"

"Well, where have you not looked? Have you looked beyond the Dead Lands? Behind the great forest? Have you truly searched to the ends of The Offset and all that we have here? You know, for every bit of space above ground in the Offset, there is an equal amount of space below." Doc winked. "They are called the Under Lands for good reason." Doc winked again. Dave wondered if he had something in his eye.

"More space? Below?"

"For every good thing that humans enjoy, there is an equal and balancing of bad energy. Car accidents, psychosis, just folks in need of a 'check up from the neck up." Doc even used air quotes to emphasize his words. "Therefore, there are equal good and bad areas of the Offset for this energy to reside."

"I thought I had searched everywhere, but now I realize I didn't know all there was to search." Dave leaned forward. "What do you mean behind the great forest? I had thought that the forest went on and on, sort of without end. And the Dead Lands too. I had thought they were at the edge of everything. And the Under Lands, how do I search all that? "

Doc stood up quickly and headed off into the stacks of books. Dave could hear him muttering to himself and walking up and down the rows. After a while, he came back holding a long tube.

Dave got up and followed Doc as he went to the center of the big room where a wide table was stacked with books. Dave noted that this was one of the few flat spaces that didn't have any chess sets, though he noticed a single chess piece sitting off in a dark corner as if someone had thrown it there. 'Chess…' Dave shook his head, but kept his thoughts to himself.

After moving the books, Doc opened the end of the tube and slid out a large map. He proceeded to spread the map out on the table. It was old and fragile, yellowed in some areas to the point of illegibility. It was so large the ends flapped over the sides of the table and nearly down to the floor. Doc poured over the big map, running his hands along as if reading the map by touch.

"Ah!" said Doc at last, "There." He tapped the paper and pointed to an area labeled 'Dead Lands.' Dave watched as Doc moved his hands over the map further, following his pointed finger as he went through the Dead Lands, closer and closer to the edge of the map. "There, you see?"

"See what?"

"Dave." Doc stood and faced him fully. "You are the Knight of the Offset. You know more about the Offset than any other human alive or dead."

"Yeah." Dave looked into the other man's eyes. "So?" He paused. Doc paused. "What am I missing?"

Doc took off his glasses and cleaned them on

his sweater. "I can't just tell you. It's something you either know or don't know. And I'm pretty sure you know it."

"Ok." Dave bent over the map. "I go down to the Dead Lands and head out across it. What's there beyond the edge of the map?" Using his phone, Dave took a couple of photos of the map for future reference. "And what about under. You said 'under'…are there any maps for that?"

"Ah, bright boy!" Doc put his glasses on and started rolling up the map. "Thinking outside the box! Now you get it!"

Dave wasn't so sure he did. He watched Doc carry the map case back into the racks and wondered what else he didn't know about the Offset.

Chapter 11

The black rock wall surrounding All Hallows Manor stood in silent testimony to Dave's study. Dave had spent a long time deciding whether or not to come here as he questioned whether or not the Headless Horseman would, in fact, tell him truthfully if Druscilla had taken up residence once again within the area behind that wall. His relationship with the entity was strained, at best.

He had watched the Horseman turn Druscilla to purple dust without so much as a second thought. The doubt collected at the forefront of Dave's current thinking was that the whole altercation between The Headless Horseman and Druscilla might have been just for show. After a lot of thought, he'd come to the conclusion that the only way to find out for sure, is to ask.

Unsure how to broach the subject, he studied the wall a bit longer before he finally approached the gate. He stood there a moment, waiting for it to open, as it had so many times before. When nothing happened, he grabbed hold of the thick bars and gave a shove. The heavy gate didn't move and he didn't see a latch anywhere where he could open it. Dave was unsure what to do next. There was no bell or buzzer, so with nothing else to do, he pounded on the gate itself. The dull sound was hardly enough to be heard all the way up to the Manor House, but before he could knock again, there came a much louder sound.

"GAH!"

Dave knew that sound. It was the Golem, Grock. Dave had encountered him in his time in the dungeons below All Hallows manor back when Druscilla had been in charge. Grock stepped out from behind the solid black wall, and approached the gate. He was taller than Dave remembered, nearly as tall as the gates themselves. Here in the endless night that surrounds the manor, his dark dirt color and musty smell gave him the appearance of a walking corpse. Unsure of the Golem's intentions, Dave stepped back from the gate.

"Out of the way, human!" a voice came from behind him.

Dave turned to find a black carriage as long as a city block and drawn by a dozen of the most incredible horses he'd ever seen. They were made of flame, head to foot with black slits for eyes. Their fiery tails whipped back and forth throwing shadows in wild patterns. The carriage was flat black, unreflecting any of the light.

The door to the carriage was open and a long thin leg reached out to the ground showing only black slacks and a riding boot. Looking into the dark interior, Dave could see the one and only Headless Horseman. His pumpkin head glowed with intensity and his eyes burned holes in the night. A skeletal hand beckoned him in. As he stepped into the massive conveyance, he heard the screech of the heavy gates being opened.

"Perhaps you need your own carriage." The Horseman smiled an obsequious smile. "I can only assume you are finally here to discuss Druscilla's demise." The Horseman spoke while the carriage pulled through the gate and began the trip up to the Manor House. The Horseman's burning eyes narrowed on Dave. "You are not here to discuss that, are you?"

"No." was Dave's terse reply.

They rode in silence to the foreboding Manor House. The All Hallows Manor House had undergone a major redesign since Dave had last seen it. Under the ownership of Druscilla, the building was a Victorian ramshackle monstrosity more resembling an empty, decaying and decidedly haunted house decorated in colors of black and gray. Inside it was mostly empty except for, as Dave remembered it, giant spiders and snakes. He shuddered at the thought and glanced around for anything that might be moving. He exited the carriage when it stopped and took in the new façade.

The new Manor House was a stately colonial with elements of Greek revival. It was still colored in darker shades, but now had an almost homey feel. In moments they were entering the big double doors, and when Dave glanced back, the carriage and horses were gone.

Inside the mansion there was now a stately design including large burnt orange couches and comfortable autumn brown arm chairs. Dark walnut and cherry accents were everywhere. As they entered the main room, Dave even saw a chess set with pieces that were witches and demons and he was unsurprised to see them turn to look at him as he walked by.

It was hard to keep up with the Horseman, as he was a good foot or two taller and moved with purpose through the room ahead of Dave. In a moment, he was gone, but he called back to Dave, "Coffee or Cider?"

"Coffee." Dave replied, "Too early in the year for Cider."

The Horseman returned, but Dave noticed his hands were empty. His confusion was cleared when a moment later a silver serving set with two cups floated out of the far door, sailed across the room and settled gently on the table between two big couches.

Sitting down beside the table, the Horseman began preparing his coffee. Dave sat across from him and did the same. It was quiet in the room and Dave could hear noises off in the big Manor House. He only hoped that none of them were related to a hiding witch with plans for his demise. His attention returned as the Horseman leaned back on the couch with his mug of coffee. The light inside his pumpkin head faded to a dim flicker as he eyed Dave.

"Well?"

Dave also picked up his mug and leaned back. "Well, Horseman -" Dave took a sip and stopped. The Horseman always had good coffee, but his mind went another direction. "Do you have a first name? Nickname? Calling you The Headless Horseman or even Mr. Horseman or just Horseman seems a bit weighty on the tongue."

There was another long silence. The Manor House continued to make noises in the far rooms.

"Rider." He said. "Call me Rider, if you must. But -" He leaned forward, "Do not mistake my acceptance of this moniker for friendship or camaraderie. You are a human. You may be able to enter the offset and be called The Knight, but you are still human. Nothing more."

Dave nodded. "Thank you. Both for the name and for the reminder." He didn't relax, but watched the entity as he sipped more coffee. "In fact, it makes my job here just a bit easier." He held the coffee with one hand and placed his other on the handle of the Knight's Sword for emphasis. "I'm here about Druscilla."

"Druscilla?" Rider waved a hand dismissively,

"She was de-created. You were there."

No," Dave was calm, simply stating a fact. "Druscilla was not de-created. AND, I think you know that." He knew he was stepping on dangerous ground here. As the Scarecrow, the Harvest Entity had been grumpy and irritable, but as the Horseman, he was downright menacing.

The Horseman's dim flickering eye holes came to life. A low glow of orange flame erupted in their hollow centers causing smoke to gently slip out the corners. "Watch your -"

"I need to know for certain that Druscilla has not taken up residence here, with or without your permission."

"I can assure you, if she yet lives, she is not here."

"Would I be insulting if I asked to see for myself?"

"Yes, you would." Rider finished his coffee and set the mug down forcefully. "But, you are The Knight," he said, putting a heavy sarcastic emphasis on the title. "I can understand the need to be thorough, so let's settle this." He stood and walked off. Dave had to put down his coffee and race to keep up.

In the front hallway, Rider stood before a massive staircase and raised a hand casually. The staircase fell back inward on itself, creating a stairway down into the lower levels.

This house is full of secrets. Dave thought to himself.

"We're starting below?" Dave asked.

Rider stopped in the middle of the stairs, turning only slightly to reply to Dave. "I'm assuming that you would expect Druscilla to be below, and not cowering in my linen closet. This way." Rider led the way down the steps into darkness. "If you wish, we can examine every inch of the place, but my patience for this charade is wearing thin. Let's get this over with."

In stark contrast to the redesign of the upper part of the Manor, the lower levels were as Dave remembered them. The darkness, the brickwork, the dank feel and smell and off in the distance somewhere, the constant noise of dripping water. He almost expected to hear the screams of captive victims being eviscerated.

They looked into odd rooms, with odder furniture. Dave used the light from the Knight's Sword to check small alcoves, rooms and even ran his hand along the walls looking for hidden passageways or chambers, much to Rider's amusement. They came upon the dungeon rooms with the glass bricks, now finished with solid unbreakable brick. They came to a 'T' in one hallway and the smell from one direction reminded him of Grock. He still checked the area, just to be sure. He found nothing of note.

Throughout their exhaustive search, Rider stood just off to one side, as if impatient for the search to end, affecting an air of aloofness; but Dave noticed something else. Rider was searching the rooms, too. Dave would catch him checking a dark corner, rechecking a place that Dave had already checked and visibly relaxing each time they came up empty.

By his actions, Dave could tell that Rider was as concerned as Dave that Druscilla had not found a way into the lower levels of the Manor. This caused Dave to smile, but he was careful to hide it as they searched. In some small regard, Dave considered it proof that if Druscilla were found here, she had not been invited by

Rider. Additionally, it proved a fact he had not thought: Rider wasn't certain that Druscilla was de-created either.

They rose from the basement by the same inverted staircase that they had used at the start. Rider turned as the stairs rose back into place. He gestured to the upper floors.

"Shall we continue this upstairs?"

"No," Dave moved to the front doors. "I think we can pretty much dispense with further investigation." Dave smiled, but quickly stopped smiling when he saw that Rider was not smiling with him. "I need to get going."

"The Under Lands."

"Yes." Dave turned to go but turned back, "Wait, how did you know I was going there?"

"Human." Rider folded his arms across his chest. "I happen to know a great deal more about The Offset than you. It is only expected that you would get to the Under Lands, the Citadel, the Dental Caverns."

"You been down there recently?"

"Me? No." Rider looked down. "Those areas have nothing to do with my area of interest, dark and foreboding though they may be."

Dave nodded, turning to the door again.

"You will… when it happens, I mean?" Rider looked off to the side, affecting more aloofness. "In case I don't feel it, you know. She was my creation after all."

Dave took in the imposing figure of the Harvest Entity and paused, before nodding again and pulling the door shut as he left.

Chapter 12

"Under..." Dave whispered to himself. He was in the dark, the area of tunnels he had used to rescue the fairies and to find the Tooth Fairy. He used the light from the end of the Knight's Sword to find his way around, though the light was, at times, dimmer than usual. It had been growing dimmer and dimmer since he had first entered. He resisted the urge to tap the side of the sword as one might to get an old flashlight working again.

Finding his original footprints he knew which ways he had turned when he was here before and now took different paths, not wanting to disturb the Tooth Fairy. Once meeting him was enough. He found the tunnels to be endless with a musty smell that he attributed to something dead. It bothered him to think something in the dark, there ahead, might be the carcass of some long dead animal, - or worse, some recently dead animal.

Along with supplies like water and trail mix, he also carried a thick piece of sidewalk chalk he had borrowed from his neighbor. The neighbor family was a man and wife with a small daughter. The daughter had seen Dave with his long white beard and immediately thought he was Santa Claus. Once that was corrected, at least to a degree, the family and Dave had become good friends. Dave kept the chalk in one hand and used it to mark his turns in case he came across the same intersections again. He smiled at his own ingenuity.

He had been walking for some time. He had taken a couple of turns, found dead ends, and returned making changes to his chalk marks. There were short tunnels, and long tunnels, some wide and some so narrow Dave had to turn sideways to get through. The more tunnels he found, the more he felt he was on the right track in looking 'under' the Offset.

Walking down one long tunnel, Dave thought for just a moment that the walls were moving. He stopped to orient himself and felt the floor tipping. In a moment he was falling. With nothing to stop him, he fell down into some unknown pit.

His feet went airborne and he bent his legs to keep from breaking a knee when he finally landed. When contact finally came, he felt coarse sand; but rather than an abrupt end to his fall, he began sliding. He dug his heels in, hoping to slow his descent. Instead, he found himself gliding along the sand through a very long shaft. He put his hands up around his head to protect himself as he was thrown from side to side down the long chute.

Finally, he found he wasn't falling or sliding any more. The sand he had dislodged piled up behind him. He checked himself for injury and found only a few bruises on his arms and back. Still in the dark, he slowly worked himself into a standing position, moving his legs slowly and checking the height so he wouldn't hit his head as he stood up.

He put his hand on the handle of the Knight's Sword and noted an dimmer light than usual. Putting two hands on it made no difference; Dave made a mental note to bring a real flashlight next time, if there was a next time. He decided he'd explored enough for the day and decided he would need to get out now, while the getting was good.

The tunnel stretched to his left and right, the slide creating a T in the juncture. There would be no chalk mark to guide him, so Dave decided he had only one way out. But before he could put the sword against the wall, there came a noise from deep in the tunnel to his right. It was a low guttural sound, like the wakening of a long forgotten beast.

Dave froze. He hadn't known there would be others down here. He shook his head at his own ignorance. He could have – should have – asked Doc about this, but in his own arrogance, felt he couldn't or shouldn't. Regardless, he didn't. And now he stood to face the ramifications of that inaction.

The Knight's Sword was about to touch the wall when a great and powerful wind blew through the tunnel. It was a hot wind reminiscent of a breath on a hot summer's day. It was wet and smelled of…Dave didn't want to know what that smell was. It was the smell of death and someting on fire.

The wind pushed Dave away from the wall and he fell onto the sand behind him. The sound grew louder. Dave looked in the direction of where the wind had come only to see two red spots in a far distance. At first Dave thought they were lights but in quick realization, Dave knew. Eyes.

There was a chuff sound and the eyes were quickly hidden behind a growing fire. Dave didn't need any more information to realize that what was down that tunnel was the one thing that so many humans had feared for so many years. Whether real or imagined, the great creatures of fable had to exist here, in this place of energy.

Dragon?

Dave scrabbled up into the sand as the first breath of fire passed him by. He could smell the melting of the rubber soles of his boots and quickly pulled them up into the sand out of the heat. The flames were blown along by the wind, and this time the smell of charred and rotted meat followed.

Unable to climb up the chute, Dave knew he would have to run. The flames stopped and he knew that the Dragon was taking a breath. Perhaps sniffing to see if some human was here, perhaps charred and ready to eat.

Now. Now was the time to get up and out.

Dave turned left as soon as he was out of the sand. He ran as fast as his old legs could muster. He mentally thanked Todd and the exercise regimen his friend had developed for him over the past year, knowing that without it, he would be just a smoking snack in a dark, long forgotten tunnel.

With one hand on the Knight's sword, he used the bit of light from it to watch for a side tunnel.

There, just ahead.

Behind, another chuff. Dave knew what was coming. He could feel the hot wind at his back and in a moment he would be engulfed in flames. He lengthened his stride and slid into the turn, rolling away from the corner just as the flames passed him by. The heat was intense and he pulled in his hands and feet instinctively and waited. The flames stopped.

He fought to his feet, knowing that he had to keep going, had to get as far away as he could, before the dragon got closer and another blast of flame turned him to - before he could move, he heard something else. Along with the breathing, the soughing of the air, there was something else. He closed his eyes and stood motionless. It came again, ever so faint.

Laughter.

Dave opened his eyes. He knew that laugh. Had

he really found her? Or was this another trick? He was questioning everything. He moved away from the turn, his steps becoming faster, knowing that if this was the still living Druscilla, she would be coming for him, and bringing the dragon.

How was this possible? The phrase repeated over and over in his head as he ran. He had SEEN her die! Rider had seen her die! Rider had DE-CREATED her, himself!

If it was possible and she was still living, how did she know he would be here, of all places? How COULD she know? How can she always be one step ahead of him? He ran down the tunnel taking the first turn, stopping to look back around the corner, judging how much time he had. He was breathing hard, cursing his age and his fitness regimen for the past, what – 60 years? Todd's help was good, but in his mind Dave knew he was just an old man with a shiny kitchen gadget.

A new sound. He heard the scraping of the dragon's skin as it pulled its big feet across the uneven stone floor, the thick meaty pulse as it hit the ground and pulled its heavy body along. He heard a voice – her voice? - speaking to it, low, urging it on. They were moving, coming this way. He looked down the tunnel again, waiting for the eyes to appear.

What could he do, how can he take on a Witch and a Dragon? Dave worked his mind as fast as he could. He held the sword in one hand, and pulled the gun in the other. A gun? Against a Dragon? Laughter threatened to bubble out of his throat. He came to a quick answer.

He can't. He couldn't. He wasn't prepared! He didn't even believe it was possible! Out. He had to get out. He didn't move, just pushed the Knight's Sword and its sheath against the wall where he was standing and the door appeared. For just a moment, the door, like the light from the sword, flickered before becoming whole. Anger, frustration and failure flooded his face making it hot. At least this heat wasn't enough to burn him. Without a second thought, he pulled the door open.

Just before he stepped through, he heard that sound again.

The Laughter.

Chapter 13

"It's nice to see you here on a regular basis," Doctor Pat began, "but I hope this is more upkeep than new problems. Everything going ok?"

"I really don't know."

Dave had decided he needed to take a day to visit his Doctor again, after spending way too much time worrying where Druscilla might be hiding. It was usually just a check in, a friendly conversation and talk about PTSD, but lately the Doctor had been more than a bit interested in Dave's supposed 'Silent Lightning.' She didn't really believe it existed, and had never seen it in action. She was balanced between understanding and having him committed. There were times when Dave, himself, was on the same fence.

The two sat in silence for a few moments, each gathering their thoughts. Dr. Pat sat in the side chair with her ubiquitous pad in her lap and a pen behind one ear. Dave could see the end of the pen had been chewed a bit. A bad habit he had noticed from the start of their relationship some 40 years previous.

"You told me about your time in Vietnam, but what about your Military time before that. You said you trained with only 5 other soldiers?"

Dave was immediately taken back to that time. He could see the big Quonset hut building with the door that didn't quite shut out the wind. There was minimal landscaping, no grass, just dirt out where they were so far from the other trainees.

"There were only six of us. I remember I told you we were supposed to go by a number, rather than a name. We may have introduced ourselves before the

Colonel got there, but I'll be damned if I can remember any names."

Dave looked up at the ceiling. His eyes took in the landmarks he'd seen so many times, the water spot that had never been painted over, the crack at the corner, the light that Dr. Pat never turned on, even in the evening.

"Wait…" he murmured. "I remember Nick. He was One, number one and only a number, not a leader by any means. Texas kid. Tall, broad across the shoulders. Spent a lot of time out in the fields, even spent his summers in a tent tending cows for his Uncle.

"Then, Two. What was his… oh, Fred. Yeah, they're all coming back to me a bit at a time." Dave even seemed surprised at that. "Montana or some place up north. His father taught him to be a tracker. They hunted a lot.

"Three. I remember three because he was African American. Back then we could call him black and didn't mean it as an insult. He was from some place in the south, but I can't remember where. Georgia, maybe Mississippi… Anyway, he was really knowledgeable about starting fires from nothing. Knew a lot about water, how to make it fresh and how to filter it in the wild. Never said how he knew it either." Dave laughed. "I'm sure we talked about all our backgrounds, but it's lost in the effect of time, I guess."

Dr. Pat sat quietly, listening intently.

"Lemme see…Four. Four, Four, Four. What was his name? …Billy! Not Bill, Billy. From Tennessee. We joked about how his middle name would probably be Bob, but he never said.

"Me, I was Five. And then there was Six." Dave stared off into the ceiling corners for a while. Dr. Pat thought for a moment he had lost his train of thought and was about to say so when Dave spoke. "Gil. Yeah, Gil, not Gilbert, just Gil. Can't remember where from. He was the last to arrive before the Colonel came in and started in on our mandate and training.

"We never used our names again. Always went by the numbers." Dave chuckled again. "By the numbers." He shook his head. "We weren't together as a group more than five, six weeks. Now this is what surprised us, and is so totally bat-shit insane that anytime I ever even tried to discuss it with some other Vet, I'm shut down.

"It's like this: Basic, I'm sure you know, was 8 weeks, some say 9. After that, a trainee is sent to Advanced Individual Training, AIT. Most soldiers in Vietnam, from the time they step off the bus to boots on the ground in the jungle was six months. For us it was accelerated. Five weeks. Hell, most soldiers didn't even get their hands on a rifle for the first two weeks. But then, they were marching and doing all that stuff that teaches them to follow orders.

"From the first day, we were trained and trained hard. Up at six, an hour of calisthenics, then a shower and breakfast. Two hours of hand to hand, two hours of survival training. An hour of linguistics, that's where we learned Vietnamese - very rudimentary Vietnamese. Then lunch. Two more hours of hard work-out, and again two hours of hand to hand, two hours of survival training. Then dinner and more hand to hand or sometimes, what we called 'Chaos Training.' Ways to create chaos all by yourself.. During our off time, what little there was of it, we helped each other with hand to hand. We truly believed that was going to be our salvation.

"The close encounter training took a heavy turn when we got the knives. I swear the man teaching us was determined for us to be wrong all the time. He could disarm us in seconds and not break a sweat. We got good at disarming each-other but when he wanted to, we were knifeless. No matter which knife we used, either. God, we hated him. He didn't come out and say it, but we felt that he really wanted us to fail.

"Then one day I got this idea. The Gerber knife was long but shaped like a stiletto in that it was a narrow double edged blade. I took a short belt off some other piece of equipment and secured the knife on my forearm. The little belt had a snap and fit like a charm. Held the knife firmly against my forearm under a long sleeved shirt. I put on a tee shirt and a loose, long sleeve jungle shirt over it. Sitting in the dark that night, I practiced unsnapping the little belt from the outside of my shirt, releasing the knife and slipping it into my right hand.

"We took turns in hand to hand training the next morning and I figured he'd call on me first because I was wearing the clean and pressed jungle shirt. I was wrong. He let me sit in the heat in that long sleeved shirt, sweating for a good hour before he finally turned to me and said, 'Dressed for the ladies, Five?' He was trying to bait me, but I just pulled the buck knife and the Pilot knife and took a stance. Tried to look ready.

When we started, I tried my best to keep the knives, but finally let him take the buck knife first. Rubbed my forearm like I had practiced, unsnapping the little belt and then lunged with the Pilot's knife, letting him take that. I came in close, knowing he'd pull me by my left arm, turning his back, spinning completely around so as to show me my own knife. It was his big move to make us all squirm.

"But not this time.

"As he took the knife, turning around, the Gerber was already sliding into my right hand. I brought my right arm up as he turned and I whipped the knife right under his chin, tapping him on the collar bone with the fist holding the knife." Dave laughed. "My god, you should have seen his eyes!"

"He quickly called an end to the workout that day. He caught me as we were leaving and looked me up and down. 'Moves like that?' he then tapped me on the sternum. 'Thinking outside the box, always having something in reserve?' Then he smiled, nothing big, no teeth, just a less serious flat lipped smile. The only time I can remember him smiling. 'That's how you will survive this. Always think ahead, plan ahead. Keep your head and give them what they don't expect.' And with that, he left. He never mentioned it again.

"The guys considered me a genius and they all asked how I did it. We talked that night for the longest time. I showed them how I had secured the knife, and we took turns trying it out." Dave smiled and hung his head. "I still remember his words and the feeling of the guys slapping me on the back. One of the few times in my life I felt like I had done something right."

"Where was the fear then?"

"Fear?" Dave looked at her, then at the ceiling. "Every night I feared what was coming. We had no fantasies about what to expect. We didn't say it out loud, but none of us expected to be coming back from overseas." He swallowed hard. "You try not to dwell on it, but sometimes, when the night droned on, and sleep wouldn't come, that's the thing that slips in uninvited. I can't tell you the number of times I cried myself to sleep with that flat pillow across my face so no one could hear me." He cocked his head to the side, "Now that I think about it, I wonder if they were doing the same."

"You have no real knowledge of the moment when the fear left you?"

Dave stared across the office. He knew exactly when it all changed. Part of him didn't want to give in, give the Doctor what she wanted, but he recalled how he had changed that before. After 40 years of refusal, he had given her the whole story in one visit. He knew he couldn't do that again.

"That moment in the jungle." Dave said. His mouth had become dry. "When I found her…" He could see the little girl's hand, the one he had accidentally dug up which indicated the fate of the villagers he found in Vietnam. "The realization that none of us, soldiers or civilians like these innocents who were just trying to eke out a living there in the jungle… None of us were…" He could feel the cold sweat collecting at the back of his neck. "Something inside me sort of… clicked… died… left." He took a breath to calm himself. That smell had returned. The mixture of dead flesh and rotting vegetation. The ravine with the bodies covered with just enough dirt and junk to… He knew he was on the edge of an episode of some sort. Fear feeds on fear and he knew if he pushed against it, he'd lose. He took a breath, and another.

The room tipped a bit and he could swear he heard those trucks on that rainy muddy back-road. Those damn trucks. Dave closed his eyes and without knowing he had, put both hands up over his ears. He knew if he heard the trucks, he'd see the people. Visions of the dead, rising up out of that ravine.

"It's ok, Dave." Dr. Pat's soft voice. "We're here in the office, no jungle -"

A tone. Soft. Unremarkable but for what it indicated. Dave broke from the vision, grateful for the tone. It indicated the end of today's session and it gave him yet another anchor to this moment here, in the present. It helped him separate then from now. Just that one thought helped to push the thoughts of the jungle, the little girl and Vietnam itself back into the box where he kept it all locked up.

Dave was up and out the door before Dr. Pat had even shut off the soft alarm. He headed to his car, thoughts of hidden knives and hidden places and lost fear swirled about in his mind, behind a growing headache.

It would take a few days and a lot of naps to get control again. Time, he felt, he just didn't have.

Chapter 14

The hill overlooking the Dead Lands was covered in a variety of green grasses, all of which made a comfortable seat as Dave studied the landscape before him. Beside him lay the knight sword and a sunhat, along with a small backpack of things he might need on a long hike: a big jug of water in a sling coupled with trail mix and a couple of sandwiches packed into the pack. Dave pulled the pack on and adjusted the straps while trying to think his way across the vividly dry landscape before him.

Opening his phone, he called up the photos he had taken of Doc's big map and looked quickly from the map to the landscape and back again, noting landmarks in his mind. He slipped the phone back in his shirt pocket, securing the button, took a deep draw on his water bottle, grabbed the Knight's sword and slipped down the hill to the edge of the Dead Lands.

He started out with an easy rhythm, walking steadily without overtaxing his legs. He didn't want to move so fast as to wear himself out or deplete his energy. After that run in the tunnels, he didn't have to remind himself that, although he was Knight of the Offset, at 68, he was no spring chicken. He remembered how his late wife would cackle like a chicken when he'd use that phrase. He chuckled at the memory. The thought of her gave him renewed energy, rejuvenating his hope to find a way to stop Druscilla.

He took note of the places he had been before, even marking in his mind where he had entered the caves. He wanted to find Druscilla without her Dragon backup, so he moved on past that area. Dave noticed that the rock outcropping was more than just a bunch of rocks piled together. The rocks were, in fact, the end of a long line of outcroppings and hills that stretched into the Dead Lands. He passed them by and continued further into the eerily silent lands. There were no birds, no bees, no wildlife of any kind. In addition, there were no babbling brooks or rivers. The only sounds came from Dave's boots that scuffed through the dry dirt as he walked.

The trees here had all stopped growing. Those that remained were far and few between, their bark dull and lifeless. All of them appeared to be the same, with black bark and sharply angled branches overhead. Dave noted that the trees didn't have any branches low enough to cause him to duck. At least that made walking easier. The ground was flat, but hard packed, dry and cracked. His steps kicked up small dust clouds which settled quickly behind him.

In his mind's eye, he tried to see the Dead Forest as it might have been before Druscilla, disguised as the Old Woman in the Caves, had leached out all the life. He could imagine the green leaves, the dark brown bark and the wild flowers growing in between. That would bring back the bees, the birds and everything else. Dave smiled. He wondered if the energy of his thoughts would somehow help the forest return to its original state after this whole thing was over.

He granted that he didn't know how the Offset would use his energy, but hope was hope and he produced a lot of it as he walked.

Walking. Looking. Hours passed. The Sun beat down. He left the trees behind and entered into a vast and barren desert. Dave raised his bottle of water and noted how it was close to being empty. He had also finished the trail mix and the sandwiches some time ago. He was tired, but felt good about his search. He figured it was time to call it a day and see what he could do tomorrow.

He raised the knight's sword to create one of the doors he used to get to and from the Offset.

Nothing.

He almost slapped his forehead as he remembered that he needed a wall, or something for the door to be created from, or on. He turned in a circle, viewing the Dead Lands and noticed that the rock outcropping that he had passed many hours ago had become a tall flat sided mesa. He turned and headed toward it, certain he'd find a place to create a door.

The mesa was further than he had thought and it was sundown by the time he reached any part of it large enough for his use. He gulped the last of his water and strode up to the flat side of the mesa, holding up the sword. He touched the silver to the side of the rocks, fully expecting the door to appear.

Nothing. He waited a bit and again touched the sword to the flat rock again. Still nothing. Dave turned and stared out at the vast plain of dry dirt with the angular black trees dotting the distance. He dropped the sword to his side, understanding dawning as to what was going on. Druscilla had drained all the Offset energy out of this land. Since it was a creation of the Offset, it was Offset energy that fueled the Knights sword, and thus, created the doors he used.

"Well," he said aloud, "at least I found her again."

He turned to his left, for no other reason than it would take him back the way he came. He knew it would take hours of walking to get back to where the

Offset energy could help him. Shadows were growing quickly, and he knew he would need shelter for the night.

Littered about the base of the mesa were rocks and boulders from small to large. Some so large, Dave felt confident he could find a sheltered spot to spend the night and try the long walk home the next day. He walked in among the boulders, stepping over the small ones and walking around the large ones in his search. He worked a winding path in and out among the boulders and rocks.

Rounding a large boulder, Dave came upon a clearing where he was surprised to find a small boy sitting before a fire. Dave was immediately wary. The boy simply sat staring at the fire, his hands in his lap. He was about 5 years old, Dave guessed, and wore a gray tee-shirt and jeans. His face was a jovial round and his hair rumpled and unkempt.

Dave approached the fire and the small boy.

"Hey." Dave offered. The boy continued to stare at the small fire.

"His name is Huck." A voice came from Dave's right. Dave glanced to the right to find another boy, a bit older. He was solid, stocky and wore a black tee-shirt over black shorts. His hair was cut short, and stood up in the front. "I'm Tom." He said.

Dave glanced back to Huck, only to find he was gone. Dave looked back to his right only to find the other boy, Tom, also gone.

"No," Tom said from Dave's left. "We're not gone." Dave swiveled his head to the left to find Tom up on a rock. Beside him was Huck. Their movements told Dave more than he wanted to know of these two.

Dave tried for nonchalance. "I'm Dave." He sat

down on a log beside the fire, holding out his hands pretending to warm them. He kept his eyes on the fire, waiting to see what, if anything, the boys did. He continued to stare at the fire, not moving.

Beyond the fire, Tom and Huck appeared. They sat and also pretended to warm their hands. Dave nodded to himself internally. So far, so good.

"So, what's two boys like you doing out here in the Dead Lands." Dave asked.

"Well," Tom smiled, "we're not dead, if that's what you're thinking."

Huck snickered and peered over the fire at Dave. "You got any snacks in there?" He pointed to Dave's backpack.

Dave spoke first to Tom, "Then, what are you?" Dave looked at Huck. "No, no snacks." Huck looked dejected. There was a feeling pulling at him that these boys wanted to be friends, or more correctly, his friend.

"You're Knight of the Offset." Tom smiled. "You can figure it out."

"Then we can be friends!" Huck said. Tom gave him a quick look which shut him up. The look wasn't lost on Dave.

Huck reached up inside his tee-shirt sleeve and scratched his arm. When he pulled it out, he was holding two granola bars. He gave one to Tom and bit into the other. Tom joined him, looking right at Dave.

Dave looked at the boys and smiled. "I never had an imaginary friend when I was a boy, at least not that I remember."

Tom nudged Huck and nodded. "He's smarter than he looks." Huck snickered with a mouthful of granola.

"He looks like my grandpa." Huck offered and

continued munching his granola bar.

"You don't have a grandpa!" Tom said tersely.

"HE can be my grandpa!"

"We're imaginary FRIENDS, not grandkids!"

The evening was getting darker, and Dave hoped to find a place to catch a few hours sleep. "Boys, I wonder if you can help me find a place to sleep before I start back toward home." This stopped the boys' bickering and directed them both back to Dave. Huck looked a bit taken aback. Tom smiled. Dave was unsure what that smile meant.

"Yeah," Tom said, "We can do that." He got up and started off into the dark, closer to the mesa. "There's a cave back here."

Dave was glad to hear about a cave. He got up and followed the boy named Tom as Huck got up and followed the two of them. Dave rounded the rocks as he listened to Tom's voice up ahead in the darkness.

With the fire light gone behind them, the night closed in. When the night became too dark, Dave put his hand on the knight's sword. Expecting a brilliant light from the end of the handle, the sword only gave off a dim glow. Tom and Huck stopped before the wall of the mesa and turned to look at the dim glow coming from the Knight's Sword.

"What's that?" he asked.

"That's the Knight's Sword." Dave replied calmly, looking down at the dim light it gave off. "It -" Dave was slammed from behind and though he fully expected to come in contact, face first, with the wall of the mesa, he instead found himself stumbling head first into total darkness.

"Huck!" Tom shouted in alarm.

"Shhhh.." Huck put his finger to his lips. "Now

he'll be our friend forever! And, maybe, protect us from," He looked around the growing dark. "You know who."

Chapter 15

Dave was in the dark. Again. The Offset had a way of putting him there and for the moment, he was frustrated. He was angry at himself for trusting the two boys so easily. He stumbled into the dark after being shoved by one of them and couldn't stop himself from running into a wall in the dark. He felt the Knight's sword dig into his hip but had protected his head and face with his arms. At least this time he could stand in whatever corridor or cave he found himself in.

He took hold of the Knight's sword's handle hoping for some light, any light. He was disappointed. The glow from the stone at the end of the handle was even less than it had been only moments before. Dave wasn't sure if the problem came from the shock the sword took against the wall, or something else. This only led to a dawning understanding of his internal power, its origins and connections to the Offset.

But that was not the issue at this moment. He needed to find out how to get out of this place without having access to the Knight's Door, as he had come to call it. The dim glow may not have been as bright as it had been in the past, but it did allow him to see a bit of what was around him as his eyes became accustomed to it. It was about half a candle power, but it was enough.

"I've got to remember to always have a flashlight handy." Dave's voice almost startled himself. He looked about, taking in the walls, the floor and his situation.

He was in another tunnel, much like the one that took him deep into the Tooth Fairy's 'Dental Caverns.' It also reminded him of his recent run in with a certain large reptile. He really didn't want to make that mistake again. Dave looked down the tunnel one way and then the other. The tunnel was wide with sloped sides that had a rough hewn look as if carved by picks. The floor was smoother, and he was glad for that. 'Less stumbling.' He thought to himself.

He took his hand off the knight's sword for a moment and looked both ways again. There was, he thought, just a bit of light coming from one direction more than the other. He listened for any sounds but heard nothing, and felt only a gentle movement of air. He took a slow sniff of the air. All he smelled was dry rock. This told him that there was, at least, no Dragon in this tunnel. With nothing else to guide his decision, he moved toward the light. He walked carefully and cautiously, taking his time. He didn't want to trip or stumble in the minimal light.

Dave's eyes were getting quite used to the almost darkness as he rounded a curve in the tunnel and came out into a vast room. This was no natural cavern. The walls were smooth, with six torches mounted on the walls to the right and to the left. Thirteen massive columns stood in a large circle holding a cupola style roof high above his head. Each column was the size of a house with hardly any space between them. Due to the low light of the flickering torches, the cupola held only darkness.

Between the columns and the walls, wide steps had been carved into the rock and rose to a level higher than Dave's head, but still far below the height of the ceiling. At the top of the steps was a wide circular door which showed only darkness beyond.

What caught his attention most was the stained altar in the center of the big room, between all the giant columns. It looked a lot like the big altar he had seen in the Tooth Fairy's domain. The main difference was that this one had dark stains that ran down the sides; stains that ranged from a black to a dark brown. He knew in an instant that this was a place of sacrifice. What kind of sacrifice was the question as the entities in the Offset were incapable of bleeding. It was not something he wanted anything to do with and decided he'd better move on. He angled around behind one of the columns and toward the steps, thinking, 'Up is always better than down.'

There was a brighter light on the stairs, being directly below the torches. Each step was quite wide due to the size of the circular room. He was halfway up the steps when the first blob of darkness slipped out of the stone walls and bit him on the wrist. Dave wasn't sure exactly what he was seeing and was totally unprepared for the thing to attack him. He cried out and beat the creature against the wall to get it to release him. Before he could accomplish that, more of the blobs slipped out of the walls and came at him. They were mostly floating, shapeless black things. They had both legs and wings and moved through the air easily, though their wings didn't flap and Dave didn't feel any air movement.

He quickly pushed his injured hand, with the unknown creature attached, against the new threat, allowing them to bite at the blob attached to his wrist. Finally, the thing fell away, but left a ghastly hole in his wrist. The bite was black at the edges and Dave had only a moment to note that there was a glowing purple center where the teeth bit into his flesh. He turned his attention to the growing threat.

Now unable to use his left hand, Dave grabbed

the knight sword with his right and stepped back down a step to give himself more room to fight. He pulled, but the sword wouldn't come out of its sheath! As he pulled and shook the sword, trying to release it from its sheath, another of the blobs came at him. Dave caught a glimpse of its purple eyes just before it sunk its teeth into his thigh. The pain was incredible!

Not wanting to go down without a fight, Dave fell back a few more steps as he pulled the bowie knife and sliced the blob in two. It disappeared in a puff of golden dust. Dave's leg was on fire, but he knew he had to keep fighting. He pulled a second blade, the stiletto. Holding the two knives handle to handle, he created a two ended fighting weapon made of steel. He twisted his right hand, spinning them high and low and knocked more of the blobs away into the dim light, killing others as they were touched by the steel, exploding in a puff of gold.

Unable to feel his left arm, he knew he had only moments to find an escape. He could feel the poison moving up his arm, nearly to his shoulder. He turned to stand with his back to the wall, but then his right leg suddenly stopped working. Dave stumbled and fell, rolling off the steps and down into the altar area, holding tightly to his weapons, careful not to lose them in the fall. When he landed, he lost his breath for just a moment, but he was quick to raise the two knives, fending off another of the blobs.

He looked at his left hand and saw it was black, misshapen, with purple lines following the veins. He was pretty sure his leg was the same. He knocked another of the blobs aside and stabbed one that aimed for his good leg. That's when one of the blobs slipped past his blades and sunk its teeth into his shoulder, but

Dave snapped his right arm back and impaled the thing on the stiletto. Dave was dying, he knew. Each time he killed one of the things, it disappeared leaving behind a golden cloud, but another immediately took its place. This battle, he knew, could not be won. He had to come to grips with that, telling himself all that he needed to hear.

Dave felt weak, his vision blurred. He shook his head to clear it. His breathing was hitched and he had little left to give in the way of strength. At the core of his being, he knew he wouldn't be making it out of this room alive. He was disappointed in himself and his actions. He should have been more prepared, should have had a plan. He wasn't some hero, he was just an old man who now lay on the floor of some ancient temple, his body no longer responding, surrounded by some strange creatures of evil that he couldn't even understand, let alone defeat. Even the Silent Lightning had deserted him.

He only hoped his wife couldn't see his defeat, watch him die from where she was. Perhaps, soon, he would be with her, and he could hold her once again, be loved by her, say how sorry he was. The emotions of the last year rose in his chest, threatening to spill out his eyes. He steeled himself for the end. Maybe in death, at least, he could keep the power from Druscilla. He looked up at the blobs, trying to count how many he could take out before he succumbed.

But they didn't attack. Instead they all turned and rotated, pointing their eyes up to the landing at the top of the steps. There, shrouded in the darkness of the circular doorway, was a tall shadowy figure. A shadowy figure with glowing purple eyes! He knew immediately it was Druscilla. He didn't know at this point if he had found her or she had found him. Part of him really didn't care.

As she approached the edge high above, the blobs moved away, leaving him alone. Dave used his good leg and just about all the energy he had left to scoot himself up against the base of one of the columns for no other reason than to get away from the altar. The light from the flickering torch high above his head gave Druscilla a ghastly yellow glow as she stepped forward into the light. Her smile of triumph made Dave hate her even more. She didn't walk down the steps. She stepped off the upper level and merely floated down. Her new magic may actually be more powerful than her old magic, Dave thought.

She stood watching him die. He knew she would gloat and he also knew he would do anything to keep her from getting the power of the Silent Lightning. In truth, he didn't know if she was able to get the power from him, but he was sure he couldn't let her try. He was as sure of that as he was sure he didn't want that Dragon to eat him dead or alive.

"Hello, Dave." She just stood beside the altar. She gestured and the blobs retreated out of Dave's line of sight. She walked slowly to where Dave lay in the last moments of his life.

Dave calmed. He knew now what would happen and how. He almost smiled at the Hallowitch. "You again?" he forced a chuckle. "I thought I killed you."

Druscilla didn't smile. In fact, she almost looked bored.

"No matter," said Dave. "Come on over here and let me do it again." With everything he had, Dave raised his left arm and tried to point two fingers at Druscilla, just as he had the last time he had seen her.

Dave knew he hit a nerve when she flinched back a bit.

"You no longer control that power." Druscilla said more in an attempt to convince herself, though Dave knew she was probably correct. In his head, Dave wondered if he ever really controlled it. "There is no Offset Energy existing in this area so there is no connection to it. IF, that is, you still carry it, and that is questionable. If you do, you will soon be without it."

She walked slowly and triumphantly to his side. Dave simply watched her, waiting for the moment to come. He had long ago wondered what he might do in this situation. How he might react, how he could keep his dignity and at the same time, keep Druscilla from getting control of a power he, himself, didn't even know that much about. One night, it all came to him. He knew that if this situation were to play out, were to have its proper conclusion, he knew what had to happen, and how to do it. He had thought it could keep that from happening. He closed his eyes for a moment, realizing how foolish he had been.

"I told you." She leaned down into his failing vision. "I always get what I want." She reached forward, her hands becoming clawed, ready to tear the power from his chest.

"And I told you," Dave wheezed and swiped the steel blades at her hand, causing her to flinch back. "Over my dead body!" All the power he had was left in his one arm. He dropped the bowic knife into his lap and without a second thought used the last of his strength to drive the stiletto into his chest.

In his mind two voices screamed. One didn't want him to do it, and the other argued that it was the only way. A third scream joined them.

"NOOOO!" Druscilla screamed.

Dave entered the blackness with a smile.

Chapter 16

"Ok, that should do it for today." Todd called out to the room of women. They gathered up their mats and water bottles and purses and carry bags as Todd made some notes about the recent class.

Todd was a man of many skills. In the spring and summer, he drove a cement truck for a local company. During those times when the weather kept him from that job, he filled in with such things as handyman projects, martial arts training, and he had just finished teaching a class of yoga students.

The big barn sat on a property just outside the subdivision where Todd's and Dave's houses resided. Todd had purchased the property on a lark and used his own labor and resources to build it into the gymnasium and offices it now housed. The main area was a large space for workouts and included climbing walls. A large workout bag hung from the ceiling high up in one corner. The back area of the big barn had been rebuilt to include showers and offices for Todd's various activities.

Todd glanced up as the last of the women left and noticed someone he wasn't expecting. Edgar, the S3HR supervisor of the Shopping Center Santas – of which he was one – stood at the door waiting patiently for the room to clear.

"Mr. Frasier!" Todd called out. "What can I do for you today?' He put down his notepad and gestured for the man to join him where he sat on the floor. Edgar glanced out the door one more time before closing it firmly and walking briskly across the exercise area.

"There's been a..." Edgar paused to look

around the area, "situation." Edgar wasn't so sure how much he should tell Todd.

"You need me to play Santa for someone?" Todd forced a laugh. "It's not even Autumn!"

Edgar tried for a relaxed posture, and put both hands into his pockets. "Oh! No, it's not that." Edgar stopped again, looked down, looked up, glanced nervously about the room. He came back to Todd, who was waiting expectantly. Finally, he could think of no other way to say it. "It's Dave."

Todd was immediately concerned. "Is he hurt? Is he ok? Is there something I can do?" Todd switched to angry. "Was it that bitch, Druscilla?" Todd was always an easy going guy, but when something threatened his friends or his family, he became a very dangerous individual. "Did she -" Todd's face darkened even more. Edgar knew Todd was as deadly with knives as Dave and had even helped Dave with his knife fighting skills. He didn't need a demonstration.

"No, no," Edgar put up his palms, hoping to calm the big man. "He's… ok. There was a bit of a… problem - but again, Dave is ok." As Todd relaxed, so did Edgar. "It's just that Dave will need to be… uh… away for a while and he needs someone to feed his cat."

"Sheldon?"

"Yes."

"Oh." Todd still wasn't sure. "Yeah…I guess I could. I think he left me a spare key. Yeah, I can run over there and feed the cat a couple times a day. Sure."

"Good." Edgar nodded. He stood there a bit longer, wondering if he should tell Todd the truth. He pretty much knew the truth already. Todd was Dave's best friend and had been privy to much of the information that Dave had about the Offset world and the entities who lived there. Edgar almost hated lying to the man. In the end, he just nodded and headed to the door.

Todd got up and followed Edgar to the door and watched him drive away. While he was watching the car make it down the unpaved drive to the main road, Carrie, his wife, came out of the back rooms and joined him at the door.

"What's wrong?"

"What makes you think something is wrong?" he smiled at Carrie as he turned to take her in his arms.

"I know you." She pushed him away. "Don't play this off. What. Is. Wrong?"

Todd stood there, wondering how much he should say, and at the same time wondering just how much he really knew. He walked across the gym gesturing for her to follow him.

"You remember Edgar? The boss at S3?"

"Your Christmas job?"

"Yeah, he was just here."

"Ok, so?" Carrie kicked off her shoes and began the slow dance of martial arts moves, known as a 'kata.' Carrie, like Todd, was also a black belt in martial arts.

Todd got up and joined her, mimicking her moves as they both worked through the same kata. And as they worked, Todd told her why Edgar had come by. He also added in the history of Druscilla, her monsters both real and nightmare, and her threat to destroy Dave and both worlds. By the time he was done talking, Carrie had already stopped to stare at him.

"Truth?" she asked.

Todd stopped his kata and looked at his wife. He just nodded. In a moment she was in his arms, but this was anything but a romantic moment. Carrie was scared. Todd was also scared, but determined. He made a mental note to buy some more steel jacketed ammunition for his guns. And maybe a few more knives.

Chapter 17

Dave opened his eyes and looked around. As far as he could see was a flat featureless plain. He looked up at a ceiling of white fluffy clouds, but no blue sky showed through. Even with the clouds, there was plenty of light. Light seemed to come from both the clouds above and the surface beneath him. He wondered where he was and how he got here.

Air pulled into his lungs as he tried to pull up his last memory. A vision of Druscilla, standing over him, there in that dark area of the Under Lands, caused his breath to hitch in his throat. He remembered his last moments in the Offset. He had been determined to keep the power of the Silent Lightning from Druscilla at any cost. He remembered his thoughts of his wife, and his promise to her. He rethought through his plan of how he would keep Druscilla from getting control of the power. He remembered his resolve as he drove the stiletto into his chest. He heard Druscilla's scream and the smile it gave him before the darkness swallowed him.

He should be dead, but here he was, very much alive. Or at least it appeared that way.

Looking down, he was a bit surprised to find that the stiletto was not stuck in his chest. He was doubly surprised to lift his left hand and find it was still black and purple. He worried for a moment that this was another one of Druscilla's tricks.

"You've been poisoned." Said a voice.

Dave sat up and looked around. Standing only a few yards away was his old mentor, Grandfather. He was not Dave's real grandfather, but the oldest and wisest of the Cherokee tribe at the time when Dave had been a boy. Dave never knew him as anything but Grandfather.

"Grandfather." Dave stood slowly, still unable to use his left hand. His right leg was also giving him trouble. He hugged the old man. "You look older than last I saw you." Grandfather had died many years ago, but had appeared twice before to help Dave in his efforts to battle Druscilla. At that time, he appeared as a young man, in counterpoint to Dave's age of 68.

"You look older, too." The old man smiled. He indicated the stygian appendage that hung at Dave's side. "The poison is killing you, you know."

"I thought I had taken care of that." Dave gave a sheepish grin.

"Yes." Grandfather grimaced at the thought. "Not really the answer to the problem, Thunder Wolf, though I must admit, I didn't think you had that in you." He mimicked stabbing himself in the chest, as Dave had done.

"It seemed to be the only way to end the fight and keep her from getting that extra power."

Grandfather merely nodded.

"What is this place? Am I dead?"

"You are between life and death." Grandfather looked him up and down. "Not really Uwasv udahisdi Suicide; but then I'm not so sure it was such a good death."

Thunder Wolf knew that Grandfather only appeared to him in times of need. He waited for the lesson, giving Grandfather the time to gather his thoughts.

Grandfather looked up from under his furrowed brow. "When you drove that knife into your chest…"

He said.

Thunder Wolf nodded, looking down rather than at Grandfather.

"You might say, it was misguided."

Thunder Wolf didn't look up, embarrassed at the mention.

"No, not that." Grandfather chuckled. "You missed."

Thunder Wolf's head shot up, his eyes wide. "What?"

Grandfather patted the air between them chuckling a bit. "Yes, the knife went into your chest, but you missed the heart. You nicked a lung and scraped a couple of ribs, but you will probably live."

Thunder Wolf now narrowed his eyes. He looked around, raising one eyebrow as if to ask, "Then why am I here?"

"Yes, why are you here?" Grandfather sighed, putting both hands on Dave's shoulders. "I needed to know you were doing the bad thing for the right reason. I needed to see you." He smiled. "I am a medicine man. I brought you here to keep you from the Kalona Ayeliski, Raven Mockers. But now, I know you won't die and the Kalona Ayeliski will not torment you. Both because I have scared them away," Grandfather smiled, "And because you fought the Uyaga, evil earth spirit, and won

"Uyaga? You think Druscilla is the Evil Earth Spirit?" Thunder Wolf asked. Grandfather nodded. Dave thought some more about this.

"I won?"

Grandfather's shoulders rose and fell. "Well, maybe not won, but she didn't win either, now did she?"

Dave shook his head. "No, she didn't get the lightning." Dave looked off into the distance, "but at what cost."

"What cost? She didn't get the power, she didn't kill you and she is now filled with anger over the loss of that battle." Grandfather mimicked reaching for Thunder Wolf's chest, just as Druscilla had.

"Were you there? Did you see?"

"Nearby." Grandfather stepped closer and hugged Dave with more strength than he thought the old man had in life or in death. "You surprise me, Thunder Wolf. I wish we could have fought side by side, perhaps against the Uktena!" Grandfather laughed and stepped back. "You and your knives and the lightning against the great horned serpent! I would pay money to see that!"

"You can't fight by my side and watch the fight from the sidelines. Besides, I thought the Uktena was just a myth." Thunder Wolf said.

"There is much you do not know, Thunder Wolf!" Grandfather smiled one of his enigmatic smiles. "And now you must go and live to fight another day."

"Another day may be a while." Thunder Wolf said, indicating his left hand.

"Do you need anything?" grandfather examined the wound closely.

"A cure for this poison?"

Grandfather shrugged and shook his head indicating he didn't know of any cure.

"Oh that's good." Thunder Wolf chided Grandfather, "a medicine man with no idea of how to cure a poisoning."

Grandfather was not amused. "That is not poison of the earth. This is a poison from beyond the earth. It is made of magic and madness. I have nothing in my knowledge that would help." He looked into Thunder Wolf's eyes. "I can sing, and pray, but to what end? You need the help of others, who know of this poison."

Thunder Wolf nodded. "Ok, then just send me those hundred warriors again, when I'm back on my feet." Grandfather had brought 100 Native American warriors to the Offset to help Thunder Wolf in his fight against Druscilla. Thunder Wolf felt like it had been a hundred years ago. His strength was fading and he felt lightheaded.

"They can only make that trip once." Grandfather said. "But I will look around for some other help."

"What about you?" Dave smiled, thinking Grandfather was pulling his leg. 'You made the trip, what… twice now?"

"I am not them." Grandfather smiled.

Thunder Wolf smiled and nodded as if this made the most sense. He pulled his Grandfather in for another big hug and held him longer than he really meant to. Finally, they stepped apart.

The two men looked into each other's eyes for a moment longer. Grandfather nodded and turned to go. "Gvgeyu'i." he said in Tsalagi, the Cherokee Language. I love you.

"Gvgeyu'i." Thunder Wolf said in return.

He watched Grandfather fade into the landscape, but squinted when he realized that both Grandfather and the landscape were fading, turning dark. He reached out with his good hand, but his vision blurred and faded to black. He lost his balance and he fell into the darkness.

Again, darkness… was the last thing Dave remembered thinking.

Chapter 18

Druscilla approached Dave's body. She didn't want to admit that Dave had actually found a way to keep her from getting control of the power he had. She looked down at his lifeless body, scowling at the knife that protruded from his chest. She smiled a tight smile at the purple lines that pulsed through Dave's black and dead flesh. She stepped a bit closer, and used the toe of her boot to kick at his feet.

Assured he was actually dead, she put her hands on her hips and sighed angrily. She tried to remain calm, but inside she was fuming. *How can a mere human keep just of of my reach time after time?*

"It's bad enough you can come here to the Offset!" She shouted at Dave. Standing next to him, she kicked Dave's lifeless body as hard as she could. The kick was so hard the body flopped over on its other side. She watched the body a bit longer and with a nod, turned to her hoard of dark blobs, which had been waiting patiently in the near dark. She waved a hand and the dark blobs disappeared and with another wave and a sneer at Dave's corpse, she was gone. Only the scent of lavender and sulfur remained.

In the darkness, things moved. Things scraped and shuffled. Other things sighed. The movement of shadow coalesced into a shape, which took in the crumpled body lying alone in the big room. The form stood looking at the Knight, taking in both his body and his actions in the battle with the witch. With a nod, the shadow moved off down the long tunnel with quickening steps.

The torches continued to burn and flicker. Blood

trickled from Dave's mouth and pooled on the stone floor. It took some time, but finally, a door took shape in the wall behind the column. It was short and engraved with an elf standing beside the North Pole. The door opened and a bright white light flooded the room, casting wide shadows on the closest columns.

After a moment, a long green arm reached through the door. The arm was almost as big around as the door itself. It slid into the room and reached across the steps to where Dave's body lay. Verdant tendrils sprouted from the finger tips and enwrapped the human. The tendrils pulled him into the waiting hand, which then picked up the body carefully and carried it back through the small door.

The door closed and faded away.

Chapter 19

"Thank you all for being here." Mother Nature began. "I have asked you here to allow me to tell you a story. One that will mean more as you hear it."

Mother Nature stood in the vast Offset forest, a head above the tall trees. Sprinkled about in the tops of the trees were the hundreds of colorful fairies, her favorite creatures.

"This is the story of Dave -"

"The First Knight of the Offset?" Mari-elle was excited and it showed. She flew about as she talked, unable to control herself. Like sparrows, the others were prone to flit and fly with her when she got excited.

"Yes," Mother Nature was always patient with her children. "You see, Dave needs our help, but I feel I must tell you this story so that you understand why he needs your help." She waited for the fairies to calm and turn their attention to her. Mari-elle finally alighted on a small branch next to her friend, Rodri-gelle.

"For a human," she began, "Dave is an old man at 69 years old."

"That's barely a baby!" said one purple fairy loud enough for all to hear. The others murmured their agreement.

Mother Nature admonished the outburst with her eyes. "Yes, but remember, Dave is a human." She waited for them all to quiet down again. "Dave is part Native American, and part something else, though it's unimportant what that is.

"When he was just a boy, Dave would visit the American Native reservations and commune with his distant relatives. They are called Cherokee or

Aniyvwiya which means 'Real People.' It was on one such visit that Dave was gifted the powers that allowed him to come to the Offset and later, to become the Knight."

"The power?" said one bright red fairy.

"Yes." She responded. "Dave calls it the power of Silent Lightning, I call it the Lightning in the Knight, for he is only the second entity in any realm which has it. Certainly, the only human."

The fairies were now enraptured to learn about Dave, the First Knight of the Offset and the power he wielded. There were no more interruptions and Mother Nature spoke on.

"Dave received the power as a child. He never really understood it, but carried it as best he could. He lost track of it after his father died the following year. Growing up without a father, for a boy, is a very hard thing to do. For one, there was a lot of misunderstanding about it on all sides. He was bullied, teased, alone. Always alone.

"Death is, at best, incomprehensible to humans. Oh, they know it. They become aware of it when they get older and even expect it. But most can handle it day to day with the support of their careers, their friends and their families. You take away one important post of that support, and the rest of it… falters.

"Dave's mother was also lost after her husband died. She had to change her entire life. She went from housewife to bread winner practically overnight. She continued raising young Dave alone. But because of her own inability to accept or understand the death of her husband, she had trouble in directing young Dave in how to understand the loss of his father, how to live with it, accept it, learn from it and get past it and so he never quite did.

"Having rarely used the lightning, and never really connecting to it, the power itself was forgotten. He used it only a few times when the power itself protected him from danger. He never learned how to call upon it when he needed it. He forgot about it as he got older and life took his attention.

"To someone like our Dave, school was almost an imposition. He was smart, but never was good at being part of a group, not sports certainly. Graduation came and went. Dave joined the army and went off to war. He did what was asked of him and returned home in short order.

"He married young. Had children. Divorced. Married again. Divorced again. He was just too young in the first marriage. He never learned to be the right husband for his wife, nor the right father for his children, though he desperately wanted to. He wanted too much to be the father he never remembered, couldn't remember. Try as he might, he just couldn't find the key.

"He moved from job to job, always trying but never quite succeeding. He felt he was missing something tangible, some unknown thing or knowledge he just didn't possess or couldn't find. In his second marriage, still lost from the first, he chose unwisely. Incompatibility caused them to go their separate ways. Dave was alone again. More alone than he could almost bear."

The fairies were caught up in the story, so much so they hardly breathed. They were enraptured with the story of the human with so much pain in his life and no one to help with the burden.

"Late in life," Gaia continued, "Dave met a third

woman who seemed to be all that he needed. He had made changes to his life as he got older, ways he thought would lead him in a relationship better. When he met his third wife, they were both surprised at the love which grew so quickly.

"They married.

"Life for Dave and his third wife became rather idyllic. They lived a life he had always dreamed of. He found a stable job that supported them, and was able to stick with this job for many years, long enough to retire. In retirement, they could then spend so much more time together.

"Dave's retirement routine was more fulfilling than anyone could ask. They spent every moment together. Shopping, cooking, doing little chores around the house. They watched tv together, gardened together and loved together. Every night, laying in bed, waiting for sleep, she would lay her head on his chest for a few minutes, listening to his heartbeat. She felt connected to life in that way, through his heart. With a lingering kiss she would then roll to her side of the bed and they would both go to sleep. Every morning, he would roll over to her side of the bed and gently wake his wife with a kiss, playfully waking her with love and the special attention he felt she deserved."

Mother Nature looked over her listeners. The multicolored fairies adorned the trees like brightly colored sprinkles on a very special cake. She knew they had trouble with human concepts such as divorce or retirement, but they listened quietly, taking in the information that Mother Nature offered.

"Then…" She said slowly, "then… came the one morning when Dave, our Dave, First Knight of the Offset…" Mother Nature didn't want to say this part out loud, but she knew she had to. She steeled herself and smiled, letting her favorite little creatures know that all was good. "Dave rolled over to his wife and kissed her ear. She didn't move." She lost her smile as she continued.

"Dave wrapped an arm around her and snuggled up to her, chuckling at her playful attempt to pretend to be asleep. … He kissed her again. … Whispered in her ear. There was still no response. He spoke loudly, saying her name, asking her to respond. He felt her neck, to see if her heart was beating. He found nothing."

Shocked by the mention of real death, some of the fairies began to cry. Even Gaia, knowing what was coming, felt tears welling in her eyes. She had trouble continuing, but she knew she must.

"Alarmed, he rose up in the bed, speaking her name aloud... louder… Shouting her name, he leaped from the bed, and ran around to her side, calling her name again and again.

"Ever the protector, the one who knows what to do, Dave called for help. He cried while he waited for them, working to revive her, himself. He cried when they came. He cried while they tried; but they were unable to wake his wife. The people left and Dave sat on the floor and cried. And shouted, and screamed and cried some more."

Mother Nature looked at the small faces of the fairies. They were all crying at the loss they felt for Dave. She hated having to use their emotions in this way, but it was the only way to get what she needed, what Dave needed, for the fairies were such happy loving creatures that asking them to create tears would be monumental for them to even consider. With a gentle gesture from her hand, Mother Nature gathered all the fairies' tears into a large lily pad leaf. The fairies were surprised at the move, but didn't speak.

The entity known as Gaia leaned down into the forest to where a bed had been set up, and now held the near lifeless form of Dave Nicklaus, Knight of the Offset. The knife had been removed from his chest and lay at the foot of the bed with the rest of his things. His clothes and the sheets on which he lay still bore the stains of his blood. In stark contrast, half of Dave's face appeared as if carved from charcoal with dark purple lines that ran haphazardly across the ashen half. The other half was as pale as the clouds above.

Dave's shirt had been ripped open above the shoulder where the shapeless blob-creatures of darkness had bit him. The bites were blackened deformed flesh and the holes were growing wider with every passing moment. The areas where he had been bitten on his wrist and thigh were also exposed, both black, with the same deformed and dying flesh adorned with pulsing purple lines.

Gaia stepped to the bed, now of a size to approach. She held the large lily pad leaf full of Fairy tears and carefully brought it closer to the reclined form. She tipped the leaf and poured some of the tears into each of the ragged holes causing them to boil and hiss. She also poured the last of the tears into the wound on Dave's chest. Steam erupted from the hole and Dave's body convulsed violently, shaking the bed and frightening the fairies nearby. As the steam and bubbles abated, the shivers and convulsions also calmed.

Setting the lily pad leaf down beside the bed, Gaia sat on a stump close by to wait. She was joined by the fairies, who all simply sat quietly on the ground or in the trees and waited with her. They all spent a long time wiping what was left of their tears and glancing from Dave to Gaia and back. Not one of the fairies uttered a word.

They waited a long time.

Chapter 20

Old Man Time sat at his desk reading a book. It was the perfect time of day for reading. No one was clamoring for his attention, or making requests for changes in the way the Offset ran. It was a difficult decision when that happened.

The book was a simple study of the history of humans and he wasn't really all that engrossed in it, which is why something behind him caused him to look up, and lay his book down. He spun his chair around and looked across the wide room. Nothing was amiss, nothing was out of place, yet he still felt something was pulling him. Was it a noise? Was it a settling of the books and shelves? Perhaps a bird had flown against one of the window panes. That happened more than he cared to admit. He stood and surveyed the big room.

The room was a large collection of things having to do with the Offset and the energy it controlled. There was an alcove of books adorned with clocks, sundials and hourglasses, another alcove of sculptures depicting clocks, sundials and hourglasses. The walls were adorned with hundreds of clocks. Sundials sat upon shelves and hourglasses hung from the ceiling.

A very large globe of the earth sat in front of one of the tall gothic windows. The room was so large that there were six tall gothic arched windows on each wall of the square room. At the moment, only one side of the room had the shutters opened to allow the sunlight in. There were clear panes and stained glass panes depicting time in some manner or other.

But the centerpiece of the office was a large

scale model of the Offset. It showed the city center, with the clock tower along with the large mansions of the Major 7 lived. Gaia along with her partner, the Green Man lived in the Great Offset Forest. There were outlying areas identified and laid out precisely. Most importantly was that the edge of the large model had no definite beginning or end; the edge fading slowly to nothing.

All appeared to be in order.

The Old Man didn't look old today. He was in his prime and warily stalked about the room. Each dark corner was examined and dismissed. When, at last, he thought he had dismissed the feeling, he turned to find Shadowman standing before the Offset Map.

"Old Man!" He spoke softly but it was obvious he was angry.

"Jack." Old Man Time greeted this intruder warmly. "What brings you here?"

"Jack. What an interesting name, I haven't heard it in a while." The Shadowman smiled, his shadow teeth filling his lightless mouth. "How long has it been, TIM?" Jack asked.

"You're the only one that calls me that, and I've told you I don't like it."

"Tim Time, Timothy Tim with an E." Jack smiled big, then immediately lost that smile. "How long?"

"How long?"

"Don't patronize me, Old Man!" Jack advanced on the older man until they were almost face to face. "You remember! How LONG has it been?"

The old man didn't answer but merely stared into the black eyes of Jack, the Shadowman. "You know how long." There was a long pause where neither spoke. "What's this about, Jack?"

Jack ignored the question. "Over one hundred years! That's how long it's been," He poked the old man in the chest for emphasis. "Tim."

The Old Man relaxed, this was an old conversation between the two. "This again? You found a way to…escape, to enter the World of Man. I had to bring you back." The old man sauntered around the scale model as he spoke. "Especially after you killed all those -"

"Escape?" Jack laughed, "Is that what you called it?" He spread his arms wide. "I called it a vacation." He stepped toward the Old Man again, "Finding that man, taking him on, visiting the dark streets of Whitechapel, oh! What a freeing feeling. So incongruous that a being of Dark would find himself in a place called Whitechapel. Everyone should have such a vacation." He stopped and looked at Tim. "Oh, Tim, Timmy, Tim! You'll never feel that. You think humans are so much in control, but when you hold them down – ahh! The glint of the blade in their eyes. The sensation of the sharp edge gliding through young firm human flesh!" Jack lost himself in memory.

"Jack -"

"A scalpel! So simple, yet so very perfect for that. It's like running your hand across silk! The scalpel, it just glides through their flesh almost effortlessly!"

"Jack. Please."

"Their flesh hearts beating so hard that the blood spurts – it actually spurts from their flesh like -"

"Jack!" The old man's patience had worn thin.

Jack paused. The two looked at each other without speaking. Jack broke the silence. "Do you remember your promise?"

"Promise?"

"Yes, when you came to bring me back. You made me a promise, TIM. " Jack paced around the big model, putting it between him and the Old man. "You promised me that if I came back of my own free will, I could have the Darkness of the Offset. Every tunnel, every cave, every dark corner in the Under Lands would be mine. MINE! And MINE alone! Do you remember now?"

"Of course..."

"And now I must share the darkness with -" Jack stopped, his anger getting the better of him. He knew he should be calm to discuss this with Old Man Time.

"With?" Old Man Time was now surprised, and he was rarely surprised.

Jack smiled, amused. "You really don't know? The Controller of the Offset, Time and All It Represents doesn't know what's going on right under his own Golden Sundial?"

"You're talking about the Tooth Fairy." Old Man Time knew all, or at least he thought he did. He tried not to let the small doubts he had creep into his voice. "He never leaves his space, which isn't really part of the darkness, so you have the rest of the Under Lands to -"

"THE TOOTH FAIRY?" Jack shouted, "This is not about that damn lunatic and his stupid mice!" He had rounded the model fully and was now closer to the Old Man.

Old Man Time had had enough. He advanced on Jack and pushed him against the globe, bending him backward. "You will be civil in this room! You will stop this vague charade and make your request and be done, or I will banish you to the citadel – permanently!"

Now it was Jack's turn to push. He stood up, forcing Old Man Time to back up. "My Darkness has been usurped for far too long. Temporary. It was supposed to be temporary. Now, I kindly request you get her the hell out!"

"Her?"

Jack, the Shadowman, knew he was bringing new information to the conversation. "Yes. Her." He paused to make a point. "Druscilla."

Old Man Time laughed. "Druscilla is dead!" He laughed some more, and laughed even harder when he saw the look on Jack's face. "The Knight saw to it just recently." He calmed his laughter a bit, "well, actually it was Scarecrow, now the Headless Horseman, but she no longer exists here. It was Christmas Day just this last year. Scarecrow returned to retake his position as one of the Major 7. As his creation, he also had the power to de-create her; which he did!"

Jack was not amused. He looked at Old Man Time blankly. "Where is the Knight?"

There was a bit of a mental disconnect in the quick change of subject, but The Old Man was quick to reply. "I can ask him to come visit you, but he will tell you the same. He was there when it happened!"

"I saw The Knight, just recently, as a matter of fact." Jack moved slowly toward a darker corner of the room. "Just yesterday he was lying on the floor of the citadel. One of his own steel knives hilt deep in his chest by his own hand. And standing over him, angry at the loss of the Knight's special power, was… a very alive HallowWitch." Jack paused and turned to the Old man. "You can verify this. Just contact Gaia and ask her what she's doing today."

"Gaia?" The Old Man stared at The Shadowman who had stepped into the darkest corner of the room. He was almost invisible there.

"And once you know the truth," Jack said, "get that damned witch out of my demesne! Or you will see a return of The Ripper, the likes of which the world of man has never seen before!!" he snarled.

Old man Time watched the corner for more, but Jack, the Shadowman, was gone.

After a moment, he turned on his heel and headed out. Gaia and the Green Man in The Great Offset Forest were about to receive a visit, and the Old Man wasn't too happy about it. In fact, he had never been this angry.

Chapter 21

Dave didn't want to open his eyes. His arm was numb, his leg was numb and the right side of his face was numb. Top that off with a pain deep in his chest and he knew if he opened his eyes, he'd find out he was dead or about dead and he really didn't want to face that.

What was it Grandfather had said? "Between life and death" He tried speaking aloud, but only a small breath escaped his desensitized lips. Oh great, what could that mean if I can feel the pain in my chest and not my face! thought Dave.

He finally decided that if he could open his eyes, he should, if only to find out if he's in heaven or hell or back home with Sheldon perched on his chest. He chuckled at the thought of Sheldon doing that, but chuckling only made his chest ache more.

He allowed his eyes to open, but just a bit. Light. Ok, not red light, so it can't be hell. It was bright —

"His eyes moved!" came a voice.

"Which one…or was it both?" said another.

Dave wondered whose eyes they were talking about and almost chuckled again when he realized it was probably his eyes. He needed to get his eyes open. He pushed himself a bit more and forced himself to open his eyes.

Blurry. Very blurry.

"Looks like he's finally coming around." Voice #1. Sounds familiar.

"Dave?" Voice #2, also familiar.

The light stung his eyes a bit, but he forced

them to stay open, squinting, forcing his eyes to adjust to the light. He blinked a few dozen times. The blur abated if only a bit.

"Who is that?" Dave's voice was rough and using it took a lot out of him. His chest ached and why shouldn't it? He'd stabbed himself in the chest with a really sharp knife. I must be alive if I can feel that, but how can I be alive if I stabbed myself? Oh yeah, Grandfather said I had missed.

"Easy there," Voice #1, "just relax. It's me, us, Edgar and Reggie."

His eyes started to clear, but he was pretty sure they weren't working properly. The ceiling was way too low and Edgar towered over him.

"My eyes aren't working…" he rasped. "Where am I?

Edgar chuckled. "You're in the Medical Center at the… well, the North Pole." Edgar looked up at the low ceiling. "The place is designed for…my people. Low ceilings. In order to fit you in, we had to put your beds on the floor. Two mattresses, end to end."

That would explain a lot. Dave moved his eyes to take in the room, pretty much a standard hospital room, but much smaller. He smiled at being able to see things more clearly. He moved his right hand slowly up to his chest. There was no bandage he could feel. "How long have I been here?"

Edgar looked at Reggie, seated by the door. The low doorway made Reggie look like a giant. "About 4 weeks. It took that long for the poison to be countered and for your other…wounds to heal. You'll feel an ache, for a while anyway, but we expect a full recovery." Edgar leaned down so that he was closer to Dave's face. "And don't ever do that again!" He stood up straight, about to speak some more.

"I have no plans to do that again…"

"Old Man Time was pretty much livid!" Edgar explained, sitting in a low chair beside the bed.

"Tell me all about it." Dave's voice was clearing and he noted that the ache in his chest was growing less with each passing moment.

Before he could continue, a nurse, also about Edgar's size, came in to check on the patient. She adjusted his pillow so he could sit up, took his blood pressure, temperature and checked his hands, shoulder and even his thigh where they had been bitten. The bite marks were no more than ragged scars.

As the nurse left, Dave could see a small collection of others grouped by the door, eager to see Dave, the First Knight of the Offset, incapacitated though he may be. Reggie noted Dave's eyes and closed the door, waving the looky-loos off.

"Ok, so let's hear your side first." Reggie said, reseating himself in the chair.

"My side?"

"Let's just take it easy," Edgar put a hand on Reggie's arm communicating in ways words could not. "Dave did what he did, and the reasons will come out in good time." To Dave, "We're just glad you're alive and getting better."

"Look," Dave said, "I had no plans to do what I did… so don't go thinking I'm trying to do myself in for any reason." He looked pointedly at the two of them in turn. "It just… happened. I wasn't…" he sighed and laid his head back against the pillow, "I wasn't really prepared to find Druscilla even though I had gone looking for her and even though there was every indication that she was still around. I had thought everyone was just a bit too sure she was there, when I had, in fact, seen her demise." Dave paused thinking back. "And then there was that laughter."

Edgar and Reggie shared a glance, which Dave noticed. He waved it off with his good arm. "When I saw her in that big room, there below ground, I was as surprised as you would have been. She stepped off that high ledge and just floated down. That's when I knew it was really her and that my chances of getting away were…pretty much nil. And that poison…"

"It wasn't poison." Edgar stated calmly.

"It wasn't?" Dave looked at him. "I was told -"

"Told? By whom?" Reggie interjected.

"And when?" Edgar again…

Dave looked at Edgar. "Sorry, by the look of it during the fight, I had assumed it was poison of some sort." This seemed to placate Edgar who merely nodded and went on.

"First, you have to understand," Edgar looked at Dave meaningfully, "we didn't know where you were. You left no notes, nothing that would tell us when to even expect you. You might have died in that citadel had it not been for – of all entities - Shadowman."

"Shadowman?"

"He was watching you, and when you …used that knife on yourself. Doing that, well, first, you gained his grudging respect. But he also knew that without you, Druscilla would continue on, so it was he who came to Reggie." Edgar gestured to Reggie sitting in the chair.

"He came to me for help." Reggie continued the story. "Scared me silly when he just showed up in my bedroom! Woke me up shouting, 'Get Help! Save the Knight! He's in the citadel!' and the only thing I could think to do was contact Gaia. I wasn't going to contact the Old Man, that's for sure. It was Gaia who orchestrated the rescue. She called on Edgar and then the two of them worked with the Green Man to get you out of the citadel."

"How'd they find me?"

"The stones on the sword come from the offset." Reggie explained. "They are part of Gaia's world and she can find them anywhere."

"Offset GPS…" Dave muttered.

"Offset… what?" Reggie asked.

"Nothing." Dave smiled and turned his attention back to Edgar.

"Once you were rescued, Gaia took you to the Great Offset Forest." Edgar nodded. "It is a place of great healing energy and growth. She also knew that Druscilla had no way of finding you there. I don't know how, but she knew that the poison was not really poison, but was magic. Fairy Magic, from fairy dust. Gaia used more fairy magic to cure you."

"Fairy Magic?" Dave blinked a couple of times.

"Yes." Edgar responded. There was a long pause, while Edgar and Reggie waited for Dave to take it all in. "Then you were brought here to heal." Edgar gestured to his own chest, indicating the self inflicted wound Dave had received. Edgar didn't want to say it out loud.

"Fairy Magic." Dave looked down. "Well, I didn't stab myself with Fairy Magic. Why am I still alive?"

"Fairy Magic is a powerful thing." Edgar explained. "I… We… don't know that much about it, but suffice to say that the way the fairies felt for you caused their magic to heal you in ways no one else could."

Dave nodded, thinking. In all that had happened, and all that he knew about the Offset, he realized he was pretty much clueless when it came to battling anything magic. "I guess what this all comes down to is… hubris." He looked up at Edgar and Reggie, both remarkably quiet. "I didn't defeat Druscilla at all. The first time or this last time. I never had the power, in fact, it deserted me in the… what did you call it? The Citadel?" Dave turned his head away from his friends. "My power, my… special power… The Silent Lightning, whatever you want to call it, deserted me in that place. It's gone."

This was the first Edgar and Reggie had heard this part of the story. Dave's power was known across the Offset and Druscilla's hunger to get that power was all part of it. Now, without that power, everything about Dave, the First Knight of the Offset, was in question. They all sat in silence for a while, Edgar and Reggie exchanging quiet glances.

Standing beside the chair where Reggie sat, was the Knight's Sword. Dave stared at it. It represented what he had done to help the Offset, but in reality, he hadn't done a thing. Druscilla had fooled him. Fooled them all. Time and time again she proved she was indestructible. The sword only represented his failure.

"I'll get that sword back to Old Man Time." Dave looked to Edgar, "And then we can go back to just being friends or co-workers."

"Dave.."

"No, it has to be this way. Without that power, and without me being able to control that power, I have nothing to give the Offset. I didn't defeat Druscilla, quite the opposite, she defeated me! She defeated all of us! I suppose the only good thing to come of this is that she didn't get control of the power either."

The group lapsed into silence again. Dave stared at the wall above his feet. A pair of purple eyes appeared in the wall. They pushed forward revealing one of the big dark blobs he had fought in the Citadel. It looked about the room, locking eyes with Dave. It darted forward, quick and sure.

Dave put up his hands shouting a warning to the others, pointing at the intruder. Edgar and Reggie bolted up out of their chairs.

Light.

Bright white light blinded them all. A bolt of Silent Lightning, the power of which was more than Dave had ever seen, burned through the blob and into the wall. It was so powerful it cut through the wall and into the next room, where it continued up and out ripping through the walls, ceiling and roof, leaving a large gaping hole.

No one was more surprised than Dave, who had thought the power was gone. As his eyes regained their sight, he smiled and turned to Edgar. He lost his smile.

Edgar was half up and half out of his chair, frozen in the moment several inches off the ground. Dave saw Reggie was leaning at an angle, also surprised by Dave's warning. He should be falling. They both should be falling, but they were motionless. Frozen. Dave was confused. The power had never done anything like this.

"I just needed a moment, Thunder Wolf."

Thunder Wolf snapped his head around to where, a moment ago, there was a solid wall. Now it was open, a vista of low fluffy clouds beneath clear blue skies. Crouched only a few yards away was

Lightning Thunderer, the mythical entity who had gifted him the power. He was exactly as Thunder Wolf remembered him, complete with the lightning painted on his face. It was that same day that he had been given his Tribal Name, Thunder Wolf.

Thunder Wolf found he was no longer achy, and easily rose from the bed, ducking as he exited through the open wall. A glance back told him that the wall remained open. Edgar and Reggie were both frozen in motion.

"Siyo!" *Hello*. He spoke in the Cherokee language, Tsalagi.

"Siyo." Thunder Wolf returned the greeting.

"It is good to see you again, Thunder Wolf!" The two sat on the clouds, Thunder Wolf remembered the feeling of sitting in the clouds so long ago. The two sat in silence, looking at one another, the bright sun on their shoulders. Thunder Wolf was bigger now than he was as a child, but the big entity was still much bigger, even sitting so close. Lightning Thunderer smiled warmly.

"You said you needed a moment."

"Yes." Lightning Thunderer said, and clapped Thunder Wolf on the shoulder. "It is the Lightning."

Thunder Wolf waited, but nodded as if he understood.

Lightning Thunderer turned and looked out of the cloud plain and at his gaze, the clouds parted. Below, Thunder Wolf could see the arroyo where his Grandfather had lived and he could even see where the lightning scorched the rocks that fateful day. It was like looking back in time. Thunder Wolf stayed quiet, hoping to draw out whatever needed to be said.

Finally, Lightning Thunderer turned to Thunder

Wolf and reached out to touch his chest. "Pain." He said, pointing to the place where the knife had nearly ended his life. "It is the great teacher." With this he smiled.

Thunder Wolf nodded again, accepting this bit of information.

"When I allowed you to take the Lightning, I have to admit, I did not expect you to be able to hold the lightning, let alone use it. The lightning has its own motivations for doing what it does. And it stayed with you all these years for a reason." Lightning Thunderer raised his eyebrows as he looked at Thunder Wolf. "Even I don't know what those reasons are. I only asked it to protect you."

"It's gone. I-" Thunder Wolf started, but stopped when he remembered what had just happened. It was the Silent Lightning that had burned through the blob and the building itself. This confused Dave even more when he considered how the lightning had not been there when he needed it.

"Not gone, disconnected." The big man said. "Because we are Legends, Beings of Lore," Lightning Thunderer smiled a bit at this, "Our Energy is Offset Energy." He looked to Thunder Wolf as if this was the piece of information he was missing.

Thunder Wolf merely nodded, still unable to put it all together. In his head, he was shrouded in the idea that he was no longer The Knight; especially so if the Silent Lightning was not his to control.

"When the good energy of the Offset was drained from the Dead Lands; your energy, the Lightning energy, had nothing to connect to. It connects through you, and through the Offset. Sort of like trying to draw on a pipe with no fire." He mimed lighting a long pipe and looked to Thunder Wolf again to see if he got it.

"The first time, though," Thunder Wolf countered, "I went down to save the fairies. The power was still there."

"Residual." Lightning Thunderer said. "You had enough of the connection inside you to do what needed to be done. But, the second time, you were out there so long, it ran short…" He looked pointedly to Thunder Wolf.

"So now," Thunder Wolf gestured to the small room behind them and the small hole which became a large hole in the ceiling. "The power returns, with emphasis?"

Lightning Thunderer laughed. "Yes." He also looked back at the room, with Edgar and Reggie still floating out of their chairs. "Also partly you."

Thunder Wolf looked askance.

"You are starting to fear again." He touched Thunder Wolf on the temple and then touched him lightly on his chest, lightly touching the scar. "Your fear of the creatures of darkness and your fear of losing the lightning caused that." They both looked again at the damage he had done to the walls, ceiling and roof. "But you should also know, fear fuels wrong choices."

"Vietnam," Thunder Wolf remembered the last time he allowed his emotions to override what he thought. "I made choices that -"

"Choices made in war are choices made for war. What you did then, you did without fear, without thought. That is when the fear left you." The Thunderer looked at Dave and smiled. "What happens in Vietnam, stays in Vietnam!" he intoned and laughed an easy laugh.

"The lightning took the fear from you to protect you." He said. "Or, at least I think that is what happened. The lightning does what it wants." He smiled at Thunder Wolf.

Thunder Wolf had never felt fear after coming home from Vietnam. He had always just attributed it to being in the military, even for such a short time. With nothing else to go on, he was really unsure what this all meant. But when the blob had poked its eyes into the room, Thunder Wolf felt instinctively that he had nothing to defend himself, nothing to fight it off and his concern over his friends overrode every emotion he had. It wasn't a choice, it was fear. Finally after all these years, fear.

"I doubt it will happen again." The big Native smiled and got up to go. "Dodadagohvi!" he stated simply. *Goodbye*. He stood without looking at Thunder Wolf again and started off across the cloud plain.

"Dodadagohvi!" Thunder Wolf watched him as he walked across the clouds and faded away. Thunder Wolf went back into the small room and crawled back into the low bed. As soon as he was comfortable, the wall reappeared.

"Look out!" Edgar shouted and at the same time Reggie fell over with a loud "Awk!" They quickly gained their feet and looked about for the blob of darkness. Edgar was the first to see the hole in the ceiling. "What the…"

"Sorry." Dave explained what had happened and even told them of his meeting with the Lightning Thunderer. He also realized that the ache in his chest had returned. When the story was over, Edgar went about finding someone to repair the holes while Reggie kept Dave company.

"I can't stay here." Dave stated flatly.

"Oh sure you can." Reggie moved to the closer chair. "It's small, but they have really good doctors here."

"No." Dave took a breath and thought a bit more before continuing. "The Blob. The creature of darkness. It's one of Druscilla's creations and now she will know I'm alive, and I'm here in bed and worse, that the power of the Silent Lightning is still here, too. She will come for it."

"We'll protect you!"

"You can't."

"But -" Reggie tried to stop him, but Dave kept on.

"Druscilla has no way to get to the World of Man. At least, not yet." He threw back the covers as he spoke. "We know this. If I'm there, I'm protected by the veil."

"She got to you once before!" Reggie stood and put both hands out to keep Dave in the bed.

"Her power was different then. Hell, she was different then, if I understand what all has been happening. But, if she does that again," Dave hesitated just a moment, "I have more to fight her off there than I do here. She will have to use a lot of her new power to get there and even more just to stay there while she fights with me." Dave rolled up and sat on the edge of the bed. "I'll have a better chance of success than I've had in the past, too." The room was so small he could easily reach the Knight's sword beside the chair. He used his good hand to be sure he could feel the sword as he lifted it up. "Tell Edgar I'm sorry about the damage."

"Dave, wait!" But Dave didn't wait. He held the

sword against the wall, the door he wanted appeared, shortened to fit the wall, and without speaking further, he used it and was gone.

A few minutes later, Edgar returned. Reggie simply shrugged and pointed to where the sword had lain. Edgar knew immediately what Dave had done.

"Let's just hope he's safe." Edgar said. "And stays safe."

Chapter 22

Dave opened his eyes to the morning. The light through the window in his bedroom told him it was late morning. Sheldon sat staring at him and upon seeing Dave open his eyes, came across the bed and sniffed his face and clothes. Dave had fallen into bed fully dressed, something which caused Sheldon a lot of interest. After a few moments, he butted Dave with his head and began to purr.

After feeding his monster cat, Dave took a hot shower. In the steaming solitude, he examined his wounds. He was amazed that the wounds had healed and become insignificant scars in such a short time, especially the one on his upper chest. The scar was merely a bump under his fingers, but the memories of how that scar came to be were stinging reminders of what he had done. His face burned in the thought of how easily he had chosen that path. He knew what it meant, to himself, to his family and to his Naquinta. With the water as confessor, he reaffirmed his pledge to the Offset and to life, regardless of what that brought.

He would not allow himself to become just another Vietnam Veteran suicide. He just couldn't.

He dressed slowly, his mind on failed works and future plans.

Chapter 23

A single candle lit the room, eliminating all the details but the table and its inhabitant. Druscilla stared evenly into the steady flame which belied her level of disgust and dismay. Her anger had subsided after learning that, once again, the human had escaped with his power intact. How he was able to do this was beyond her comprehension. She was so certain he was dead by his own hand when she left him lying in the citadel; his life gone, his power gone, her plans... also gone.

She scoffed at her own mistake and doubly at the loss of her magic accouterments, created and gathered over so many years, now sitting useless in the black mansion on the hill. She needed them now, but where were they? Most likely stored in the basement and there was no way to get into the mansion without discovery. She boiled at the thought. Anger flooded her once again at the thought that the Horseman might even have destroyed them all. Her hands clenched into fists of rage at the very idea.

A light breeze through the window brought her back to a level of control. There was one thought and one thought only that echoed in her mind. She must find a way to get to him, even in the human world. The power he carried must be hers!

Putting both her hands to the sides of the candle, she began to concentrate on its aura. The glow grew and waned, grew and waned, and finally the flame itself snuffed out, but left the golden glow like an ethereal frame. As once before, she sought out the humans she could use to gain the power that she felt was rightfully hers.

Who to pick this time? Who was close to The Knight?

#

Mike was not working in the fabrication shop. He was involved with paperwork as paperwork always seemed to pile up. He sat on a tall stool at the counter of the shop and sorted papers into stacks for payment or delay, making notes on each one.

For a moment or two, he felt dizzy, like he might fall off the stool. He looked around feeling as if someone was standing right next to him. He found no one there, of course. He gripped the edge of the counter with both hands and planted both feet on the floor just to center himself. The feeling passed.

As the world returned to its rightful place, he noticed the ring on his left hand was hot – almost hot enough to burn him. He touched the ring with his right hand and found it to be no more than body temperature. Luke warm at best. Now he was convinced something was wrong. He just wasn't sure whether it was physical or mental and really didn't want to know for sure.

The bell above the door chimed as Dave pushed open the door.

"Well, Hello again!" Mike was happy to have a distraction from whatever was going on with his perceptions.

"This is new." Dave looked up at the old style bell which hung over the door.

"Yeah, got tired of the old bell, which is good since the old bell broke!" The two men chuckled as Dave put his canvas bag on the counter.

"I need some of your skills again." Dave got down to business. He pulled open the bag and fished out the sword. He lay the sword down on the counter and began explaining the issues. "This filigree here, you see where it's been…mashed?"

Mike nodded, remembering the filigree from before.

"Currently, it's keeping the sword from being extracted." Dave explained demonstrating the effect by attempting to pull the sword from its silver sheath. The sword wouldn't slide out at all.

"Well, that's a problem." Mike took the sword gently and examined the filigree and the sheath. "If you removed this altogether, the sheath would open a lot easier, and wouldn't seize up on you when you… uh… drop it?" Mike's eyebrows went up in a question.

"Ran into a wall." Dave smiled big and shrugged it off as if this were all some joke.

Before he could continue, Mike felt the heat around his ring again. Dave noticed the discomfort the man felt as he fiddled with his ring. Worse, Dave could see purple sparks where the ring met his skin. He could also see that the sparks were invisible to Mike.

"What's with the ring?" He tried to remain calm and hoped his question would stop him from removing his ring.

"Don't know." Mike felt the ring with both hands and shrugged. "When it's on my hand, it sometimes feels like it's hot, like red hot. But when I touch it with my other hand, it's not hot at all." He grabbed the ring as if to take it off.

"No need."

Mike looked at Dave for a moment.

"I… uh, I can see it there." Dave tried to change

the subject. "What's it made of, if I may ask?"

"Steel." Mike proudly held up his left hand, "made it m'self." He indicated a new display of rings which hung on the wall. "I just started making these steel wedding rings for people who aren't into gold or silver. It's a big new thing."

Dave now knew what was up and he was sure he didn't want Mike taking the ring off when he was around. He chuckled a bit, "Better not take that off when you're around the wife, then."

Mike chuckled along with him and the subject was lost to discussions of the sword Dave had brought in.

"I have some more thoughts on what I really need in this, along with the changes to the filigree." Dave spoke while Mike worked the filigree with his hands. After a moment, the sword came free. Mike lay the sword down next to its sheath and the two continued to discuss what would make the sword better. Mike took down notes of what to change and how.

"You sure you want those kinds of changes?" Mike looked at his notes. "If it's just a ceremonial sword, I mean? Might be expensive?"

"You know me and my blades." Dave didn't want to tell Mike about the history of the Offset and his position as the Knight. "I'd just like it to be more like an honest to goodness sword, y'know?"

"You came to the right place." Mike looked over the sword some more, turning it up and feeling the blade. "I was going to suggest a jeweler might be better with all this silver, but…"

The two men nodded and Mike made more notes about the sword. After a deposit and a handshake, Dave was out the door. About to get into his car, Dave stopped when he heard a familiar sound and turned to find Todd arriving in his big truck.

Dave waited while Todd parked his truck and met him as he exited the cab.

"What you doing out here, old man?" Todd joked.

Dave didn't take the bait. "Brought that stupid sword in again. Banged it and it locked up. Wouldn't even let me slip it out." He chuckled a bit. "Decided I'd better have a few things done to it to make it easier to carry around, easier to keep from locking up." The two laughed.

"Hey," Dave spoke when the moment became quiet. "I need to tell you something." He glanced around to be sure they were alone, then looked at the easy going handyman and knew this would not go well. "You remember the altercation we had with Miss Merry last year?"

"Yeah." Todd nodded, unsure where this was going.

"It happened again."

Todd was now on alert. "What? Where? Who was it this time? Mike? You ok?" He looked Dave up and down.

"Well," Dave started slowly, filling in everything, finishing with the truck nearly missing the turn. Todd just stared at him, unable to speak. When Dave finished, the two men didn't say much for a while.

"I know." Dave turned to lean against the truck. "But I just learned something that may help in the future." Todd was still silent, but listening.

"Mike makes steel rings. You know, like jewelry, wedding rings and the like. Get one for yourself, and one for Carrie. Don't ask me how I know this, just get them and wear them and don't take them off, even to shower. Especially if the ring feels hot."

Todd stayed silent, but nodded. Dave gave him a terse nod, slapped him on the shoulder and headed to his own car. As he drove off, in the rear view mirror he could see Todd still standing by his truck.

#

Druscilla screamed and threw the candle out the window! She was beside herself with anger at the fact that she had been thwarted with something as simple as a ring. "A Wedding Ring!" she shouted in the dark.

Chapter 24

In the middle of the night, the wind blew and the trees rustled. Dave awoke, sure he was needed. The dark was more menacing than he remembered and he turned on a light. He found Sheldon at the foot of the bed, now awake and blinking at the light and its intrusion on his night.

"Ok, so nothing evil," Dave chuckled, "is that what you're telling me by not being a giant killer cat?" Dave patted the big cat and decided that since he was awake, he needed to go on patrol. A quick once around the house would at least belay any fears that he was feeling. He pulled on a pair of cargo shorts and a tee-shirt. He slipped one of his knives, the USN knife, out from under the mattress, where he now stored it just for emergencies like this. He stuck the knife into the deep front pocket of his shorts, making sure to keep it handy.

Ever since the night he had been awakened by a giant Sheldon, he had kept a knife in every room and his gun always ready. He snapped off the light, glancing back at Sheldon one more time and began his circuit of the house.

The office. Light on. Nothing of note. He checked the blinds to make sure nothing was waiting in the night beyond their wooden slatted protection. Light off.

The front bedroom. Light on. Nothing to see here. Nothing out laying around, this room was rarely used. The closet door was always ajar so that Sheldon could climb up on the stored blankets when he so desires. A quick check of the closet and blinds and he was back on patrol. Light off.

The basement was the easiest. Check the big glass sliding door, making sure it was locked and a 2x4 sitting securely in the track. Dave studied the small forest behind the house, remembering just a few months ago when a monster had come out of it. Dave shook his head at the thought. Monsters, here in the Midwest. He could see there was nothing moving out there tonight, but he checked it carefully just the same. The rest of the basement was just so much dust and open rafters. Nothing moving around. He headed back up the stairs.

The big open kitchen/dining room/living room was also empty of any threat. Lights on. A quick glance out the back window, make sure the back door was locked and Dave was satisfied that all was well. That uneasiness that had felt earlier was still with him, however. Returning to the back window, he studied the dark forest again for a few minutes. When he was sure nothing was moving, nothing new crawling out of the trees, he turned his attention back to the house.

He stopped at the last check, the front door. It was locked. Lights off. He looked out the window in the door and was about to turn away, when something caught his eye. Movement. He looked back, studying the suburban landscape.

Four houses down the street a second street light illuminated the corner. It was there to help people who got off the bus or had a ride share drop them, but at this moment, there were no buses or cars. Movement again. Just outside the light. Dave was certain that someone – or some thing – was standing just there in the darkness just close enough to the light to become noticeable.

He unlocked the front door, stepping out onto the porch and shutting the door behind him. The night was clear, stars spun in the heavens devoid of concern for Dave or his situation. Indecision filled him. It was not something he was used to.

Whatever it could be was at least fifty yards distant. It was on the outside of the light, thus hiding or trying to hide from being seen. Why? He thought. There on the corner lived a family, but the kids were too young for some late night Romeo in search of his Juliet. Next to them, another family with kids even younger. Next, a retired woman and her middle aged daughter. Lastly, - Dave stopped – Lastly there was the family next door. There was Lori, the little girl who lived next door who thought he was Santa Claus. He stroked his long white beard absently thinking of her.

Ok. Not a Romeo. But it may still be a threat. Dave had a long time hatred for anything that threatened little kids. Little girls, especially. It stretched, he knew, all the way back to Vietnam when he had found a fresh mass grave where an entire village had been murdered to make room for a temporary military encampment. The first thing that had clued him to the grave was a little girl's hand.

He could smell the vegetation again. Taste it. No, not that, not tonight. He shook his head, determined to remain in control. He wasn't going off half crazy like that very night after he had discovered the remains. He had gone… what was the phrase? Yes, Jungle Crazy. He had stalked off through the thick vegetation and had killed 24 men in their sleep.

He shook himself all over, to bring himself out of the past, and took a few deep breaths with his eyes tightly shut, concentrating on the face of his late wife. Naquinta, his anchor to the present, his protection from the past. Soon, he was back in control. He looked up at the street light, and decided he would check it out. He slipped his USN Knife out of his pocket, slipping the blade from its worn sheath. He held it with the blade up, hidden behind his arm and started down the driveway.

Moving slowly, like out for an evening walk, he turned to his old training. He tried for an easy gate, just a man out enjoying the night, but he was determined not to be blindsided as he had been in the past. Head on a swivel. Check all points for the enemy. Left, center, right, center, left. Shadows are not your friend.

It was a very short walk. He got to the light and turned, skirting the dome of brightness looking for whatever moved. He walked all the way around it until he was back facing his house. He let out a breath he didn't realize he was holding.

Chuckling to himself, he stepped into the light and leaned against the street light pole. He was about to put the knife back into its sheath when the voice spoke.

"Knight of the Offset." The voice was low and guttural, almost a growl. It seemed to come from everywhere and nowhere. It caused the hairs on the back of Dave's neck to stand up. He stepped away from the light pole trying to see everywhere at once.

He turned in a full circle, eyeing the darkness. "Come on out and talk." He studied the area just outside the darkness. He saw nothing. He turned again studying both the lighted and unlighted night. Squinting just a bit, he saw what he needed. Down the street another street light stood sentinel to the darkness. When Dave moved, something blocked the light of that streetlight.

Dave could see the light pole, but the light was much dimmer. This told him all he needed.

"Shadowman." Dave waited. Silence. "We

haven't met." Dave waited longer, and was about ready to call it a night, thinking that Shadowman had left.

"I'm surprised." The voice again. Not as guttural, the tone more congenial. "But then, again, you are the First of your Kind to have invaded the Offset."

Dave watched the shadows in the darkness. They seemed to turn to dark smoke, shifting and creating shapes. Into the edge of the light stepped the figure of a man. Tall, with no discernible attributes other than he had two legs, two arms and a head. On the head sat a wide brimmed hat and he appeared to be wearing a long topcoat. The rest was smoke, darkness and nothing.

"You are what I assumed." Dave smiled. "Shadows." He nodded, trying to keep his composure. He glanced about the neighborhood, making sure no one was up at this hour.

"You know NOTHING!" Shadowman shouted and slipped out of the cone of light. "Shadows are a trick of light and dark. I am more than that. I am what grovels at the bottom of every heart of every man and woman and yes, every child that hates, angers at another, kills, murders, harms, wishes demise on another. I am the racist, the bigot, the vainglorious conceited leader!" He leaned back on his heels. "I am more than just... shadows. Druscilla harnessed the power of fear. The energy of fear is powerful, but the energy of WHAT to fear is more powerful. That energy is mine. Terrorism is my drug." Shadowman's chuckle died in the night.

The two stood opposite, one fully in the light, the other just outside its uneven boundary. They studied one another and imagined scenarios of attack and defeat. Dave decided he needed to get this ended quickly. He took half a step forward, inclining his head as if speaking conspiratorially.

"Why are you here?"

Shadowman took a long time in answering. He, too, inclined his head, "She needs to be eradicated." They both knew he spoke of Druscilla.

"That's a given. But more, I wondered how you are here. Why aren't you in the Offset?"

Shadowman chuckled, which was more of a low growling noise. He held his arms wide, "Old Tim has no real hold on me. I come and go where and when I want." He quickly closed the distance between them. As he entered the dome of light, the streetlight dimmed creating more shadows than it chased away. "And I do what I want!"

Dave stood his ground, concerned for the neighborhood, but also not wanting to let Shadowman loose. Moving closer, he didn't flinch as the cold slimy shadows slipped slowly up his arms. "Tim?"

"Tim?" Shadowman stood so close, he could feel the heat from Dave's skin. "Tim Time, Timmy Timey, the Old Man with a small clock." He laughed as his own crude joke. It was a quick laugh which stopped just as quick. "You… Knight. You need to get rid of the Hallowitch."

"Do you know where she is?"

"Yes. She's in the Offset, you pulsing flesh sack!"

"Enough." Dave knew he wouldn't get much more from Shadowman, but he needed to make sure he went back to where he belonged. "You need to go back."

Shadowman leaned in and laughed in his face. Dave was ready; he flipped the knife in his hand forward and drove it into the Shadowman. He nearly fell over as his knife touched nothing. Dave looked down as his extended arm, which went into and out the back of the shadow form in front of him. Shadowman laughed again.

"Your steel cannot touch me, as I really don't exist here, at least - not yet!" Shadowman floated up and away joining with the darkness outside the lighted circle. "Find her as you found the Scarecrow and remove her, Knight!" Just before he faded to nothing, he added, "You won't want to see what happens if you fail!"

Dave stepped out of the light and into the dark street. He looked up and down the street, looking for moving shadows, but saw only the dark hulking forms of the houses shouldered up one to another, all dark.

He slipped his knife into his pocket and hurried back home, more than a little motivated to find both Druscilla and this new threat, Shadowman.

"I'll eradicate them. I'll eradicate them both!" he said as he closed the front door and locked it firmly behind him.

Chapter 25

It was a few weeks later that Dave returned home with the Knight's Sword in hand. Mike had returned it to him with all the new changes and had even created a thick and soft carry case because, as he put it, "I'm tired of you damaging it!"

Even though it was expensive and cut deeply into his budget, Dave was thrilled with the carry case, hard plastic on the outside and soft faux lamb's wool on the inside. He could slide it out easily and there was even a shoulder strap. It was the best way to carry the sword when he wasn't using it.

Rather than go into the house, Dave decided he needed to work out, and the best place to work out was Todd's barn. He grabbed his workout bag and the knight sword in its carry case. At the last moment, he also grabbed the Zombie Killer ax, or Zeke, as he had come to call it. Rather than take his car, he decided to walk. It was an easy walk down the creek bed, the back way to Todd's.

The door was unlocked and Dave entered as he always did. He was surprised to see Todd with another group of women working out with Todd in the lead. He waited until they were done and Todd had time to talk.

"What's going on?" Dave set the sword carry case on the floor.

"Word got out." Todd laughed. "No one else has the space or the openings, so I'm going full time with the exercise barn. My boss at the cement factory is giving me some time off to see if it's viable. He hates to lose me, but he's a good guy."

"Is now a good time for me to come in?"

"Oh yeah, next class isn't until after lunch."

"Um." Dave began, "You gonna charge me now, Sensei?" Dave smiled as he bowed.

"Yeah," Todd headed back to the changing area. "Twice what I have been charging you!" The two men changed and started in their standard exercises, including the knife katas Todd had designed. They were half way through when Todd noticed the case.

"What's that?"

"Mike made that for me to carry the Knight's Sword." Dave stepped over and pulled open the case to show Todd. He slid the sword out of its case to show the improvements that Mike had made. The case worked like an oversized scabbard.

"You gonna use the sword more?" Todd looked at Dave closely. "I mean as a sword, not just a door stop or cat toy?"

"Yeah, I have a planned use for it, if you know what I mean." He smiled grimly at Todd, both of them knowing he meant Druscilla. "It's not much more than a long knife, though, so it shouldn't be hard to match with what I already know."

Todd went back into the storage closet and produced a couple of short wooden poles, about the same length as the Knight's sword. "Let's work out with these." Todd began to show Dave some new moves designed to use with the sword.

"You always keep wood bits like these around?" Dave smiled

"I somehow knew you'd be up to this one day. I made these two myself out of some aged hickory left over from a job. They should do the trick." He stood in the middle of the room and held the sword out. "This is called Kodachi, or short sword form. We'll call it a

Kata, so you don't get confused, old fella. I'll do it once and then we'll do it together a few hundred times."

Dave smiled and moved to one side. Todd moved smoothly through the Kodachi short form, calling out names for each position to Dave to help him remember the movements. When he was done, he worked with Dave to get the form down. As the two had worked together before, this was an easy adjustment for them both.

For the remainder of the hour they worked out with the swords. When they were done, Dave had more than a few bruises, but felt better about using the sword for more than making doors or lighting tunnels.

"I have something else new." Dave went to the wall and picked up the sheath that held 'Zeke.' He pulled the wicked looking weapon out of the sheath in one smooth move.

Todd's eyebrows went up. "You're getting strapped for bear!"

"I don't want to rely on just my knives and… well…" Dave remembered back to the day he bought the ax, and the hope he wouldn't have to use it on Todd. "You know any 'katas' that use an ax?"

"You're really pushing my skills!" Todd laughed. "Well, there are some. The two that come to mind are Wushu and Choy Lay Fut. There are also some moves to learn from Western fighting techniques made for the billhook and glaives." Todd took the ax from Dave and swung it a few times. "By the next time you come by, I'll find some to help you. Work on the Kodachi for now."

Dave nodded, putting Zeke back in the sheath.

"Now, I have something to show you!" Todd went back to the storage closet and came back with a small sheath. It looked to Dave as if it was a thick knife of some sort. Todd slipped the sheath onto a belt and stepped to the center of the room.

"Watch." He pointed to the far end of the room where some pieces of wood had been laid against the wall. Todd pulled the knife from the sheath and snapped his hand forward. A knife hit the wood a little off of dead center. Todd held up a finger and reached to the sheath again, pulling another thin knife. In all there were four steel throwing knives and Todd hit all of them in the wood target.

"Impressive." Dave shook his head. "I don't think I could do that." The two laughed as Todd retrieved the knives from the targets.

"I picked these up from Mike, the day I last saw you." He held up one hand on which Dave could see a steel ring, also purchased from Mike. "He said the knives are high quality steel, weighted and do most of the work, so I just sort of taught myself to do this." He looked at Dave, who was nodding along. "Just don't go looking at the wall too closely, I haven't fixed all the misses yet." The two chuckled at that.

There was still some time before the next class, so Todd demonstrated the throwing technique one more time, laughing when Dave suggested using one of his knives. They were still laughing when people started filtering in. Dave said his goodbyes and headed back to his house. Todd gave him the short wood sword to take home for his own workouts.

As he walked in the door to his house, Dave was brought up short by Sheldon. Sheldon was perched on the dining table in hunt position. His tail was flipping back and forth and his eyes were locked on his target just a couple of feet away. His target was a short metal soldier standing on the center island of Dave's kitchen.

It looked like an old soldier styled nutcracker, complete with the tall hat, straight long coat and even a long rifle held at parade rest. More amazingly, however was that the entire soldier was made of gleaming metals. Gold, silver and copper adorned his shiny structure.

"What's this?" Dave chuckled as he closed the door. "Some gift?"

"Sir Dave!" The Soldier turned to Dave and saluted.

Dave stopped and blinked at the metal soldier. He was speechless.

"Sir Dave?" The soldier repeated. "You are hereby requested to come to the Time Tower in the center of the Offset to meet with the King, or as you know him, Old Man Time."

Sheldon leapt across the space to tackle the soldier, but with a quick move, the Soldier dodged the cat easily. Turning back, the soldier knocked the big cat completely off the island. Sheldon was more than a bit put out and jumped back up on the dining table to study his adversary a bit more.

"Sheldon!" Dave moved between the cat and the soldier. "Who, or rather what are you?" He spoke to the soldier.

"I am Captain of His Majesty's Guard." The soldier saluted again. "We have little time, Sir Dave. We must adjourn this place." He eyed Sheldon who had moved just enough to watch the soldier on the counter. "Old Man Time has summoned you and now awaits."

Dave wasn't so sure he liked being called on in this manner, but he also knew he needed to get back to the Offset in search of Druscilla, who had been suspiciously absent of late. He moved away from the table, stopping just before the hallway. The fact that Sheldon didn't grow larger in the presence of this Offset energy was part of the giant puzzle, but he just didn't have time to think about it. "I need a shower first. You two going to be ok for a few minutes?"

The soldier spun his rifle in a quick circle and faced Sheldon. "We've been at this for about an hour. He's big and fast, but," The soldier gave Dave a wink over his shoulder. "I'm faster."

Dave shook his head, but went off to the shower. A few minutes later, he was ready and came out of the bedroom to find Sheldon in the arms of a now six foot metal soldier. Sheldon was purring.

"What -"

"We seem to have an accord." The soldier put the big cat back on the table and retrieved his rifle from where it was leaning. "All set?"

"My how you've grown." Dave picked up the sword case and slipped it over his shoulder grabbing his leather bag from the front closet. He had become inured to the magic that fueled the Offset.

"Belief." Said the soldier simply and held his rifle up to the wall. In a moment, a large wood door appeared, complete with a full sized carving of the same soldier. "When you first saw me, you were in disbelief. Now that you have accepted the existence of Offset metal soldiers, I can be any size needed. I feel better full sized." He pulled open the door and the two disappeared.

Sheldon watched the door fade away and went off to find a place to nap.

Chapter 26

"This is UN-AC-Ceptible!" The Old Man was livid. He had never been this angry, but as angry as he was, he was also trying not to take it out on Dave. "Druscilla? Alive? Why wasn't I told of this?"

"Well -" Dave sat in one of the big side chairs scattered about the big room at the top of the Offset Clock Tower. He had the sword on his lap, and his leather bag of 'tools' at his feet.

"It's not you, Dave. It's this whole debacle!" The Old Man paced quickly back and forth across the room. "Fairies being kidnapped and maimed, Druscilla attacking me here, in the tower and now I hear the formerly thought dead Hallowitch is now apparently very much alive. Not to mention, Shadowman threatening me. ME! Of all entities! I had to use a good portion of my energy to create my own guard out there." He pointed toward the anteroom, where the Captain of the Guard now stood. "And You! The Knight! Nothing!"

Dave waited for the right moment that he could speak without having to shout. He knew his place but he wouldn't be blamed for any of this.

"No." was all he said.

The Old Man stopped his pacing. "No? That's all you have to say for yourself?" he came back to the chair where Dave waited. "You are the -"

"NO!" Dave said louder. This brought the Old Man to a complete stop. Dave just waited for him to calm down a bit before continuing. "It's not me you're angry at, so just calm down a bit and let's discuss this."

It took the Old Man a minute or two to calm

completely down, at least to a point where they could talk. He finally sat in a chair next to Dave, though he said nothing. The two sat in silence for a few moments.

Dave turned to the Old Man and held up the Knight's sword. "You want this back?" He waited for a response. Getting none, he continued, "If you don't want it back, then I have to assume that I'm still 'The Knight,' is that right?"

The Old Man nodded. "It's just that -"

"No." Dave held up a finger. "I'm not done." The Old man was a bit startled by this, but kept quiet. "You gave me this sword and this title and basically nothing else. If you expected certain things to be taken care of by me, as the Knight, no one told me. No one. Not you, Not Edgar, not Santa Claus! I was given a sword and a title, that's it."

"Oh."

"And, if you want me to continue as the Knight, I'm going to need some…instructions." Dave threw a hand out to one side palm up, "I don't know what I mean here, but something in the way of a mandate, a set of rules, and information I can use to do what I need to do."

"Yes, of course…"

"And a list of duties would be helpful, too." Dave held up the sword again, "This is nice and everyone seems to know that it means I am the First Knight of the Offset, but there is nothing else that comes with that. You know what I mean?"

The Old man held up both hands in front of him, telling Dave to stop. "Yes. I know. Here in the Offset, we all seem to know what we're supposed to do without instruction. I forget you're new to this place. You are correct. It's perfectly reasonable to want some sort of instruction here. And I intend to see that you get it. Especially now with so much seemingly in chaos."

"Ok, then where do we start?"

The Old man looked at Dave and Dave looked at the Old Man. "Well, I suppose we need to discuss what being The Knight means. What you do for the Offset."

"I'm game."

The Old man got up from his chair and paced across the room. This time he wasn't angry and Dave could see that. He was trying to put things into perspective and in a way that Dave would understand.

"You know about the Offset." The Old Man paced and talked, stopping now and then to make sure Dave was following along. "You know the energy of Man is sent here, divided and then used or sent back. There is a balance. A give and take."

Dave nodded. This was old news to him.

"You also know that there are certain kinds of celebrations that give this energy to us. There are the Major Seven – eight if you count Mother Nature and the Green Man as two – but I digress. The Major Seven, which you now know appear as the World of Man wishes them to be seen.

"The changing of Scarecrow into the Headless Horseman, you were there for that. Reggie was once the Goddess Oester. There is Val and of course Santa, but once they were known as -"

"This is nothing new!" Dave was getting exasperated. It seemed that no one in the Offset knew how to give information quickly and succinctly. He saw how this affected The Old Man and tried to backpedal a bit. "Nothing against you or the Major Seven, but what does all that have to do with The Knight?"

The Old man just nodded, and looked down as he returned from across the room. He again sat in the chair next to Dave. Looking up, he again nodded, as if making a decision.

"There are other energies." He started slowly. "Energies of darkness. Energies of despair and loneliness. Energies of hate, violence… even death. These are energies having nothing to do with what we do here, what we are here. Dangerous, unwanted energies."

The room had become quiet. Dave had never considered much more than what was on the surface of the Offset. The Major 7, the fairies, all the light, good energy. He remembered what Doc had said about 'balancing energies.' He waited for the Old man to continue.

"You remember how Druscilla changed her Quedret to collect the energy of Fear? Well that energy has always come here, to the Offset. Druscilla just figured out how to collect it for herself. It is a powerful energy, as are the rest." He looked off across the room, out the windows to the bright sky outside. "Before that…before that, dark energies collected here were relegated to the Citadel. You recall, that's where you…"

Dave nodded, remembering the giant empty room.

"Over a hundred years ago, all those dark energies sent to the Citadel were discovered by the Shadowman. No, not discovered, became; the energies coalesced into what became Shadowman. HE is The Dark Entity. Everything that humans fear, whether it is the dark, the wild beasts, the things that go bump in the night – even the mysterious 'monster under the bed' that all children fear…all that is what creates Shadowman. But then there's more. Add in all the energy that people use against one another. Hate, anger, murder, it's all the same darkness when it gets here. Shadowman is made up of all that. He is the ying to our yang. The bad to our good. And he knows it. And once he found a way to control that energy, he used it… to escape."

"Escape?"

"Yes." The Old Man seemed to be getting older by the minute. "He found a way to… leave the Offset and somehow, enter into a man's body. He doesn't exist in the corporeal sense. He can't be killed, can't be stabbed." He looked at the sword longingly. "But that also means he can't interact with your world. Unless…he was inside a human.

"He found a way to do that. I don't know how. The last human was a doctor, I think. It doesn't matter, except that the doctor had access to such things as scalpels. Shadowman used them – used him." He looked at Dave and waited. "He was never caught. I had to go to the world of man myself. Tracked him down in England one night. Brought him home, here, to the Offset. But there was nothing I could do about what he had already done. " He really didn't want to say the name out loud. Dave just looked at him, unwilling to give him anything.

The Old man sighed, "The human became known in your world as Jack the Ripper."

Dave nodded. It all made sense. For all good energy there must be bad. They wouldn't want to send that energy back to the World of Man, so the next best thing is to contain it. No one here wanted it, so just putting it aside was all they thought was needed. Until

Shadowman found it.

"He has threatened to do it again."

"Then I better get to work." Dave stood up, sliding the Knight's sword belt over his shoulder and clipping the sheath to his belt. The old Man noticed this and put out a hand, touching the sheath.

"You changed it?"

"Yes." Dave stopped, hoping the changes didn't anger The Old Man. "The filigree kept locking it shut, and it was rather cumbersome to keep a hand on it. Is… that ok?"

The Old Man stood, looking Dave in the eyes. "Yes. You are the Knight. That is the Knight's Sword. If you feel it needed improvement, far be it from me to disagree." The two men again stood silently looking at one another. Dave felt finally that he had received the recognition he deserved or at least recognition the position deserved and that the changes to the sword wouldn't be as big of a deal as he had thought. Internally, he let go of a heavy sigh.

"Your first instruction, Sir Dave." The Old man put his hands behind his back and spoke officially. "Is to find and get rid of the menace known as Druscilla, the former Hallowitch. Once that is done, we can discuss the rest, guarding and confining the Dark Energy, but for the moment, taking care of Druscilla is your only instruction." He looked at Dave and nodded. Dave nodded back. The Old Man glanced about the big room before leaning forward a bit. He smiled, "We good?"

Dave nodded. The Old Man let out a "HA!" and slapped Dave on the shoulder. The two walked shoulder to shoulder out of the main room and into the anteroom.

In the corners, the shadows watched them go.

Chapter 27

"It's so nice to have you visit!" Jan said. She picked up the stacked dishes and headed into the kitchen, refusing Dave's offer of help. Since it was early in the summer, Dave had taken the four hour car trip to visit Jan before the traffic got bad on the holiday weekend. Just for kicks and for Jan's two kids, he brought along Sheldon, who was now tired from playing with the two boys and overfed with treats. He could be found sleeping it off on the back of Jan's couch.

Dave was about to inquire about after-dinner coffee when one of the boys wandered in. Jake, the oldest, was about nine years old, if Dave remembered correctly.

"What's up, Jake?" Jan said across the sink full of dishes.

"I want cake." One of the reasons that Dave had made the trip was the offer of a Birthday celebration in honor of Dave's 69th birthday. Jan had a chilled chocolate cake waiting in the fridge.

"We'll have cake in just a little while."

"I want it now."

"No." Jan smiled, hoping that Jake would understand. "I need to get these dishes in the dishwasher and Grandpa and I want to talk for a bit. Please go play and I'll call you when it's time."

Jake stomped off into the living room, shouting "I WANT CAKE! I WANT CAKE, NOW!" Jan gave Dave a look of frustration and Dave shook his head in a 'do what you gotta do' gesture. He figured it was better to stay out of family issues since he had just renewed his position as Grandpa, even if it wasn't a blood relation.

Jan wiped her hands and headed to the living room. There she found Jake jumping on the couch from one end to the other shouting "CAKE, CAKE, CAKE! I WANT CAKE!"

"What are you, three?" she folded her arms across her body. Jake stopped jumping, but didn't relent.

"I want cake!"

"Sit." Jan pointed to the couch and waited for Jake to sit down.

"First, you know better than to jump on the couch -"

"But I want cake!"

"Second, I told you we would have cake later."

"I'll just go to my Dad's!" He got up to go to his room, most likely to get his phone and call his dad. Jan and Joe were divorced and had been for a year or two. She still had troubles with the way in which Joe parented their child, giving Jake whatever he wanted whenever he asked.

Jan sighed heavily. "Well, that's your choice, but I'd hate to put him in such a position to be in contempt of the court."

Jake stopped at the door to his bedroom. "What?" He may not have known what it was to be in 'contempt' but he caught the word court and knew that was important.

"Your dad and I had to go to court to file papers." She sat on the couch. "You know we both love you, and we both wanted you with us so much of the time that we had to go to court to agree to what's called a 'Parenting Plan' in order to get those days and dates and all laid out. If you call your dad to come get you, well, I'm sure he will come right over – BUT, that will put him in a situation of going against the Parenting Plan. You see?" She waited while Jake took it all in. "Do you want to be the one to do that to your dad?"

"You just don't want me to leave." Jake was a stubborn kid. "I want cake, NOW!" To emphasize his displeasure, Jake picked up a throw pillow and threw it as hard as he could. His aim wasn't very good, in fact, he didn't aim at all, but the pillow did sail across the room right at Dave. Only mildly startled, Dave easily swatted at the pillow to keep it from hitting his face.

The pillow trajectory was changed, but Dave saw something he hoped the other's had not. A very bright light he knew as Silent Lightning. He looked down at the pillow, which had been thrown against a lamp, and now lay on the floor by the back door where it sat smoldering. Without a second thought, Dave snatched up the smoldering pillow and tossed it out the back door, onto the patio.

"DAVE!" Jan shouted. "Are you ok?"

"No problem." Dave shrugged. "Lamp must have a loose connection, or at least if it didn't, it does now." He forced a chuckle.

Satisfied at Dave's explanation, Jan turned back to Jake. She took his startled expression and sat back down on the couch.

"That could have been worse." Jan said. "Not a good thing to do, as we've discussed throwing things before." Jan stared at the boy, uncertainty written on his face. "Let me make this easy for you." She patted the couch next to her and Jake moved across the room slowly while she spoke. "I've always told you that life is a matter of choices. It's in our own best interest to make the best possible decision in making those choices. So, here's your choice. You can call your dad, get him to take you out for ice cream or something, OR you can stay here and have cake."

"I want cake!" Jake jumped up off the couch.

"Is that your choice?" By her tone of voice, Jan was making sure the boy knew what that meant. When he didn't respond right away, Jan took this as a good thing and moved on. "Ok, so here's what we're going to do. You can read clocks, so what time is it?"

Jake looked at the big clock on the wall. It was analog, the kind with hands. "It's 6:05." Jake said.

"Ok, so you watch the clock and when it says 6:45, you come in and tell me it's time for cake, got it?"

"But I want cake now!"

"Another choice." Jan nodded as if this was expected. "If your choice is to continue to whine, I'll pack the cake into Grandpa's car and there will be no cake. Leon and Grandpa and you and I won't get any, well Grandpa and maybe Sheldon on the way home, but the rest of us, no cake. BUT, wait until 6:45 without whining and you get cake. It's up to you, which choice will it be?" Jan was a no-nonsense kind of parent.

Jake knew she didn't threaten lightly, and if he continued, he knew she'd put that cake into Grandpa's car. Jake didn't want to lose out on cake, so he quietly got up and trudged into his bedroom. In a moment the sounds of video games could be heard.

Coffee was poured and Jan and Dave sat at the table and had their time alone.

"You handled that pretty good."

"If only Joe would do the same." Jan gripped her coffee a bit tighter. "He's… he's…"

"He's not you."

Jan looked at the man who was not her father and relaxed just a bit. She tried to see what her mother had. The big furry beard belied the gentle man she had come to know.

"Enough about me," she said, "tell me about you. How are things? Better, I hope?"

Dave knew she wanted to change the subject. The divorce, like the loss of Naquinta, was still an open wound and would affect both their lives from now on. He demurred and the two quickly filled in the past year with thoughts, memories and emotions. Their conversation waxed and waned and at 6:45, two boys came racing into the kitchen chanting "CAKE! CAKE! CAKE!"

The birthday celebration was wonderful and Dave, like the boys, ate his fill of cake, and Sheldon ate even more treats. Dave opened gifts and enjoyed the feeling of family as much as Sheldon enjoyed the treats he just couldn't seem to get enough of.

\#

Early the next morning, Dave was just finishing up repairing the lamp. The lamp was in perfect shape, but he wanted Jan to believe that the sparks came from the lamp so a bit of 'repair' was in order.

A noise caused him to look up. Jake was walking through the living room, headed toward him, wearing his sleep clothes, a tee shirt and pajama pants, rubbing the sleep out of his eyes.

"Morning." Dave offered.

"Hey."

The 'fixed' lamp was put back in its spot and Dave packed his tools into the small case he had brought in from the car.

"How'd you sleep?" Dave pulled out a chair at

the kitchen table and sat across from Jake. His heart jumped into his throat. Jake sat across from him with a wicked smile; one that showed a mouthful of sharp, black teeth. His eyes were black, even the whites, making them a deep hole, which no light could find. The skin around the eyes was cracked like an old ceramic plate.

"First Knight of the Offset." That voice. Low, guttural, and Dave knew it in an instant. It took a moment or two before Dave could breathe enough to actually speak.

A big headed Sheldon peered over the top of the couch. He was growing with the presence of evil Offset energy.

"What are you doing here?" Dave said, his voice low, menacing, his eyes darted to the bedroom door and to the hall, making sure they were alone. He also didn't want Sheldon to continue to grow and have to explain it all.

"Slacking off on your duties, Good Sir Knight."

"You are not welcome here." Sheldon was almost twice his original size, and a low growl came from his throat.

"Do Not Dictate to ME!" Jake's body stood up. Dave knew it wasn't Jake; it had to be Shadowman controlling him. "You are mandated to find and destroy the HalloWitch and here you sit, belly full of sweets and playing repairman? You disgust me!"

"Again, You are not welcome here!" Dave tried to keep his voice low.

"Dave?"

Dave looked up. In the doorway to the main bedroom was Jan, her eyes wide. Dave realized that he had gathered up Jake's tee-shirt in his fist. He looked back to Jake, who's eyes had returned to normal, except that now they were also wide, confused. Across the room, out of Jan's sight, Sheldon slunk down the stairs toward the basement, returning quickly to normal size.

"Jake was so sleepy he nearly fell off the chair." Dave faked a laugh and let Jake slip back into the chair.

"I don't remember that." Jake looked around the room.

"You were half asleep, bud."

Jan took the silence to mean that the issue was solved. In a few moments, Sheldon, back to normal, returned to the back of the couch and stretched out. Dave showed Jan the lamp and made up some explanation for the sparks. Since it was Sunday, breakfast was pancakes with plenty of syrup. The boys ate more than their weight in pancakes and the rest of the morning was filled with relaxation, coffee, and family. Dave kept looking from Sheldon to Jake, checking both every chance he got.

Just after noon, Dave packed his overnight case for the trip home. He took the case out to the car along with left-over cake. When all was ready, he put Sheldon into a special big carrier for the trip home and said his goodbyes.

"You can stay longer, if you want." Jan had tears in her eyes. Having just reconnected with Dave, and in some small way, her mother, she was reluctant to end their short weekend. Connection to him was connection to her Mom. Dave knew this, and felt himself tearing up.

"I've got some things that need to be done." Dave said, hugging Jan with all he had. With a touch of side-eye, he was also checking Jake's eyes for the thousandth time. He hugged both boys, who, for some reason, began to cry as he got into the car. He made a mental note to visit more often.

The street was clear as Dave backed out of the driveway. He put the car in gear and glanced back at the small family waving to him. He raised a hand to wave back and stopped. Jake's eyes were black again. That evil smile was back, too. Before Dave could decide what to do, Jake's eyes cleared and his mouth full of sharp teeth returned to normal.

More determined than ever to find and eradicate both Druscilla and Shadowman, Dave nearly floored the big SUV and headed home.

Chapter 28

Dave stood at a crossroads in the Offset, with his phone in one hand, scrolling through the pictures of the big map Doc had shown him. He had spent the morning walking along the roads that lead to each of the homes of the Major 7 and now stood only a few yards from Doc's great library.

"Somewhere," he squinted at the screen on his phone, tipping it back and forth trying to reduce the glare from the bright sun, "there should be a way into the Under Lands."

"No, there shouldn't."

Dave turned around to find Doc coming his way.

"Good morning, Doc."

"Good Morning, Sir Dave!" Doc was about out of breath from the short but quick walk. He took a moment to catch his breath before continuing. "Now, why would you want to go to the Under Lands?"

The comment caught Dave off guard, causing him to pause a moment before replying. "Well, I do have to find Druscilla."

"And you have faith that is where she is?"

The conversation was getting to him already. Doc's habit of speaking in circles was not something Dave felt he had time for or even wanted. What he wanted was just to get on with his hunt. He was also aware that a quick temper was one of the facets of his PTSD, and he worked to bring it under control, with quiet thanks to Dr. Pat.

"Yes, Doc. The way I see it, she's using some dark or fairy magic that can only come from her connection to the bad energy that is diverted to the Under Lands. I've not been able to find her anywhere else, so I have to go to the Under Lands to find out if she's there."

"I see."

The two moved to the shade of a large oak tree, Dave looking at the photos on his phone and Doc staring out at the well maintained park. Finally Dave couldn't take the silence.

"What is it, Doc?"

"It's just that, well..." Doc shoved his hands into the pockets of his baggy trousers, "You see, there really isn't a way into the Under Lands. Not here. Not like there is in the Dead Lands, anyway."

The phone forgotten, Dave gave his full attention to Doc. "So?" Shaking his head as if to clear it, "what are you trying to tell me? Or better yet, what aren't you telling me?"

"The way into the Under Lands that the Shadowman used is really a way into the tunnels that lead to the Tooth Fairy and his work in the Dental Caverns. Shadowman - and Drucillia, it would seem - used that area to garner both the energy and a safe space to work where no one would suspect."

"But there is a place beneath the Offset, right?" Dave held his phone out with the big map on it.

"Oh yes." Doc nodded without looking at Dave.

"And, there is a good reason for me to believe that Druscilla is there, right?"

"Yes, that is a good conclusion."

"So if Druscilla is there, and we both agree she may be, how did she get there?" Dave pulled his argument full circle. Doc merely glanced his way.

"Oh I have no idea. You have faith in that

regard, and I truly want you to have some faith of some sort."

"Faith." Dave shook his head again.

"It is one of my energy sources." Doc puffed up his chest as his clothing changed from Professor to clergyman, complete with a clerical collar He tugged at the white collar to loosen it a bit.

"Gotta say, that's one of the things I don't understand about the Offset." Dave fully faced Doc. "I mean, how is it that so many people in the 'human realm' have religion and yet there are none of the many religious characters from the Bible or other religious books?"

"That is a very good question, Sir Dave." Doc now turned to face Dave, both shaded by the large tree.

"One which deserves an answer, wouldn't you say?" Dave felt his face grow hot challenging the man in such a way, but, in spite of his efforts, his anger and frustration gained control and he couldn't stop it. At this point, he wasn't so sure he wanted to.

"Yes, but you know the answer." Doc didn't flinch.

"Oh no! Not this again!"

"Dave," Doc's voice became soft, friendly. "All those people you expected to see here. What do you know of them? Did they exist? Do they exist?'

"Well, to someone of faith, yes, they did…do."

"This is a place of energy and of beings that humans believe to be real, but not really. The icons here represent certain things, garner certain energies, but more importantly, they are never seen. Mother Nature, the Green Man, even Reggie, in either of his forms. If you ask anyone about them, they would agree they exist, but in some form which no one can see, or rather, has never seen. If those of faith, those with true believer faith, believe their religious icons to be real, flesh and blood, either now or in the past, it goes without saying that they wouldn't be here, now would they?"

"Well, no?"

"Flesh and blood real people like Saint Valentine or Jesus, or even Mohammed have all gone on to their own accepted rewards. And this is not heaven."

"Ok, that makes sense."

"You see?" Doc smiled, the lines beside his eyes crinkling with mischief and joy. "You did know the answer!" And he laughed. His laughter was infectious and Dave ended up laughing along with him. "How about a nice glass of lemonade?" Doc began walking back to the library without waiting for Dave's response.

"Doc…"

Doc turned back to Dave.

"How would Druscilla have gotten to the Under Lands if there is no entrance here?"

Doc put his hands on his hips, exasperated at the question. "How do you think she did?"

Once again put on the spot, Dave shook his head. "I don't know! Did she make her own way in?"

Doc took a step toward Dave. "And just how would she do that?"

Dave realized that Doc was leading him to come up with the answer. He almost threw up his hands in frustration when it hit him. "Magic?"

Doc made a gesture as if presenting him with something.

"Fairy magic." Dave said again. "She made a door some place I wouldn't think of, you wouldn't think of, no one would think of. It's here, but it's not on the map." Dave smiled at Doc. He didn't want to actually admit that he had had the answer all along.

Doc nodded and turned back to the library. "Lemonade?"

The two men walked across the road and up the path to the big Library. The shadows beneath the bushes slipped away.

Chapter 29

Dave spent way too much time waiting at the front door to Reggie's mansion before finding the note which said "We are around back….go to the left, though the gate.." The note was lying on the ground, which is why it took so long to find. Dave crumpled the note and headed to the left, around to the back.

Once in the gate, it was a long walk around the side to the big patio where he found his two friends, Reggie and Edgar, drinking iced tea under a wide shade umbrella. A third glass waited on the table, its sides sprouting moisture droplets so big they were visible at a distance. Just the sight of it made Dave's mouth dry up. The lemonade he had at Doc's was too sweet to finish.

His big frame fell fairly heavily in a lounge chair and took a long pull on the iced tea. "Searching the Offset is getting to be a fool's errand." The sun was warm and the breeze cool making for a beautiful, late summer afternoon. It coupled perfectly with the iced tea.

As conversation waxed and waned between the three friends, it finally circled back to the subject of searching for Druscilla.

"Druscilla is somewhere in the Offset and yet, I can't find her again, no matter where I look." Dave said.

The three began discussing places Dave had looked and places he hadn't. The only places he hadn't looked were obviously places that Druscilla wouldn't hide like the mansions of the Major Seven or the North Pole. "She hates the cold." Edgar had explained.

They discussed the forest at length, the animosity between the HalloWitch and Mother Nature and the furthest parts of the Dead lands, but came to the conclusion that Dave had just looked in just about every area of the Offset that Druscilla might be found. Every time Edgar mentioned a place, Dave would go into detail of how he had searched it. Edgar interrogated him on every area and then Reggie would make a comment and the two argue over details. They all knew few arguing was getting out of hand.

"Well," Edgar looked out across the gardens, "There is one place you haven't looked…" He turned to Dave.

"If you say 'Where she is' I'm going to throw this drink in your face!"

"Ah, I see you've been talking to Doc about this."

"Doc also said think outside the box, another of those phrases which makes me want to throw this drink at someone."

"Hey, it wasn't me!"

"All right, you two!" Reggie held up both hands to keep the two quiet. "This bickering is getting us nowhere. And, by us, I mean Dave. He's the one charged with finding and dealing with her.

"We're not bickering!" Edgar laughed, but acquiesced.

The three friends sat in silence for a few

minutes, each thinking of a way to find the Hallowitch. Dave turned to the other two and blinked a couple of times. "Where she is." He said simply. His eyes got a far away stare, looking at nothing in particular. "Where. She. Is!"

"I think he's lost it." Edgar looked at Reggie.

"No, no no!" Dave stood and walked about, his excitement suddenly peaking as he came to a wild thought. "This is so simple!" He turned to the other two. "Where she is! Where Druscilla is!"

"You getting any of this?" Reggie turned to Edgar.

Frustrated, Dave returned to the patio table and sat. He put out a hand to keep the others from speaking while he put his thoughts together. They waited patiently. Reggie refreshed the ice teas from a pitcher. Just as he sat back down, Dave spoke. "When I was a kid I would visit the Cherokee reservation." Dave's vision became unfocused as he remembered his childhood. "The kids would always wind up playing games together."

"This is not a game." Edgar inclined his head in Dave's direction.

"Along with the big games, like ''the little brother of war'- what most would call stickball or baseball," Dave went on. "We played typical kids games. We'd race, play tug of war and -" he stopped to make a point. "Hide and Seek." We played it a lot because it took so long and could eat up an afternoon.

Edgar and Reggie simply waited for Dave.

"You ever play it?" Dave looked from Edgar to Reggie and back again. Before either could answer, he went on, "Simple game, really. They choose a wide open place as 'home base' like a tree, or a bale of hay, and choose someone to be IT -"

"Does this have anything to do with scary clowns?" Edgar made a half hearted joke, but Dave continued as if he hadn't heard.

"The person who is IT, hides their eyes while they count to a hundred, and the rest quickly and quietly hide. When they're done counting, IT has to find the others before they can get back to the home base. If they make it home, they can't be chosen to be IT in the next round."

"We would all play this down at the big tribal barn where everyone kept their horses and tack. There were a lot of places to hide in and around that big place. We usually did this on the weekends, so all the horses and tack were there in the barn. Parents hated that we'd go in there, but there was never an injury, so we kept doing it. I think the horses sort of enjoyed the attention. All of us were really gentle around them.

"There was this one kid, Crows Wing, we called him just Crow, or Kâgû. Small, but fast and he was never caught."

"Crows Wing?" Edgar interrupted.

Dave allowed the interruption. "Cherokee children's names come after they are born, but within the first seven days. It's important to give the right name because it is their belief that a child will grow up to become that name."

"And they wanted him to be a Crow's Wing?"

Dave chuckled, "No, his mom left him sitting outside one day while she was hanging laundry and when she turned around, she found a Crow's Wing in his lap. Just a wing, no blood and the bird with the missing wing was never found. Someone decided it was an omen, and thus the name. To the Anniviya, the

Cherokee people, Crows are a symbol of wisdom, and this kid was smart, I'll tell ya that!" Dave laughed at the memory.

"You see, inside the barn, the saddles were all kept on saddle stands right outside each of the horse's stalls. Not much more than a 4x4 fastened atop two 4x4 posts, but they did the job. Since each horse belonged to a particular member of the tribe, they kept their saddle right there, too. That way they wouldn't have to lug it back and forth, home to barn. Under the saddle was usually a blanket. Depending on the size, it could hang all the way to the ground. That was Kâgû's secret. I never knew how he never got caught until one day I happened to see it from where I was already hiding. Talk about out of the box thinking!

"When IT would start counting, Kâgû would run straight to the barn and to one of the saddles about half way down the line of them. I think there were about 10 to 12 on a side. He'd then slip his little frame up under the saddle and blanket on the stand, his fingers and feet gripping the 4x4 under the saddle blanket. He just hung there, hidden by the draped blanket, totally hidden. He was very quick and very careful and the saddle never fell off, either. No one would take a second glance at the saddle sitting just a bit taller than the others. They weren't right next to each other, so nothing out of the ordinary. Even more, when IT came by looking for hiders, Kâgû could see their feet walk by from where he was hidden behind and under the blanket.

"Now, this is where his wisdom came in. And my point. Once they went by, checking each of the stalls and the hay and such. Kâgû would allow himself to slip out from under the saddle, and then silently run into one of the stalls where the seeker had already looked! Invariably, he was the last one to be searched for and everyone would be calling Olly Olly In Free - and there he'd come sauntering out of the barn. He never told and I never told on him."

"Olly Olly?"

"In Free?"

"End of the game, IT gives up and calls everyone in to start over." Dave explained quickly.

Reggie and Edgar stared at Dave as if he had three heads.

Dave shook his head at the two. "Druscilla is not some place I haven't looked! She's someplace I've already looked!"

Chapter 30

Just outside the main doors to the building where he visited with Dr. Pat, Dave sat on a long bench, watching the comings and goings of the motley mixture of people. He made a mental game of trying to identify which branch of the military each person was, and any leftover he'd figure they were office personnel.

Dave had no appointment today and had just dropped by in hopes of popping in to see Dr. Pat. He discovered she had a full schedule with no room to include him, which was probably for the best as he really wasn't sure what he could tell her. If he told her he had stabbed himself in an attempt to keep a witch in another realm from stealing his super power, he was pretty sure he would be in a rubber room faster than he could say "Knight of the Offset."

A man exited the building and upon seeing Dave, turned toward the bench, taking a seat just a few feet down. Dave noted he was rather typical, he guessed Army, with a baseball style cap emblazoned with 'Vietnam Veteran' and a double row of ribbons engraved between the two words. Dave didn't want to stare at the cap and discern what the ribbons represented; he just accepted that the man was proud of his military service.

"Vietnam?" the man said, trying for conversation.

Dave didn't know how to respond.

"The beard." The man pointed to Dave's long white beard. The two chuckled a bit at the observation. Their conversation stalled, but Dave had a thought he wanted to share. If he couldn't talk to Dr. Pat, perhaps a total stranger would give him some insight.

"Can I ask you something?"

"Sure," the other man grinned, "just don't ask my age or my weight." They again shared a chuckle.

"You know any vets from our era, you know: 'Nam, that…" Dave didn't know how to word this correctly, "put themselves on the casualty report?" Dave noticed that the army terms came easier when he was around other soldiers.

"You're talking suicide before ETS." The other man turned and studied Dave for a bit. He looked away and then back. "I've known several who did so afterward. One during. Why the question? You thinking of taking that route yourself?" The question was simple, but it brought Dave up short, giving him no time to put words together.

"Wish I knew how to say this." Dave folded his hands in his lap, thinking on the whole subject. "In 'Nam -"

"Vietnam was another world and a lifetime ago." The man said. "I don't want to become your shrink, but that is one tough subject."

Dave nodded, still unsure how to discuss this with a total stranger, but at the moment, needing to discuss his thoughts with someone. He was saved when the man put out a hand.

"Captain Lance McCall, retired."

Dave looked at the hand and decided he wanted this to continue if only to know what the man would say. "Corporal David Nicklaus, likewise retired." The two men shook hands. It was one of the first times since his return from Vietnam that he had shared his rank and name in association with the Army. It was a weird feeling for Dave.

Again, the conversation stalled, until it was Captain McCall who started speaking.

"We may both have been in that... action..." McCall fairly spit out the words. Dave could read the heavy sarcasm in his voice. The U.S. never declared war on Vietnam or any of the countries involved in the conflict.

He spoke without looking at Dave. "But we're probably as different as night and day. Similar in a lot of respects, too, I imagine." He stopped talking so long that Dave thought he should maybe say something.

"I come here for me. At least that's what I tell folks. 'Gotta go see the VA Doc, get a checkup from the neck up' is what I tell 'em. But really?" he looked at Dave. "I come here to see and talk to others. Guys like us. No one, but no one knows what we went through. Not even the Docs, really. They like to say they do, and they nod their heads and speak the words, but when it all comes down to the zulu? They don't. They can't."

The mention of 'zulu' brought Dave back to the days he spent locked up, while the brass tried to figure out what to do with him. Zulu was the last letter in the military phonetic alphabet, but it was also the nickname for the daily casualty report. He remembered his last days in-country, locked in that room waiting for the call from his CO, harassed by the guards. They would express their opinion again and again of how he should be on the zulu. A miracle he wasn't. McCall's voice brought him back.

"We had this guy," McCall said, looking out at the day, "Greg. Private Greg Wilkins. Little fella, probably no more than 90 pounds soaking wet. Didn't want to be there. Scared like crazy the moment he got off the plane. Practically wet himself every time a gun went off. He went to the CO asking for a transfer back to the states within the first 8 hours. They laughed at him. He went to the Chaplain and tried the same. Didn't get him anywhere.

"We went out on daily patrols, close in. We were support basically; but the day that sticks in my mind was when we were changed to lrrps and sent further in to support the taking of some stupid pile of jungle muck. Hill Number Blah Blah Blah. It was a good strategic point for both sides, so we were ordered to take the stupid little hill.

"Charlie had a nest at the top of the hill and had a mounted machine gun up there, an old ZB VS26. They had built up a berm enforced with loose rocks around the whole thing. The rocks were hand placed, so the wall was wide and tough. They had cut down trees all around the top of the hill down about half way, so that no one could get close enough to lob a grenade without being shot. Not even sure Glen Gorbous could have tossed a grenade that far, uphill.

"We piled out of the truck as soon as it stopped. As you'd expect, Greg usually stayed with the vehicle, using it as both a shield and security blanket. Not this time. Something in him changed that day, and I look around and there's Private Gee-Willikers so close behind me, he could have given me a proctology exam. I don't think much of it; in fact, I figure he's finally come to his senses and turned into a real honest-to-god soldier.

"There were two squads already engaged, but nothing much happening. We huddle up out of sight, near the bottom of the hill, with the guns going off now and again. Both sides, just taking pot shots, hoping for something. No one had any idea how to get up there.

The VC were happy to just sit and wait us out. We couldn't call in an air strike because we were all just too close. I'm not even sure the action rated any air support. We check our equipment and I still wonder at the fact that of three squads supporting this clusterfuck – sorry, telling this story always gets to me - not that I tell it that often. "

Dave smiled and nodded. The term clusterfuck was one that seemed to be custom made for military use. Hearing it took him back to those days in the military, both good and bad. He shook his head a bit to clear the dark webs growing in his vision.

McCall didn't notice and continued. "Out of the two or three squads supporting this action, not a single M79 blooper was in working order. Not one. This was before the widespread use of the M203, too, so no grenade launchers of any sort were available. All we had was what we were carrying.

"One of the guys, rank above me, muses out loud, 'If only we could get someone close enough to lob a grenade over that wall' and before anyone could say a thing, Private Gee shouts 'Yes, SIR!' and is off like a shot.

"I tried to order him back, but that only alerted the zipperheads at the top of the hill. We could see rifles being hefted over the rocks and getting ready to fire and I could almost hear the VS26 turning our way. I shouted 'COVER FIRE!' and the jungle filled with smoke and steel jacketed rain.

McCall took a moment to remove his hat and scratch his scalp. He continued a moment later.

"My God, he was fast! Like Water Payton running through the Giant's secondary, sidestepping every obstacle like it wasn't there. He cleared the trees at the bottom of the hill and made it halfway to the top before he was shot." Captain McCall took a deep breath and glanced at Dave, who was hanging on every word. "But, he kept going."

"The bullet tore through his left arm; I could see the blood come out the back of his greens. He was already carrying a live grenade but it was in his right hand. A couple of men began cheering him on, moving closer through the trees to give him better cover. By the noise, you'd have thought we were in a major skirmish. The cover fire did what was needed, keeping their big gun from being used.

"Little Greg was a jackrabbit. Even with his left arm useless, he burned a zig-zag path up that hill and lobbed that grenade over the wall, falling against it. We all knew that the grenade would kill some and send the rest scurrying to safety. That would give us enough time to get in close and sure enough, we took that hill." He took a long breath and let it out. "That stupid little hill."

McCall let the moment pass, honoring a fallen soldier who never wanted to be. The breeze carried his words away and he watched them alight in the trees. It was a long wait before he began speaking again.

"When we got the place secured, we found that Wilkens had a total of four bullet holes in him. The arm, two in his chest and one in the hip." McCall touched each spot on his own body as he spoke. "I have no idea how he made that run. He was awarded The Purple Heart with three Stars, of course, and a Bronze Star for meritorious and heroic service in the face of the enemy. Buried with full military honors. Every single one of the men I commanded that day saluted him as he was put into the back of a truck. None of them smiled when they did it. The name Gee-Willikers was never uttered when talking about him again. A hero. A dead hero."

A cool breeze floated across Dave's neck. He didn't realize he was sweating until that moment. He looked up at a cloudless summer sky and watched a few birds coast on the thermals. Tried to get his heart rate to cooperate.

Captain McCall turned in his seat. "Now, here's the part of the story that makes this a bit apropos. The day before, Private Wilkins confided to me that he wanted to take his own life, but that he couldn't seem to do it. He had put his service weapon up to his temple several times; but couldn't pull the trigger. Couldn't bring himself to take his own life." He looked into Dave's eyes, hoping the message got home.

"Suicide by Enemy Fire." Dave whispered. McCall merely nodded.

"I told him to see the camp doc. He wouldn't." Another long pause and the Captain's head swiveled back to Dave. "No one knows what I've just told you, and I hope I can rely on your discretion."

It was Dave's turn to nod.

"That was the one I knew during." McCall sat back in his seat, looking out over the people coming and going. "From what I understand, there were about 18 in every 100,000 soldiers that committed suicide while in the service. That was about 1975 if I remember my figures right. And, if you asked any one of them why, they would each give a different reason." McCall smiled a gentle smile. "If you could ask them."

"There have been a lot of studies and reports of the number of Vietnam Vets who have committed suicide in the years after the war with vastly different numbers. Some estimate as high as 60,000. What we can say is that any suicide of any soldier, for any reason, before or after service… is concerning, or at least it should be.

"I am not going to say that any one of them was wrong or right, just that war is hell. You understand that, I'm sure. But in the years since that day, the death of Private Greg 'Gee-Willikers' Wilkins has brought me to one conclusion. A soldier's death, regardless of how, is important. We need to spend as much time thanking them, supporting them, accepting them while they are here, as we do anything else. Especially those who have been in combat. Double those who were in that damn jungle. You catch my drift, Soldier?"

"Yes, Sir."

McCall rose to go. "When were you discharged?"

"Middle ages." Dave smiled as he stood, also getting ready to go.

"Before or after the fall of Saigon?"

"Before."

"That was a bad time. Bad for everyone." McCall put out a hand. "Let me personally thank you for your service." It was no big thing to McCall, he had a way about him that said he did this regularly.

A lump formed in Dave's throat. Because he had hidden his military service from everyone for so long, he had experienced very few 'thanks' over the years. Dave stared at the hand.

"It won't bite." McCall smiled. Two hands came together in friendship and thanks. Dave thought he'd never forget this moment, the first time someone actually thanked him and meant it.

McCall pulled out his wallet and extracted some

bills. "I normally like to take old soldiers to coffee or lunch, but today, I just don't have that much time. I'd like to pay for your lunch, if you'll let me?"

"No, that -"

"Corporal…" McCall put his wallet away. "I'm an old man with no kids. My wife passed a few years back and my bills are few. If I don't give some of it away now and then, well…" He held out the bills again.

Dave smiled, "That would be fine, but there's two of us." He said. "Another old soldier from that damn jungle."

McCall smiled, pulling out his wallet and extracted a few more bills. He stuffed the wad into Dave's shirt pocket and, without another word, walked off into the day. Dave watched the man until he was out of sight.

The cool air conditioning felt wonderful on Dave's neck as he entered the building's cafeteria, taking note of the new tables and chairs along with the new patio for public use. The building's original cafeteria had been only for employees who worked in the building, but someone finally figured out that they could make more money by providing for the public at large. He purchased two burgers and fries and three drinks. He snatched a couple of granola bars off a rack and added them. He paid and took it all out to his SUV, placing the two bags on the seat.

The SUV knew the way; Dave was just along for the ride. Just down from the VA building, the streets connected with the highway system. Between the street and the highway was a long chain link fence protecting a narrow sidewalk. Dave knew that one particular Vietnam vet lived on the streets down here and whenever he could, he'd bring coffee, snacks or cold drinks to the man. Thanks to Captain McCall, he was able to bring a full lunch for both of them.

Pulling the SUV up to the curb, Dave saw the mound: sleeping bags, garbage bags in which were kept clothing, and, of course, a shopping cart. The man sat along the fence watching the cars go by. As soon as he saw Dave, he pulled himself up, stepping out to the curb to greet his benefactor. He was a typical homeless man, with two to three weeks of unshaven cheeks and unkempt hair, which he smoothed back with both hands. He had on baggy jeans, dirty boots, a tee shirt that had once been white covered by an Army jacket. The jacket was in surprisingly good condition. It was, as Dave knew, his most prized possession.

"How's the patrol going, Private Stanis?" Dave said.

"Corporal Dave!" exclaimed the man. He came over to the SUV and shook Dave's hand. "Things are good, Corporal. We patrol regularly through this area." Dave knew that when Stanis said 'we,' he meant himself alone.

"That's good, Private." Dave turned and looked across the street, where a swath of weeds and dirt held a small group of homeless, identified by cardboard boxes and threadbare camping tents in haphazard array. "I've brought you lunch and a bit extra." Dave had met the man years ago, on one of his trips to see Dr. Pat. They had bonded over shared stories and Dave tried to help the man whenever he could. Wounded in the war, his resultant scars weren't all visible. He was unable to hold a job, or even communicate to anyone who was not a superior in the Army hierarchy. Dave, being a Corporal, garnered his respect.

Dave had found out early on that the man had

been in and out of hospitals since he came back stateside in the mid 70s. No amount of pills or therapy made a difference. Dave had been unable to do more than befriend the old soldier, but rather try to force the man to do something, he joined in the fantasy that they were both still in the Army, still doing what was ordered. This gave the man a feeling of being needed, being productive, and it gave Dave a chance to be there for him.

"Nothing to report?"

"No, Corporal."

"That's good. At ease. Let's have some chow." The two old soldiers ate their burgers in silence, watching the encampment across the asphalt. Dave hung around, trying to get some more information, always looking for a way to help the guy, but in the end, he got nothing new. Stanis lived in his own world where the Army and the war were a reality.

"See you next time?" Dave made it a question, patting him on the shoulder and slipping the change from lunch into his jacket pocket.

"Always, Corporal."

Dave nodded and moved to go. Stanis got up and came up beside him.

"Corporal? You seem like you got internals. Something going on?"

"I'm good." He replied. "Heard a story today that just got me thinking." He looked up into the other man's eyes. He took in the long, gray hair and the deep crevices around his eyes, wondering how much of that reflected in his own. "Too many of us taking a... we're losing too many the wrong way, Private."

"Don't worry about me, Corporal." Stanis responded and nodded hard. "I made a commitment. I honor that commitment every day while on patrol. I'm diligent, careful and nothing gets past these eyes." He backed up to the fence. "I'll be here, Corporal, ready to give you my report any time you need."

Taking in Stanis's commitment to a long forgotten war that never was, Dave was nearly brought to tears. He looked up and down the road to give himself a moment to swallow the lump in his throat.

"That's good." Was all he could say. He looked over the old man, not much different than himself, but for the way in which a war had taken its toll. He noted, not for the first time, the Vietnam Service Ribbon adorning the proper spot on Stanis's coat, something he was never awarded.

As Dave got into his SUV and started the engine, Private Stanis stood tall and straight and gave him a salute. It was perfect, belying the age and mental status of the man himself. Dave smiled, knowing that a PFC didn't salute a Corporal, but he still saluted back.

Chapter 31

This basement was unused. Reggie rarely went down there and couldn't remember much about it other than it was there. To him it was nothing more than red brick walls surrounding a large open and mostly empty space. Dave checked each wall, pushing and knocking here and there, searching for an entrance to the area Doc had told him existed, The UnderLands.

"Ok, are we sure she's not come through here?" Dave glanced at the other two, Reggie and Edgar, sitting skeptically on the stairs to the upper levels. "This is the only place that I know of in the Offset that even has a basement level."

"No one comes down here." Reggie scoffed. "Not even me. In fact, I don't recall ever designing this area, let alone having someone build it."

"Were you naked at the time?" Edgar could never resist a joke at Reggie's expense.

"Are you still on that?" Reggie scoffed and turned away. Edgar chuckled as he got up and joined Dave in his search of the big open basement.

Dave smiled at the two friends, and went about tapping on the walls, looking for some sort of passage. "Where she is." Dave muttered, his eyes checking the corners and moving side to side. He had already checked the dust on the floor and found nothing that would indicate that either Shadowman or Druscilla had walked through. But Dave didn't put anything past Druscilla's abilities. He had seen her float once before, so he kept looking.

"Now that I think about it," Dave turned to Edgar, "would Druscilla need a door or something?

Couldn't she just walk through the walls, or slip through a crack like those places in the Dead Lands? Wouldn't she be able to do that?"

"With her new 'fairy magic' abilities," Edgar said from across the space, "I have no idea. When she held the Quedret, she could easily go wherever she wanted, especially in the Offset. It makes sense that she would create invisible entrances like the ones you found in the Dead Lands. Even more so considering how she, most likely, created those before she lost the Quedret. Now? Unknown."

"Too much unknown." Chimed in Reggie.

"Planning ahead. Maybe that's how she's stayed ahead of me all this time." Dave muttered. He dropped his hands and backed to the center of the big space. "This is fruitless! She -"

Dave found himself on the ground. He knew it was the ground because beneath him wasn't the smooth cool feel of concrete that was in the basement where the three of them had been only moments before. He felt gritty dirt, asphalt and the smell of…what was that smell?

Looking around, Dave couldn't see much at all. He could make out a dim sky above an outline of trees, but there were no stars, no moon and no lights. The air felt humid, heavy. He breathed it in, again wanting to identify that odd smell.

He reached to his belt for the Knight's sword and taking hold of the handle, a bright light filled the area. He relaxed just a bit to see that he was near bushes and trees, thus placing him squarely in the center of the Offset just outside the park.

Standing up, he began to realize that nothing he could see had any color. Everything seemed to be shades of darkness, shades of black and of gray. The charcoal tree trunks held ashen leaves. The sooty grass beneath blackened bushes all were so out of place. Even the inky shadows seemed to swallow both color and light.

"Where…?" Dave turned, taking in all the scenery he could. All piceous edifices surrounded by pitch black night. Even the light from the Knight's Sword seemed insufficient to the colorless landscape.

There came a chuckle.

"Where, indeed!" A voice from the darkness, the voice Dave had grown to know in a very short time. Shadowman.

Dave stepped forward, his foot crunching on the stiff grass, puffs of black powder blew forward from his decimation of the field. "So, this is the Under Lands." Dave examined the featureless vista a bit more closely. He was taking it in, but at the same time, watching for Shadowman to appear, as he knew he would.

"You are a bright one." Shadowman's voice seemed to come from everywhere and nowhere in particular. "still, though, all flesh and pulsing plasma."

Movement from one side caught Dave's eye. The shadows began to move, to grow together and become a single entity. In a few moments, Shadowman stood before him, just as he had beneath the light on Dave's street. Had that been a dream, or reality?

Shadowman took a quick step forward, tipping his head down in a conspiratorial gesture, "She's dead?"

Dave didn't answer right away. He studied the vision before him, looking for anything he could use to his advantage and for just a moment, the pause was all he had. "No." Cautiously, as calmly as he could, he turned to look about. "I'm still hunting her." He turned back to Shadowman. "You have no cause to be dealing with my grandkids. I -"

"What's taking you so long!" Shadowman's shout should have echoed off the nearby buildings, but even the air was dead here. "Surely, you don't expect her to be here, in my realm? What kind of a Knight are you that you can't find her?"

"If you can do better, find her and kill her yourself!" Dave countered hotly, his anger spilling over before he could stop it. He didn't expect his response to make any difference and he was right. Shadowman didn't flinch. Instead his shadowy arms reached out to Dave's and caressed him. It was like the cold tendrils of a draft on a dark and chilly night.

"Maybe I should." Shadowman paused, reaching up to Dave's neck. "I could probably do a better job of finding her at least!" Shadowy tentacles probed through Dave's beard. "I'd at least know how to kill her permanently." He ripped Dave's shirt open with both hands. "But I'll start with YOU!" He put one hand on Dave's neck holding him still and reached forward with another tentacle.

Dave struggled in the grasp of the entity, pulling this way and that, unable to wrench himself away. The ropy shadow around his neck was like iron, unmovable.

"I do so enjoy the way in which you humans pulse inside, pushing all that hot coppery smelling blood around. And I do so love watching it squirt all over the ground." He met Dave's eyes, "that power you carry will be quite the prize, too!" His fingers stopped at the scar over Dave's heart. "Ah, you're so inept you can't even kill yourself properly!"

Dave tried to pull the bowie knife from its

sheath, but it wouldn't budge. Somehow, Shadowman had control of the leather sheath and was holding the knife in place. Dave was about to pull the Knight's Sword when Shadowman screamed. The entity pulled back, falling to his knees, releasing his grip on Dave. "WHAT HAVE YOU DONE?" His hand was on fire, burning with a white flame.

Dave pulled in breath after breath, ignoring the smells and enjoying the feeling of being free once more. He looked at Shadowman, careful in his approach.

To stop the white flame, Shadowman disappeared, the darkness inside him flying out in all directions. Once the flame was out, the Shadowman reappeared, the shadows congealing in a moment. He held up his hand, now complete, unburned. "After all I've done for you!" He screamed, "You attack me in this manner? STEEL? In the Offset? Steel in MY realm? In your SKIN??" He appeared at Dave's side, carefully avoiding his open shirt. "You will rue the day you took on Shadowman! My oath is rent! I am my own again!"

And he was gone.

Dave was as perplexed as he ever had been. He used one hand to feel his chest where Shadowman had touched him. He could feel his skin, and the scar from when he had used the knife on himself, but otherwise his skin was unblemished.

Steel he thought. In my skin?

Dave glanced around and found a featureless wall of black. He walked to it quickly and held up the Knight's sword. The door appeared and with a cautious glance over his shoulder, he entered and was gone.

Not far away, the Shadowman seethed with

anger. "I warned him. I warned them all!"

Chapter 32

The sun was a relaxing warmth as Dave sat on his back porch, but he was anything but relaxed. Coffee had been a couple of hours before. Todd had told him a new joke before heading off to teach a new group of karate students.

Because of his errors, Dave wallowed in indecision. How long had he searched for Druscilla? And yet, she remained hidden in the Offset, still working, no doubt on a way to come across the veil and take over the world. Dave shook his head. My lord, if I said that out loud to someone they'd lock me in a rubber room. He was angry, too. Angry at himself for the way in which he constantly seemed to be up and down, up and down about the whole thing. Yes or no, good or bad. Either he was capable and would find and eradicate – who'm I kidding? I need to kill her - or he'd never find her and should return the sword.

"So," he said aloud. "Either I need to find and kill this witch, or give up and wait for the world to be destroyed." He shook his head. No way can I do that. He shook his head again, both in a defiant NO and to clear his thoughts. "How in the hell do you kill a witch from another realm?"

He leaned back, looking up at the clear fall sky. In only a few short weeks, there'd be ghosts, witches and trick-or-treaters galore. If Druscilla is using the bad energy, or even the 'fear' energy, she's going to have to have enough by then to make her attempt on the veil. Dave absently rubbed his hand across the scar on his chest. He could still remember his feelings of defeat and shame as he drove the blade home. He never had been suicidal, he just felt so out of his depth and unprepared. The whole thing wasn't planned so much as just happened. He made yet another internal promise to never let it happen again.

Dave took a deep breath and closed his eyes, letting the cool fall breeze play over him. He rested his head on the back of the lounge, wishing for a moment that he was far away, with his love, Naquinta, the dangers of the Offset and all it represented just a bad dream.

Sleep had been light these past few weeks, maybe just a nap for a while. He could hear the gentle buzz of the hummingbirds at the feeder and the rustle of the leaves as the breeze blew them out of the trees and played with them on the floor of Naquinta's little forest. The warm sun and cool breeze were just the ticket and he felt himself slipping into that perfect nap.

Something touching his cheek. Hummingbirds were a curious lot. He brushed his hand across his face to chase them away but came in contact with something else. Unsure what it was, he opened his eyes in reflex.

There, sitting on the side of the lounge was his late wife. Again. This time he didn't question, but raised his arms and allowed her to scoot under them. He wrapped her up in a hug, careful to stifle the tears that pushed at the corners of his eyes.

"Am I dreaming?" he murmured.

"Yes, but don't stop on my account." Her voice filled him with memories. Her laughter, her conversations with her grandkids, her moaning those nights the two of them were alone in bed. She snuggled her head familiarly against one shoulder and the two lapsed into silence, enjoying the moment.

After a bit, she looked up at him.

"You're all clenched." She put her head down again on his shoulder. "What's that about?"

Dave chuckled. He could never keep anything from her, even in dreams.

"Something happened recently," he offered, "I'm still wrapping my head around it all."

"Ok, I'm listening."

"I met with Shadowman, down in the Under Lands beneath the Offset itself. Did I ever mention him?"

"No, but I know about him." She leaned up, looking into his eyes. "He's basically an Asgina." Evil Spirit. Naquinta lapsed into Tsalagi, the language of the Cherokee, now and then. "He's not to be trusted." She lay back down

"He touched me and had a reaction."

"Ooo I know the feeling!" Naquinta rocked her hips against Dave's side. The two of them giggled like kids at that. When their giggling died off, Naquinta sat up and swung a leg over Dave, straddling him. She grinned an evil grin.

"Show me where the bad man touched you, Liver."

Dave looked up at her. The emotions he had felt when he lost her rose up in him again, and spilled out his eyes. He pulled her to him, kissing her with a passion he had not enjoyed in many months. He needed her and breathed her in. She gave him so much by just loving him, both in life and in death. She was demonstrative with her love, touching him, holding him. She would walk by and run her hand over his shoulders silently, simply stating the obvious. I love you this much. At night, in bed, she would slide a foot across and caress his leg, just to feel his presence, make that connection once again.

Naquinta pushed herself back up, slowly, not wanting to stop the kiss.

"Ok, now," She brushed her hair back with one hand. "Let's get back to this." Dave slipped his hands up under her tee-shirt, but she stopped him, smiling. "No, not me, you."

"Here, on my chest." Dave relented, tapping a finger against the scar.

She slipped her hand up under his shirt, and ran her hand over his chest. She stopped when she was over the point where he had stabbed himself. "Wait. What's this?" She ran her fingers over the scar. "This. It's new. This is what he touched?"

"Yeah, the scar." Dave's feelings of inadequacy rushed over him thinking of that moment. He didn't want to tell her, didn't want to admit what he had done. He was ashamed of it, as well as ashamed that he couldn't share this with her easily.

"There's steel in here." She sat up and put both hands on his shoulders. "Did you do that on purpose?"

"Do what?"

"You've somehow embedded some steel in the scar itself. Not A lot, but enough that I can feel it."

"How on earth…" Dave lost focus remembering the day he had last sharpened his knives. Taking them to Mike was expensive, so he worked with them himself in between having them professionally done. Using one of several sharpening stones, he would hone them himself, working slowly so as not to make mistakes. It helped him relax, working with the knives one at a time, to clean, sharpen and polish each one.. He would sit down in the basement at the little workbench with a whetstone positioned just so with a cup of water handy.

A moment floated back to him. He was on the last one. The Gerber Combat knife with the extra long blade. This was the same knife he had used on himself in the Citadel with Druscilla reaching for him. He had worked the edge across the whetstone, adding a few drops of water to help carry away the excess material, called 'swarf.' Swarf is a nickname for the mixture of steel, whetstone bits and water. When each blade was finished, he would carefully wipe down the blade with a soft cloth, cleaning it, removing the swarf, checking the blade for imperfections.

But at that moment, he was interrupted by a big idiot named Sheldon who wanted attention and jumped up on the workbench, knocking over the water. Dave remembered jumping up, sliding the knife into its sheath quickly so he could clean up the water. He hadn't wiped the blade off! When he had pulled the blade from the sheath there must have been small amounts of the steel laden swarf left on it. Running the blade into his chest, the skin had acted like the cloth and pulled the swarf off; later healing over it.

"That's it!" he looked up at his late wife and explained what he had remembered. She, always understanding, didn't discuss the actions, but Dave could see her admonishment in her eyes. He pulled her into another hug and, holding her close, the two fell asleep once more.

When he awoke, he remembered everything. He lay there a bit, savoring both the memories of her, and the information he had gleaned during the dream. If he could only figure out a way to use this information. After a bit, he had worked up a plan and with a gentle pat on the lounger, headed to the basement.

Chapter 33

Checking the address for about the hundredth time, Dave slowed the car and turned down the radio. In his head, the familiar argument played where he and Naquinta would playfully argue which music was better. She loved heavy metal, Dave loved oldies. The click of the radio shutting off brought him back to the moment.

He had driven out here into the sticks looking for this particular business and figured he'd finally found it. Like Mike's sharpening business, this place was located out in the country and probably needed a guide for most people to find it. Off the beaten path is one thing; this, to Dave, seemed almost strategically hidden.

The ramshackle building looked like something thrown together with boards found after a hurricane. Nothing matched. Above the door was a wide piece of wood with the bark left on the edges. Crude carved letters spelled out "Lost in the Country" and in the window was a neon sign that said "TATTOO."

A single vehicle sat in the parking lot, and Dave could see two more parked around the side as he ambled up to the door. The sound of a bell came just above his head as he stepped through the door. Dave stopped to take in the décor. He was stunned. Totally opposite to the outside look of the building, the insides were professionally put together with modern design. If he hadn't just spent the better part of an hour trying to find the place, he would have expected this to be in the middle of the city.

"You found us." A beautiful young woman

seated on a tall chair greeted him from behind a counter. She was scantily clad; her tee shirt cut too short here, and too low there. Dave figured it was only to show off the myriad of tattoos she sported. Dave didn't want to gawk, so he kept his eyes on hers.

"Yeah," he pulled out a small packet, "I called earlier, spoke to - I think he said his name was Eddie?"

She checked a schedule open in front of her, "Yeah, you're Mr. Nicklaus? …Like Saint…"

"Yeah, beard and all." Dave let out a chuckle.

"Eddie is just finishing up, he'll be right out. Have a seat!" She indicated a group of chairs by the front window. Two of the chairs were taken up with two young women going over tattoos. Dave sat down and picked up a tattoo magazine to have something to concentrate on.

The two women went back and forth looking for the right tattoo. Dave wondered how anyone would go into a tattoo shop basically hidden in the woods an hour from the city and not know what they wanted. After a bit, he realized that they were a couple, and wanted something special to commemorate their wedding that was just a few days ago. They had just about decided to leave and come back when Dave spoke up.

"Butterflies are great." He said looking down at the sheets of designs. "Nobody is going to ask what a butterfly means. If it were me and my wife, we'd get them on the same side of the neck, angled the same. Then when we hugged, and pressed our necks together, the butterflies not only touch, but form an X, like a kiss." He looked at the two quiet women and realized he may have spoken out of turn. One of them had picked up the butterfly designs again when –

"Dave?" came a voice.

"Yes!" Dave nearly jumped out of his seat, anxious to be away from the indecisive girls.

Eddie was a solid man with a powerful handshake. The two went back into a private room and Eddie closed the door. Dave sat in the chair while Eddie prepared the equipment.

"You got the right stuff?"

"Yeah, I gave it to the girl at the front."

Eddie smiled. "That 'girl' is my wife and she's nearly 40!"

A knock at the door interrupted. Before Eddie could respond the door opened and there was the 'girl' from up front.

"Hey." She said softly.

"Hey." Eddie responded. "Dave, this is my wife, Natalie. Natalie, Dave thinks you look like a young girl."

She smiled really big. "Well, thank you, Dave. I also want to thank you for your help earlier."

"My help?" Dave looked a bit lost.

"Those two up front, the girls?" Natalie reminded him. "They've been here all morning trying to find the right tattoo. Both of us have suggested and discussed designs with them till we're blue in the face and you get them all decided in a matter of seconds. Thank you Thank you Thank you!"

"Anytime, I guess."

Natalie closed the door and Eddie finished his preparations.

"Ok. First tattoo?"

"Yeah."

"Portrait." Eddie angled his head, "Gonna take about five or six hours. You up for it?"

"A year or two ago, I would have said no."

Dave began removing his shirt. "Today is a different matter." Using a rubber band, Dave positioned his long beard away from the work area.

Eddie carefully shaved away the excess chest hair so the stencil would stick better. "I'm glad you told me about this scar on the phone. I've worked this design of your wife so that the scar will not stand out. Scars don't take inking well. Some not at all."

Dave really had begun to hate the scar and what it stood for. After his dream with his wife, he had decided to have a portrait of her tattooed over the scar. It would stand as both a remembrance as well as a reminder of what he had been and where he would end up one day. As Eddie applied the stencil, he smiled at the thought of covering it up.

When the stencil had been positioned and the paper removed, it was time to start. Rubber gloves were put on, ink dribbled into small paper cups and the light adjusted. Eddit prepared everything with the careful eye of a consummate professional. All was ready as Eddie picked up the tattoo machine and stepped on the pedal. He checked the workings of it, and checked everything once again before dipping the needle in the prepared ink.

Six hours later, Dave exited the shop carrying a tube of gel and instructions on how to care for the tattoo while it healed. There were times he wondered if the pain was worth it, but was determined to get the entire tattoo in one sitting. At least Eddie and Natalie were impressed. It was his first tattoo after all.

As he drove back through the country roads, hoping he remembered how to get home, he reached up and felt the bandage that covered the portrait tattoo of his wife. When he had looked at it in the mirror, there at the shop, he was actually stunned. It literally looked like the photo he had sent Eddie. It looked so much like his late wife he had actually cried.

To cover the whole area over his heart, Eddie had added in a dream-catcher design behind her, creating the entire tattoo in only black and grays. Dave was just amazed at both the effect and the talent of this man who hid himself in the woods.

When researching the tattoo shops, Dave learned that some people look at tattoos as mainly art; but many choose to have a tattoo as a memorial. Having them applied becomes a cathartic experience. Dave didn't realize how much the image of his wife now being permanently applied to his skin would affect him. As he drove, he used his right hand to check the bandage Eddie had applied. He didn't realize that he rode the entire way home with one hand on his heart.

Chapter 34

The bandage sat in the trash, where Dave had thrown it. The weeks had passed too quickly and the tattoo was healing nicely, so Dave decided it was time to get back on the hunt. Time was growing short. Druscilla would not have stopped working on her plan, so Dave shouldn't stop either.

A soft loose tee-shirt over the partially healed tattoo would help. With jeans and his boots on, he added his 'tools,' his knives, and of course Zeke, the new hand-ax. Dave felt he had to take everything he had in order to not be caught unaware or unprepared should he finally find Druscilla. She wouldn't be unprepared either.

Sheldon followed Dave around the house, watching him load up his tools, pack food in the backpack along with a couple of water bottles. Part of the preparations was to also feed Sheldon and change his water, an ever present check point on any day's list.

While Sheldon ate, Dave added one new item to his preparations. A flashlight was stuck in one of the big pockets on his cargo jeans. He made sure he could reach it easily and even added a second set of batteries to another pocket. He would not be caught unprepared!

Finally, he was ready and pulled the Knight's Sword from its carry case and slipped the long strap over his head and shoulder. The sheath was clipped to his belt and he checked himself in the mirror as he touched each of the knives, thinking of anything he could add to the array.

He looked at his reflection and felt like a damn fool. He remembered the conversation with Todd about crime fighters with powers and shook his head at the belt of tools. As a crime fighter, he would have some sort of nemesis, and Druscilla was certainly that. Thinking of her brought his musings back in a circle. Even as he pulled the knight's sword out of its sheath just enough to check it for problems, he couldn't help but think where in the hell is she hiding that a simple human wouldn't be able to find her? She's a witch, after all. She follows a pattern of behavior, which should be – no, not all that again!

Today he wouldn't let the feelings of inadequacy affect him. It needed to be done, and he was the one chosen to do it. He remembered, for just a moment, about that first day he landed in Vietnam. The jungle was worse than anything he could have imagined. As he had crawled out of that cave the first morning, the fear in him rose to a shrill level in his mind that was almost debilitating. He staved off tears, screams and a case of the shakes; but in the end, against the odds, he had done what needed to be done. And survived! It had to be that way now.

The Knight's Sword slid shut and he unclipped it to position it on the wall once again, thinking of where he wanted to go. He remembered the last place he had wanted to check, the UnderLands. The only way into the UnderLands he had found was an entrance of sorts in Reggie's basement. Start there. The door appeared and he slipped through.

Amazingly enough, Reggie was there waiting.

"I thought it might be you." Reggie said.

"What gave me away?"

"Ever since Druscilla all but destroyed my home, I keep track of energy coming and going through here. When energy affects my home, I always know."

Reggie hesitated. "Well, at least I had thought so. Knowing Druscilla used this basement to get access to the Under Lands without my knowledge has me even more on guard."

"I can imagine." Dave checked out the corners of the basement with the flashlight. "Druscilla originally used the dungeons of 'All Hallows Manor,' the mansion in which she lived, now looked over by the Horseman." He came back to Reggie. "She needed some other way in, and you have the only other 'dungeon' in the Offset."

"Dungeon?" Reggie looked aghast.

"Ok," Dave chuckled, "basement. An area closer to the UnderLands which she could use to gain access. Better?"

"Much." Reggie didn't seem too placated, "Just let me know when you're done. I may have this whole basement filled in."

"Jelly Beans and Chocolate?"

"Rocks and cement." Reggie turned to head up the stairs, but was stopped by what he saw. "Where did that come from?" In the center of the room was a trap door. It was wood, and set into the cement floor.

"That wasn't there when we were here before," Dave came across the expansive room slowly. "And, it wasn't there when we started looking just now." He looked at Reggie.

The two friends examined the trap door, walking around it silently. Dave cautiously took hold of the recessed handle and pulled up. The door lifted easily, but unsure what to do, Dave closed it again.

"If anything in the Offset smells like a trap, this is it." Dave stood and backed away from the trap door. "I've not been briefed on the use of the Knight's Sword doorway. Couldn't I just create a door that takes me down there?"

"Well," Reggie started, "I would say yes, but I really don't know. The doors can be created to go from one place to another here in the Offset or to anyplace on the Human realm. Dark Energy places are another thing entirely. Even the Green Man had issues in his rescue of you in the Citadel."

Dave paused for a moment, reconsidering what he was doing, and what it had taken for the Green Man, et al, to rescue him. He didn't really want to go head first - or in this case, feet first – into another problem with either Druscilla or Shadowman or something else the two of them might have cooked up. He also knew he was the only one who might even have a chance of stopping Druscilla from destroying the veil.

The entry beckoned him. Dave stepped forward and again lifted the trap door, pulling it completely up and open. When he let go, he expected the door to fall to the floor. It didn't. The door stayed open, as if it contained sentience of its own, and was waiting for him to enter. Reggie joined him at the edge of the dark maw, both peering over the edge into the opening. They could see a ladder with wide steps leading down into the darkness. They could not see where it ended.

"Twice I've used the sword to call up doors to get out of the areas of Dark Energy. The first when I was by the Tooth Fairy, and the second when I ended up down there." Dave indicated the darkness below them. "I don't see why that would stop working now, do you?"

Reggie hesitated. "This has got to be a trap of some sort!" He pointed to the door, standing waiting. "Trap door? Trap!" He waited for Dave to nod before returning his attention to the darkness below.

The two stood staring at the opening in the floor. It was quite obviously there for Dave to find and use, and Dave knew it. He also knew he had his knives and his internal power and he could handle just about anything thrown at him. Just about.

Without a word, Dave stepped into the opening and onto the top rung.

"If I'm not back in a couple of hours," Dave looked up to Reggie, "get someone to feed my cat again." Dave forced a laugh, trying to be cavalier. Reggie didn't respond.

The darkness swallowed Dave as he went down the ladder. His head no sooner ducked below the floor when the trap door swung shut, startling Reggie. In a moment, the door was gone!

"Dave?" Reggie called. "Dave!" He left the basement in a hurry. "Oh this can't be good."

Chapter 35

"The optimum word is trap." Dave muttered as he turned on his flashlight and stuck it back in his pocket for some light while he climbed down. With the door closed above him, all light was cut off and he had to create his own. He looked down. A hundred rungs on the ladder, maybe more, Dave counted as he descended.

Half way down the ladder, Dave had to stop and rest. Don't remember it being so big last time. The light shown across the vast cavern. So wide, the light barely made it to the outer edges. Just visible were sconces in the walls, giant things, easily bigger than a man. Currently, they were unlit. Not very welcoming. Dave chuckled.

More rungs…deeper into the darkness…Dave lost count, but finally stepped off the ladder and took a slow look around. The word big seemed somewhat ineffectual in describing the size of the space. He looked up and was unsurprised to see that the ladder was gone. He wasn't too concerned as he felt he could create one of the doors he had used to get out of here. He patted the Knight's Sword on his hip.

"Ok, Druscilla," Dave announced out loud, "let's see where you're hiding." He slipped the flashlight out of the pocket in his cargo pants and grabbed the bowie knife with his other hand. A boy scout is always prepared. He joked to himself. In truth, Dave was feeling more unsure of this adventure with every step.

He walked in a large circle, wondering if the cavernous space had any natural ways out. There, in the far end, he saw that the pattern of big wall sconces had a space. Darkness beyond must be some sort of entry or maybe even a connecting hall? Dave started toward the area, walking with a hesitancy he hadn't felt before.

Moving the light left and right, he kept his gaze moving, always on the lookout for movement, or trouble. Several minutes passed and he didn't feel he was even that much closer to the dark space on the far wall. Ok, more than big, it's very, Very big, but also... He felt something. A feeling he had felt before, but still unable to identify it. He stopped walking.

The first sconce blazed to life. It sat beside the area Dave had aimed for, the fire in the sconce lit the wall and ceiling where they met so high above. As big as the fire was, it wasn't enough to light the entire cavern, but it did show that there was, indeed, an entry or connecting hall there. He could make out a rounded arch in the half light. Smiling to himself, he started again.

Another sconce blazed to life. This one on the other side of the arch. Dave stopped again. There wasn't a lot of light, but what light there was showed Dave that this was not the Citadel. There were neither the massive columns nor the stairs behind them. He also noted with a smile that there was no altar.

All of the sconces came to life, one by one around the giant room. They were high on the cavern's curved walls, but gave only the barest of visual acuity. Dave waited until they had all lit. He turned back to the arch, now able to just make out that the arch was around a large set of doors. By their size in comparison to the vastness of the room, he figured them to be 30 to 50 feet tall at the center. A pair of handles dead center marked where the doors would open.

A loud clank, followed by a clunk that echoed

across the vast space and the doors began to open. They opened inward, away from Dave, pulled by someone or some thing. There was just enough light beyond the doors to see a silhouette of someone visible in the half light just beyond the moving doors. Dave recognized that silhouette. Druscilla.

The bowie knife slid into its sheath as easily as it came out. Dave waited, knowing this was the moment of truth.

"Hello again, Dave." Druscilla stepped into the room; the light from the sconces above her head allowed Dave to see that this was indeed the HalloWitch. He waited. She walked toward him slowly. The distance Dave knew to be long, but she seemed to walk it in only a few steps.

He knew she was after the power he carried, and wanted it to use it to cross the veil. The veil was a simple explanation for the barrier between their worlds. Dave wouldn't allow that, couldn't allow that. He watched, waiting for the dark blobs that she used the last time. There were none visible, but that was not enough to relax him.

"I don't know whether to congratulate you on finding me, or laugh in your face."

"Maybe you should just -" Dave wasn't much for small talk today. He relaxed enough to allow his power to grow and with a gesture from one hand the room filled with light. It was powerful, brief and perfectly aimed.

The bolt of silent lightning tore through Druscilla's sternum, ripping her limb from limb. The black tarry stuff that he had come to recognize as dark energy splashed across the walls behind her nearly as high as the wall sconces. It only took a second, maybe less.

Dave stood with his arm up, looking where Druscilla had stood. He didn't like killing, and even though she was a creature of evil energy, having to kill her took a lot of mental control. His eyes glanced left and right. He was frightened, and knew that came from the PTSD that was part of his very being. He didn't want little Vietnamese girls waltzing around the cavern.

Just to make sure, he took a sniff. No fetid vegetation, no jungle sounds, no trucks. He was fully in control. He lowered his arm, still watching the place where Druscilla had stood. He even let out a breath he didn't realize he had been holding.

There came a new sound. What was it, a slap? A clap? A slow clap? What in the hell?

The doorway still had just enough light to show a silhouette as it stepped into view.

"No!" Dave was aghast. It was the same silhouette and he cursed himself for not knowing this might happen.

Druscilla stepped into the dim light. She was clapping very slowly. The giant doors closed behind her.

"How that must have felt!" She said as she floated across the cavern floor. "And I mean how it felt for you," She looked down at the viscous dregs of what was left of the other Druscilla, "certainly not for her." With a wave of her hand, all the back spots, drips and steaming tar slipped out under the massive doors.

Dave didn't hesitate; he raised his arm, pointing two fingers unsure if he had enough power, but determined to use it all.

"No." Druscilla waved her hand again, as if directing some arcane orchestra.

Dave felt a punch to his entire form. He flew backward, across the distance he had walked and then some. Further and further finally slamming against the wall beneath one of the burning flames. His knives and even the hand ax dropped off him, thrown from their sheaths as if by an invisible hand. It left him held to the wall, defenseless. He saw stars for a few moments. When his vision cleared, he looked about frantically. Druscilla crossed the massive space in seconds. She stood right there in front of him. Dave hung several feet off the ground, yet Druscilla stood face to face with him.

"You had your chance," Druscilla seemed very satisfied with herself. "I've studied you, Dave. You only have one chance to use your power… whatever it is you call it. Then, you need to rest, wait, recharge. Fear. I know Fear. Fear makes you do things to protect yourself and, well… we both know how that worked out last time." She looked him up and down. "Was it fear you used this time to get the power stoked? Call on it to protect you? "

Dave was held to the wall unable to move, unable to act; he couldn't even have snapped his fingers. There were none of his tools handy either. He could see them lying about on the floor where they had been thrown. He tried not to berate himself for his lack of success.

Druscilla grabbed his shirt in the middle and ripped it open. She looked him in the eye. "This is always the best part. Being able to look into someone's eyes when you kill them." She looked at Dave's chest and stopped. "What?" She stood back getting a better look. She threw one hand up and a bright violet flame appeared in it, illuminating the area. She could see the finished portrait of Naquinta tattooed on Dave's chest, right over his heart.

"Oh, how lovely!" She laughed in Dave's face. "I get to destroy the two of you at one time!" She brought her other hand up in front of Dave's face, her fingers forming into obscenely large, sharp claws. "Goodbye, Sir Dave, First Knight of the Offset. I'd like to say it's been fun, but you've been a pain in my ass for far too long!"

She plunged her hand into his chest –

-and screamed.

Druscilla pulled her hand back from Dave's chest without leaving any damage, not even a scratch on his skin. Each of her long sharp claws was melting, black smoke pouring from what was left of them. She stumbled back in shock. Her violet flame went out and she grabbed the melting wrist. "WHAT HAVE YOU DONE??" she screamed.

The power that had held Dave to the wall let go and he slipped to the floor. "I learned a long time ago to keep something in reserve. I had that tattoo done with black ink and titanium powder." He scanned the floor quickly for a weapon while he talked. "Used sandpaper on an old titanium fishing rod. Had to do a lot of research to make sure it was an alloy, too. Titanium, in case you didn't know, is the hardest metal on earth, combined with…well, I won't go into that. It was tattooed under the skin, so you wouldn't feel it until -" Dave made a claw with his hand, "and now you pay the price!"

Druscilla screamed incoherently at him while he gathered up his knives, quickly sliding each into place. He turned to her, ready to finish her off. He saw murder in her eyes. What else?

"You have not won!" Druscilla, backing away, gestured again with her good hand, "Not by a long shot!"

The door, far across the cavern exploded inward with a spray of rock and wood. Dave's mouth fell open. Charging through the opening was a very large Minotaur. He was reminded of looking up at the bones of dinosaurs he had seen in museums as a kid. This put them all to shame. The creature was so tall and the horns were so wide they took out the rock arch above the door. Its hooves splintered the doors as it stamped across them. The ground shook with each step. Its eyes were glowing red and it was headed right for Dave.

Dave turned to find Druscilla gone. He cursed his age, his speed, everything that prevented him from taking her down this one last time. But he also cursed his predicament.

The Minotaur was making quick time across the floor, so Dave tried the one thing he thought might help. Steel. He slipped the bowie knife out of its sheath and flipped it over in his hand catching the blade by the back. He had never thrown a knife, either for fun or practice; but he knew it was his only chance now. The memory of Todd throwing the knives at least gave him a starting point.

He took a stance, brought the big knife over his shoulder, unsure of how to accomplish the task, he took a step, balanced his body, and threw the knife with everything he had. He turned and ran to one side, out of the path of the Minotaur.

The Minotaur didn't see the knife, nor did it see Dave run off to the side. It had lowered its big head as it charged across the wide floor. Dave stopped after a short run and watched the big blade and the beast come together. The knife flipped over and over and finally struck – amazingly enough, just below the big behemoth's eye. It struck flat and the blade didn't stick, but it was enough. The steel scratched it and that touch jarred the Great Beast. Its concentration faltered and the trajectory of its path changed. Uncertain on its feet, it stumbled to the side, away from Dave.

The wall held only a bit as the Minotaur struck it sideways. Rock and rubble rained down. Unable to keep running, The Minotaur fell and rolled, passing Dave where he stood by mere inches. The big form of the monster struck the curved wall again, and rocks began to fall. Dave knew it was time to get out. He wouldn't leave his knife behind, so he ran to find it, scooping it up as he did.

Back along the opposite wall, he stopped to create a door, holding up the Knight's Sword just as the Minotaur gained its feet. Pulling the door open, Dave glanced back, noting that the sconces were going out. But there was enough light to see that one side of the Minotaur's face had already begun melting, turning black.

Dave heard the rumble of the cave-in mixed with the roar of the Minotaur as the door closed behind him. He was not surprised to find that he was covered in sweat.

Chapter 36

"A Minotaur, you say?"

"Yes, that is what I said. Giant thing, arms like a bodybuilder, head of a bull with horns nearly scraping the ceiling of the place." Dave stopped his workout and flopped down on the padded floor of Todd's workout barn. "Imagine something tall enough to look down into that skylight up there." Dave pointed to the skylight 3 stories above.

"Yikes." Todd joined Dave on the floor. He looked up at his wife, climbing the wall. "I'm not spotting you. You be careful!"

Carrie glanced down at the two men and shook her head. She was on the way down anyway and soon joined the two in relaxing.

"And you just threw your big bowie knife at it?" he paused, smiling, "with no prep or nothing?"

Dave hung his head. "Yeah." He looked at Todd, raising his eyebrows, "but, it worked. What else can I say?" The two men laughed. Even Carrie chuckled at the idea. They lapsed into a comfortable silence.

"It's coming to a head." Dave looked at the other two. "I can feel it." There was a moment of silence as they contemplated what this might mean. "I need to find her before she finds a way to cross the veil. If she does that, then all the lightning in the world won't stop her."

"We'll do whatever we can on this end." Carrie rose and went to the wall where there were several katana swords on a rack. She took one down and pulled the long blade out in a quick move. She began her kata, spinning swiftly between moves, the blade almost singing through the air. Spinning, Carrie appeared to barely touch the floor, the blade flashing in the light. It was a sight to behold.

"You've been practicing!" Todd watched the moves from the floor at the side.

When Carrie was done, she sheathed the Katana and returned to the floor with the two guys. "I want to be ready, that's all." Her eyes went from one to the other. "For anything." She shared a look with Todd.

Dave noticed the look. "What?"

"I don't want to reveal anything, you know, in case it… well, gets out." Todd looked at Dave.

"Druscilla doesn't read minds." Dave cocked his head thinking. "At least I don't think she can. No, she can't. I'm pretty sure of that. If she could, she would have known about the…" he tapped his chest in emphasis.

After a moment or two of silent conversation with Carrie, Todd got up. "Come on, then." He said, and headed to the back room. "You may as well see."

The back room was just that, mostly just a back area where extra mats, exercise equipment and even paint had been stored. Everything was on shelves. Dave looked about for something new, but didn't see what Todd had meant.

Todd walked to a back corner and turned, making sure Dave watched. He pulled at the shelves there, and the whole unit moved easily. Behind the shelves was a doorway. The door looked solid, with a keypad just above the handle. Todd punched a few numbers and pulled the door open. He slipped in first, followed by Carrie and Dave.

The light overhead was fluorescent and filled

the room with a bright almost blue light. Dave was dumbstruck. The walls were simple, the room narrow, like a closet. Mounted on the long walls were automatic weapons. Four of them to be exact. Above the four was mounted a very long rifle.

"I don't think you ever knew what Carrie did in Afghanistan." Todd pointed to the long rifle at the top. Next to the rifle was a set of military marksman awards and patches. "She's nationally ranked. No one is going to get near this barn." Todd smiled. Carrie leaned against her husband in solidarity, her arms crossed in front of her.

"I wasn't a sniper, those guys go through more training than I had." Carrie said. "But, I'm good. Damn good."

Dave nodded sagely. He turned and noted a cabinet at the end. "What's in there?"

Todd didn't hesitate; he opened the cabinet to show a rack holding two AK-47s. He didn't smile, but the look of pride on his face said it all. He was going to be ready for anything. On the lower shelves were boxes and boxes of ammunition.

"Steel Jacketed Ammo?" Dave asked.

Todd nodded. "Nothing to chance. Wish we had a small squad of marksmen, but we'll make do." Carrie gave him a high five.

"Look, Dave," Carrie stepped forward. "I'm not one of the best, but I do have military people stopping in from time to time checking on me. They know what I'm capable of and until now, it was more of a minor inconvenience. Now, I feel I can… well, I can be of service again, but this time for the right people and the right reasons."

Dave nodded. In the back of his mind he was

starting to worry about what he might have dragged his friends into. He had made a sort of peace with what he had to do, himself, but knowing his friends were now a part of it almost made him want to quit. But the echo of Private Stanis' words about commitment and honor floated back to him. There was no turning back, regardless of what lay ahead, they had to try.

"The veil." Dave's mouth was getting a bit dry talking about this. "We know it's getting weak. I have no idea how, but we certainly know why." In his mind's eye he saw his friends lying in a shallow grave, with just enough jungle dirt and foliage to cover their bodies. The smell… No, not that. Not now!

He could feel a small hand slip into his. The small voice, a little girl, speaking Vietnamese. "Đừng để họ chết!" Don't let them die. Her voice pleading.

"No, I won't." Dave forced out the words, barely audible.

"Won't what?" Carrie. Standing in front of him. She put her small hands on his arms. "You ok, Dave?"

He squeezed his hands into fists. The small hand which had been there was gone, the smell of the jungle rot fading, his breathing coming a bit easier. A swelling headache and the sweat under his arms a cool reminder of what had just happened. The anger and tension abated as he took in a deep breath, concentrating on the here and now.

"Yeah." Dave's voice was gruff, his throat dry. "Need some water, I think." He turned and left the small room quickly, remembering a bottle of water in his bag out where they had been working. The room temperature water refreshed him.

Todd and Carrie joined him. Carrie seemed a bit reserved, as if revealing the stash of weapons deserved more of a positive reaction than Dave had given. She wasn't going to let it go, Todd could tell.

"Been collecting them for years." Todd stated rather easily. "Carrie started it some time ago, after she got out." Todd waited for a response from Dave. Seeing none, his eyebrows came down a bit, concerned for what his friend was thinking. "Dave?"

Dave turned, the nearly empty bottle halfway to his mouth. In a moment, he knew what was up and there was only one way he felt he could go. Truth. He sat on the floor and motioned for the two to join him, which they did, only a bit reluctantly.

"Everything is good." He started. He looked at Todd and Carrie, making eye contact to see that they got that one message. "What's up, is that this shouldn't be happening." A quick glance around the room to make sure there were no Vietnamese children lurking and Dave finished his water.

"If Druscilla does what I think she will," Dave looked down at the floor. "We are in for a larger fight than we've seen in the past." He waited for nods of agreement. "I...can't lose you two." He reached out across the short distance between them and put a hand on each. "I lost Naquinta, I can't lose you and I can't lose you to something like this."

"You won't." Carrie was stalwart, determined.

"I could." Dave relented. "I lost Naquinta through no fault of my own, but this...this is something that I seemed to have brought to us all, and I'll be damned if I lose you because of it." The quiet was softened only by the breathing of the three of them. "I have no idea what is to come and I can't ask, won't ask you to join if there is anything that could at all... I mean..."

Carrie reached out and took Dave's hand. "Dave. We know all this." She took Todd's hand with her free hand. "We are responsible for us. Not you. And if you need to be the thing that stands in harm's way, then we are behind you, not because of you, but because of what you mean to us. We're more than friends, I hope you know that."

"But -"

"No." Carrie stopped him. "When I joined the Army, I made a commitment to protect this country. That commitment doesn't end because I left the service. I know I'm not alone in that. We're here for you, but we're also here because this is where the fight is. I don't leave my friends, and I don't run from a fight!"

Dave was overcome with emotion. He hadn't felt anything like this since his wife had died, and hadn't thought he would feel it ever again. He loved these people. Perhaps that's why he wanted to protect them. In the end, he knew he couldn't stop them and only hoped he could help prepare them for whatever it was that was coming.

He didn't speak, but simply held their hands until the doors opened and a couple of women came in, indicating a new class was scheduled to begin..

Dave walked the back way to his house, tired but determined to protect it all, his house, his cat, his friends, and if need be, the world. He started to plan in earnest.

Chapter 37

Dr. Pat stopped just outside the doors to the new patio at the building where she worked. The patio was newer than the old utilitarian style building, and held a small array of tables for both the workers and visitors to eat lunch or just grab a coffee. Normally, Dr. Pat would eat at her desk, but today, she's been called here.

The sun warmed her after all morning in the air conditioned building. The breeze was uncharacteristically warm for late September. She scanned the tables and benches to find her appointment, Dave Nicklaus, in the far corner.

"Dave!" She approached the table and set down her notepad and lunch. "This is odd. Why did you want to meet out here?"

"I have a few reasons," Dave hemmed a bit, "but it's a beautiful day, so why don't we enjoy it?" He lifted the specially made carry case and set it on the table in front of him.

Dr Pat gave him a bit of side-eye, but sat down opposite him. She pulled her notebook out and asked, "So, what's going on that you needed to talk…out here on such a beautiful day and not in my delightfully decorated but stuffy office?"

"I've grown to dislike dim or dark places."

"My office is dim and dark?"

"The whole building is dim and dark." Dave tried to chuckle, but he knew it was more true than he wanted.

"Is this something new you need to talk about or…?" Dr. Pat made some notes in her notebook.

"Yes. No." Dave looked up at the wall which

separated the eating area from the parking lot. Cement block, 8 x 16. "I had an encounter I need to tell you about." He looked to the Doctor. "I'm not sure if you really want to hear it."

"Dave, I always want to hear what you have to say."

Dave glanced around. He had chosen this time because it was at the end of when most of the folks in the building took lunch. What he had planned, needed to be done with as few extra eyes as he could manage. Currently, it was just him and the doctor; but Dave also noticed two men just inside the glass doors eyeing them. Dr. Pat had brought backup.

"It was a couple of nights ago," Dave began, "I was just coming home from working out with some friends. We were making plans for…Halloween.

"The sun had already set, but there was still enough light for me to find my way home the back way. Their place is just down the wash and I knew the way, so the oncoming dark didn't bother me.

"I suppose, all in all, I should have guessed something was up. Sheldon usually meets me at the door, or stands on the cat tower by the back window when I approach. He's very aware of what is going on out in the yard. After the first attack, he's been even more diligent, especially during the night.

"As I came up the back, I looked for Sheldon in the window and didn't see him. I didn't think much of it, and just headed in the back door. The lights were on a timer, so I had no problem with my keys and in no time, I'm calling for Sheldon and tossing my keys on the kitchen table.

"Sheldon was nowhere to be found, but I kinda lost interest in that when I noticed two young boys sitting on my couch. I told you about these two, I think. Tom and Huck. They are from the Offset, and represent all the energy children put into Imaginary Friends."

Dr. Pat looked like she was having trouble with the story, but Dave knew he had to tell her the whole thing, so he continued before she could speak.

"They were dressed just as they had been when I saw them out in the Dead Lands. The older of the two, Tom, was sitting up on the back of the couch, his feet on the cushions. They both looked at me as I came in.

"Tom shouted 'it's about time!' and hopped down from the back of the couch, using the cushions as a springboard.

"He grew as he jumped. I'm not just saying he grew in size, though that is most assuredly what happened. But he also grew from a young boy of about 10 into a full sized adult taller than me. Huck stood up, doing the same thing.

"What faced me now were two huge adults and they were both coming at me. No intro, no threats, they just started across the room. I had my bag of tools and the Knight's Sword," Dave patted the knight's sword in front of him, "but I knew I didn't have time to get any of my tools out.

"The kitchen island was there, so I stepped behind it to keep it between us. I thought that might slow them down a bit, but it didn't. Tom literally stepped right up on it. He took a step forward coming across the island, and was now between me and Huck, so I grabbed the knight's sword, in its case, and knocked Tom's legs out from under him as I headed to the hallway. He came down face first.

"Huck started in making these strange noises. 'Ca-KAW Ca-KAW!' and then Tom, lying face down on the island, also started shouting, 'Ka-GUU Ka-GUU.' I rounded the corner to the hallway, opening my bag on the way.

"Glancing over my shoulder will give me nightmares for the rest of my days. Both of them were growing beaks. Their arms were growing longer, becoming wings. They grew in height even more and their now clawed feet scrabbled across the floor in my direction. Giant eyes with no color still seemed to focus directly on me."

The pounding of a headache began at the base of Dave's skull. It was, as he knew, the precursor to a full blown panic attack brought on by his PTSD. He tried to concentrate on what he was saying, keeping himself in control. The headache ignored him.

"Halfway down the hall, I tripped and fell. I could hear them behind me. My saving grace was that they were now too large to fit into the hall! They tried to force themselves into the hall, scraping the walls and gouging huge holes with their feet and their beaks. I thought for a moment, they would bring the house down around us.

"The whole time they are screaming 'Ka-GUU! KA-GUU!' It was deafening.

"The gun, my gun, the 1911 was shaking in my hand. I have no idea why or what, but I had to figure out how to stop them or I'd be dead. I steadied the gun with both hands and waited for the first one to try again to get down the hall. I didn't know if it was Tom or Huck, but I knew the second one would be directly behind the first and I knew I was loaded up with steel jacketed rounds. Steel is deadly to creatures from the Offset."

He stole a glance at Dr. Pat to gauge her

reaction. As usual, she was stoic.

"The gun erupted twice. It did nothing. The two giant black birds were now even more determined to get to me, now knowing the steel couldn't touch them. At this point, I was dazed, I couldn't understand why the gun hadn't worked. They're still screaming "KA-GUU! KA-GUU!! I fired again and again, but they just kept coming.

"They were in the hall, wiggling their big feathery bodies down the hall to me. I backed up all the way down until my back hit the closet. I could see them both now in the hall. The one in the lead opened its mouth and snagged my shoe! I could see the look of triumph in its dead eyes.

"At that moment, I was pretty sure I was seeing things, as a giant furry paw reached out of the bedroom and snagged the first one with some wicked long claws. It pulled him screeching and kicking into the bedroom where I heard a flurry of feathers, howling and kicking against the walls..

"Still fighting, the giant bird crawled out the door where it had been dragged. It was missing a lot of feathers, and it was still fighting whatever was behind it, but I could see in its eyes it was coming for me, no matter what had ahold of it."

"Danger is the thing which has always fueled the silent lightning. I know you don't believe in it, but it's real and at that moment, I dropped the gun and put out both hands and a bolt of white lighting ripped the two birds to shreds. Feathers turned to tar and my walls burned through, up and out, through the garage and out the top corner of the house. The lightning is stopped by nothing."

Dave stared at the Doctor. He knew what she

was thinking. She thought he had gone into some schizophrenic fugue state and was seeing all this in his head. He pulled out his phone and showed her the photos he had taken of the walls. They were scratched, gouged through to the studs. Another showed a hole that ran through the house and showed the black night sky beyond.

"I don't know how long I sat there. I was brought around by my neighbor pounding on the door. I got up and walked to the door looking for those bits of tar that I had seen spread about. They were already gone. Faster than before, too. All that was left was the damage. Theirs and… mine. Sheldon was unharmed, sitting on the island in the kitchen, waiting for treats.

"My neighbor had called the cops. I should have expected it, since he works for them. Works for the county anyway, he's in forensics. He recognized the sound of the gun going off and dialed the phone before the second volley.

I told the cops that the gun had gone off while I was preparing to clean it. They gave me some looks, like 'yeah, the gun goes off that many times while cleaning? Yeah, sure.' Thanks to my neighbor, they took my word. They looked at the holes in the walls or the blackened hole that was still smoking. They asked a lot of questions, like 'what caused that big hole' and I told them there was a small fire which was what caused me to accidentally fire the gun. They looked dubious, but there were no bodies, no other damage I needed to claim, so nothing for them to write up other than a standard call report. "But that's all done. I needed you to see these photos and hear the story."

Dr. Pat stood up. "I'm really sorry Dave, but this is for your own good." She turned and nodded to the two guys waiting by the doors and in a moment they were moving in among the tables, making their way to where Dr. Pat and Dave now stood. They moved in a way that would block any exit Dave tried to take.

"That giant furry paw?" Dave spoke to the Doctor while watching the guys approach. "I forgot to mention, that was Sheldon, my cat, grown to the size of a horse. Took him a while to get turned around in that small bedroom and grab the bird in the hall. The evil energy from the Offset does that to him. Oh, and he talks, too. But, that's a story for another day."

Dave held up his hands, smiling to the two guys. MPs. Not orderlies. This ought to go down well. As the two men approached, he turned his hands around showing he was unarmed. When they reached out to take him by both arms, Dave casually reached out to touch them.

Both men immediately stiffened. Dave grabbed their shirt collars and gently eased them to the ground. He turned to Dr. Pat, showing her he was not holding anything.

"I'm getting better at controlling it." He looked down at the two men. "They should be fine in a few moments. He picked up the carry case and, snapping it open, pulled out the Knight's Sword. "I'm doing much better at everything, Doc. I'm keeping the visions at bay and controlling my… my destiny."

Dr. Pat looked at the two men on the ground. They would be ok, she was sure. "This will be difficult to defend."

"Everyone just needs that one person to believe in them." He walked to the cinder block wall and held up the sword. "I need you, above all, to believe me and maybe even believe in me. I suppose it has to do with

Naquinta being gone and me feeling a bit… alone." In a moment, the Knight's Door appeared. Dave smiled at the fact that the door's visage was no longer a knight with a helmet on. It now showed the knight holding his helmet at his side, the carving clearly showing Dave's own face on the door, long beard and all. Perhaps I am getting the hang of this.

"I'd take you along, but honestly, I don't think you'd survive." Dave pulled open the door, and a white light illuminated the patio. "Keep the faith, Doc." Dave nodded to Dr. Pat and entered the light. In a moment, the door had closed and the whole thing had disappeared, like a mirage in the desert.

20 minutes later, Dr. Pat was standing in the security office for the building watching the video from the cameras mounted in the patio area. She watched Dave take down the two large security personnel without a weapon, lowering them carefully to the ground. She almost smiled when she realized that he had chosen the place to call up the door right below the camera so that there was no record of it, except maybe for the bright light which lit up the patio.

"I'll need to report this." The one MP said. This one was standing beside the door. The other was seated at the console for the video cameras.

"And I'll need a copy of that video so that I can show my friends how a 69 year old Vet takes down two young MPs without a weapon." Dr. Pat turned to the standing MP. "Whether you decide to report this or not, I will need a copy of that video."

When she left a few minutes later, she was carrying a small USB drive with the video on it. She left the two men arguing quietly. She was still on the fence, but now, at least she had some small evidence of

the power that Dave carried.
    It scared and thrilled her.

Chapter 38

Martha Claus brought the small tray with the three steaming mugs into the ornate study at the Grand Lodge in the North Pole. Walls of books on Christmas traditions filled shelves on both sides of the big fireplace. In front of the fireplace were two very large and very comfortable chairs, perfectly positioned to enjoy the warm fire. Seated in the chairs, warming themselves with the fire were Dave and the Big Claus Man himself. Martha waited while each took a mug and before she set the tray on the small table. She lifted her own mug, but rather than sit, she leaned over and kissed his husband on the cheek.

"I'll leave you two to discuss things." She said.

"Thank you, my love." He turned to watch her as she walked out. It did not go unnoticed that, contrary to many depictions of Martha Claus, she was not an old frumpy woman with gray hair. She was actually quite attractive, and she well knew it. She turned at the door, knowing that The Claus had watched her walk away, and giving him a sly wink, closed the door.

Dave smiled at the interaction and blew softly on his hot mug. He tried not to think of all the times he had had similar interactions with his own wife, now gone. He shook his head to clear it and brought the steaming mug up to his nose. The aroma of rich chocolate tempted him. The crackle of the wood in the fireplace, burning brightly, added fall flair to the room and helped him stay grounded. Knowing he was actually in an alternate realm, talking to a being of energy was not helpful in that grounding.

"It's snowing outside." Santa gestured to the big

window, the gentle fall of snow evident by the build up on the frame, "but, it's most always snowing here." He turned to Dave. "So, what brings you here, Dave?"

"Druscilla." He said without preamble.

"I had heard, but thought this was some odd Offset Urban Legend, like that old story of the human raised as an elf." He chuckled a bit. "Didn't she get… what, de-created last year? Didn't you -" He stopped speaking, looking at Dave.

"No." Dave said simply, looking down into his mug. "She's very much still with us. She's been living under the Dead Lands for many years. As far as I can tell, the Druscilla that lived in All Hallows Manor was not the real Druscilla. Perhaps at first, but somewhere along the line, after she discovered the power of fear… things changed. She created a clone and the two changed places whenever it pleased her."

The two sat in silence for a few moments, sipping chocolate.

"Why come to me?" Santa finally said. "Wouldn't the Horseman be a better source of information?"

Dave set his mug on the tray half finished. "That's part of the problem." He stood and paced in front of the great fireplace. "He created her. He has the same powers as she does. I really don't know where his loyalty lies. His dislike of humans is well known. Is he really acting in our best interests or is he, in fact, hiding her? I've searched the Under Lands, the Dead Lands and honestly, I found evidence of her in every place I dared to look. Where is she now? I could ask the Horseman, but if she works for him or is working with him, I won't know if he's telling me the truth or not." Dave stopped pacing, facing the big man in the bigger comfortable chair.

"I think you're overthinking this a bit." The big man sipped his chocolate. He took his time allowing the moment to pass slowly. Dave stayed by the fire, allowing the heat to help him relax. The fire ignored them both.

Finally, touching a napkin to the long white mustache, Santa set his nearly empty mug on the tray, taking his feet off the footstool and leaning forward to make his point. "We, the Majors, are beings of energy and purpose. Created by the Old One. Don't mistake our purpose for your beliefs or miss-beliefs."

Confusion drew Dave's eyebrows down. "I'm not sure what that means."

"Simply," Santa sat back in his chair, laying his arms on the sides. "We can only be what humans 'expect' us to be. The majority of humans. Nothing more. In fact, we are basically incapable of being anything else."

"Druscilla intends to enslave humans. Is that what humans expect?"

"Ah, but Druscilla was not created by the Old One in the old ways. She, if you remember correctly, was created by -?" He smiled, waiting for Dave to complete the thought.

"Scarecrow." Dave was more confused, but felt he was on the edge of understanding.

"Yes." Santa smiled and stood. He gathered the mugs onto the tray.

"So Scarecrow, or the Horseman, didn't know how to create a being, properly…and made mistakes, is that it?" Dave's mind reached for the gold ring.

"Perhaps you should be talking to him about his purpose and his… well, ok, let's call it his mistake."

"But I -"

"Dave." Santa smiled, understanding of what Dave needed, clouding his own needs and desires. "What exactly is the problem as you see it?"

"I need to find her before she finds a way to cross the veil." Dave hesitated. "And I need to… kill her, I guess, before she can do so. If I destroy her on this side of the veil, I can protect the division of the two realms." Dave leaned back against the fireplace mantle. "Even when I say that out loud I sound like some sort of fool reading a bad script in an even worse movie."

"HA!" Santa laughed. "You don't sound that bad to me. But listen, it seems to me that every time you go looking, regardless of where you go looking, that you have a habit of finding her - especially in the Under Lands." He looked up at the ceiling, thinking. "She really won't be there anymore, she knows you're looking. She will be here, above." His hands slapped down on his thighs, emphasizing this point. "Yes! You'll find her the same way you found the Scarecrow that first time." He stood, picking up the tray and mugs.

Dave stood gape mouthed as he realized the truth. Yes, here above. Wherever I go looking.

"Now, forgive me if I don't show you out," Santa walked to the door, "but when she winks like that at me, I know exactly what's waiting for me upstairs and honestly, we were done a long time ago." He opened the door and headed down the hall carrying the tray of mugs. "You'll… show yourself out, won't you?" His boisterous voice carried from far down the hall.

Dave held the Knight's sword in its sheath against the wall and the door appeared. He could hear the Big Man's footsteps as he headed up the stairs to the warm bed and warmer company that awaited him.

He looked at the door, and considered what waited for him.

Indecision and PTSD collided and froze Dave to his spot. He stared at his own visage on the door, unable to pull it open. What? He asked himself. What am I doing here? Am I really the only person, the only human able to do this? Am I destined to do this, take the life… kill… de-create this being of energy? His anger bubbled off center in his brain. In his mind, he again saw the line of villagers in Vietnam, each one crying, holding one another. The enemy holding weapons on them, the smoke from their weapons as they erupted in death.

Discovered in the shallow grave, Dave had never seen the action which caused the deaths of the small group of villagers. PTSD had only created this visceral scene in his mind, using his own fears and misgivings. No. I could not have saved them. I was not there when they were killed. But, why do I feel I should have? Why do I feel I have to do this to avenge a group of people on the other side of the world 40-odd years past, that I never knew?

And the answer came. If not me, then who? In the jungle, after having discovered the recently buried bodies, Dave had gone over the edge. He had gone on a killing spree in the nearby Viet Cong encampment. 24 dead by his hand in one night. Not fulfilled, he had gone back and carved the letter V in each of their foreheads. V, the Roman numeral for five.

Five. V. His squad nickname. A signature. A way of taking the shoulder of vengeance. Not hiding. It wasn't his to do, but if not him, then who? Dave had avenged their deaths the only way he knew how. If he had been there before they were killed he might have done something and there was his answer.

He was here, now. He was capable, now. If he didn't act now, the entire planet of humans may well be killed or worse: enslaved, living each day in fear. Every man, woman and – Lori! The cute little girl that lived next door with such a pure heart that she asked Santa to bring his late wife home to him for Christmas.

All of them, the rest of their lives. Ever afraid, feeding that energy to a being who wanted only power. He couldn't, he wouldn't let that happen.

With a firm grip on the handle, Dave pulled the Knight's Door open and dashed through, more energized and determined than ever.

As Dave passed through the door, the shadows cast by the fire danced a bit quicker and slipped under the hall door.

Chapter 39

Dave was enjoying the breezy day, walking in the Offset. He had determined the meaning of his meeting with The Claus that looking for Druscilla was, in itself, finding Druscilla. So, much like he found the Scarecrow that first time, he only had to think of finding her and she would be found.

He had been walking for more than an hour, still unsure where he might end up; his only thought was finding her, dealing with her and getting things back to normal in the Offset as well as his own life.

The clouds had begun to meander in, causing shadows to float across the countryside. Soon, there were more cloudy spots than blue sky. Dave took this as a sign he was close. He checked his knives, wondering if he had made the right choice by leaving both Zeke and his handgun at home.

The blue sky finally hid behind an even blanket of gray. The road became gravel, and the gravel became rutted dirt. Dave carefully watched his step, knowing Druscilla's penchant for traps and tripwires.

Crossing over one hill, Dave was reminded of the day he had met Scarecrow. Across the fence, he could see the far-off fields appearing the same brown turned earth dotted with the remains of recently harvested crops. The fences were the same, but worn, broken in spots. It was a moment of déjà vu and he stopped beside the fence to get his bearings.

Turning around he was even more surprised to find, not only the tall pole with the scarecrow perch, but also the older man standing off across the open space. He was exactly as Dave remembered him, down to the worn overalls and faded hat.

"You again?" the old man said, coming across the gravel.

"Scarecrow?" Dave was confused. In his own mind, the Scarecrow was no longer the persona of the Scarecrow, the old Halloween entity, but had changed to the Headless Horseman. Dave's head felt light, off balance.

"Yes." Immediately the old man with the straw colored hair became the Scarecrow. Gone was the ball cap and overalls. The entire being gave the appearance of a man made out of burlap, including the featureless face. A slash for a mouth and a pair of dark hollow eye holes with nothing in the centers.

Dave stared at the Scarecrow wondering what this meant. "This is all -"

"Look, you, I told that winged pest that I wouldn't help you get rid of the holder of the Harvest Quedret no matter who made her, and that includes me."

Dave's head swam. He remembered getting Val to fly to the Scarecrow with a message about the night they took down Druscilla, and how the Scarecrow, as the Headless Horseman, had shown up at the right time, and literally destroyed her. If what this Scarecrow said was true….

"Humans." The Scarecrow spat into the dirt and turned to go. He walked briskly across the gravel and opened the gate.

"Wait!" Dave quickly joined the Scarecrow at the gate. "I just needed to know a little more." He stared at the burlap entity and the dark hollow eyes stared back. "I need help and you are the only one that knows her. Druscilla, I mean."

The two stared at each other for a few moments more. Déjà vu again as the scarecrow said, "I need a hot cup of coffee." With that, he passed through the gate and headed down the path. To no one in particular he added, "You coming? You're not going to get any information out here!"

Dave followed behind, still wondering what was going on. Soon they rounded a corner and there was the same well built cabin he had spent the afternoon in over a year ago. Nothing much had changed. The outside of the cabin was well fitted with the same logs he recalled; inside was still modern drywall, with the same modern furnishings. Dave could almost swear that the fire in the fireplace was the same size as before.

In the kitchen, Scarecrow poured two mugs of coffee. Dave picked up and examined the mug, noting it was the same exact mug he had used before. Dave took a moment to prepare his coffee and after taking that first sip, sat back and eyed Scarecrow. The Scarecrow poured his coffee, replaced the carafe back on the stove and leaned against it sipping his coffee.

"So, did you take care of the Hallowitch?"

"Yes and no."

"How human of you." Scarecrow smiled a flat smile.

Dave didn't take the bait. "You've been out here all this time? I mean, since I last saw you?"

Scarecrow nodded and took another sip of coffee. "Your idea to take her down was without merit, or at least I thought so." He set his coffee down on the breakfast bar across from Dave and sat facing him. "She's crafty, but that's probably because I made her so." He looked down into his coffee as if remembering his efforts now as failures and not successes. "I felt the humans wanted A Witch, and I did the research, learned what they wanted, how they wanted it and went about creating it. She's perfect." He looked up at Dave again, who was studying him with steady eyes. "Your plan would have failed if I had been there. She knows me, she would have known! She would have…What are you looking at?"

Dave started. "Sorry, I was merely wondering.."

"Wondering what?"

To give him a moment to think, Dave took another sip of coffee. "You don't know what happened. You weren't there."

"No, I wasn't."

"I'm not sure how to describe what happened." Dave looked up, trying to remember how it all came about. "She was there. She was going to take the power I carry using one of her purple flames, when… well…" Dave looked at Scarecrow. "YOU showed up!"

"Me?" The lines above Scarecrows hollow eyes went up.

"Well, at least I thought it was you. It was… how can I put this? It was bigger than her, dressed or at least resembling the Headless Horseman of Sleepy Hollow…" Dave looked to see if Scarecrow was following along and seeing a nod, continued. "He talked like you, sounded like you and he simply took Druscilla and turned her to dust!"

"Dust?"

"Yes, purple dust! He took all the black stuff on the floor, created when I… well, I killed Jungar, not once but twice… with help…" He waved a hand as if to push the thoughts away. "He turned all that into Daredevil, the Horseman's haunted horse!"

"I don't like horses." Scarecrow leaned forward

a bit. "Horsehair gets into burlap way too easily."

"Who was that then?" Dave almost shouted, frustrated.

"You fool human!" Scarecrow scoffed. "Isn't it obvious?"

Dave looked at the entity with wide confused eyes, knowing in his head what was coming, but wanting to once again not hear the truth. Truth had a way of harming him lately that was best left unknowing.

"It was Druscilla!" Scarecrow shouted and threw back his burlap head, mouth wide, laughing loud and long. "I told you, SHE'S PERFECT! She knew you'd try to fool her so she fooled you first! And second! And, most of all, LAST!" He laughed and laughed.

Dave's anger built to a head. "ALL THIS TIME?!" His anger pushed him off the stool and into the living room, both hands on his head, trying to keep it all inside. "HOW? HOW? HOW?"

Scarecrow slowed his laughter. "Calm down, human. You're not the first to be bested by the best." This made him chuckle a bit more. He waited for Dave to calm even a bit, and rejoin him at the breakfast bar. He gestured to the lukewarm coffee and Dave nodded. Scarecrow got up and brought over fresh hot coffee, warming the mug.

Once seated again, Scarecrow looked over his mug at Dave. "Have you met the Tooth Fairy? Not the cute little fairy of fable, the Tooth Fairy we have here in the Offset is a much different creature."

"Yes, I came upon him not too long ago."

"Crazy thing."

Dave had calmed down enough. "I think I know

what you mean."

"Well, you may not know this. Druscilla scares him something fierce. She forced him to teach her how to make clones, replicas." Scarecrow looked to Dave to see if he understood completely.

Dave stared at the burlap face before him, his eyes wide. "She wasn't disguised as an old woman in the caves. She had used part of herself to create several clones. One to battle me at Christmas and then created another to use a…spell?…to look like the Horseman which would turn the other clone to dust!" Dave was amazed to hear it all come out of his own mouth. "She's been ahead of the game since before I came along!"

"Don't blame yourself," Scarecrow sipped coffee. "You're only human after all."

Dave pushed his quick anger back and stood. "And now, no longer in the caves, she's disguised as the Horseman, living at All Hallows Manor! The only place in the entire Offset that I didn't think I needed to search to find her!"

Without even saying goodbye, Dave ran out the door, and up the path, leaving Scarecrow laughing as he watched him go.

"Humans." Scarecrow shook his head and closed the door.

Chapter 40

The wide putty knife dipped into the trough of mud and quickly went to the wall; covering the paper tape carefully, leaving a smooth surface. Excess mud scraped off the putty knife went back into the trough.

"Hey."

The putty knife went back across the area with a gentle scraping sound, smoothing carefully.

"Hey!"

Dave looked up from his work. "What?"

"Toss me that paper tape, will ya?" Todd was up on a ladder, working on the wall where the silent lightning had cut a hole. The two friends had already replaced the ruined section of roof and shingles along with the end roof joists and were now fixing up the interior. Todd had already cut out the damaged wallboard and set in a new piece.

"Here ya go!" Dave tossed the roll up to him from where he stood working on the deep gouges left from the giant birds. The deepest part of the damage had already been replaced and now he was just smoothing out the wall. The bedroom, where Sheldon had taken on one of the birds, received similar treatment.

The two worked in silence until Todd came down. "Now, we just wait for the mud to dry." He pulled two bottles of water out of the fridge and handed one to Dave, looking over their work. "Then prime and paint."

"Ka-Guuu!" Dave said, and knocked his water bottle against Todd's. It was another beautiful fall day, so the two adjourned to the back patio.

The two friends sat in companionable silence for a bit. The cool fall breeze danced among the fallen leaves in the little forest. Dave was thinking again of cleaning the clearing where he had placed a bench with the cement stepping stone over Naquinta's urn. The broken stone was a scab his thoughts picked at.

"Tell me all of it again." Todd spoke softly. "Druscilla is the Horseman?"

"I just don't know." Dave sighed. "If I say it out loud, it's just… crazy!" He looked at Todd, who gestured to 'go ahead.' "Ok, When I found the Scarecrow the second time, in that cabin out in the Offset boonies, it all seemed so obvious. Druscilla, working under the Dead Lands, uses some new magic taught to her by the Tooth Fairy to create clones of herself. At Christmas last year, what I thought to be Scarecrow who had changed himself into the Headless Horseman, came in to 'save the day' by killing Druscilla, was basically just a Druscilla clone. Ah, but the Horseman was nothing more than another clone that Druscilla used to kill one of her other clones all in an effort to fool everyone." He took a deep breath and let it out. "If I say that one more time, my head is going to explode."

Dave looked at Todd, and they both began to laugh.

"That's CRAZY!" Todd stood holding his arms wide. "Hey, maybe I'm just another clone!" The statement caused them both to laugh even more.

When the laughter died down, Dave went in and got some more water. When he came back, he said, "You're NOT a clone, are you?"

"Don't think so…" Todd stopped. "But that's the question, isn't it?"

"What do you mean?"

"Well, who is a clone? Sure, maybe the Druscilla who turned to purple dust last Christmas was a clone, especially since we know she – the real Druscilla - is not dead. BUT, who else?"

"I don't -"

"Let me get this all out, it's all part of the crazy talk."

Dave smiled and gestured for Todd to continue.

"Everything you said is logical, if you think that Druscilla planned all that the way it came out. But, and this is just more crazy talk, what if Druscilla is actually Scarecrow? Not the first one, the second one. What if she disguised herself as the Scarecrow just to put this whole Headless Horseman Clone thing in your head to throw you off the scent?" Todd laughed.

Dave wasn't laughing. He stared out at the forest, the water bottle hovering half way to his mouth.

"Crazy, right?"

"No." Dave put down his water and stared more at the forest. In his mind's eye, he could see the value in both arguments. The problem came in knowing which was the right one to pursue. "Not Crazy. It makes perfect sense."

"Wait, what?"

Dave took a moment to gather his thoughts. He looked at the way the light filtered through Naquinta's forest. He wished for just a moment that she was there with him to add her own level headedness to the discussion. Not that Todd was the wrong person to talk to, it was just Dave missing the input from her own lips.

Her lips….Dave smiled remembering her-

"Earth to Dave…"

Dave turned to Todd. "Oh sorry, my mind

was… wandering." He smiled. "Ok, so the problem lies in that both these arguments have merit. And both rely on acceptance of Druscilla disguising herself as either the Horseman or Scarecrow, the second one. This argument is based on the fact that the Real Scarecrow, having changed himself to the Headless Horsemen, is the one who showed up at Christmas to destroy the Druscilla clone. After gathering enough magic from the fairies, she has disguised herself – not as the Headless Horseman, but as the Scarecrow and is now residing in Scarecrow's cabin unbeknownst to anyone. SHE then puts this idea into MY head that the Headless Horseman is actually Druscilla in an effort to get me to – what, destroy him?

So which is it: Druscilla disguised as Headless Horseman, or Druscilla disguised as Scarecrow? This is not a simply a matter of picking one, either. What I have to do now is find a way to be sure who is who and what is up. If I pick the wrong one..." He looked at Todd.

"I didn't really think that would come out so serious, but I agree. You have to find a way to get under the disguise. The question is how and which one?" Todd crushed his water bottles for recycling as he talked.

For the next couple of hours, the two discussed ways of examining both the Scarecrow in the cabin and the Headless Horseman in All Hallows Manor. It came down to asking a few directed questions that would prove who is the real owner of the Harvest Quedret. They tried writing down questions but everything they could come up with could easily be guessed by anyone with any knowledge.

Dave shook his head. "This is going to take

some time to think through. You think the mud is dry yet?"

"Yup, let's get the paint."

An hour later, the two sat drinking water again, staring at the completed repair jobs in the bedroom, hall and in the living room. Anger flittered across Dave's mind at the casual destruction of Naquinta's home. She would have been livid.

"I need to get back to Carrie." Todd rose to go. "You got any idea how to do this? I mean, I wish I could go with you, sort of back you up, but…" he left the statement unfinished. Both knew there was no way for him to get to the Offset. "Just let me know if you need someone to bounce ideas off of." Dave showed his friend to the door.

As he stepped out onto the back porch, Todd stopped. "Dave," he started, "I want you to know that both Carrie and I have been working out, both with the katana and the guns and if you need us to help in any way…well, we want you to know you can count on us. We're yours to command."

Dave was choked up a bit, but nodded and gave Todd a firm hug. In the middle of the hug, Dave stopped, frozen in thought.

"Dave, this is getting a bit awkward."

Dave pulled back, staring at his friend. "Command."

"Oh geez, you've done fried your brain."

Dave pulled Todd back into the house and shut the back door, first glancing about to make sure nothing was outdoors watching them.

"Something you said." Dave said quickly. "Command. Something or someone commanded this to happen." Dave pointed at the repair jobs. "The two boys-turned-giant-birds didn't just decide to do this on their own. For one thing, they wouldn't know where to go, or why… unless…"

Todd nodded thinking along with Dave. "Had to be Druscilla."

"But, again, which one?" Dave paced, thinking. "Ok, one: If Druscilla-disguised-as-Horseman is the one who commanded them to come here, why? What could he possibly gain by sending them to me at that time?"

"Nothing!" Todd's eyes grew wide. "She already had command of All Hallows Gate, so there was no need to get rid of you. Unless… unless she thought you were getting too close? All Hallow's Manor is the only place you had yet to search!"

"Ok, So…" Dave looked up at the repair job on the wall. "The other side of this is why would Druscilla-disguised-as-Scarecrow need to send them?"

"Again, getting too close?" Todd was coming up dry. "Having you show up out there at the Scarecrow's cabin must have been quite a shock."

"No." Dave smiled. "And yes. I think I see it. I'd gone looking and FOUND Druscilla everyplace I had gone looking. The ONLY place I hadn't looked was All Hallows Manor! Not going there means I was NOT getting close, at all! So, the logical conclusion is that Druscilla is NOT at All Hallows Gate! If she was, then she'd be happy with me not looking there, no reason to send the Ka-Guu Brothers."

"Scarecrow!"

"Yes, that's probably it! It all makes sense."

"Unless she wanted to throw you off?" Todd suggested.

"This is getting as complicated as a bad mystery

novel!" Dave sighed. "And just when I thought I had figured it out."

"That's it!" Todd pointed at Dave. "That's why she sent them, to keep you guessing!"

"Yes, and it sure worked." Dave and Todd laughed and high-fived so hard they both nearly fell down. This caused them to laugh some more. After some quiet moments of thought, they discussed what might work to finish this whole fight. A few minutes later, Todd was headed down the back way to his house and Dave was collecting his tools.

He made a quick list of errands he needed to get done before this whole thing came to a head; and, in truth, he needed to know for sure who was who before he put his plan into action. He had to make one more visit.

Chapter 41

Dave stood behind a big tree at the edge of the great offset forest. He leaned out just enough to get a look at the dark edifice standing behind the black All Hallows Gate. The structure stood in the dark, surrounded by a landscape of gravestones and mausoleums.

He leaned back against the tree and again went over his knowledge, inferences and solutions to what has been almost a long year's worth of thinking, questioning and searching. He knew in his gut that the Headless Horseman was, indeed, the owner of the Harvest Quedret. He just couldn't shake the idea that somehow, Druscilla-

"What's this all about?"

Dave looked across the park and spied Doc headed his way with a hurried gait. "Doc?" He left his blind by the tree and moved to meet the entity out on the grass.

"Are you having some sort of crisis?" Doc asked, "A crisis of faith versus knowledge, perhaps?"

"No, I -" Dave noted how Doc was dressed. Worn jeans and dock shoes were fine and he usually saw them when Doc was viewed in his 'professor' clothes. But oddly, today Doc also wore the black vestments with a white collar and black coat of a catholic priest.

"Yes, it seems things are a bit confused," Doc mused, looking down at his own clothes. "It's never been mixed up like this. I can only figure … well I don't know what I figure, that's why I'm here."

Dave led Doc out of the view of All Hallows

Gate. "I'm having issues with my own faith in myself, I guess."

"How so?"

Dave looked at the entity, whose vast knowledge rivaled the greatest minds in the human world. "It's not so much faith, like in God, it's faith in my own being. My abilities, my thoughts, my conclusions."

An annoyed tone entered into Doc's voice. "Tell me."

"Ok," Dave looked about putting his thoughts together. It did not escape Dave that the entity wanted succinct information and yet was unable to give it at times. "Let me get through this entirely, if for no other reason than I need to spell it out for myself. Ok?"

"Ok." Doc blinked a few times, but leaned against a nearby tree ready to listen.

"This all comes from the confusion planted by Druscilla. From what I understand, Druscilla has been living under the Dead Lands for some time. She has come out to visit humans on Halloween, but for the most part, hides in the caverns around the citadel."

"The citadel was created many -"

Dave held up a hand, stopping Doc from continuing. "Not yet. I'll let you know when I've got this all out."

Doc closed his mouth and nodded, not the least bit ashamed of his interrupting.

"So, Druscilla has been hiding, coming out only at Halloween. Along comes Dave, First Knight of the Offset, to do battle with her in order to retrieve the Quedrets she had taken from the others. Yours, Val's and Reggie's. Somehow, she is always one step ahead of me. Always.

"I find Scarecrow out in the boonies and persuade him to return and claim the Harvest Quedret. The end, or what I thought was the end, came at Christmas of last year. I'm sure you've heard the story a hundred times." Dave checked to see if Doc was truly listening. Doc nodded, very aware of his own part in the drama that unfolded last year. Assured, Dave continued, "In an attempt to think ahead of her, I bring in help. Sheldon, my cat, and Scarecrow, who had become the Headless Horseman. The Horseman takes back the Quedret and destroys or what he called 'decreates' the Hallowitch, Druscilla." Dave holds up his hand again. "Or so I thought."

"It has now come to light that the Druscilla destroyed last Christmas was not the real Druscilla. Somehow, the real Druscilla has found the secret to making clones of herself, taught to her by or stolen from the Tooth Fairy. But now, with all this cloning, and the knowledge of Druscilla not being killed last year, I'm questioning everything and everyone. Is Druscilla disguised as the Scarecrow, back out in the farmlands living in the cabin there, or has Druscilla really been The Headless Horseman all this time, laying out this convoluted plot to keep me from knowing the truth? I thought I had figured it out, after the two Imaginary boys came to my house and tried to kill me, but now… now, I just don't know if I can trust my own thoughts, my own conclusions." Dave looked at Doc, who dutifully said nothing.

"Ok, I'm done." Dave leaned around the tree to glance again at the All Hallows Gate.

"Occam's Razor." Doc replied.

"What?

"Oh, don't tell me you've never heard of Occam

and his razor?"

"Yes." Dave replied. "That's the idea that the simplest solution is, most likely the right one?"

Doc scoffed. "Occam's Razor or the principle of parsimony or law of parsimony is the problem-solving principle that 'entities should not be multiplied beyond necessity,' sometimes inaccurately paraphrased as "the simplest explanation is usually the best one."

"The simplest explanation is that Druscilla was killed last year." Dave was not impressed with Doc's explanation.

"Not if you include all that you've learned this year." Doc leaned out and looked at All Hallows Gate with All Hallows Manor standing ominously behind it. "Perhaps another adage will help you in your search."

Dave didn't respond, sure that Doc would give him the adage regardless.

"I've learned through my different sides, faith or knowledge, that with Faith, one never needs to increase their understanding of faith. Many do, studying their respective religious texts, but Faith is never in need of more information. With knowledge, however, it's exactly the opposite. One can never have enough information when it comes to knowledge." He turned back to Dave. "Which means -"

"Which means," Dave nodded, "that I am going to have to go in there and ask more questions if I'm going to be sure."

"Hoc est rectam conclusionem" Doc waited for Dave to agree, and when he didn't, added "Yes, that's pretty much it."

Dave nodded in understanding, and this time he didn't hesitate. He walked off in the direction of the black castle on the hill known as All Hallows Manor, in front of which was All Hallows Gate. He turned back to wave a thank you to Doc, noting in passing that Doc's priestly coat and collar had been replaced by a turtleneck sweater and a dark tweed coat.

"At least that problem has been corrected." He muttered to himself.

Chapter 42

The katana sword whistled as it cut cleanly and quickly through the air. Todd sweated with exertion, having spent the better part of his day off working out and practicing with the long sword. He was determined to be ready should Dave need him in any way. He knew he couldn't help in the Offset, but if anything tried to come after his friends or his wife here, they would be in for a fight.

He closed his eyes and just for the experience, ran through the Kata again slowly, whispering each move which made up the Kata. Each move, each thrust or slice had its own separate name, but created the Kata or form when compiled together. He finished by sliding the long two handed sword into its wood Saya or Scabbard.

"Impressive." Carrie had been at the door, watching the entire time.

"More impressive with two…" Todd gestured to the mats. Carrie dropped her bag by the door and joined him, picking her Katana off the rack. They stood still for a moment, focusing on the task at hand, and as one, began to move, staying far apart.

Two swords sang in the large barn room. Their katas identical, moves precise. When they were finished, Carrie continued working out while Todd relaxed by the big window. He wiped his face with a towel, looked from Carrie to the window, suddenly aware that the sun had gone behind the clouds.

This time of year, he knew clouds had a habit of showing up unannounced, but this was something different. The clouds were darker, thicker and had an almost malevolent look. He leaned close to the panes of glass, checking the horizon to the east and west. The angry gray clouds seemed to cover the sky completely.

"Going to be a bad Halloween this year." He spoke to no one, but Carrie had finished her Kata and came to his side.

"I grew up in the north." She sighed and turned to lean against the wall. "We had to design our Halloween costumes with snow in mind. Snow White loses her definition with a pink parka and a hood."

"I know what you mean," he continued studying the clouds, "but this is more than snow. Those clouds almost look like tornadoes or, god forbid, a hurricane."

Carrie laughed, turning to join him in looking out the window. "Hurricane, this late in the season?" but her laugh caught in her throat when she saw the clouds. "They weren't there when I came in." The two looked at each other for a moment and without a word headed to the door.

Todd and Carrie went outside to look at the clouds. He almost turned on the radio to hear the weather, but the windswept waves across the sky told them more than the weather report could. He stepped away from the building, looking up. The low ceiling of dark vapor swirled and bucked closer and closer to one spot in particular: the forest behind Dave's house.

Thinking about what this might mean, Todd had a thought. "Come on." He opened the door to his truck and without a word, Carrie got in the other side. In moments they were headed through the subdivision, out of the area.

Once they turned onto the two lane highway outside the subdivision, Carrie was surprised to see that the sun was shining, and a blue sky overhead. Todd pulled the truck over to the side of the road. In the rearview mirror he could see no clouds.

"You knew this." Carrie turned to look out the back. "What's going on?"

"I'm not sure, but I think this means we've got a bigger problem this Halloween than having enough candy." Todd looked at Carrie and took her hand. Turning the truck around, they returned to the small suburban streets where they lived. Immediately the clouds returned, horizon to horizon. The light became a diffused dimness.

"For the time being, this may only be visible to us." Todd leaned forward to check the clouds again. "Though I'd be hard pressed to tell you why." He watched kids playing in the dim streets who all acted unaware of the lack of light, the wind which swept the streets or the bitter chill in the air. "Somehow, we're connected to it."

Parking the truck out behind the big barn once again, Todd turned to Carrie. "I may not get this chance again, but I need to tell you -"

Carrie put a loving hand over his mouth. "You don't need to tell me anything. Everything I've ever needed, I can feel in you every day, every moment. A lot of other women may need their men to vocalize what they are feeling, but with you, I can know it in everything you do when you're near me and even when you're not near me."

Tears threatened the corners of Todd's eyes. He grabbed her wrist and kissed the fingers that covered his mouth. Carrie giggled and reached for the door handle. She hopped out of the truck, and turned back as she closed the door. "I had better get Cassandra out and ready." The door shut and Carrie disappeared into the barn.

Looking out the windscreen, Todd remained in the truck. He thought back on their life together, which, if he was honest, wasn't that great. He had spent way too much energy and time focused on himself and not on his family. When he finally woke up and saw the result, it was already too late. Divorce hung on the horizon.

Todd wouldn't take a thing from a divorce, letting her take it all. He would live in his broken down van, an old 1965 Ford panel van, with more rust than metal. At his core, the feeling of needing to be punished for how he had treated both his wife and his daughter took more control of him than he might have wanted. All he asked her for was a place to park the van during the day.

Back then, they had an old house with a creaky floor, drafts that came out of nowhere and they were plagued with the three M's: mold, mildew and mice. Part of Carrie's anger was at Todd's inability to prioritize their own home over the little projects he would take out of desperation when the bills came due. Unemployed and living in the van gave him ample time to rip out and replace just about anything he could. Hard work was his penance.

When they sold the house, they made a heavy profit, getting more than the market price. Todd may have had problems in his relationships, but when it came to fixing up old houses, he was one of the best.

Then Carrie dropped the news. She wouldn't go through with the divorce if he could continue to prioritize his life the way he had the house and by extension, his family. Todd felt he had been given a reprieve from the hangman's noose. He redoubled his efforts, increasing their meager profit on the first house, and buying a brand new house in the small rural subdivision. He continued to improve on himself, getting the job driving a cement truck for many years, which, in turn, allowed them to buy the property with the barn.

The second chance. He knew she loved him and he knew that the second chance was her way of giving him time to show how much he loved her. He never stopped doing things for her and never let a day go by without telling her how much she meant to him.

A smile played at Todd's lips thinking of how much he loved his wife. He would bring the pain to anyone or anything that threatened her. He popped open the door of the truck and smiled a bit more thinking about what Cassandra would bring.

Chapter 43

All Hallows Gate loomed before him. He looked at the thick solid iron bars with the hinges set in wide brick columns. For just a moment, he wondered if the gate was to keep visitors out or other entities in. The dark façade of All Hallows Manor loomed above the hill with a monochrome air. Dave watched the clouds swirl about with no real pattern.

His hand grasped the bars and gave a tug. The gate didn't move. From behind the brickwork came a loud "GAH!" Dave stepped back. Trundling into view was Grock, the very large misshapen Golem. Once again Dave hesitated while he waited to see what the big creature's motives were.

"Hi, Grock." He tried to sound casual.

"GAH!"

"Is he in?"

"GAH!" Grock grabbed the thick bars and with a mighty groan, the gate swung inward.

At first unsure, Dave took a hesitant step toward the opening. When he was sure nothing was about to happen, Dave slipped on through and Grock worked at closing the gate. With a shake of his head, Dave started up the new black cobblestone walkway which led directly from the gate to the front door. He could see the old path that ran around the back of the house as he went up the hill.

Dave had been walking for a bit when he realized that he wasn't getting any closer to the front door. Stopping for a moment, he looked back, and found Grock standing vigil right where he had been before, behind the brickwork next to the gate. He didn't look that far away. Dave turned back to the path and looked at the big structure. It didn't seem that far away, either. But Dave knew things here were not always as they seemed behind the gates of All Hallows Manor.

"Rider!" Dave called out. "You got a few minutes to spare for the Knight?" he held out the Knight's sword, still in its sheath. The jewel on the end emitted a bright light. Dave waited for some sort of response. He didn't want to be battling some strange magical walkway all afternoon.

Dave heard a clank and the front doors swung open. From the dark interior a pair of glowing orange eyes appeared and came forward. Stepping from the dark was the large and imposing figure of the Headless Horseman. He was dressed exactly as always, long cloak and all. His large pumpkin head glowed with malice.

"You are once again disturbing my work!" he shouted, as he continued toward Dave.

"Your work doesn't really come to a head until Friday." Dave lowered the sword, but kept an eye on the black clad entity. Dave tried a different angle, going for friendly. "You had time for a cup of coffee when we first met about a year ago. I just need to get some questions answered, that's all."

The giant figure of the Headless Horseman stood before him, both of his boney hands in fists on his hips. Without a word, he turned and strode back up the path to the door. "You won't get any questions answered out there!" He shouted as he disappeared into the dark entryway.

Dave shook his head, remembering the bristly attitude of the Harvest Entity, then known as Scarecrow. He wondered if this was his attitude most of the time. With a shake of his head, as if to say This is a bad idea, he hurried up the path and into the door before it closed.

Inside, he followed the sound of the Headless Horseman's loud footsteps. Dave discovered the main room was empty. With an uneasy feeling he crossed through the entryway, but kept to the side, remembering the trap door he had discovered there once before.. Dave took in the room, totally redecorated, without a single snake or spider. He shook his head at the way in which Druscilla seemed to know so much about him. His thoughts were interrupted by the sound of the Horseman calling from an adjoining room.

"In here, human." The sound directed Dave to a room off to one side, opposite the room where they conversed last. He found himself in a parlor of sorts. The walls were covered in tapestries, bookshelves and in one corner, standing incongruously open, an Iron Maiden. In the center of the room, as before, a set of twin Queen Anne couches in burnt orange faced each other across a matching dark brown coffee table. A fireplace sat empty and cold.

The Headless Horseman, his back to Dave, pulled his large pumpkin head off and set it on a side chair. He gestured with one arm and his long riding cape floated to a far corner and hung itself on a waiting coat rack. Without the cape and its high collar, Dave was surprised when the entity turned and revealed himself anew. In place of the pumpkin head, was a large skull, pale off-white with deep, dark crevices, giving it a distinctly malevolent expression.

"That's new." Dave nodded to Rider, indicating the addition of the Skull.

"As I told you before," Rider, the Horseman, sat

on the couch across from Dave, "I needed to make it my own."

"It looks good."

"Enough." Rider waved his hand, dismissing Dave's comment, "What is it you needed from me, that couldn't wait until after my time?"

Dave bristled at the remark. As he had remembered outside, the Scarecrow had been irritable when they first met out at the Farm Cabin. This attitude seemed the same which only cemented the fact that Dave needed confirmation of who was who.

"It's Druscilla…"

"Druscilla is not here." The Horseman's skull displayed emotion like a human's face. The eyebrow ridges curled down, showing displeasure. "You can't be here for that."

"No," Dave stepped lightly through the minefield, doing his best to keep his anger under control. "As we discussed when last we met, Druscilla was not de-created. AND, I think you know that." He watched Rider for reaction. The Horseman's dark eye holes came to light. A low glow of orange flame erupted in their hollow centers causing smoke to gently slip out the corners.

"Watch your -"

"THAT is unimportant." Dave said, casually leaning back in the Queen Anne. "What is important is that I have found her. But, there is a complication. I -" Dave stopped, watching the entity, hoping for some sign that this was the real Harvest Entity, not the Scarecrow in the farmlands. He needed more time. "Did you say you had coffee?"

The smoke from the skull's eye holes dissipated some, but the glow remained. It took him a moment or two to respond. He finally lifted one boney hand and gestured to the coffee table. A pot and two cups appeared. The pot was the same silver set from their last meeting. Two mugs appeared, but instead of fine bone china, these two were ceramic mugs of a general cylindrical shape, one with skulls on it, and the other with pumpkins.

The pot rose up into the air, and poured steaming coffee into each of the mugs before setting down where it started. Dave waited for Rider to reach for the mug with the skulls before taking the one with the pumpkins. At least, internally, he still understands Halloween.

Dave watched the Horseman cautiously as they both set about adding cream and sugar, adjusting for taste. Rider finished with a small shaker filled with brown powder. Once used, the mug gave off the scent of pumpkin spice.

They both sipped their coffee, both eyeing each other over the top of their mugs. Dave waited; he did not want to be the first to speak. In the back of his mind, he wondered at how a skull could sip coffee. Magic, of course.

"So." The horseman said over his mug. "Druscilla."

"Yes."

"Still alive." Though hollow, the eyes settled on Dave.

"Yes." Dave set down his mug. "At least, for the moment." He hoped this would cause the Horseman to respond in kind if he was truly Druscilla. The big entity didn't move.

"Tell me all you know."

Dave was afraid of this. If this was Druscilla in

disguise, he didn't want to be giving out all his information on the situation to her. He hesitated, stood, paced.

"It all comes down to these events. First, every time I've gone looking for her, no matter what I thought I'd find, I did find Druscilla, in some manner or other. She cannot hide from me, it would seem." Trying for another dig, Dave paused for reaction. None came. He continued. "Below the Dead Lands, in her hidey hole by The Tooth Fairy and," Dave hesitated again. No guts no glory. "and, out in the farmlands at the cabin where I first met you."

"Druscilla? At the Farm Cabin?" Rider set down his mug rather forcefully. "She has no business out there."

"I'm still not sure it was her." Dave said, again watching Rider for any indication he was in league with the Hallow Witch. His pulse rose and his hand strayed to the Knight's Sword.

"She's rather easy to identify," the big entity sat back on the sofa, spreading his arms wide across the back, "even for a human. Tall woman, thinks she is fashionable, oh and purple hair. I'm sure you may remember." He sneered at his own sarcasm.

Dave was well aware of how the Harvest Entity viewed humans. His loathing of humans was well known throughout the Offset and it was not something he felt he had to hide, especially from Dave, the Knight of the Offset. If mere dislike is what he felt for most humans, the fact that Dave, a human, could come and go to the Offset caused Rider no end of both disgust and frustration. Dave wouldn't take the bait.

"Second," Dave ignored the insults, "the imaginary boys, Tom and Huck. They showed up at my house and attacked me. Which really muddled things, especially since the attack came after I had been here looking for her." Dave again watched the Horseman carefully. "I had originally figured that Druscilla had sent them thinking I was getting too close, finding her every time I went looking." Dave paused again, still pacing, still waiting, still watching. "Last, finding her out in the... Farm Cabin, as you call it."

"And you didn't take care of her then and there?" Rider turned his head to say this directly to Dave, his contempt on full display. "How pathetic."

"Therein lies the problem." Dave almost jumped at the insult, but, instead, sat back on the couch, replacing his empty coffee mug on the tray. "What I found was not a tall, somewhat fashionable woman with purple hair. What I found was... you or rather I found the Scarecrow." He calmly and carefully folded his hands across his lap.

The room was quiet. Dave thought he might have gone deaf as there was no sound at all. There was no fire to crackle in the fireplace and no sounds of the building around them.

"But I am here." Rider finally said.

"That, in a nutshell, is my dilemma." Dave slowly placed a hand on the knight's sword and leaned forward. "If the Scarecrow I found in the Farm Cabin this year is the same Scarecrow I met last year, and therefore is also the real holder of the Harvest Quedret, who, then' is residing at All Hallows Manor?"

The two stared at each other for a moment or two, long enough for tension to mount, and for Dave to begin to sweat just a bit. When Dave was about to do something he would regret, Rider threw back his big skull head and laughed loud and long. Dave wasn't sure if this was laughter at the situation or at him. He waited. His anger boiled, causing the threat of a headache. Damn you, PTSD!

"So, you came here to what?" Rider stood, leaning over the antique coffee table. "Question me? Play detective and find out the truth of who is residing in All Hallows Manor?" Rider laughed again, standing and moving away from Dave. When he finally calmed, he looked at Dave with disdain. "So, what is the answer, Knight? What have you learned from this little visit? Who is who? Prove your worth! Prove you are deserving of the title of Knight of the Offset." He leaned against the fireplace, throwing his arms to the side, resting them on the mantle, just as he had on the couch.

Dave looked down at the coffee table, both angry and embarrassed at this entire endeavor. He felt out of his element once again, unable to find the clue which would lead him to the answer. He felt it was just there, out of reach, on the tip of his tongue. If only he could put it all together. His anger took control of his thinking and he again considered just going home, dropping off the Knight's Sword on the way.

Who was he, anyway? Who mandated that it should be Dave Nicklaus to the rescue? Certainly not him! All he wanted was to bring in a bit of extra cash, spend his last years with his cat and drink a lot of good coffee. Now, it seems he's got the fate of the world on his shoulders and no idea of how to handle it. His head pounded telling him his blood pressure was spiking.

Rather than respond, he tried to get himself under control just a bit more. He took a deep breath through his nose. He could smell his own acrid sweat mixed with the leather smell from the books, with just a light tinge of pumpkin spice from the little shaker.

Pumpkin Spice. He thought. Everything froze as he grasped at the thought. What? The connection was there, if only he could- Coffee with Pumpkin Spice! All at once the knowledge hit him and he stood quickly. Even Rider was thrown a bit off and started.

"Pumpkin Spice!"

"Ok…" Rider replied, unsure of what Dave was going on about.

Dave was flustered and held up both hands. "Wait." He grabbed Rider's empty coffee mug. "You drink your coffee with Pumpkin Spice!"

"Yes, So?" Rider's patience was wearing thin. "Lots of humans do. It's a Harvest tradition." Again, the sneer, the sarcasm. "I could go with Spiced Cider, but the coffee is just-"

"Every time, right?" he persisted, "Every time you have coffee, you use that spice shaker and have Pumpkin Spice, yeah? Any time of year?"

"YES!" Rider took a threatening step toward Dave, "I drink coffee with Pumpkin Spice all year long. It's not illegal! Just what are you getting at?"

Placing the mug back on the tray, Dave stepped toward Rider, their faces nearly coming in contact. "The Scarecrow at the Farm Cabin drinks it black." He raised his eyebrows as if this said it all. "When you and I first met, we talked over coffee and you also drank your coffee with Pumpkin Spice in it. I remember the room filling with the smell. Cloves, Cinnamon, nutmeg?" He turned and pointed to the tray again. "Same little shaker, too. Right?"

Rider looked from Dave to the shaker and back again. A small bit of his anger drained away. "Maybe you are a bit of a detective." Rider folded his arms in front of him. "But, what are you going to do with this bit of information?"

Dave turned and headed to the door. "I'm not sure, but at least now, I know who is who and that puts me one step ahead of where Druscilla wanted me." Dave was almost running by the time he hit the front door.

The Headless Horseman with the big skull floating above his shoulders leaned against the fireplace and watched the human until he had left the Manor. He turned his head to look at the coffee tray with the little shaker filled with brown powder. Chuckling just a bit, he muttered, "Pumpkin Spice."

Chapter 44

Walking up a rocky path behind and above the Farm Cabin, Druscilla looked up at the gray ashen clouds. The longer she stared at them the more they became darker and thicker until most of the light had been blocked out, turning the countryside to indiscernible shadows. Shadows which moved. She didn't care about the shadows; she was concentrating all her powers to try again to open the veil one last time. She was almost out of fairy dust and needed to get the veil open before that happened.

She approached a large flat area. Knowing this would work for her needs, she held the small vial of golden powder up in the near dark to see how much she had left. She didn't need light; the bottle's contents glowed on its own.

Her eyes could see that the bottle was less than half full, but she felt it would be enough. Digging a small hole in the dirt, she poured the contents into the ground. Replacing the stopper in the now empty bottle, she tossed it away, into the bushes.

From the folds of her coat, she produced a knife. It was the obsidian dagger that was her favorite. The dark glass blade was perfect for this project. She rubbed the dark amethyst stone embedded in the handle, speaking to it softly, as one lover speaks to another in moments of intimacy. The stone came alive and pulsed rich purple light with each stroke of her hand. The blade carried strands of the purple light all the way to its tip.

Kneeling in front of the buried dust, Druscilla began drawing in the dirt with the tip of the dagger. For the next few hours as she drew in the dirt, she spoke in languages both unknown and long dead, writing in runes, hieroglyphs and even putting her own sweat, spit and blood into the ground around the bottle. She drew in a spiral, moving out from the center, further and further, her voice growing louder and harsher; her actions becoming larger and wilder.

Inside the cabin, sitting in a circle around the dining table, a quorum of twelve purple haired clones worked in tandem with their leader at the top of the path. Each took the hand of the one beside them, and began to chant in the same language moving back and forth as one. Their iconic black witch's hats identified them easily. Their faces were all identical. They moved and spoke the same languages in unison with Druscilla, moving back and forth, to and fro, their grip on one another tight and unyielding.

Druscilla screamed at the ground, carving deeper and deeper, chanting and cursing. Finally, with a loud cry, holding the dagger with both hands, she jammed the knife into the ground at the end of the long spiral using almost every bit of energy she had left. The dagger glowed and the buried powder glowed and the spiral of symbols and runes burst to life giving off a telltale purple light. The light swirled around the symbols to the center where an explosion of gold powder filled the sky. Druscilla's face shown with sweat and her eyes gleamed with satisfaction. The spell had worked!

She sat back, turning to look down to the cabin, to see the twelve through the window. They also glowed as they were part of the elaborate spell Druscilla had concocted to break through The Veil. She could feel the power emanating from them and knew, at last, that she would succeed. She had to succeed! Everything that she was had come to this point in time. She would either be successful, or be banished to the citadel.

Moving back from the growing light, Druscilla waited to see the spell work. She knew the spell backward and forward, but didn't really know exactly what would happen at this point. Her smile was filled with both joy and awe at the swirling glow before her.

The glow coalesced into an ethereal flame burning softly but growing ever brighter. The flame was as wide as the spiral of runes and taller than the trees. For just a moment, Druscilla thought she may have made a mistake. A flame was not what she was after.

The flame grew so bright it was difficult to look at. With one incredibly bright flash, the flame changed from bright light to more than darkness. The flame was coal black night, much darker than the surrounding cloud muted countryside. The giant dark flame also changed shape, going from flame to something more sinister, something with intent.

Great thick arms shot out of the shape, reaching upward. Three arms each with three joints at irregular intervals, reached up toward the shrouding clouds. Three giant feet sprung from its base giving it an awkward mobility and even more height. In the center of the shape, dozens of eyes of different sizes opened and looked about, finding and locking on Druscilla. Without hesitation, the giant creature bowed to the HallowWitch.

Druscilla smiled. She stepped forward, nearly touching the thing which stood before her. "The veil." She said simply. "Rip. It. Open!"

The big thing bowed again and turned away. Reaching out all three of its arms, it spread its wide hands, each with two thumbs and 6 long fingers. Stretching up into the dark sky, it appeared to grip nothing, yet like viewing a mirage from a distance, the air rippled and moved. The big thing continued to work pulling and twisting.

Druscilla knew her spell would finally work and she carefully made her way down the dark hillside. With one last look up at the monster on the hill working to open the veil, she went inside to consult and instruct the coven of twelve. She smiled as the word 'coven' slipped across her mind.

The monster worked without stopping. The large hands pulled and stretched the very heavens in its effort to do what Druscilla had commanded. Above and to one side, a stand of trees proved the perfect spot for two small pairs of eyes to view the events as they took place. Mari-elle and Bari-elle were quite hidden behind the branches of a thick needled pine tree.

"This is not good!" breathed Mari-elle quietly. "We must tell someone! We cannot allow this to be!"

"The Witch has gone," Bari-elle moved to the end of the branch. "We can go now, unseen!" Without another word, Bari-elle jumped off the branch and flew up into the night, with Mari-elle right behind him.

Eyes. Not all the eyes of the beast were watching their hands wrench at the sky. Some saw the two fairies slip from the trees and across their vision. One of the big hands reached out to catch them, missing one, hitting another. Bari-elle was knocked out of the sky and into a tree.

"NO!" screamed Mari-elle, dodging the big hand mid-flight and slipping down into the branches of the tree. Bari-elle lay next to the center of the tree, Mari-elle ran to his side. She saw his wings were crushed.

"Get the knight!" Bari-elle sighed, "I'll be ok, but we need help. Go!"

Without hesitation, Mari-elle fled the tree flying high up over the reaching hands of Druscilla's monster, skimming the low ceiling of clouds and headed off to the center of the Offset.

Without another thought, the monster went back to work ripping open the veil.

Chapter 45

In the hills beside the Farm Cabin, Dave crouched behind a stand of thick bushes. The little cover they offered came from the few brown leaves left on them. Dave couldn't see as much as he wanted to see. He glanced up, cursing the waning light amid dark clouds. The cabin across the field was dark, no lights. Behind the cabin and up into the rocky hills, Dave could see something quite large moving about, three long arms reached into the night sky. A breeze blew down the mountain bringing with it the unmistakable scent of death.

"About now I could use those hundred warriors again, Grandfather." He whispered.

"And I told you I could not do that again." Came a voice.

Dave turned to find the apparition of his grandfather, just as he remembered him. Grandfather knelt behind the bushes to one side, also peering through them at the Farm Cabin.

"Why are we studying this house?" he whispered.

"Osiyo!" *Hello*. Dave said to Grandfather.

Grandfather turned his head to reply, "Siyo." Hello. He looked back through the brush and whispered again, "Now, why are we studying this house?"

"Druscilla, the Hallowitch, is in there."

"No." grandfather made an annoyed face, "What I mean is, why are we here, behind these bushes just looking at the house? Shouldn't we be there, at the cabin?" His hand made a fist and moved forward and back a couple of times. Dave recognized the sign language of Native American Tribes known as Hand Talk. Grandfather wanted to fight.

Dave sat back, crossing his ankles as he leaned against a tree. He knew he had to come to terms with his own doubts about being the Knight of the Offset, but he didn't think he'd have to share those doubts with, of all people, Grandfather. And he certainly didn't want to be doing that right now. He watched as Grandfather joined him in sitting, first glancing through the bushes one last time.

"Honestly," Dave looked everywhere except at Grandfather. "I'm not sure." He was about to start telling Grandfather about his own level of self-trust and misgivings, when some noises drew them back to the bushes.

Through the thick branches, nearly devoid of leaves, they could see easily across the recently harvested field. Dave wondered for just a moment if the Horseman still worked the land. He dismissed the thought when he saw what was coming out of the cabin. Druscilla stepped out into the wind and darkness, but she was not alone. Dave and Grandfather watched as Druscilla exited the main door, followed by 12 more witches, single file. Conical hats, black outfits and purple hair.

"Clones!" Dave whispered, "Druscilla has been busy!" The procession walked around the cabin and up the back path, where they were lost from sight. In only a few moments, they were at the top of the path, near the thing tearing at the sky.

Dave sat back down by the tree. "We have to stop them." Grandfather glanced toward Dave and gave a nod. Dave continued, "Even if you could bring a hundred warriors like last time, there is no way we could assault the top of that path easily. Not with a dozen more just like her waiting for us."

"No," Grandfather moved away from the bushes, but he did not sit down. "What you need is a small specialized team."

"Oh?" Dave raised an eyebrow. He noted the twinkle in Grandfather's eye and waited for the punch-line. Grandfather merely moved further away, into a small clearing near the bottom of the small hill. Dave followed. In the small clearing, Grandfather revealed five people waiting for him.

Dave looked at the five and knew immediately who they were. He hadn't laid eyes on any of them since jumping out of the plane over Vietnam, yet they were indelibly placed within his memory. Each about 18 or 19 years old, wearing the fatigues they died in.

"Damn, Five," the closest one stood up and lightly touched Dave's beard, "you got old!"

The tension Dave had been keeping in his neck and shoulders drained out of him with a stifled laugh. He couldn't express what it meant to be near these five again. They had only known each other for a few weeks before being inserted into the war in Vietnam, but there was something about them that couldn't be forgotten. He took in the old fatigues, boots and each wearhing at least two fighting knives.

"Listen, Punk -"Dave was about to give the guy a scathing comeback when he noticed the man at the back. "Wait." Dave stepped over to the man noting that he wasn't wearing fatigues, and was easily twice the age of the young men assembled. There was a light gray at the temples of the man, who just smiled at Dave.

"Yeah, Five." The man said, "It's me, Six." He

looked down at his own clothes, a faded pair of jeans and a tee-shirt with an elephant on it.

Dave pointed to the elephant, and the odd looking letters above it. "This looks like…Thai?" Six nodded. Dave sat down next to the others. "I was told that you all died, one way or another."

One spoke up first. "First morning there, I got into a firefight. Alone and outnumbered, you can guess the outcome. Our whole project was a shit-show from the get-go."

Two chimed in. "Me too. And I see your shit-show and raise you a cluster-fuck."

Three smiled. "Oddly, I never got to see action. I was killed by a snake the first night. And no, I don't know what kind." He grinned at his own demise, but the ghost of disappointment flitted across his face.

Four added his demise. "I died coming down." He didn't offer much else.

Dave nodded and looked at Six. "Ok, so what happened to you? And where were you for the next, what, 20 years?" He felt the call of the Farm Cabin, but felt a greater need to reconnect with these apparitions from his past.

Six had sat apart from the others, but came closer to tell his tale.. They formed a circle of sorts. "It's not as cut and dried as you may think." He said. Taking a few minutes, the area was quiet enough they could hear the chanting of the coven of purple haired witches across the barren fields.

"I didn't plan it." He started. "Like the rest of you, I fully planned to be the soldier they wanted me to be. I jumped out of that plane with my head held high and my stomach in my throat. Praying I didn't puke on the way down." There were a few chuckles and nods of agreement.

"I came down in the trees. The two 'chutes caught in two trees next to each other and when I shined a light, I found I was only about six feet off the ground. I pulled on the rope that connected me to my supplies and cut it loose first. Then I quickly cut myself loose, dropping and running into the shadows. There I waited a good 30 min before I was sure I hadn't been seen.

"For that first day, and into the next week, I was a good little soldier. I worked at finding the enemy and worked at a plan to cause some chaos as our 'shit-show' commanded. I found nothing. At night I wondered at the 'why' of it all. Why was this war happening? Oh yeah, not a 'war', it was a 'conflict.' The more I thought on it, the more disgusted I became. At the US, the ARVN, the Viet Cong, the Chinese, Colonel Fartface… and myself.

"On about the ninth or tenth day, I found a well worn path. Examination showed me that this was Viet Cong patrols. The boot prints." The others nodded, remembering the information they had been taught. Six looked at Grandfather's confusion, "Most were worn, made from tires. Our boots, the jungle boot, had a very easily spotted tread. There might be a couple of US boots in among the others, if, say, those boots were stolen off some poor grunt. But, it's the smooth boots and the tire treads that indicate it was the enemy." Grandfather nodded, grateful for the information so he could keep up.

"We were all inserted north of the major fighting, that much I remember. At the moment, standing there in that goddamn jungle, I couldn't remember where I was. I mean, I knew I was north of

Phnom Penh, but how far north or how close I ended up was totally lost to me. If I were closer, I'd have expected to see more activity. After a week, zip. So this was a major find to me. It also scared me silly. How had I missed these patrols so often? Better yet, how had they missed me?

"I knew immediately what I had to do. I spent several hours setting up a booby trap using every grenade and toe-popper I had. Spread them out along the path and some beyond. I remembered the punji stakes they used on us, and decided I'd return the favor and set some of my mines a few feet off the path." A couple of the others nodded emphatically that this was a great idea.

"Then." Six took a deep breath. "I'm sorry, guys. I… I… ran." The six men sitting in the near dark were quiet. Dave knew he had just about done the same thing, but didn't say it. Where would he be if that patrol hadn't found him? The war in Vietnam was not a regular war, at least not to the six of them. Their involvement had been a bad plan poorly thought out and maladroitly enacted by people with little forethought except for their own reputation. In short, a shit-show.

"I was far behind enemy lines. That, I knew." Six went on, attempting to fill the silence. "So I pointed myself northwest and started walking. Kept out of sight, even when I passed some nondescript village. I hid every night. Slept with my gun in my hand, though I'm not really sure I slept much at all.

"The first river I crossed I tossed everything out except for my MCIs and my gun. I wanted to travel light, but be protected. When I could, I stole clothing that was left out. I changed my look so I looked like some lost traveler rather than a soldier. I wasn't fooling anyone but myself. I was six foot tall and white and wearing US jungle boots. I only hoped I could just make it to Thailand. They were the largest backer of the war behind the US and Korea, so I hoped I'd at least find sanctuary there.

"Then I ran out of food. It was starting to get cold at night, really cold. I found an abandoned cabin. Not much more than a few boards set up on a few more boards. But I found an old moldy blanket and that helped keep me warm while I kept walking. Always through the jungle, not on the roads. I'd step out on the road only now and then when I spotted some kind of sign. Usually just a post with a… a symbol or number and an arrow. Stupidly, I expected English.

"Finally, the signs began to change. Those weird letters?" Six touched his tee-shirt, "I knew I had entered Thailand. What would now take you about 12 hours to drive took me the better part of 4 weeks. I was nearly dead. Honestly, at times I thought I should just let myself die. I was that low. With the combination of no food, thoughts of dessertion, my own self worth, it's just amazing I didn't just eat a bullet."

He let a moment pass in silence, allowing everyone to ponder that singular thought.

"Just outside a small village, I ran out of… everything: food, water, energy, life. I sat down and wrapped myself up in that blanket and just willed myself to expire.

"The next morning I open my eyes and there, staring back at me is this old woman. She's forcing a bowl of food at me, and I didn't hesitate, I took it. Once I ate, she grabbed my arm and forced me to follow her." Six looked at the others, who were watching him, listening to the story they felt he needed to tell. "Her name was Adranuch and… she saved me.

"I stayed with her for several years. We had a great friendship. She taught me the language. Every chance I got, I'd do what I could to thank her for everything she had done. I never left that village. Married a girl there about my age and we moved Adranuch in with us. Me, Chailai, that's my wife, and Adranuch, we made a great little family. Never had any kids, but we really didn't need any. We were quite happy.

"Then." Six took another deep breath. "1999, just a week after my 48th birthday, I died of a heart attack. I hate like hell that I left them like that, but we had almost 20 years together. I miss them both so much."

Dave looked at the other 4 men. "No judgment here. Anyone else?"

Four began chuckling. "Judgment? I steered my chute carefully clear of any trees and landed on a mine and killed myself. I ain't judging no one!" They all began laughing. "I mean what were the odds?" More laughter.

Before they could offer up much else, the chanting across the way grew loud enough to draw their attention. Dave turned in his seat and looked over the mound of dirt behind them. "Ok, reunion is done." Dave slipped one of his knives out and handed it to Six.

" It's time to make a plan."

Chapter 46

Druscilla watched as a foul wind blew the clouds back and forth above the clearing at the top of the hill. She studied the clouds with a flat smile. The coven of purple hair also looked up and smiled. Druscilla knew things were going to work this time. Her eyes glowed as the coven circled the creature, chanting to give it power and encouragement. As the giant creature pulled and tore at the sky with its wide paws, light flashed across its fingers.

In the distance, Druscilla could see the tower that marked both the center of the Offset and the home of Old Man Time. Once her plan was complete, the entire offset might implode, an effect of losing any and all energy being sent by Man. She didn't really care about that. She had been created to be an evil witch and tonight, she was living up to that decree.

Along the path behind the cabin, a six man team moved along as fast as the dark allowed. The trail was narrow and the wind made their efforts even harder. Just before the final bend, five of them turned and without so much as a backward glance, slipped silently into the woods. Each carried at least one long steel knife, ready for action. They were quiet, determined and deadly. The plan was that each would take out two or three of the clones while Dave took out Druscilla. Though he didn't know for sure, he expected that once Druscilla was killed, the others may die with her, thus making their efforts much easier.

Dave was the only one not to enter the forest at that point. He took a breath before rounding the last bend, trying to calm his nerves. He knew he had the lightning, but always considered it as a last resort, for defense rather than offense, if he could use it at will. He carried a knife in each hand and could feel the weight of Zeke on his back. He was ready.

Rounding the corner Dave looked up and there at the edge of the clearing was Druscilla, arms crossed as if waiting for him. Not stopping, Dave continued up the path toward her. As he approached, the situation at the top of the hill became clearer. The coven also faced him, arms crossed. Must be some sort of puppet arrangement. Dave considered. Time to take out the puppeteer and cut the strings!

Dave stopped a few feet from Druscilla. The two adversaries eyed each other across the small space.

"Dave." Druscilla tipped her head to one side. "Such a surprise to see you here."

"Sarcasm does not become you." Dave paused, unsure of what was going on, or how to approach the battle to come. "You know why I'm here." The wind snatched at his breath and nearly knocked him over.

"You cannot harm me." Druscilla waved a hand and Dave's knives were torn from his grip. He also felt the weight of Zeke lifted from the sheath on his back. He turned and watched them sail up and into the clouds, blown far across the cabin, gone from sight.

Without thinking of his plan, he pulled the Knight's Sword. This only caused Druscilla to laugh even more.

"How many times have I told you that Offset Silver cannot touch me." She stepped closer, both arms out. "Now, if that was Human Silver, which is never 100% pure, then maybe you'd have a chance, but with that -"

Dave wasn't listening, he stepped forward

closing the distance between them. He didn't look into her eyes, but concentrated on his movements. The sword came up. He rotated his body. Aiming for the center of her chest, even slightly to the left-

The sword stopped in mid air.

The five men in the forest appeared at the edge, their knives out. They came at the coven as one. They didn't shout, but were as silent as they were sure. As deadly as their intent.

Without even a glance their way, Druscilla waved a hand. All five men were turned to dust, carried up and away by the shifting winds. Watching the dust circle up and into the dark clouds, Dave lowered the sword. He looked back at Druscilla and lifted his other hand, reaching out feeling until – he felt something solid. Invisible. Druscilla laughed at his endeavors.

Some sort of magical shield! Dave's face fell. He stepped back and sheathed the Knight's Sword. He was so tired of her laughter. Taking a step back, he raised both hands, each hand pointing toward Druscilla. The laughter stopped and Dave almost laughed himself at the look of terror that crossed her face.

The lightning would finish this.

And. Nothing.

Dave tried again. And again, and even a third time. Nothing.

Druscilla was laughing even harder now. "You never could control it, and it seems as if you've lost it entirely." She watched Dave try one more time. "Now, there is no reason to kill you, Dave. When I have taken control of the World of Man, perhaps you can live as my pet." And she laughed. The Coven of the Purple Hair laughed with her.

Turning toward the monster with the three arms,

Druscilla stopped and pointed a finger at Dave. In a moment, Dave was flying up and over the trees, over the farm cabin and headed for the field he had so recently crossed. He knew this time may be a bad landing and tried to relax, hoping for the best.

He came at the ground obliquely, skipping across the furrowed fields like a stone across a pond and coming to rest against the hill of dirt that had hidden him so recently. Dirt and rocks rained down on him, kicked up by his landing.

His breath was knocked out of him and it took longer than he felt was normal to get it back. Finally, he inhaled a deep breath, acknowledging he was actually still alive. When he rolled over, he saw Grandfather's face, looking down on him with love and concern.

"I can take it." A cough, a breath. "How bad is it?" His left arm was under him, and he couldn't seem to get rolled over to free it. One leg was hurting, but all in all, nothing felt broken, a feat he could only attribute to the fact that this was the Offset and things happened differently here. Maybe it was the fairies…

Grandfather worked quickly, checking Dave for injury. Once he was sure Dave was going to live, he scavenged some wood and created a travois, loading Dave into it slowly and carefully. Dave had no idea where Grandfather got a horse, but he could hear it thudding gently across the field and clip clopping along the hard path toward the center of the offset.

"The tower…" was all Dave could get out before he passed out completely.

Chapter 47

Opening his eyes, Dave was not sure where he was. In fact, he was rather surprised to even find himself abed.

"Wha…where…"

"Easy there, Good Sir Knight."

Dave blinked a couple of times, to bring back his vision. Blurry turned to less blurry and he turned his head to look around. There beside his bed stood a metal soldier. Dave had a vague blurry memory of knowing something about this soldier in particular. He did a slow blink again. The soldier was gone. My imagination is better than my vision, he thought.

Inhaling deeply, Dave took stock. He moved his hands and fingers and wiggled his toes and feet. He was amazed that everything moved, and he could even move his elbows. In all that, he could feel nothing untoward. No pain, nothing wrapped in gauze; he could also detect no smell of iodine or other disinfectants found in most hospitals. Looking again at the walls, he could pretty much be sure he wasn't in a hospital or Doctor's office. By the size, it was most certainly not the hospital he had been in before. This place had room to spare.

His vision cleared more as he took in the room itself. He noted that the walls were a medium gray, and even a bit reflective. He forced himself into a sitting position, sliding his legs over the edge of the bed and pushing himself up. Muscles groaned and tendons screamed, but he made it.

Once he was upright, sitting on the edge of the bed, he again took stock. His left side felt bruised and his left leg ached at the knee. Old age, hopefully. He rubbed his knees and stretched his aching back. More bruising, no doubt. He couldn't believe that nothing was broken.

The door opened and in walked Old Man Time.

"Good to see you up and about." The Old Man said. Dave's vision had cleared completely and he noted that The Old Man's beard was much longer than he recalled and seemed peppered with gray.

"How long have I been here?"

"Only a few hours." The Old Man took in Dave's wide eyes and added, "It's early morning of All Hallows Eve, if that helps. Just after 1:00 in the morning in your world."

"Time is on my side." Dave looked askance at the entity. "I'm feeling pretty good for having been tossed a couple hundred yards into a field just a few hours ago. Ok, a plowed soft field, but I remember feeling I had broken at least one limb before I passed out."

Old Man Time laughed lightly."I'm sure you did!" When his joke didn't go over as expected, he sat in the chair beside the bed. "You have healed rather quickly."

"Exactly my point." Dave bunched his fingers into fists a couple of times to stretch the muscles there. "I expected to wake up in a full body cast. Now, I know you don't have an actual hospital here, at least not for humans, and I'm not dead, so… what?"

"You're alive. Druscilla did her worst, but… let's put it his way: her worst just wasn't bad enough." Old Man Time leaned forward a bit. "Your body still contains the Fairy Tears." He paused, allowing Dave to catch up. "Remember the poison? Fairy Tears healed you and they are healing you now. They were poured into your wounds and into your bloodstream. You will never be entirely rid of them."

Dave nodded. "So Lightning Man has a new super power?"

"No, just Fairy Tears." The old man smiled.

Dave didn't want to push the subject, and it was just a joke anyway. The conversation waned and the Old Man broached a new subject. "I hear the Lightning failed you. Is that true?"

Dave had to get up and walk around. His legs ached a bit, but the more he moved about, the better they felt. "I'm not entirely sure." He paced one end of the room to the other. "When I needed it, when I thought I could count on it to take down Druscilla," Dave threw his hands up in frustration, "nothing."

The old man narrowed his eyes, "But she didn't kill you." He noted.

Dave looked at the floor. He felt like this was the moment. He had to admit the Lightning was actually gone and that fact meant that Druscilla wasn't after him. There was, in fact, no reason for him to be the Knight of the Offset. He tossed his hands again, at a loss of what to say.

Sitting back down on the bed, Dave looked at the Old Man. "I cannot express to you what this has all meant." Dave frowned, "What do I call you? Calling you the Old Man seems a bit odd."

The Old Man laughed. "If you must use a name, use Ben, like the clock."

"Big Ben?"

"Yes, but just Ben."

Dave smiled. "Well, Ben," he nodded to Ben in emphasis, "This whole thing has been a, well, a God send. It came at a time when life seemed to be kicking me a bit more than usual. My wife had passed, and bills were coming due. Friends that were friends of the two of us had seemed to drift off, not wanting the reminder of her death – or theirs, I guess.

"Other than my cat, I had nothing. Nothing fulfilling, anyway. Joining S3 gave me new friends, a job that paid those extra bills and yeah, even a bit of adventure."

"But…?" Ben asked.

"Yeah, but." Dave shook his head, "Maybe a bit more adventure than I bargained for." Dave paused, gathering his thoughts. Ben waited patiently. "Well, I.. I don't think I'm really the man for the job." He glanced at Ben, and returned his eyes to the floor. "Druscilla has bested me over and over from day one. We found out about the bug in Edgar's office, sure, but now, I get up there, back behind the cabin, my chance to take her down for the final time…and…."

"And you can't."

"Can't is the best word for this, because it's not from lack of want. I wanted so badly to take her down, Ben! It's what you knighted me for! It's what I deemed I was ready for! It's what I knew the world of man needed! I figured the lightning was the best bet. It just…wouldn't… But…" Dave trailed off. "It's gone."

Ben brushed a bit of lint off his slacks. "AND, you feel you've failed."

"Yeah." Dave didn't look up.

"Failure is -"

"Oh please!" Dave closed his eyes. "PLEASE don't give me some strange Offset philosophy like 'Failure is when you stop trying' or 'I don't know the meaning of the word fail' or anything like it." The room got very quiet and Dave looked up at Ben.

Ben knew what Dave needed and yet he felt he couldn't be the one to give it to him. At the moment, it was apparent that Dave didn't want anything more than to return to his cat in defeat and forget all about the Offset. Dave didn't know it, but Ben couldn't allow that. The two men stared at each other.

"What?" Dave broke the tension. He felt a bit belligerent and tried not to let it get out of hand. He knew Ben and the others had accepted him as one of their own and never once questioned him on his ability nor his suitability to the job for which he had been chosen.

"Humans have quite a lot of effort built into the word fail, don't they?"

"We don't like to fail."

Ben leaned back in his chair. He knew that as long as Dave was talking, that he would be open to just about anything; but it was a slippery slope. "I'd like you to keep an open mind while I suggest something." He looked at Dave.

"Ok," Dave relented. He knew that Ben and all the entities here in the Offset had never treated him poorly, not given him bad information. He could still turn in his sword at the end.

Ben sat quietly for a few moments before continuing. If he was going to support his Knight, he'd need to do it right. How was the question.

"Humans," he began, "are all caught up in the idea that they must not fail. Success is achieved at whatever level because of assumed potential. Isn't that about right? If you live up to your potential, then you'll be successful."

"Well, yeah..." Dave shrugged. "Teachers in

school are always going on about 'living up to one's potential'."

"The problem is, then, that no one is able to tell you or anyone else, for that matter, just what that potential is. It's as if the potential is the same for everyone and no one knows how to attain it, how to live up to it. Potential is a magic word used only by teachers."

Dave laughed out loud at the simplicity of it. "Yeah, you got that right."

"So what happens?"

Dave blinked at the question, unsure of where Ben was going.

"Humans, people, even children, all working hard to achieve their potential, without knowing if that level of potential is theirs or not. School age girls working long hours in gymnastics, working themselves into anxiety over succeeding. Men in the army, trying to live up to the phrase 'Be all you can be' but if you can't meet our level of what to be, you're discharged." Ben tipped his head to the side. "And then there's you. YOU think that just because you were unable to stop a powerful witch with magic on her side, you have failed, when in fact, the opposite is exactly true."

"I didn't stop her."

"No. Not yet."

"Oh, I get it, " Dave leaned back on the bed, leaning against the wall. "This is the old 'You only fail when you stop trying' sort of lecture, is that it?"

"Yes, and no." Ben got up and pulled out a pocket watch. He checked the watch, thinking. He nodded and looked at Dave. "What a lot of humans regretfully do not understand is that not achieving a goal does not mean failure."

"How's that?"

Ben held up the watch. "If I expect this watch to fly and throw it across the room, and it smashes into the wall, has the watch failed?"

Dave narrowed his eyes. He was sure Ben was up to something.

"It comes down to this." Ben placed the watch back in his pocket. "The watch flew but only because I made it fly by throwing it. I forced it to achieve something watches were never supposed to achieve. And in the doing, probably broke the watch. By the same token, if I expected the watch to talk to me, and tell me the time, I'd say the watch failed that expectation, too; wouldn't you?"

Dave stayed quiet.

"A great man once said "If you judge a fish by its ability to climb a tree, it will live its whole life believing it has failed." Ben watched Dave, waiting for some reaction. "Let me teach you another phrase, one I particularly like. 'All you can do is all you can do.' Do you understand?"

"All you can do is all you can do." Dave repeated the phrase, listening to it as he spoke.

"All this watch can do is tell time, but only if I look at it. All it can do is all it can do. It is living to its full potential just by being what it is. If you think you have lived up to your potential, done all you can, then there you are. All you can do is all you can do. I've never expected you to do more than you can, to be more than you are or achieve more than you are capable."

"It seems rather defeatist, though." Dave sat up again. "If I didn't want to do something, then I could say I've done all I can do and let it go."

"Then you'd be a liar, as well as a failure."

"So each of us has to find our own level of potential and do our best to use it fully, is that what you're saying?"

"Yes. Pretty much. It also comes down to not expecting the fish to climb the tree in the first place. The watch knows nothing of my expectations, all it knows is to be a watch. We, each of us, must rely on what we know of ourselves to know if we've reached our potential, if we've done all we can do - expectations be damned. Which means perhaps I shouldn't have expected you to be the one to take down our errant witch if you didn't feel your potential was up to the task." He paused and looked Dave over. "So…" Ben smiled. "Tell me Dave, what do you think? Have you done all you can do? You ready to turn in that sword?"

Dave studied the Old Man a while, thinking of all he had done and wondering if there was more he could do before Druscilla brought destruction to both worlds. Who's expectations was he really trying to live up to, his own or…?

"I don't want to force you to decide." Ben stepped to the door. "If you leave the sword here, I'll know your answer and I'll not think less of you." He opened the door and stepped through. "I can always have a clone made and continue fighting the witch." He smiled a grim smile. "She's not achieved her potential, either."

Dave watched the door close. He picked up the sword and ran his hands over the engraving on the sheath. There were no clocks for him to check, so he didn't know how long he sat and thought about the information Ben had given him. He went over it all in his mind again and again, questioning everything about himself, the Offset, his entire approach to the task at hand.

It didn't seem to be part of the conversation, but he also noted how his own battles with depression and the ever present PTSD had abated with the work to be done in the Offset – to some degree anyway. Sure, frustration caused headaches and the anger spiked occasionally, but really, the PTSD wasn't as bad as it had been in the past. Was it his own doing, or was the Offset somehow blocking these issues in him? Or was it helping? He would never know, but he decided that his expectations on those two subjects should be changed.

"Expectations. All you can do is all you can do." He repeated. "Rely on what you know... Expectations... Rely on... wait..." Dave's eyes narrowed, focused on a distant point. A plan was coming together.

Dave rose and paced the floor again, pointing with his hand, gesturing and muttering. He stroked his long beard and paced again, reforming and rethinking. At last he stopped and looked at the Knight's Sword where it lay on the bed.

Ben was not surprised when he returned to the room and found Dave and the Knight's sword gone.

Chapter 48

Dave sat on a lounge chair at the back of his house. Off across the top of the small forest he could see something happening within the colorless clouds. Lightning flashed in a rainbow of colors. That most of them were shades of purple was not lost on him. This, he was sure, was evidence that Druscilla was about to split the veil. For about the thousandth time, he looked up at the boiling dark clouds overhead. The wind had threatened to knock him and his chair over numerous times, but he was confident in the fact that once Druscilla opened the veil, the wind would die down, though the clouds would remain. The clouds were Druscilla's distraction, of that he was sure.

He took a deep calming breath. "Expectations." He breathed. "All you can do is all you can do." The memory of the day came back to him as he went over the plan in his head for about the hundredth time.

It was still early morning when Dave had returned home. He was exhausted, but alive both in body and in mind. The bed was calling him but he took the time to call Todd and explain his plan.

"Walk me through this plan, again…" Todd laughed at some of it, but in the end promised to be at the house by midday to prepare. Dave sharpened his knives, polished the Knight's Sword and took a power nap.

Midday. The sleep refreshed him. Dave was up and ready for anything. Todd arrived more than ready to prepare for the confrontation with Druscilla. He had already built the platform Dave's plan required and with Dave's help, they got it into position. Todd also had rounded up some hay bales which were positioned at the north end and south end of the house along with some rolls of bright yellow caution tape to keep any 'tourists' from meandering where they shouldn't. This was strung between the houses to the north and south. The last of the hay bales were stacked two high in front of the Lawn chair.

The backyard was wide open between the house and the forest. More planning went into preparing a reception there. Empty cans loaded with gun powder and steel nails were buried at the edge of the forest to take out as many of the Coven as possible. Todd got great pleasure in making up the cans, placing the gunpowder to one side and the nails to the other. By burying them at the bottom of the hill, facing the forest, he had created his own hand-made claymore. Dave smiled thinking of the amount of work they had done, with extra care on the special surprise just for Druscilla.

About an hour before sundown, Carrie arrived with Cassandra. Cassandra is the name she had given to her most prized possession, a Barret M82 Sniper Rifle. The weapon's magazine holds 10 rounds and she had two extra magazines in a canvas carry case. She spent a long time arranging her sniper hide.

"You sure the other guns won't be needed?" Todd asked. "I have them locked in the back of the truck, just in case. Plenty of steel jacketed rounds, too."

"The only time I got close enough to use a gun on Druscilla she anticipated it and had on a vest." Dave shook his head. "I also don't want the noise to bring the authorities storming in here before we can take her down. But… keep them handy, as a last resort."

They finished the preparations just before dark, and after they had checked and rechecked the list and the plan, there was nothing to do but wait. Waiting was the hardest part. In the Army, Dave had not had long periods of waiting. He remembered the one night, his first night in the jungle, unable to sleep thinking he'd be spotted. He thought of his five squad members and how they had died. All but Six, who, like Dave, had found a way out of the Army and into a life they could call their own. Thoughts like that could spiral, and he tried to think of something else to get them out of his mind.

He checked the time. "It's late." He spoke aloud. The ear piece he was wearing connected wirelessly to his phone. The screen said CONFERENCE CALL IN PROGRESS. "Everyone ready?" Seven voices responded affirmative. He tucked the cell phone into a pocket, securing it with a button, leaving it on for direct communication with his team.

Waiting and more waiting. Just above the forest, the sky flashed and the clouds danced, but the wind through the forest and across the lawn slowed to almost nothing. Dave knew things were coming to a head.

They all watched and waited as the flashing lights in the sky got brighter and quicker, short blasts of lightning shot from one dark gray cloud to another while the clouds whipped at one another with wild abandon. There came one bright flash and the light show stopped. A piece of the cloudy ceiling fell in on itself and there appeared in the sky a wide black hole, darker than the surrounding dark clouds. At this distance Dave was unable to tell how big the hole was, but he knew it would be at least big enough to let through anything Druscilla could dream up. Dave watched the black hole wondering what would appear first. He didn't have to wait long.

The black blobs. Featureless creatures of

nothing but dark energy. They spilled out the opening like a black waterfall, hardly more visible than the night sky itself. Their movement is what caused them to be seen. They fell, flew, and crawled down the sky and into the forest. In the Offset, they floated. Here, in the Human world, they had substance, and weight. He could hear them crunching down through the branches, across the dry autumn leaves, stumbling over smaller sticks, headed their way.

Dave could feel the tension mounting. He again cursed silently knowing that once again Druscilla somehow had known his plans. They would have to change things on the fly. At least the blobs were headed toward them, and not away. They could be seen as moving shadows coming through the forest, headed for Dave's back lawn.

"Carrie." Dave didn't move. "Wait until they are almost on top of it." The blobs slowed near the edge of the forest. Dave took this to mean that the blobs were as cautious as Druscilla when it came to coming after Dave. This might work in their favor.

The blobs began pushing against one another as they moved through the forest. There were sounds that Dave couldn't identify coming from beyond the trees. The movement and sounds went on for some time, and without cause, stopped, leaving the scene as still as a graveyard.

Dave was about to say something into his mic when one of the blobs stepped into view. The blobs were no longer blobs, but were now much larger creatures with long spindly arms and legs. Their heads were all eyes with an immense mouth full of sharp black teeth. Another creature stepped out of the forest, and then another, and another. The blobs had been busy in the darkness. They had joined together and created larger but still inky black creatures. For just a moment, he acknowledged Druscilla's tactical thinking.

These creatures were larger, more formidable, nightmare inducing; but Dave had thought ahead and was ready for it all.

Dave wanted to end this, but waited for the right moment. He counted 6, no, 7 of the massive creatures, but waited to see if more were hiding. The thing in the center stepped purposefully out into the open. Its head moved side to side, looking for prey, coming to a stop when it found Dave. A quick scan of the forest told Dave this was it. The fight was…

"Now." Dave said.

On the platform Todd had created and placed on the apex of Dave's house, Carrie lay prone with Cassandra cradled in her arms, the long barrel of the gun resting on a small pile of sand bags. Todd held a pair of binoculars and scanned the woods for threats. They both wore all black outfits and black balaclavas. Totally hidden behind a plywood sheet covered in black tar paper, they'd been watching the activity of the blobs; but Carrie kept her sights locked on one target in the center, just outside of the forest. When Dave gave the command, Carrie took in a breath and let half out. She squeezed the trigger on the M-82 Barrett rifle.

Thanks to a suppressor, the sound of the Barrett rifle was no more than that of a book being slammed shut. A millisecond later, the .50 caliber BMG Tracer round struck the can in the center of the line. The tracer round ignited the gunpowder and the can exploded erupting in a cloud of steel blown back into the forest. In an instant, the big black creature in front of the first can was obliterated.

Also ignited by the explosion was the detonation cord wrapped around the can. Todd had brought the cord, explaining to Dave that when the first can ignites, the cord will also ignite, traveling its length at 6000 meters per second. This caused all Todd's hand-made claymore mines to go off almost at once, creating a hail of steel nails across the face of the forest.

The nails did their job. Some of the creatures were disintegrated by the volley as it tore through the forest. As they were steel, they didn't need to strike the creatures in a vital organ to kill them. A nick here, a scratch there, and quickly, all the creatures were reduced to an oily mess. In moments, the leaves and branches were covered in the black tarry stuff that Dave remembered from his first experience with Druscilla's creatures.

With practiced ease, Carrie swapped out the magazine containing the tracer rounds for a magazine of regular steel jacketed rounds. She pressed her cheek to the side of the rifle and used the high powered scope to look through the forest for any remaining creatures or blobs.

Todd caught movement at the opening in the sky. "We have incoming."

"Ok," Dave said, "let there be light."

Todd flipped a switch on the side of the platform. The switch connected to the floodlights Dave had for the backyard. The flood lights filled the area with light, even up to the hole in the clouds. Dave could see activity through the gateway in the sky, imagining all sorts of creatures that might come through.

Before he could say anything to Carrie and Todd, the sky filled with the coven. They burst through the opening flying across the boiling sky and down onto the lawn. They remained wary, after having witnessed the demise of the first wave of their attack, flying this way and that, in an effort to disguise their movements.

One of the coven, landing at the far end, away from the opening in the sky, exploded into an oily black mess, falling where she used to stand. Carrie and Cassandra didn't wait for instructions. Another of the witches fell, splashing into a dark puddle as she hit the ground. Carrie racked another round into the M-82 and pulled the trigger. She was surprised to see that the witch she had targeted was still standing.

Both Dave and Todd knew Carrie was a good marksman. She wasn't the best in the business, but she was good. Honored. Decorated. For her to miss at this short distance was unheard of, confusing. If the bullet missed its mark, there was only one reason: something stopped it before it got to the target.

"Dave?" she looked at Todd while she spoke.

"Yeah, " Dave responded. "I can pretty much guess. Stay ready." Dave reached over and picked up a rock, one of those used in laying of the foundation and the patio. It was a rough aggregate rock not much larger than a golf ball. He stood and threw the rock, and watched it arc over the heads of the witches. "They know where you are. They've set up some sort of shield, probably magical. For now, just… hunker down and stay safe."

Dave stepped out from behind the hay bales. All the witches that were left watched him with a careful eye.

"Team Two. Team Three." Dave smiled at the military vernacular. It had been more than 50 years since he was in the army. From his spot in the center, Dave looked to his right. Todd and Carrie stood up from behind the stacked bales of hay. He looked to his left, and watched as Todd and Carrie came from behind the bales of hay there.

"This is too weird." Carrie's voice came from the ear piece in Dave's ear.

"Weird is as weird does." Dave's voice came through her earpiece. "Or… something like that." They all watched the coven for danger as he stepped out from behind the hay bales and advanced on the witches. In a moment, he saw they each had their own sword of glowing purple fire. "Swords of fire. I figured as much."

The two Todds and the two Carries didn't hesitate stepping into the line of fight with the coven. Their training had prepared them for something such as this, and the witches were just unprepared for such a fight. They would expect to use magic, the purple fire, or tricks of some sort. Dave figured they were untrained in the use of their swords. They were good, but with their opponents using steel swords, the fight was over in a matter of minutes.

The two teams of Todd and Carrie moved backward toward the bales of hay, their tar covered swords at the ready. Dave nodded, telling them they had done well. He remained closest to the forest, knowing that the big fight would be next.

Dave was almost surprised to see a crowd off behind the team at the south. A group of kids had amassed behind the yellow tape, watching what was going on. He worried about their safety, but didn't have time to dwell on it. In the forest, there came a rustling, a few uneven footsteps and with a flourish, Druscilla stepped out of the woods and onto the back lawn. Out of the corner of his eye, he saw one of the Todd clones step forward, but he was stopped by a shield, invisible, but nonetheless effective.

If the shield kept the clone at bay, it would at least protect the kids, too. Dave was a bit relieved at that thought. He looked at Druscilla. "So, now you'll blast me with your famous purple fire and be done, is that it?"

Druscilla felt in complete control. She looked up at the platform on the house, and to each of the teams of clones, stopped by the shield. She lingered on the crowd of kids, now with a couple of adults watching the 'show.'

"I've spent almost a year planning to kill you, Knight." Her eyes leveled on Dave. "You no longer have the power I sought, so I have no need to kill you. I thought I might just keep you as a lapdog, making you watch the rest of the world suffer." She raised one hand and waited. "But then…."

Leaves crunched in the forest as Jungar stepped into view. His hulking form muscled its way into the area and looked to Druscilla for orders. There was still the memory of last Christmas between Jungar and Dave. Dave was almost surprised that the evil beast took the time to get orders from the Witch.

Behind him, Dave heard a crash, like something being thrown through a window. He worried that the kids behind the yellow tape might be injured. He was about to turn and look when Jungar disappeared in a flash of black and white. Even Druscilla looked back in shock at the giant figure of Sheldon ripping Jungar in two.

"You're next!" Sheldon said and finished off the jungle cat, shaking his head to clean off the tarry residue.

Druscilla clenched her fists in anger. She pointed to the big cat, her hand shaking, her eyes flashing purple. Nothing happened.

Realization hit Dave. He smiled. "You have no more power." He slowly pulled the Knight's Sword from its sheath. "You've used up all the power you gained from the Fairy Dust and are hoping to scare me, and maybe those kids up there." Dave hooked a thumb over his shoulder, toward the group of kids, now quite large. "But, it seems my buddy Sheldon is still standing; which means, you can't do a thing." Dave swung the Knight's Sword toward Druscilla who jumped back.

"You fool!" Druscilla screamed as a flaming purple sword appeared in one hand. It flickered to life slowly, like an old fluorescent light, once again proving how low she was on magic.

Out in the forest, Sheldon turned to take on Druscilla, but was stopped by another of her invisible walls. Dave wondered at the amount of power she had left, keeping all these shields up, but didn't have time to study it. She swung the sword hard at his neck. He slapped the sword away with the Knight's Sword and stepped back. For the next few minutes, the two danced across the lawn, thrusting and parrying. Dave kept busy dodging both the sword and the holes left by the land mines.

Druscilla was more than angry at the amount of time it was taking, and her anger caused her to swing harder and harder. Dave was doing everything in his abilities to keep out of the way of her sword.

"You cannot win!" Druscilla stopped fighting. "Even if you were to get close enough, the Knight's Sword is Offset Silver. It cannot harm me, even here!"

Dave thought on this a moment, but came for her anyway. She parried his move and swung again, hard. This time the purple sword snapped the Knight's sword in two, breaking it off at the guard. Dave watched the entire blade sail off into the forest. When he turned his eyes back, it was just in time to see Druscilla slip the sword into his chest, between two ribs, and into his heart. Dave smiled, and fell back, dead before he hit the grass, the sword still where Druscilla had left it.

The group of children and adults gasped as Druscilla stepped toward Dave and leaned over his dead form. "You humans are so..." she spat on his lifeless form. "And that's for losing the lightning!"

The ground beside Druscilla erupted. For a moment she thought that the woman with the gun, up on the roof, had found a way to slip a shot under the shield. Before she had time to consider it, something large hit her obliquely, picking her up in its momentum and carrying her back toward the trees. She was stopped when her back hit a large oak, almost taking the breath from her. She blinked and looked down.

Dave raised his head and looked into Druscilla's purple eyes.

"Dave?" she sputtered. "But, -"

Without comment, Dave pulled the real Knight's Sword from its sheath and jammed it into Druscilla's chest, through her heart, with such force that it embedded in the oak tree behind her.

Druscilla grabbed the sword with both hands, laughing. "One last time, human, this is Offset Silver -" Druscilla's eyes grew wide, looking down at her hands - hands which were starting to melt. "No!"

Dave stepped back. "I must have forgotten to

mention, I had that blade replaced with a high grade steel alloy some time ago." Rather than be upset, Druscilla laughed a long and evil laugh. Her laugh didn't stop until she totally exploded in a puff of gold dust.

Dave was only a bit unnerved by the laugh. He could hear the cheers of the kids on the hill. They must think this is all some Halloween show. He stepped out of the trees and raised a hand to the crowd. But the crowd was not looking at him; they were looking up at the opening in the sky. Dave stepped up far enough onto the grass to look up and stopped. He almost couldn't believe what he saw.

"Of course…" Dave was quick to give instructions. "Everyone get ready. Sheldon, inside where it's safe."

"But -" Sheldon looked up at the sky and was back through the broken window in a flash. The dark Offset energy flowing across the lawn kept him in his large form and able to talk, but even Sheldon knew he couldn't take on this new threat.

Pushing out the opening was a giant serpent's head. Its wide snout and jaw were covered in a pattern resembling Cherokee beadwork. It was working hard to get out of the opening, because its two long sharp horns were not fitting through. It pushed and worked and finally the two horns came free, allowing the serpent to glide out and down into the forest.

"Dave?" Carrie's voice over the headset. "What the hell is that?"

"Uktena." Dave was mesmerized by the giant serpent. "Cherokee serpent of lore. Only killed by… true heroes." The serpent raised its massive head into the light from the flood lights. Dave could finally see that all the patterns on its head and skin were purple.

"Druscilla." Dave said and headed to the forest. "She's fooled us again! She didn't have any power because that was a clone I just killed. She also knows that the Lightning has left me."

With sudden insight, Dave remembered the issues Mike had with the steel ring and knew exactly where Druscilla got her information. "And she also knows that the blade I have is steel." Dave grabbed the Knight's Sword by the handle and tried to work it loose from where it was stuck in the tree. It wouldn't budge. He cursed once or twice and stepped back, looking up at the head of the serpent as it rose above the treetops.

Dave watched it, but it wasn't watching him. He stepped back a bit. No, the serpent wasn't moving. Glancing around, he also noticed that the crowd, which had been cheering and making lots of noise, was quiet. He turned, looking up at the group of kids. They seemed frozen. No one was moving.

It wasn't a long distance, but Dave could see one kid who had been jumping up and down was now floating, mid jump, his feet in the air, a couple of pieces of candy were motionless, falling from his bag. Behind him there was an adult who was smoking a cigarette, the smoke a ghostly statue.

"Carrie?" Dave spoke into the microphone attached to his phone. There was no response. Thinking this was a plot of Druscilla's, he looked back to the serpent. The serpent hadn't moved. Dave didn't know what to do. He turned a full circle, looking at everything. Nothing stirred, even the clouds had stopped.

To the south, on a neighbor's lawn, in the half light thrown by Dave's flood lights, Dave saw a figure.

Visible in the wan light were the bare arms and only a couple of feathers tied at the crown of the head, which told Dave that this was a Cherokee. Not sure why or who, Dave walked cautiously across the lawn and into the half light. When he was close enough, he recognized Lightning Thunderer.

"Osiyo." Dave visibly relaxed.

"Siyo." The lightning Thunderer looked up at the serpent standing still in the sky. "Quite a show you have here."

Dave decided he didn't need to explain what was going on. He was pretty sure Lightning Thunderer knew the full story. He also turned to look at the giant figure of lore and simply nodded.

"I needed to share something with you." Lightning Thunderer turned to Dave, reaching out to his heart. "He is still there." The Lightning Thunderer turned to go.

"No. It's not."

Lightning Thunderer turned back, a quizzical expression on his face. "There are three who know the Lightning, its place and its life. The first is me. The second is Unetlanvhi. (Creator)"

"And the third?" Dave smiled, "Not me."

"The Lightning."

"No," Dave persisted, a bit ashamed of losing the power he was gifted. "The Lightning left. I tried to use it and it was gone."

Lightning Thunderer chuckled. "Lightning is not a weapon, Thunder Wolf." He touched the breastplate he wore. "This is not a weapon, but it does what he needs to do when it is needed." He touched Thunder Wolf's chest producing a couple of sparks.

"It is there, and will do what it needs to do when

you need it." And with that he turned and walked off, fading into the shadows.

Dave turned back to the forest and trotted over into the light. The moment he got close enough to the trees, the noise from the crowd returned. He looked up at the Uktena as the big head of the creature turned to look at him.

"The time has come, the walrus said," The Uktena spoke, using Druscilla's voice, which wasn't surprising to Dave at all. The serpent dipped its head down and grabbed hold of one of the big trees with its mouth. It ripped the tree up out of the ground and tossed it into the yard, over Dave's head, where it landed with a loud crunch.

Dave stepped into the forest. The cheers of the crowd behind him were both unnerving and encouraging. The tree that the Uktena had uprooted was from the edge of the clearing where he had laid his late wife's ashes. The cement plaque was missing and a huge hole was all that was left. He knew Druscilla was trying to get him off center, angry so he wouldn't think straight.

As Dave stepped into the clearing, his head began to pound. His blood was boiling at the thought of where his late wife's ashes now resided.

"Druscilla!"

"Ah," the big serpent head dipped down into the clearing, close enough for Dave to reach out and touch. "The human figures it out."

"I figured you out a long time ago."

"No, Knight." The corners of the serpent's mouth turned up slightly. "I saw the look of surprise on your face. I know you."

"And I know Wetiko." Dave nodded.

"Wetiko?"

"It's a word from the Native peoples." It was surreal for Dave to be speaking to a giant Serpent in his backyard with his wife's ashes just steps away. "It's a term which means inherent evil, I suppose. Some embody it as Wendigo, Wiindigoo and even wīhtikow." Dave waited a few moments, knowing finally what was needed to get rid of the curse of Druscilla completely. "You. You are evil and need to be stopped. And we are going to stop you.

The Uktena laughed. "Let's not banter, human." The serpent's head reared back. "I have much to do with my new world of slaves." It opened its mouth, showing two rows of long sharp teeth. In a flash, the head snapped forward, opening wider to make room for Dave's entire body.

Watching a giant serpent try to eat him is not an easy way to stay calm, but Dave tried to concentrate on what Lightning Thunderer had said. "It's there when you need it." So Dave merely raised his hands as if in defense. The Uktena's mouth opened and came close, slipping over Dave's head. He could see the long thin tongue of the Uktena, he could smell the foul breath she let out, and he could almost hear the muscles tense as they tightened to close, bringing the teeth into Dave's body.

Dave's hands were up, pointed toward down the throat of the Uktena when two bolts of blinding white light leapt out of his palms and screamed up through the mouth of the beast and into its throat. In the flash of the lightning Dave saw the face of Druscilla, her eyes wide, her mouth open in shock and disbelief, her plans for world domination burned with her. The lightning went down the witch's ophidian throat and followed the twisting turning flesh all the way to the tail. In a flash, the Uktena exploded like a water balloon flooding the forest, this time with dark purple syrup. Druscilla was finally de-created.

Dave stood looking around, and could only see the dark substance sliding down the tree trunks. The purple tar was turning quickly to black. He alone was untouched. In the near distance, he could hear the noise of the kids and adults cheering at what they could only imagine was a very good show. All that concerned Dave was that Druscilla was actually, physically, undeniably dead.

Making his way out of the forest, Dave once again raised his hand to the crowd and was again surprised to see them looking up at the opening. Shaking his head, Dave prepared for the worst. He turned to see what the cheers were for and found the Headless Horseman atop his steed, Daredevil. Daredevil reared up, blasting twin flumes of fire out his nostrils. Together, they jumped off the edge and rode across the open vista down to Dave's back lawn.

Turning to the lawn, Dave found himself face to face with his clone. The clone pulled the purple sword out of its chest and tossed it aside. In a moment, Clone Dave was gone and in his place was the very diminutive Rodri-gelle, his fairy wings aglow. From their places behind the hay bales, the two sets of Todd and Carrie also trotted up. In moments they disappeared and revealed themselves also to be fairies.

"Thank you." Dave said.

"Don't thank me," Rodri-gelle said. "Thank the Tooth Fairy. He's the one who made all these clones!"

Mari-belle was about to speak, but had to fly out of the way of Daredevil who had just landed. As the

Headless Horseman slid off his mount, the five fairies gave a quick salute and headed off to the Offset, flying up and through the open hole in the quickly dissipating cloud cover.

"Knight! You have succeeded!" Rider shouted.

"Rider, good to see you."

Rider retrieved a large clay container from his saddle bags and went to the forest. He set the clay container on the ground and with a few odd gestures; all the black and purple residue left over from the fight ran quickly down to his feet. From there, it funneled itself into the vessel. Rider pulled a wide cork out of a pocket and stopped up the top. It didn't seem possible to Dave that all that odd stuff would be contained in such a small container, but he knew better than to ask.

Rider placed the container back into the saddlebag. He noted the crowd of spectators watching.

"What's with this?"

"They must think it's some sort of show."

"Indeed?" Rider mounted Daredevil and turned to go.

"Want to have some fun?" Dave stepped close. "Circle up closer to the crowd and take your pumpkin head off and toss it at them."

"Just like in -"

"The story." Dave nodded, smiling.

Rider laughed. "Come see me later this week. I need you to teach me about this new thing, Trunk or Treat." Without needing to kick him into action, Daredevil took off at a dead run. The pair circled up nearer the crowd, who shrank back at his approach. As expected, he removed his head and threw it at the crowd. There were a lot of shouting and excited kids, and a few fearsome moments, but when the pumpkin head exploded against the corner of Dave's house without creating any damage, they knew it was only 'part of the show.'

The crowd cheered as Rider and Daredevil rode back up across the sky and through the opening in the veil at full gallop and disappeared from view. Dave wondered for just a moment at how the veil might get closed, but got his answer quick enough. Three large hands, each with two thumbs and six fingers reached up and through the opening, taking hold of the edges and pulling the entire thing closed. There were a few flashes of light and a distant rumble of thunder from what was left of the clouds as the sky cleared completel.

The crowd cheered and Dave waved. Approaching from the north end of the house were the real Todd and Carrie.

"Quite a show!" Todd slapped Dave on the back. Carrie gave him a high five.

Before he could say anything, Dave was nearly knocked down by Sheldon, now his regular size, though still quite a large beast. Dave held him in his arms and carried him along, making a mental note to repair the back window before bed tonight.

"I couldn't have done it without all your help." Dave hugged them both while Sheldon climbed up on his shoulder, which at h is size, was not easy. "Now, what's say we go hand out some candy?"

"You mean hand out what's left, right?" Carrie elbowed Todd in the side.

Dave and Carrie laughed while Todd tried to explain why so much candy was gone. He tried all the way up the hill to the crowd behind the yellow crime scene tape.

Before they headed to the front porch, Dave

stopped to study the forest. Above it, the sky was clear and a beautiful moon reflected on the stillness. Dave only hoped it would stay that way.

He reached a hand up and scratched a purring Sheldon on the neck.

Chapter 49

Looking through the newly repaired window that overlooks his backyard, Dave checked the recent work that had been put into the other needed repairs. The holes from the hand-made claymore mines had been smoothed over and, time and weather permitting, he would work on the big hidey-hole next. Dave narrowed his eyes a bit and imagined the fresh grass that would be planted in the spring which would complete the restoration. In the back of his mind, he also noted that the trees, every single one of them, would need to be examined for embedded nails. Dave sighed at the amount of work that would take.

Sheldon stood on the cat stand and also looked out the window, but not at the yard work. He was looking for anything moving. A breeze played among the fallen leaves in the forest and Sheldon's eyes locked in on the movement, quickly determining which was or was not a threat.

Looking around the room while absently scratching Sheldon's ears, Dave was at peace. It was Thanksgiving and Dave knew the day after would be when he started his job as a Shopping Center Santa. He had already spoken to his kids, grandkids, and Naquinta's kids and grandkids; so now he was just enjoying the day. Alone, perhaps, but it was a good day anyway. He grinned a bit realizing that he also looked forward to being part of the big Christmas Day Delivery that S3 was founded on, even if he could never tell anyone about it.

He settled himself on the couch and Sheldon followed him, making himself at home next to Dave.

Running his hand absently down Sheldon's fur, Dave studied the papers sent over from S3 about where he would be working, the team he would be with, and the hours. He was glad to know he'd be working with the same girls he had the year before. He smiled at the memories. Yes, all was good.

The doorbell rang. Sheldon put his ears back, proving how much he disliked it when the bell rang. He growled low to express his displeasure further.

"Easy there, big fella." Dave patted the big animal. "Don't go killing anyone today, ok?"

Dave opened the door to find Todd and Carrie.

"Hot Stuff!" Carrie pushed past Dave carrying a large casserole dish. "and I don't mean you!" She laughed as she made her way to the kitchen, placing the casserole dish on the stove. She turned and headed out to their car for more.

"Yeah," Todd said as he passed Dave, "I'm the 'hot stuff' she was referring to."

"Wait," Dave closed the door as Carrie passed by with another armload. "What's going on here?" Dave smiled, because he knew what was going on.

"We know you wanted Thanksgiving alone," Carrie pulled a treat from her pocket for Sheldon. Sheldon rubbed against her legs so hard she almost fell over.

"But," Todd pulled Dave over and pushed him into a chair beside the dining table, "We are also alone and so we thought we'd just all eat together."

"Don't know how it worked this way, but at the last minute Lou canceled." Carrie opened several cabinets until she found the plates and began serving things up. "This is a special meal, just for us. Turkey, dressing and gravy all in a casserole, along with mashed taters. Oh and we got some yams and green beans and…" She reached both hands into one of the bags, "THIS!" Two bottles of win appears from the bag.

Dave looked at his two best friends. "I'll get the wine glasses!"

They ate, they toasted and they joked and laughed the afternoon away. When they were done, both with the food and the wine, they all agreed that the dishes could be picked up in the next few days as Todd and Carrie headed home.

The night was just beginning as Todd and Carrie headed home. Dave was careful not to let them drive if they had had a bit too much wine. Todd was adamant that he was ok to drive and made a loud mention of how little of the wine he had drunk compared to the other two. Carrie snorted and laughed as she crawled up into the cab of Todd's truck. There was no question of who had the most wine.

Once they were gone, and the inevitable text assuring they had made it home safe, Dave cleaned all the dishes and stacked them. He pulled his Santa Suit out of the closet, in preparation for the next day, removed the plastic suit cover and hung the outfit so that the wrinkles would be gone by morning. Moving to Naquinta's side of the bed, he sat and looked out the window. With the flood lights off, the little forest was clouded in shadow. He wasn't sure why, but he was more concerned than ever that the shadows remain right where they were for the rest of the night.

Dave was circumspect about what the future held. This whole Offset adventure may have helped and hurt him. Memories of the knife going into his shoulder surfaced with a vengeance. His eyes squeezed shut in an effort to push them back where they belonged.

Visuals like that now belonged in the same internal chest where he locked the nightmares from Vietnam.

Vietnam. Smells of the jungle, voices of the dead.

Long slow breaths dragged into his throat. Breathing came easier, long slow breaths. Sheldon's head bumped against his shoulder letting him know it was time for bed. Without looking, Dave's hand found the furry beast and felt the purring inside.

"Ok, big fella." Dave pulled himself up and across the bed. "Thanks."

Once Dave was under the covers on his own side of the bed, Sheldon plopped down next to him. The two were soon fast asleep.

Out in the forest, the shadows did, indeed, move.

-   End –